THE ROGUE

"Once you've read a Liar's Club book, you crave the next in the series. Bradley knows how to hook a reader with wit, sensuality (this one has one of the hottest hands-off love scenes in years!) and a strong plot along with the madness and mayhem of a Regency-set novel.

—*RT BOOKclub Magazine*

"Bradley continues her luscious Liar's Club series with another tale of danger and desire, and as always her clever prose is imbued with wicked wit."

—*Booklist*

"Celeste Bradley's The Liar's Club series scarcely needs an introduction, so popular it's become with readers since its inception . . . Altogether intriguing, exciting, and entertaining, this book is a sterling addition to the Liar's Club series."

—*Road to Romance*

TO WED A SCANDALOUS SPY

"Warm, witty, and wonderfully sexy."
—Teresa Medeiros, *New York Times* bestselling author

"Funny, adventurous, passionate, and especially poignant, this is a great beginning to a new series . . . Bradley mixes suspense and a sexy love story to perfection."

—*RT BOOKclub Magazine*

"A wonderful start to a very looked-forward-to new series . . . once again showcases Celeste Bradley's talent of creating sensual and intriguing plots filled with memorable and endearing characters . . . A non-stop read."

—*Romance Reader at Heart*

"Danger, deceit, and desire battle with witty banter and soaring passion for prominence in this highly engrossing tale . . . Bradley also provides surprises galore, both funny and suspenseful, and skillfully ce so as to make this story more

—*Road to Romance*

MORE . . .

"A fantastic read . . . Bradley successfully combines mystery, intrigue, romance, and intense sensuality into this captivating book."

—Romance Junkies

THE CHARMER

"Amusing, entertaining romance."

—Booklist

"Bradley infuses this adventure with so much sexual tension and humor that you'll be enthralled. You'll laugh from the first page to the last . . . The wonderful characters, witty dialogue, and clever plot will have you wishing you were a Liar too."

—RT BOOKclub Magazine

THE SPY

"Only a clever wordsmith can make this complex, suspenseful tale work so perfectly. Bradley pulls us into the wonderful world of the Liar's Club and gives us a nonstop read brimming with puzzle after puzzle."

—RT BOOKclub Magazine

"With its wonderfully witty writing, superbly matched protagonists, and intrigue-steeped plot, the third of Bradley's Liars Club historicals is every bit as much fun as *The Pretender* and *The Impostor*."

—Booklist

"A must for readers of the Liar's Club series and a good bet for those who haven't yet started . . . I unhesitatingly recommend."

—All About Romance

"Ms. Bradley has an effortless style to her prose."

—The Romance Reader

"A Top Pick . . . the best of [the Liar's Club] so far. Bless Celeste Bradley . . . She just seems to get better at it as she goes along."

—Romance Reader at Heart

THE IMPOSTOR

"Bradley carefully layers deception upon deception, keeping the intrigue level high and the tone bright . . . Readers will race through this delightful comedy of errors and eagerly anticipate the next installment."

—*Publishers Weekly*

"With delicious characters and a delectable plot, Bradley delivers another enticing read brimming with the mayhem and madness that come with falling in love when you least expect it. The devilishly funny double identities, witty dialogue and clever twists will captivate."

—*RT BOOKclub Magazine* (Top Pick)

"Don't miss this second book of the Liar's Club series. With humor, passion and mystery, it's absolutely delightful in every way! I can't wait for the next one.

—*Old Book Barn and Gazette*

THE PRETENDER

"Totally entertaining."
—*New York Times* bestselling author Julia Quinn

"An engaging, lusty tale, full of adventure and loaded with charm."
—Gaelen Foley, *USA Today* bestselling author of *Lord of Ice*

"Bursting with adventure and sizzling, Bradley certainly knows how to combine engaging characters with excitement, sensuality, and a strong plot."

—*Booklist* (starred)

"Bursting with adventure and sizzling passion to satisfy the most daring reader."

—*RT BOOKclub Magazine*

"A charming heroine and a dashing spy hero make *The Pretender* a riveting read . . . [E]ntertained me thoroughly from beginning to end."
—Sabrina Jeffries, *USA Today* bestselling author of *After the Abduction*

Seducing
the
Spy

Book Four in the Royal Four series

Celeste Bradley

ST. MARTIN'S PAPERBACKS

This book is dedicated to my dear friend and fellow writer, Cheryl Lewallen. Friends like you don't come along often enough in a lifetime.

SEDUCING THE SPY

Copyright © 2006 by Celeste Bradley.

All rights reserved. No part of this book may be used or reproduced in any manner whatsoever without written permission except in the case of brief quotations embodied in critical articles or reviews. For information address St. Martin's Press, 175 Fifth Avenue, New York, NY 10010.

ISBN: 0-312-93967-1
EAN: 9780312-93967-0

Printed in the United States of America

St. Martin's Paperbacks edition / August 2006

St. Martin's Paperbacks are published by St. Martin's Press, 175 Fifth Avenue, New York, NY 10010.

10 9 8 7 6 5 4 3 2 1

Every ruler needs a few men he can count on to tell him the truth—whether he wants to hear it or not.

Created in the time of the Normans, when King William the Conqueror found himself overrun with "advisors" more concerned with their own agendas than with the good of the whole, the Quatre Royale were selected from the King's own boyhood friends. Lords all, and bound by loyalty rather than selfish motives, these four men took on the names of ruthless predators while acting as the Quatre, keeping their lives and identities separate from their true roles . . .

. . . to act as the shield of deceit and the sword of truth in the name of the King.

Courageous as the Lion
Deadly as the Cobra
Vigilant as the Falcon
Clever as the Fox

The appointment is for life—the commitment absolute. Bonds of family, friends and even love become as insubstantial as a dream when each hand-selected apprentice takes the seat of the master. All else is merely pretense, kept for the sake of secrecy and anonymity. For it is true that the iron bars of duty cage the hearts and souls of . . .

. . . THE ROYAL FOUR.

I would like to acknowledge the hard work contributed by some people we could not do without—our teachers. Many thanks to the creative and committed women and men who help us raise better human beings.

Seducing
the
Spy

Prologue

ENGLAND, 1813

Lord Wyndham,

I am writing to you because you appear to be a somewhat lesser idiot than other gentlemen. The gossip sheets have made much of your cousin Lady Jane Pennington's marriage to a common gambler, yet you continue to acknowledge her, exhibiting excellent judgment for one of your species.

Therefore I choose to trust you with something which has recently come to my attention. I believe there is a plot against the Crown brewing at this moment, the details of which I shall delineate on the following pages.

What you do with this information concerns me not at all. I do not care to further waste my time on the affairs of men.

Lady Alicia Lawrence

1

Stanton Horne, eleventh Marquis of Wyndham, member of the Royal Four—cadre of the most powerful men in England—esteemed scholar of historical documents, and a damned handsome bloke to boot, looked down at the mess on the floor of his grand hallway and bit back a helpless sigh.

"I'm sorry, milord," the servant said quickly. "I'll clean that up right away, milord. So sorry, milord!" Stanton's stammering footman backed away from him rather like one would back away from a dangerous man-eating beast. Stanton raised a hand carefully to make an easing gesture, but the man squeaked and paled anyway. "S-sorry, milord!"

Stanton gave up. There was no reasoning with some people. He'd only meant to apologize to the fellow for rounding the corner of the hall so suddenly and sending his own tea crashing to the floor. Now, the footman would doubtless carry tales of a close call with the master's notorious temper, and of escaping a blow by the nearest margin.

The fact that he'd never raised his voice in this house in his considerably exact memory seemed to have no effect on the awe that his own dependents held him in.

Yes, he could be a demanding master. True, he was not one to socialize with . . . well, anyone, actually. Still, he considered himself a fair and equable fellow, not a great hairy beast who frightened beardless young footmen out of their wits and—apparently—their ability to carry a tea tray.

"Young man—"

"Dobbins, milord!"

"Yes, Dobbins, of course." Stanton took another calming breath. "When you've done here, I would appreciate another tea tray shortly."

The man dropped to his knees as if he'd ducked a bullet and began to frantically gather the broken crockery. His hands shook so badly that the dripping shards flung droplets of tea onto Stanton's boots.

The fellow nearly fainted at that. "Milord! Oh, milord, I—"

Stanton could bear it no longer. He turned on his heel and strode away. Nothing useful would happen while he was present anyway. It seemed all that was required to send his household into spasms of terror was for him to walk into a room of his own house!

It was always thus. Wherever he went, mothers urged their children from his path and even the most belligerent of men averted their gazes. No amount of careful grooming seemed to erase their impression that he was actually a foul and frightening ogre.

It was enough to give a fellow self-doubts.

So perhaps he'd been a mite tense lately. Why wouldn't he be, when the mightiest spy England had ever faced had escaped him and his fellow members of the Royal Four yet again? True, at least this time the Chimera had come out somewhat the worse for wear, scarred and run to earth, hiding from their search efforts, only one step ahead of their best men.

The thought of the evil French nobleman—who had passed among them so easily as a young Cockney valet for so long—hurting and run ragged was a pleasing notion, but what Stanton truly wanted was to have the man's cold dead body laid out in front of him.

Alas, that cherished hope was proving difficult to fulfill. Though the Chimera's talent for disguises had been destroyed with the slashing of his face, there was nothing wrong with the man's brilliant mind.

Furthermore, the war against Napoleon had come to a troubled standoff with both sides taking heavy losses. Swords drawn at each other's throats, England and France currently stood equal, each uneasily waiting for some factor to tip the balance.

Thus the ample excuse for Stanton's touchy behavior lately. He was simply a bit . . . tightly wound.

As he walked away, he heard another footman join the first. Their dread-heightened whispers carried clearly down the hall.

" 'Imself 'as been a right terror these past weeks, ain't 'e?"

Dobbins grunted in agreement. "I thought I was a goner, I did!"

"If he was t'ask me, I'd tell him to find himself a woman, I would. Bloke needs to let steam before 'e blows!"

"Won't 'appen. The master's not likely to find a bird who wouldn't run screaming from them cold eyes! Ain't no lady I've ever seen got the heart for someone like that bleak bastard!"

Bleak bastard? That was a new one. Colorful, if a bit alliterative. Stanton found he rather preferred it to "demon's spawn" and "ice-cold devil." He continued on his way without comment. What good would punishing them for their disrespect do him but create yet more fear?

Still, as he settled into his study to await the next version of his tea tray, it was hard to shake that last comment.

"Ain't no lady I've ever seen got the heart for someone like that."

Unfortunately, that appeared to be precisely the case, although not for quite the reason the footman assumed. If his presence ignited fear in the sturdy East End souls of his staff, it was nothing to what his presence did to the tender sensibilities of lovely and eligible young Society ladies.

Not that he was without fault there. He was not a smooth and flirtatious fellow, nor was he able to set ladies at ease with humorous anecdotes—for he could never think of any at the necessary moments. His lack of the pretty conversation that women set such store by did nothing to dissuade them of his reputedly sinister nature.

Still, what did it matter? Stanton had given up on women a long time ago and found himself better off.

The very last thing he needed in his complicated existence was a woman.

The door knocker rapped sharply three times, sending a resounding noise through the largely silent house. Stanton started, for he was unaccustomed to the sound. Voices came from the front hall through his partially open study door.

"I wish to see Lord Wyndham." A woman's voice, clear and strong. "He wishes to see me as well. He simply doesn't know it yet."

"I'm sorry, madam." The butler's tone was frigid. "His lordship is not inclined to be at home to uninvited guests."

Stanton twisted his lips. He rarely had guests at all, invited or otherwise, which was why the knock on his front door was such an unusual occurrence. Fortunately, Grimm wasn't the sort to disobey strict orders. The person would be gone in moments and Stanton would be able to return to his work.

"I cannot see that he is all that busy. He is sitting in his study, staring at the ceiling. I know because I looked through the window before I knocked."

Grimm, the most ruthless butler money could buy, was reduced to sputtering at such a scandalous statement. Stanton found his own well-cultivated curiosity was aroused. He rose to his feet, drawn by his own need to know. Who was that making such a commotion in his front hall? He leaned partway through his study door.

She was somewhat less than tall and very oddly dressed. Her shapeless gown was too long and dragged the ground, as evidenced by the street muck that the hem was now transferring to his own carpets. Her head was crowned with a hat several decades out of date, which sported a heavy veil that hid her profile.

An unworthy supplicant, Stanton had no doubt. Grimm would handle it.

He moved to step back into his study. Her head snapped around and he could nearly feel the glare piercing that dark veil.

"There you are," she snapped at him. "Tell your man to let me in at once. I must speak to you." Her voice at least was cultured and melodic, despite the irritated bite of it. She was entirely odd, with her commanding manner and her bizarre appearance.

Grimm sent him an agonized look. "She refuses to identify herself, my lord." Grimm looked as though another minute of the creature's company would cost him a major portion of his sanity.

Stanton decided there was no need to cause the butler to have some sort of apoplectic fit. It was hard enough for Wyndham House to keep good help as it was.

The fact that his growing curiosity was doing much to ease his bout of restless dissatisfaction had nothing to do with his decision.

He bowed to the woman and waved his hand to another door. "If you would do me the great favor of awaiting me in the green parlor, I shall be happy to attend you in just a moment."

She didn't curtsy back, or make any of the usual social noises. Instead, her veil remained facing him for a long moment.

"If you think I will simply leave eventually, you are quite mistaken," she said flatly. "I have no pressing plans for the rest of the day. In fact, I have no pressing plans for the rest of my life, so I would advise you to adhere to your word and take no more than a moment."

With that, she turned briskly and put herself in the green parlor, unassisted by Grimm, who was surprisingly slow on the take.

"Hmm." While the woman might appear to be an escapee from Bedlam, she more sounded like a short-tempered army captain. Stanton slid a glance to Grimm, who was staring after the woman with a mixture of glowering hatred and—unbelievably, since Grimm bowed to no one but him—a tinge of respect.

"Grimm, have tea and cakes brought in. Ladies like tea and cakes."

Grimm said nothing as he turned away, but as he walked down the hall, Stanton was fairly sure he heard his unshakable butler mutter something about serving "venom tea and dragon cakes."

Stanton returned to the study just long enough to shrug himself into his coat and tuck the papers he'd not been reading into a securely locked drawer. Depositing the key into its usual home in his weskit pocket, he strolled to the green parlor and let himself in.

Lady Alicia Lawrence turned from her position at the window to greet the man she had come so far in the rain to see. Stanton Horne, Marquis of Wyndham—the only man in London who might possibly listen to what she had to say before throwing her back into the street.

He was a handsome one, to be sure. She could safely admire the symmetry of his rather sharply chiseled features without any worry as to whether he found her similarly attractive.

It was uncanny, really, how much more time she had on her hands since she'd stopped worrying about such things. Of course, she had very little to do with that accumulated time . . . but there was no point in crying over milk already spilled.

She found her gaze lingering upon the rather sensual curve of his bottom lip and snapped her attention back to more of an overall view. What sort of man was this Lord Wyndham, whom everyone knew of but no one knew well?

Even she, cut off from Society as she was, knew that he was as wealthy as a king and as mysterious as a dark wizard in his tower. She did not believe the rumors of virgin sacrifices in the attic, but then again, what did she know of virgins?

He looked normal enough, if devastating dark eyes and an iron jawline could be considered normal. His thick, nearly blue-black hair was pulled back into a perfect queue, adding severity to a face that might otherwise be called beautiful.

She admired his adherence to a classic style rather than the tousled Byronic mop most men were sporting these days. Those who adopted any new fashion that came around tended to be easily manipulated. She ought to know, having been such a person herself once upon a hundred years ago. Lord Wyndham did not look as though a hurricane could push him about.

He bowed to her, a correct but minimal bow. She didn't bother returning the nicety. He'd quit such nonsense soon enough when her reputation came forth. "I am Lady Alicia Lawrence, daughter of the Earl of Sutherland. I have information about an attempt that will be made to kidnap His Highness, the Prince Regent. Are you interested in hearing it, or shall I find someone who cares?"

Stanton felt his curiosity seep away. Oh, drat. She was one of those, the sort that saw conspiracy about every corner. He'd dealt with a few of those irrational people in his years as the Falcon, but this was the first time one of them had sought him out directly.

Which posed yet another question. What had made her think the reclusive Marquis of Wyndham would be interested? Stanton decided that he would very much like to know the answer. After all, he made no practice of publicly being seen to be involved in anything even faintly political.

Perhaps he ought to take Lady Alicia more seriously. "May I have my man take your bonnet?"

She touched her gloved fingertips to her mildewed veil. "I would rather it remain."

He ought to insist, but she might ask the one question he did not want to answer.

Why?

He had no desire to explain himself, for to do so would only land him in Bedlam. How could he tell this woman that he needed to see her face in order to tell if she was lying? She would ask him how he could possibly know that, and he would not be able to reply with any sort of truth, for he did not know how his peculiar talent worked. He didn't even much like to think on it, for he took pride in being a rational man, and he was . . . but for this one thing, this ability that he believed in wholeheartedly, for it had never failed him.

For Stanton's entire life, he had somehow known when he was being lied to. As a child, he had detected the easy lies adults tell children as a matter of course. He had known he would not be stunted if he neglected to drink his milk, he would not die if he ran with scissors, and as much as a young lad might abuse himself, he would never, ever go blind.

As he matured, he found that he could detect even the withheld truth, or at least the act of withholding. He learned the lies people told to spare themselves shame, or effort. He became familiar with the lies they uttered in pursuit of money, or of love.

Veil or no, even he could tell that the person before him was losing patience with his inattention.

She waved a folded sheaf of paper at him and tilted her head. "If you had read my letter—for which someone in your household refused to pay the post—you would already have a full account of what I overheard," she said shortly.

She was annoyed with him. Stanton couldn't begin to describe how much he didn't care. "Lady Alicia, perhaps you might recount it for me now."

In a moment he was going to recall where he'd heard of Lady Alicia Lawrence before. He himself hadn't refused her letter, but he was sure Grimm had, under orders. Anyone with news of importance knew better than to trust the post with it, therefore it followed that there was no reason to clutter up his existence with letters and invitations he had no intention of responding to.

Lady Alicia seated herself at last. "Four nights ago, I overheard a conversation. Three men discussing the 'relocation' of the Prince Regent. They intend to capture him at a house party to be held at the estate of Lord Cross." She hesitated. "Do you think it's possible that the Prince Regent would actually attend such an affair?"

Not only possible, but probable. Cross's parties were notorious for the lascivious madness that went on. No one ever actually admitted attending, but rumor abounded concerning the nature of events.

"I think it is a certainty." George was not a man to pass up licentious diversions. Moreover, George's recent disaffection—to put it mildly—with the Four meant that they were overdue some royal misbehavior.

Relocation. George could be in trouble. Again.

This was not something Stanton would want to leave to commoner hands—and what could the Liars do? Only those of his rank and higher—not many of those either—could get close and stay close to the Prince Regent if the man didn't wish it, not even his bedmates.

Bedmates.

Licentious diversions.

Suddenly, Stanton remembered where he had heard of Lady Alicia Lawrence before.

Five years earlier, a young debutante had been caught with a stable boy in her bed—a simpleton stable boy at that. Bloody hell.

Stanton's carefully polite expression soured. This faded and ill-fitting disguise concealed one of the most notorious women to scandalize Society in a generation.

In typical Society fashion, the young lady's wild ways had become the stuff of legend. The uproar had cast echoes into all reaches of Society and the well-bred daughters of England had been guarded much more closely since that day.

The woman before him was a discredited wanton. What a waste of time, time he did not currently have to spare.

He stood. "Thank you ever so much, my lady. I shan't keep you any longer."

She stood as well, but remained where she was. He could feel her gaze piercing him from behind the veil.

"I see your memory is not faulty, Wyndham. I take it that you've just recollected my reputation."

He bowed perfunctorily. "Lady Alicia, I am a very busy man—"

"Of course." She did not curtsy, but merely turned and walked from the room. "You needn't see me out. I made sure to remember the location of the exit. 'Tis always best to be prepared." With that she was gone.

What a stunning bit of rudeness. He was well shut of her. He turned to leave the room himself. Now he could turn his attention back—

Damn. His curiosity continued to twitch despite the fact

that the woman was obviously disturbed. He wanted to know more, but shuddered at the thought of inviting the creature back into his house.

Where was that letter? Ah, she'd left it on the side table.

Stanton picked up the folded sheets of paper and flicked them open in one motion. Ah, she had indeed written the entire account for him. She certainly was putting a great deal of effort into fluffing up her story.

Then his gaze caught the words "scarred man."

Bloody hell. There was only one scarred man on his mind at the moment.

The Chimera.

He turned abruptly and ran from the house after the woman, but she was well gone. There were no hackneys on the street, nor any shabbily dressed pedestrians.

Lady Alicia had disappeared.

2

As soon as Stanton had given up on following his odd visitor, he had set about investigating the woman. His first stop, Diamond House.

"Lady Alicia Lawrence?" Stanton's cousin Lady Jane—or Mrs. Damont as some might consider her but no one did—knitted her brow. "I may have heard some gossip . . . but I really didn't pay attention." She poured tea, then smiled up at him, her green eyes gleaming. "Why? Has someone finally caught your eye, Wyndham?"

He blew out a breath. "A world of no." He took the offered tea absently and settled back into the wide wing chair Jane had offered him. Taking a breath, he allowed his shoulders to relax slightly.

Jane's presence was rather soothing, at least when she was alone. She had never said as much, but he knew she completely disregarded his reputation. Stanton had the thought—which he'd had many times before—that he wished he'd had more exposure to young ladies like Jane in his youth, sensible ones with good minds and steady nerves.

Well, perhaps not as much nerve as the creature who had called on him today. "She came to my house this morning to berate me and men in general," he told Jane. "And to give me some disturbing . . . political news."

Jane's gaze brightened further. "A new case for me?"

"*No.*"

The flat refusal came from both Stanton and from the doorway behind him.

Jane's eyes went from bright to shining as she looked up at the newcomer. "Hello, darling."

Stanton didn't stand, or even turn. "Damont."

Ethan "the Diamond" Damont, former useless card cheat and now rather annoyingly useful spy, came around to sit upon the arm of Jane's chair. Seeing as Ethan was a big lout, the chair gave a creak of protest. Damont dropped a kiss on the top of his wife's head and let his fingers toy with a wayward strand of strawberry-blond hair.

To Stanton, the gesture didn't seem so much a territorial gambit as it did a "so mad about his wife he couldn't keep his hands to himself " motion.

Stanton was himself rather fond of his brilliant cousin. He was somewhat less fond of her choice of husband, although he reminded himself—often, daily even—that Ethan had been an exemplary spouse . . . so far. Perhaps it was fair, then, that Damont was none too fond of Stanton either.

Now, Ethan watched him through slitted eyes. "Jane, I can't do a thing with Cook," he said. "Everything I tell him goes in one ear and out the other. He'll only listen to you." He sighed. "I miss my old cook."

Stanton grunted. "Your last cook was a Liar's Club operative sent to keep an eye on you." Something that in Stanton's mind could have been continued indefinitely. "She has better things to do now than bake your crumpets."

Ethan sighed. "Oh, but the crumpets . . ."

Jane patted his hand and rose. "I'll fix Boxer for you, pet. Were you still after those little lemon biscuits?"

Ethan nodded eagerly. "Yes, please."

Jane smiled at Stanton. "I'll be back in a moment, after Ethan has his little talk with you." She slid a knowing glance at her husband. "Not subtle, my love. Not one little bit."

Ethan shrugged, then took the opportunity to slide down into the vacated chair across from Stanton.

Stanton never quite knew what to make of the irreverent gambler who had captured, and been most thoroughly netted by in return, the indomitable Jane.

Ethan had no respect for authority—after all, here was a man who called the Prince Regent himself "Old Codger" to his face. He was entirely without restraint or social compunction, but there was no denying his effectiveness. After all, who would ever expect a layabout gold digger who'd married above himself to be a dangerous counterespionage operative?

Stanton had not been wrong about Ethan, exactly. The fellow was without scruples or honor. Yet those same shady tendencies had made Ethan a valuable member of the Liar's Club, the ring of spies and criminals that was the hand of the Royal Four.

Still, Stanton had no illusions that the dog had changed his spots. It was only Ethan's consuming adoration of Jane that kept that particular hound on the leash.

Stanton felt a moment of envy for Damont's insouciance now, for he couldn't remember the last time he'd slid into a chair with such fluid relaxation.

With Ethan, however, languid ease never lasted long. He leaned forward, elbows on knees, hands dangling casually, and fixed Stanton in his suddenly fierce gaze.

"No, no, a thousand bloody times *no*."

"No, what?"

"No, you are not going to involve Jane in another of your 'deadly consequence be damned' cases. She barely survived the last one." His gaze went dark and inward. "When I saw her burns . . ."

Stanton had been spared such visual confirmation of the deadly error that had nearly cost Jane her life at the hands of the Chimera a few months ago, but he had not forgotten his own guilt in the matter. He'd thoughtlessly sent Jane into the thick of conspiracy with no way to reach him quickly enough to help her, should things go wrong—and they had.

Still, he found himself defending his position yet again. "She was only supposed to observe her uncle's household, not involve herself."

Ethan grunted. "Then you didn't know her very well."

Another regret. "No, I'm afraid I didn't." Young Lady Jane and her delicate, emotionally unstable mother, the previous marchioness, had been banished to a life of poverty and neglect when Stanton's father had become the new Marquis of Wyndham. Not Stanton's fault precisely, but then he'd never bothered to ask what became of them either, until he'd taken over the title two years ago and discovered the appalling conditions the two ladies were living in.

He'd done what he could to make the late Lady Wyndham's existence more comfortable for her last days. Jane, however, he'd immediately seen as valuable and had promptly put her into use for his own ends. England's ends.

However, Stanton wasn't about to let the irritating Ethan in on his personal misgivings. "You seem to have no objection to Jane's working within the Liar's Club."

Ethan didn't back down. "It isn't the spying, and it isn't that Jane isn't more than capable. The problem is you and your willingness to sacrifice anything and anyone to achieve your ends, you cold bastard."

There it was again. "Actually, I prefer 'bleak bastard,'" Stanton muttered faintly.

Ethan didn't slow his attack. "Sometimes I wonder if you think everyone has your lack of interest in life—or if you simply think so little of the welfare of others that you expend them like lamed horses or soiled gloves!"

The shot went deep. Stanton felt himself grow colder as Ethan went on. "I do not consider Jane expendable," he said stiffly. "And I do not need her for this mission."

Ethan leaned back, only partially mollified. "So you have someone else to sacrifice this time?"

"Lady Alicia is not going to be sacrificed," Stanton said tightly. "She is merely the source of some information that I am not yet sure merits investigation."

Ethan raised a brow. "Lady Alicia? Not Lady Alicia Lawrence?"

Stanton tilted his head. "What do you know of her? I remembered her being involved in some social mishap a few years ago."

"Mishap? Debacle, more like. She wreaked havoc at a house party in Devonshire, taking on three men in one night—and her a mere maid of eighteen too. Actually, I was there, although I missed the worst of the uproar. Apparently several reputable witnesses found her—in all her tumbled glory, mind you—in the arms of a simpleton stable boy."

Ethan raised a finger. "I never held it against her, myself. She was a good sort before all this—always game for a laugh, not above a bit of harmless flirting with the common gambler. Not that she ever did anything out of bounds, until that night."

"It might have gone easier for her if she'd not denied it all so vehemently," Ethan mused. "She claimed that she had thought the stable boy to be someone else, a lord I think, although anyone could see he was a homespun horse boy without the sense to keep his hands off a titled lady. Then it came out that someone saw two other fellows leave her room in the wee hours. The man she claimed to have been ruined by—Lord Almont, that was it—denied having anything to do with her. Came up with a witness who said he'd been at the cards all night."

Ethan shook his head. "Poor lass. I suppose she was trying to save herself from the worst of it, but being a wanton is bad enough without making a reputation as a world-class liar on top of it."

Stanton grimaced. Hellfire. It was every bit as bad as he'd thought. He was basing a time-consuming investigation on the word of a well-known fraud.

He rubbed a hand across his face. Perhaps he ought to toss the entire "kidnapping" matter into the rubbish bin at once and wash his hands of the irritating Lady Alicia forever.

But what if it were true?

There was just enough fact in her story—fact that she could not have otherwise known—to keep him dangling on the hook of indecision for an uncharacteristically long moment.

No. There was no help for it. He was going to have to track down Lady Alicia's conspirator or else establish his lack of existence.

So you have someone else to sacrifice this time?

There would be no sacrifice. Lady Alicia, wanton liar or not, would come to no harm at his hands.

He would see to this matter personally.

Out of curiosity, and to verify the facts—for Stanton never credited gossip as truth—he took himself off to Sutherland House to speak further to Lady Alicia.

She was not there. In fact, the butler went completely ashen at the mention of her name and seemed to actually be considering the wisdom of slamming the door in the Marquis of Wyndham's face. Stanton took the agonizing decision out of the man's hands.

"I suppose I shall have to contact the newssheets, then, to see if they can tell me her current whereabouts . . ."

In seconds he was invited in and closeted with a red-faced Lord Sutherland and a pale and shaking Lady Sutherland.

Alicia's father was a large fellow who had perhaps once been of a hearty mien, but now seemed gray and bloated. Alicia's mother was thin and weary-seeming, as if she'd not much left to her.

They could hardly bear to speak of their infamous daughter long enough to inform Stanton that they had forced to deny her entirely in order to protect their other two fine and virtuous daughters from their sister's unholy influence.

Interestingly enough, they were lying. Lord Sutherland glanced away often, although that could be from shame. Lady Sutherland, on the other hand, gazed at him solemnly, scarcely blinking. Was she so practiced in the art of lies that she could seem so truthful? Still, they lied. He knew it.

Yet, they'd told him nothing but that they had shut out their wayward daughter. Now what could be untrue about such an obvious statement? Still, they lied. He knew it.

"She turned on us then," Lord Sutherland said with a tremor in his voice. "She looked at us as if we were the ones committing the crime and declared that *she* would no longer know *us*!"

"So you can see why we do not care to speak of her . . ." The pale and breathy Lady Sutherland fluttered her hands, unable to finish.

That, at least, his senses told him, was true. Which was all very tragic and pitiable and reinforced Stanton's opinion that marriage and offspring was a province best left to men with much more time on their hands, but Stanton still hadn't an answer to his question.

"Where will I find Lady Alicia?"

"We've only this Season felt able to show our faces in Society again," Lady Sutherland said tearfully. "Five years we've hidden out in the country. Now, our daughters—good, virtuous girls!—might still make good matches but only if Alicia remains out of sight and out of mind."

She sniffed and blinked at Stanton woefully. "Lord Wyndham, you do not intend . . . you do not intend to bring up such painful history again? Why do you need to find Alicia? What is she to you?"

Stanton could not tell the woman that he was the Falcon, one of an ancient secret cabal of lords known as the Royal Four—king makers and king breakers all.

That information was kept in the closed hands of a very few trusted individuals, the Prime Minister and the Prince Regent among them. Knowledge such as that was not for the weak, mortal members of Society at large.

So he merely said, "I have a small business matter to discuss with Lady Alicia."

He waited and the couple responded as people usually did, gradually becoming more restive and apprehensive under his even gaze. His eyes did seem to have that effect on people.

"Barrow Street," Lady Sutherland blurted finally. "In Cheapside!" Then she clapped a hand over her mouth and shot a mortified glance toward her glowering husband.

Truth. Stanton stood and bowed. "Thank you. Good evening." He turned on his heel and left, not terribly concerned what befell the lady. They were liars both, although they didn't seem to be lying about Lady Alicia's location. He made a note to himself that Lady Alicia's parents had more to tell him if he so required it.

After Lord Wyndham left them, Lord and Lady Sutherland sat in tense silence for a long moment, then began to discuss his lordship's visit in whispers.

Should they feel relieved that the man was gone, or should they be alarmed that Alicia had brought new attention to herself and consequently to them?

They both agreed however, that they had done the right

thing not mentioning to Lord Wyndham the other man who
had so recently come seeking information about Alicia.

"That business is best left alone."

If only they could make it all simply go away.

3

Hours after leaving Lord Wyndham's residence, Lady Alicia Lawrence entered her small, shabby house and threw her hat and veil onto the side table with enough force to send it skidding across the invitation-free surface and off the other side to the floor. She closed her eyes for a long moment, seeking fortitude, then bent to retrieve the borrowed item and place it gently on the side table once more.

Millie had not many fine things, and while the hat was nothing that Alicia would have once called fine, it was Millie's. Alicia's elderly former governess was much beloved, despite her sad lack of taste. Alicia looked down at the borrowed gown's hem and sighed. She would be up late scrubbing the soil from the ancient silk, that was very certain.

Millie came tottering down the hall on her cane, her gaze brightening when she saw Alicia. "Well, did he let you in? Did he believe you? Is he as handsome as they say?"

Alicia smiled. "Yes. I don't know. More so."

Millie nodded and smiled back. "Then it's a good thing you wore my fascinator, isn't it?" She picked up the hat lovingly.

"I had many a fellow cast me a second glance while I was wearing this."

Alicia suspected the second glances had been ones of disbelief, but she would never say so.

"Of course, my current gentleman friend needed no such influence. He says he knew the moment he saw me in the garden that I was a lady to be reckoned with. Of course, he's not much to look at himself, but I'm long past caring about that sort of thing."

Alicia was happy that Millie was happy, even if the "gentleman caller" was as imaginary as their "garden"—a stony pit behind the house that intimidated even the weeds from intruding. Imaginary callers were better than no callers at all.

She turned to the speckled mirror gracing the hall and peered closely at her face. The hives were still quite apparent, though thankfully less florid than they had been last night. Her face was still very puffy, unfortunately, and her throat was still quite sore.

It seemed that she could add strawberries to the list of things she could not eat. That was a pity, indeed, for there were still several pints of strawberry jam in the pantry. Millie's even more elderly cousin had sent them from her home in the country as a gift, and Alicia had been glad to have them. It had been a long time since she'd been able to spare the coin for nonessentials like jam.

She straightened and examined the rest of her reflection. Her entire body had swelled, not dangerously, but too much to wear her own things. She'd had to borrow the gown from Millie as well, for her own could not be buttoned round her puffy midriff. Her skin had been far too sensitive to bear the tight binding touch of too-small clothing.

It looked as though she might be able to wear her own things tomorrow, if she drank a great deal of water and took herself directly off to bed. First she headed off to the kitchen to make an oatmeal paste to ease the itching of her skin.

When the paste had cooled enough to spread over her burning skin, she dabbed it thankfully on her forehead and cheeks.

The door knocker rapped sharply, three times. Alicia started, for she was unaccustomed to the sound. Bloody hell. She didn't have enough oatmeal to spare for another batch, since porridge constituted their main meal every morning. She stepped quickly in stocking feet to open the door as she was.

The Marquis of Wyndham stood outside, all six-feet-and-then-some splendorous male, calling on *her*.

Without the obfuscation of the veil, she was finally able to see—and appreciate!—him fully.

He wasn't a beautiful man, at least not in an easy, golden way. He was dark, with the stern, arrogant strength of an archangel—the avenging sort who carried a sword and had a tendency to smite things.

His height added to that impression. He was broad of shoulder as well, although not brawny. He had large, well-shaped manly hands with long fingers—the sort of hands that knew how to tease music from a pianoforte, yet could easily wield the above-mentioned sword.

In other words, he was entirely to Alicia's taste.

Pity that. What a waste. What was she to do with the man of her dreams—who conversely would want nothing to do with said dreams—now that he had finally come to call?

It was if the devil himself had devised the perfect earthly torture for Lady Alicia Lawrence.

"Now how will I occupy myself when I get to hell?" she muttered under her breath.

Then he obviously took his first good look at her and stepped back. Oh, bother. She'd not covered her face. Alicia stifled a moment of regret that such a man was not seeing her at her best and raised her chin, defying him to view her in all her allergic-bedaubed vividness.

He blinked twice, then bowed. "Lady Alicia, I am happy to find you at home."

Alicia folded her arms and scratched idly at a bothersome patch on her elbow. "Of course I'm at home. I already informed you that I have no plans. Ever."

"Er, yes. Well." He straightened and gazed at her for a long moment. "You are wellborn, you have an education, yet you do not seem to know the slightest of the social graces."

Alicia tilted her head. "Oh, I know them. I simply don't bother to use them." She turned and walked away, leaving him standing in the open doorway. She was already seated by the meager fire in the parlor when he found her. She looked up briefly when he entered. "Are you still here?"

Stanton reined in his irritation with an effort. Obviously, there was something wrong with the woman, possibly even something that was not her fault. One had only to look at her to see that. What a sight—she was positively scaly! Delusional, certainly. He'd just discovered that her background was peppered with such things. He should find her pitiable, not irritating.

It irritated him that he could not pity her.

She sighed and flopped back in the chair. Folding her hands over her stomach, she gazed up at him with half-lidded eyes. "I'm very tired today. State your business or go away."

He found it difficult to tear his eyes away. She was idly scratching her belly through her gown—appallingly rude to be sure, yet his attention was caught by the way the fabric was stretched against her figure. If he was not mistaken, the woman was carved like a statue of a Greek goddess beneath her reptilian scales!

Discomfort seized him. He shut his eyes. He was not here to eye her curves. He was here to get to the bottom of this conspiracy madness. "Why are you weary?" he heard himself ask.

Wait—that wasn't what he'd meant to say at all. Damn his curiosity. It had a life of its own sometimes.

She leaned her head back and shut her eyes. "I'm weary because it is three bloody miles to your house from here and I was not feeling well to start."

Stanton blinked. "You *walked* three miles? From Mayfair?"

She opened her eyes. "No. However did you pass your mathematics courses in school? I walked six miles—three to Mayfair and three back. I would count it on my fingers for you, but I have only five." She shut her eyes again. "I shouldn't be at all surprised if you possessed one extra on each hand, however. Something must have been holding you back from your studies."

Stanton was not accustomed to being mocked. In fact, he had very little experience with it at all. It was most unpleasant, yet curiously stimulating. He could quite honestly say, if he were asked, that he was not bored.

The woman sighed and stretched, right in front of him. "I'm bored. Go away."

Stanton had not been asked to sit and he had the feeling that he never would, should he stand there until he was white-haired. So he sat, for possibly the first time in his life, uninvited. "Lady Alicia, you came to me with a wild story about overhearing a conspiracy—"

She grunted. She actually grunted. Distracted, Stanton lost his train of thought. Then he shook off his revolted fascination and found the thread again. "You give me the sketchiest of details and then you turn right around and walk out of my house. It took me hours to track you down. No one seemed to know what happened to you after—" He halted. Perhaps that was best not mentioned.

Her eyes flew open. "After I whored myself to a simpleton stablehand, you mean?"

"I do not mean to offend—"

"Oh, bother. Of course you mean to offend! Why else bring it up? It didn't work, for it was a pathetic effort indeed. Your mother must be proud to have a son so thoroughly mannerly that he cannot insult even when he tries." She pushed herself wearily to her feet. She staggered slightly and Stanton swiftly rose to help her. She snatched her elbow from his helping hand. "Don't touch me. It only makes it worse."

"Makes what worse?"

She widened her eyes at him. "Goodness, six-fingered and nearsighted. No wonder you live alone." She turned her face back to the fire. "I'm ill, you cretin. My head is pounding, my throat is on fire, and if you don't leave now I'm planning to vomit on your boots."

"You never told me how you came to hear of this conspiracy." .

She closed her eyes and leaned her head carefully against the back of her chair. "You never asked."

She would try the patience of a stone. Stanton forced himself to harden. "How did you come to hear of this conspiracy, then?"

"While I was vomiting."

Stone. Cold, hard, impervious stone. "And where did this take place?"

She wrinkled her brow, thinking. "The majority of it took place in my bedchamber. Then, when I could not bear the chamber pot any longer, I took it to the privy."

What an outlandish idea. "Why did you not have your maid take it to the privy?"

Her eyes opened. "Ask Millie to go out in the dark when she can scarcely see her way in full daylight? Nor is Millie my maid. At one time she was my governess, then my companion, but I do not employ her now. I support her. She had nowhere else to go when I was shunned. Even if her professional reputation had survived the ruination of mine, she is too infirm to begin again."

So she was at least responsible to her dependants, which was the first intimation that there was anything admirable about the creature.

While he regarded her silently, she rubbed at a crumbling bit of paste on her nose. It fell, leaving the tip of her nose ludicrously bare, pink in the midst of the white mask. He had the sudden image of a white cat, glaring at him through mystical green eyes. All she needed was the whiskers.

He probably ought not to look too closely. He might find them.

"So, you took the noisome pot to your privy . . ."

She wrinkled her nose. More dried paste drifted to the floor. "Not to my privy. I took it down the alley to the public house. I thought they might not notice a bit more filth in theirs."

A highborn lady, in her nightdress no doubt, weak and ill, stumbling about the rear yard of that rowdy public house he'd seen on the street corner? "Are you completely without sense? You could have been killed, or worse!"

The green cat eyes regarded him calmly. "Worse than killed? Are you sure there is such a thing?"

Stanton did not relent. "Yes, there is. A lady's virtue is beyond price."

"You're boring me again." She stood. "Go away."

Stanton stood as well, automatic in his manners. She laughed. "You'd make a proper puppet." She turned that eerie green gaze on him once more. "I wonder who would be powerful enough to pull your strings?"

There was no such person on earth, but this strange woman had no need to know that. Stanton bowed. "If you wish me to leave, I must." He straightened. "I will return tomorrow."

She blinked. "Truly? You will keep returning and returning, all this inconvenient way, until you know the entire story?"

He nodded. "Precisely."

"And your poor coachman, sitting out there in this horrid weather? What of him? What of the valet who must clean the filth from your boots and the laundress who must brush the mud from your trousers?"

Stanton nodded slowly. It seemed he had found the lady's weakness. She cared overmuch for those being vastly over-paid to serve him. "Do not forget the horses, forced to stand in the chill and wet, and the grooms who must rake the mud from their coats—"

One crusted brow rose. "Don't overdo," she said causti-cally.

Stanton knew when to stop. He bowed silently and waited. He wished he could read her expression. Then again, remembering her blotched and scaling features, perhaps not.

"Oh, sit down, you bothersome bulldog!" She flopped back down into her own chair. "If you'll shut it for five entire minutes in a row, I shall tell you everything as it occurred." She pointed at him. "No questions until I'm done."

He nodded again and returned to his own seat. If he could learn all she knew now, he might never be forced to put him-self in this revolting person's company again.

4

Across from Stanton in the tattered parlor, Lady Alicia Lawrence sighed.

"I ate strawberry preserves. Sometimes I discover that a food I was once able to enjoy will suddenly cease to agree with me ever after. Thus with the strawberries. I knew after four bites that such was the case."

Stanton could read her rue even through the clay.

"They were rather large bites. I ought not to have been so gluttonous, but it had been so long—" She shook her head. Fragments of oatmeal went flying. "I induced vomiting at once, hoping to stem the damage. Once begun, I was not able to stop."

What sort of lady discussed such things with a strange gentleman?

This sort of lady, he soon discovered. He was treated to a blow-by-blow account of her encounter with the deadly strawberries, and soon knew more than he ever wanted to know about such illness.

"Thus I found myself by the privy of the White Sow when I heard voices approaching. As you might imagine, I thought it wise to hide myself. There were three men—I saw them sil-houetted against the pub lanterns, although I could not see their faces. One of them lighted a cigar but the other two did not. I thought they were merely having a smoke and settled myself for a wait of only a few minutes. I was rather weak-ened and I feared I would give myself away by stumbling in the dark."

He watched her tell her story with a growing sense of un-ease. She spoke simply and convincingly, though her story was outrageous.

Her delivery was not the problem, nor was he particularly disturbed by the story so far. What bothered him was the fact that he felt entirely blind . . . or perhaps "numb" was a better word.

He couldn't tell.

Truth or falsehood, fact or fiction, he could always tell . . . until now.

It would be easy to blame the crusting paste that coated her features, but he'd seen worse. In the past, men had lied to him while covered in mud, blood and even coal dust, yet Stanton had effortlessly perceived the truth written on their faces.

What sort of creature was she, to defy the ability that had brought kings to their knees? Her immunity to his talent did one thing that, if she had realized it, might have alarmed her considerably. He was now completely and totally focused upon her, like a hawk upon a rabbit.

As she went on, she told the story logically and with good detail. "Two of the men sounded well educated, one with dis-tinctly highborn tones. That alone was surprising, at an estab-lishment like the White Sow. The others didn't actually say 'my lord' but one could almost hear it in their pauses. The third still possessed a hint of Cockney, as if he were perhaps of the servant class. Without preamble, they began to discuss something I thought was a business plan. They spoke of 'arrangements' and 'schedules' and 'delivery.' I listened with only half an ear, for I was feeling more ill by the moment."

Her story was going to grow stomach-churning again, he just knew it. He was already regretting his large breakfast.

Fortunately, she went on without detailing her digestion further. "It was only when someone mentioned the Prince Regent that I realized what I was hearing," she explained.

Every fiber of Stanton's being was on full alert now.

"They spoke of Lord Cross's house party and of the Prince Regent's expected appearance there. There was speculation on how His Highness tends to dismiss his guard at such events and how one might take advantage of such moments to get close."

Now Stanton was doubly concerned. If what she said was the truth, the Prince Regent was in terrible danger.

If what she said was true.

Bloody hell. His instinct had never failed him before—yet it failed him now when faced with a potential disaster! He could not swallow this—this affront to his reliability. Admittedly, a lifetime of having the upper hand made such a humbling moment go down doubly ill.

Yet what truth could there be here? The girl was a known liar. She resided here in this rat hole, in a ruin of her own making, bored and doubtless resentful. Only someone desperate for attention and notoriety would have done what she did five years ago—and that desperation was merely erupting again, only this time she was trying to drag him into it.

That was another thing . . . why him? Her reasoning that he had proved himself to be open-minded was plausible enough. God knew he'd exercised the greatest breadth of his own tolerance when his very worthwhile cousin Jane had decided to wed that worthless, Jack-of-all-crimes gambler, Ethan Damont.

So to the outside world, Stanton probably did seem to exemplify the height of social tolerance—and who better to turn to when one was an outcast, exiled by one's own unseemly tendencies?

It wasn't true of course. Not only was Stanton not tolerant of such misbehavior, he was harshly judgmental of even the smallest weavings of untruth. He'd grown up in a house of lies, existing within such a morass of heaving untruth and secrets that he'd sworn never to believe anything he could not prove with his own observation.

However, he could hardly explain that to this woman. She was gazing at him now, waiting for his response to her story.

Damn. He would love to dismiss this insane creature, to get up and leave this hovel without a single doubt that this was merely a pathetic attempt to regain something of Society's regard . . .

But he couldn't. As long as there was some shred of possibility that she told the truth, he would be remiss in his duty if he did not investigate thoroughly.

He was never remiss in his duty.

"They spoke of another man with great respect. 'Monsieur' was how they referred to him. Apparently, Monsieur is ready to implement a plan that has been brewing for some time. I was listening very hard by that time, you can be sure." She stopped and coughed dryly.

Stanton remembered her sore throat and rose. "Let me ring for some tea," he said. Her choice to fall from grace was no reason for him to abandon his own good manners.

She snorted. "Ring whom? If I want tea, I must make it myself."

Frustrated, Stanton wished he could offer to do so, but he frankly had no idea how. "Water, then?"

She tilted her head as she looked at him. "You would fetch a glass of water for me?"

"Of course."

Her lips twisted. "You truly do want to hear this story, don't you?"

Stanton felt his irritation rise again. "Can you not allow anyone to help you with anything? Direct me to the kitchen at once!"

She sighed gustily and leaned back in her chair. "Down the back stairs and to the right. It's the odd-looking room with the great stove and sink in it."

Stanton didn't bother to answer the jibe, but merely turned and left the parlor. He returned in a few moments with the water. "Here you are. I managed to find the kitchen, the glass, and work the pump all by myself."

Her jaw dropped as she automatically reached for the glass. "Was that a joke? Do heroic Greek statues joke? I don't believe it," she stated firmly. "Nowhere in your reputation has anyone ever hinted that you own a sense of humor."

Interesting. For all of half an hour, Stanton had forgotten his blackened reputation. He bowed. "My apologies. I shall strive not to disappoint you again."

She was sipping the water and choked slightly. "Stop it," she gasped. "It's unnerving."

Stanton was actually a bit surprised at himself. He was normally much more focused, especially while on a case. She was obviously driving him out of his senses. "If you are well enough, I should very much like to hear the rest—"

"Too many words," she interrupted. "Simply say 'continue.'"

Stanton nodded with a twist of his lips. "Continue. Please."

She scowled. The clay on her forehead cracked. "Mummy's proper boy." She took another sip of water and set the glass aside. "The two men refused to join the nobleman's cause, claiming the plan too dangerous. The stout man declared that 'the scarred bastard is welcome to any bounty Napoleon might pay him, but that doesn't mean I'm willing to die for it.' Then they left, passing my hiding place. I ducked down until they were gone. When I looked again, the nobleman had gone back inside—or at least, he did not pass me."

"No names were used? You have no idea of their identities?"

She shot him an ironic glance. "Oh, so sorry. Was I supposed to approach them and ask?"

"What of their statures? Were they large men or small?" The Chimera was a small man, although able to disguise nearly every other aspect of himself.

She squinted up at him. "That I did not see clearly. The nobleman was hooded and stayed in the shadows. The man with the cigar was somewhat stout and the Cockney fellow was not."

"What of their clothing? Was there anything distinctive in their clothing?"

She sighed. "It was too dark. The only things I remember as being distinct were the stout man's tobacco and the nobleman's voice."

Tobacco? That was an excellent clue. Many a gentleman ordered a signature mix from the tobacconist, as individual as their names. If he could bring her a selection of cigars—

"What of this supposed nobleman? What was so singular about his voice?"

She shrugged. "He had a peculiar twist to his pronunciation."

"Can you mimic this peculiarity?"

She shook her head. "I am a terrible mimic. I will only mislead you." She shrugged. "I would likely know him if I heard him again, but I cannot describe it properly."

Frustration rose in Stanton. Not only was this the best clue in the entire matter, his every instinct told him that the "Monsieur" the conspirators spoke of was none other than the Chimera himself.

The enemy of the state was at work once more . . . and this rude, uncooperative, unsightly madwoman with the soiled reputation was the Royal Four's best and only hope of capturing the French spymaster who had cost them all so much.

If only Stanton could find the nobleman doing the Chimera's recruiting.

"I would likely know him if I heard him again."

If only he could bring her back into Society . . . Stanton stared unseeing at her as his mind swiftly ran scenario after scenario through his mind.

She glared at him. "What is it you are thinking? I can hear the gears turning from here."

"There must be some way to get you back out into Society where you could help identify the nobleman from the plot."

"Oh, shall I don my best dress and meet you at the soonest musicale?" She shrugged dismissively. "I cannot make any such appearance and you know it."

"Perhaps you could pose as a servant?"

She shook her head. "I'd be recognized. Open a dictionary to define 'notorious' and there's an image of my face listed there."

"You could go to Lord Cross's party with Lord Wyndham."

Both Alicia and Stanton turned in surprise to see Millie seated comfortably in the chair nearer the door, her folded hands resting primly on her cane.

Lord Wyndham's brow clouded. "When did you enter the parlor, madam?"

"Oh, I've been here for ages. But do not fret, my lord. I've heard the story already. I was the one who told my lady to write to you." Millie's face creased happily. "What fun you'll have, my lady! You'll be the belle of the ball once again!"

Alicia slid her gaze sideways to see Lord Wyndham's reaction. He was gazing at Millie with a glaze of horror in his eyes. Then he looked at her and the horror increased tenfold.

"She's teasing," Alicia said hurriedly. "She's mad. Senile. Truly, she'll begin to drool in a moment."

Unfortunately, the horror was fading from Lord Wyndham's expression, to be replaced by calculation and consideration. "It could work."

"No." Alicia held out both hands. "Absolutely not."

He stood, then bowed deeply. "My lady, would you do me the honor of becoming—" He halted.

She was pressing back against the chair, regarding him with confusion and the dawning of pure horror. Under the onslaught of her aghast expression, the clay was crumbling and drifting to catch itself on the sagging bodice of her hideous gown. Oh, God help him. There must be another way.

He loved his country more than his own life, but . . .

He cleared his throat. "The honor of becoming my mistress?"

5

She stood and paced before the fire. "I can see how you came up with this plan and I suppose it makes sense to you." She scratched at her chin. Snow fell. "It is obviously now my place to shoot great gaping holes in your arrangement."

She turned. "Firstly, who would ever believe a man like you could develop a passion for a woman like me?" She didn't wait for him to respond. "Secondly, why do you care so much to find this nobleman? Why not simply tell someone who takes care of such things?"

Because he was the one who took care of such things. "I cannot take such a slim possibility to the authorities. Besides, it is my responsibility as a nobleman to protect my ruler." It sounded pompous even to him.

She merely gazed at him oddly. "Thirdly," she said, "Why should I?"

That was the easiest answer. "For your country."

She folded her arms. "Hmm, yes. My country. Because England has done so very much for me. My paradise." She narrowed her eyes. "Know this, Wyndham. I would leave England in my wake in a split second had I the resources to go. Leave and never, ever come back."

He drew back, repulsed by the very idea. She could not be serious. "Yet you came to me with this story, out of concern for His Highness."

She shrugged, her gaze on the glowing coals. "I dislike conspiracies and traps. Unjust and despicable. One cannot fight them, for one cannot find them to face them down." She turned back to him. "However, I did my part. I told you. I've no more interest in the matter."

"Why not?"

"I owe you no explanation. I simply refuse. That is all you need know."

Perhaps if he begged on his knees, the heavens might drop an anvil on this poisonous creature's head in the next few moments.

Unfortunately, he wasn't the begging sort. He stood and regarded her from his greater height. "I will pay you a considerable bounty if you can identify this mystery lord—so that I can do my duty and turn him in to the proper authorities. With that, you can sail off to any shore you like and have plenty left to start anew."

Alicia's heart nearly stopped. As easily as that? All her troubles, all these years of deprivation and ridicule, blown away by a wealthy gentleman's easy declaration?

Part of her hated him for it, for treating her like a commodity, to be bought and sold.

Another part of her—the sensible, canny woman who had survived that "fate worse than death" he'd spoken of—that woman made her stick out her hand right then and there. "Wyndham, you have made yourself a deal. Twenty thousand pounds . . . plus expenses."

He hesitated. "Expenses?"

Alicia smiled. She might be a poor, ruined woman now, but

there had been a time when she had been the toast of London. She knew precisely what it cost to be that sort of woman. "You don't expect me to appear in Society like this?"

He eyed her narrowly for a moment, then let his gaze travel down her body. It was rude and assessing, but she didn't blame him. There was no sense in buying the horse without checking its teeth. He took her hand in agreement.

"Are you sure you can you pull it off?" He wasn't trying to be insulting, that was the amusing part.

She threw back her head and laughed. She felt suddenly as light as goose down. "Just you watch me!" She began to pace the room. "I shall need a new wardrobe of course."

"Of course."

"A very fine one, I should think—for verisimilitude, you understand. No one would believe a man like you would keep a woman cheaply."

"Why, thank you," he said dryly. "I think."

She nodded thoughtfully. "And I shall need transportation befitting my new life . . . and of course, I can't get by with only Millie. She simply isn't up to that sort of work." She gazed at him severely, as if she expected him to demand that the elderly woman step to work at once.

He bowed in concession. "I wouldn't dream of troubling Millie from her well-deserved retirement."

She turned to gaze at him with her fists on her baggy hips. "I'm not sure you understand what is required here, Wyndham. I must look fabulous."

Impossible. He cleared his throat. "I assure you, no expense will be spared in that . . . attempt."

She grimaced, shedding flakes of dried he-didn't-want-to-know-what in the process. "I'm not at my best right now, but I assure you, Wyndham, I can hold my own against any woman in Society."

Since she appeared to truly believe that, and since she

was going to need every ounce of confidence to pull this off, Stanton only made a noncommittal noise and changed the subject. "About your reward . . ."

"Twenty thousand pounds." She locked her gaze to his. "Nonnegotiable," she said quickly. "Payable whether you find your mystery lord or not."

"Entirely negotiable," he said easily. "It will be ten thousand pounds guaranteed. I will not reward you the full twenty thousand unless we find precisely who you described—a man with designs against the Crown."

She looked displeased beneath her crusty mask. "I don't know . . ."

"But of course, you'll be allowed to keep the wardrobe and accoutrements."

She took a deep breath and let it go slowly. "Agreed." She stuck out her hand. Stanton pressed it quickly and let go.

Something nagged at him, however. "Why did you finally agree? It cannot merely be the money. Do you have some fantasy of regaining your place in the world? I doubt one woman can expect to reform Society so profoundly."

She scoffed. "Not at all. Why reform something that isn't worth the effort? Society will not change, for people will not change. Since the day we left Eden, there has been some form of Society wherever more than three idiots come together."

He released a short bark of laughter at that.

She looked at him oddly. "You might want to oil that. It seems to be rusting." Then she threw herself down on the seat to lounge nearly horizontal. "No, I do not want reform. I want revenge. Pure, simple, untarnished by higher motives—sweet, sweet revenge." She rolled her head and smiled at him slyly. "And you're going to help me get it."

"Revenge upon whom?"

"My family, the ancient and noble Sutherland line."

"What has your family to do with this matter?"

Her gaze slipped to the window, unseeing. "My ho—my family's home is in Sussex. Lord Cross is one of our closest neighbors." She drew a breath. "My parents are all that is proper and respectable. More now than ever, I'm sure, to compensate for their notorious daughter." She tossed her head, putting on a wide smile. "Have you never wanted to undo time? Have you never turned around and said, 'What was I thinking?' "

"Everyone has regrets."

She rolled her eyes. "Wyndham, I didn't ask if 'everyone' had regrets. I asked if *you* had regrets."

Lady Alicia fixed her gaze on his. He could not lie. "I do," he said gruffly. Then he looked away to resist the probing in her eyes. "I simply do not feel the need to make others pay for my mistakes."

She didn't let up. "But what if what might have been a simple mistake, one that has been made by others but that ended happily enough for them—what if that error was vastly magnified by the actions of others who acted with intentional evil?"

She twisted her feet beneath her and raised herself onto her knees in her urgency. "What if those people not only lost nothing, but gained a great deal while you alone suffered?"

"Vengeance is not—"

"No!" She smacked the chair cushion with one hand. "No more homilies. What would you want, in that case? If you were, after years of being powerless, suddenly offered an ideal opportunity for lovely, public, perfect vengeance?" She gazed at him without relent. "Would you resist?"

He could not tear his gaze from hers. What must she have suffered over the last five years? He could see the prim squalor of her home, imagine her life next to the filthy little pub. He'd seen the care she still lavished on her old nurse, though she doubtless would have survived better on her own. He could imagine the hopelessness of her future.

For Lady Alicia Lawrence, there would never be a husband, children, or any sort of social stature. As notorious as she was, she would be scorned by the lowliest shop girl.

She was watching him. "I used to love Christmas." Her voice was flat. "There were cakes and pies, and my mother would do her best to fill the tree with small gifts she'd purchased with the pin money my father allowed her. My sisters and I would light the little candles on the branches on Christmas morning. The servants used to sing for us then, and right then, for a moment, we were as loving a family as you might ever see."

She tilted her head. "I don't know if they still light the candles. I don't know what Alberta and Antonia find on the tree. I'll never taste our cook's raisin pie again. When my sisters marry, I'll not be invited. When my father passes on, I won't be wanted at the funeral ceremony." She struck the seat again, with both fists. *"They threw me away, Wyndham! One day I'm a cherished daughter, the next day I'm nothing but rubbish!"*

There were bright tears of fury and pain swimming in her emerald eyes, but she was too proud to let them fall as she glared at him. "What would you do, my lord? Would you let that lie? Would you turn the other cheek, or would you take up that perfect opportunity for vengeance?"

He could not answer her . . . for he truthfully no longer knew the answer. He looked away, shutting himself off from the aching vividness of her pain.

"Do not allow your . . . your purpose to interfere with my requirements, Lady Alicia," he said without inflection. "Or our agreement will come to an end."

He turned away, ending the discussion. His thoughts swirled, his usual calm disturbed.

He was not a family man. His mother was a shallow, flighty woman who had kept to her own glittering social life even during his childhood. His only other relation, his cousin Lady Jane Pennington, he'd never met until a few years past. He'd never known that sort of Christmas himself.

Yet for one, endless, breathless moment, he'd longed for it with such a passion that he'd wanted to snatch up a sword upon those who'd stolen it from Lady Alicia.

However, he was no knight intent upon saving maiden fair. He could not allow emotion to sway his strongly held beliefs. He would not aid Lady Alicia's cause.

But, he decided with abrupt inadmissible relief, neither would he stand in her way.

He frowned and turned back to her. "I have no interest in furthering your sinister plans. You are going back into Society for one purpose and one purpose only—to find that man."

She nodded. "I know. That's what so lovely about your plan. It fulfills my plan with no extra effort at all. My very presence at your side will be quite enough to engulf my late family in a storm of gossip and controversy. Their dearest wish is for me to disappear forever. I aim to make that impossible ever again."

Then her weariness seemed to overwhelm her once more. She stood shakily. "You might want to leave soon, if you're squeamish." Millie came to her side at once, a frail support herself.

He stiffened. "I am not."

She shook her head. "If we are to be convincing, you do realize that you'll have to unbend enough to act like an actual lover, do you not?"

He gazed at her expressionlessly. "I shall escort you to and from every event. I shall stand at your side. I shall dance with you. I shall treat you precisely as I would a lover."

She squinted at him, tilting her head. "Which illuminates your solitary state as no other explanation could."

She wobbled from the room on her companion's arm, her ill-fitting dress sagging on her weary form.

"I shall see you in a week's time," Stanton repeated. "Do contact me if there are problems with the arrangements."

She waved back at him weakly without turning around and disappeared. Stanton found himself alone in the tattered parlor, abandoned to make his own way from the house.

Rude, contrary, and vile—his new mistress was going to make quite the splash on Society.

Stanton only hoped he, and the Royal Four, would survive the experience.

When Stanton stepped into the Chamber of the Four, he let the mantle of Lord Wyndham slide from his shoulders and moved easily into the familiar, comfortable role of the Falcon. More and more it seemed his true life began and ended with this room and the other Three present within it.

The room itself was nothing special, for it was a small, non-descript chamber paneled on all four sides with insipid mural work and contained only an elderly table and four rather unusual chairs.

He let one hand slide casually over the carving on the back of his chair, taking comfort in the subtle depiction of a falcon's acute gaze represented there. The Falcon had saved him, given him reason to see each day through, until it became his true life—Lord Wyndham falling aside as necessary with greater ease every year.

He glanced about to see if the other three had noticed his uncharacteristic gesture. The Lion, a great blond giant, had already taken his seat and had leaned his wide shoulders back into his own carved alias while he perused the latest reports from the Liar's Club on the search for the Chimera.

The Cobra, dark and allegedly very handsome, must have read them previously, for he sat with arms folded and a half-smile upon his face as he gazed into space. Then again, the Cobra was recently wed.

So was the Fox, but there was no dulling of her sharp

gaze as she raised a perfectly arched brow at Stanton. Damn, she'd seen the gesture after all.

"Wyndham, your chair will not be growing softer, if that's what you're waiting for," she said crisply. Her protégé and husband, Marcus, took his own chair to one side of hers.

The Cobra blinked and fixed his gaze curiously on Stanton. The Lion glanced up from his reading to grin at him. The Fox—that is, Lady Dryden—was the only one yet comfortable with their new policy of dispensing with the ancient code names. "If anyone is close enough to hear our plans, they're going to be able to identify us anyway," she had argued. "Enough of this boys' club nonsense."

So it was Lord Greenleigh, Lord Reardon, Lord Wyndham and Lady Dryden who sat about the table, or, when things became more heated, as they sometimes did, it was "Dane," "Nathaniel," "Stanton," and "Julia."

All of whom now watched him expectantly.

Stanton cleared his throat. "I have called you all together to inform you of a new development. Someone is trying to round up support for an attempt against the Prince Regent."

Dane narrowed his eyes. "Then we contain him until the danger has passed."

"That will be difficult," Nathaniel said. "George has been planning to attend for months. He has even ordered a fireworks display arranged by our own resident genius, Mr. Forsythe."

"Forsythe?" Stanton lifted a brow. The elderly inventor rarely left his messy laboratory in the White Tower, where he worked on various fascinating—if hazardous—projects for the Crown. "At an orgy? He must be close to eighty years of age. He'll kill himself."

Dane snorted. "No danger of that. If there were gunpowder and fuses about, I doubt Forsythe would notice Aphrodite herself."

Julia tapped a finger to her lips. "Would repression not only push George to step farther out of bounds?"

Stanton nodded ruefully. "I believe it is possible. He is still furious at our meddling with his . . . er, mistress selection."

Dane raised a hand and nodded. "I take responsibility for that one. It seemed like a good plan at the time."

Julia slid him a sideways look. "Perhaps if you had had a woman's opinion on the matter, you might have thought twice."

Dane grinned at her companionably. "Hindsight is perfect, Lady Julia, but it's never much help at the time."

Nathaniel leaned forward. "The cause is moot. George is thoroughly infuriated with us four and not likely to listen to any advice we offer."

Dane cut in. "What of Liverpool? Do you think he could influence George?"

Nathaniel shook his head. "Liverpool is even farther in the hole than we are. George is extremely unhappy at the moment. His outrageous behavior is becoming less and less predictable. He is drinking more and gaining weight. His new mistress reports that he is indulging in progressively more debauched behavior."

Stanton nodded. "Hence the attendance at Cross's orgy." He stood, feeling absurdly discomfited by what he was about to report. "That is why I have decided to attend Lord Cross's house party. My informant will pass as my mistress, giving her the opportunity to identify the voice she overheard."

Dane blinked. "You're attending an orgy? *You?*"

Stanton clasped his hands behind his back. "I believe I have all the required equipment for the mission. What's more, my informant will only be posing as my paramour."

Nathaniel blinked. "Well, I suppose bringing a mistress will appear less odd than showing up by yourself."

Julia narrowed her eyes. "How can you be sure you can trust this woman? Who is she?"

"It is not a matter of trust, Lady Dryden. She is there only to point out the alleged conspirator. I will do the subsequent investigating. She doesn't know anything but that I am a concerned and loyal Englishman who wishes to avert a disaster."

Julia crossed her arms and regarded him with raised brows. Nathaniel and Dane exchanged glances.

Stanton waited. Eventually, Nathaniel leaned forward with his fingers clasped beneath his chin. "Wyndham, you still haven't told us her name."

Damn. This was going to be more difficult than he'd realized. "My informant is Lady Alicia Lawrence."

The uproar was immediate.

"Lady All-three-cia? You cannot be serious!" Dane's bellow threatened to shake the spiders from their webs in the rafters.

Nathaniel was suspiciously silent. Of course, he would not be one to hold someone's reputation against them, his own only recently having been restored to him.

On the other hand, Julia was icily appalled. "You are making such a break in your cover on the word of the most notorious liar in Society?"

Behind her, Marcus was hiding a smile behind his hand. "Don't believe everything you hear, my dearest lady."

Julia shot a glance behind her. "Shut up, darling." She turned back to Stanton, her horror somewhat abated. "Forgive me, Wyndham. I should have realized that you would know whether or not she was telling the truth."

Nathaniel was watching this exchange quietly. Now he sat back, his head tilted curiously. "I've been hearing about this skill of yours, Wyndham. Can you truly be sure she's not a liar?"

Julia turned to Nathaniel. "I trust Wyndham's instincts. You should too."

Stanton could not let it lie. "There seems to be a problem there," he murmured.

Nathaniel went on. "I'm not sure I believe in such a thing."

Julia wasn't backing down. "Well, it was instrumental in the determination that you had no real part in the conspiracy of the Knights of Fleur."

Nathaniel scowled. "I was operating covertly. For the Four, I might add."

Dane raised his hand again. "We all know that, Nate. But I have to say, Wyndham's skill is pretty impressive. I've never seen it fail."

Stanton rubbed his head. "Until now," he said reluctantly. "I cannot read her."

Dane leaned back. "Well, hell."

Julia frowned. "You cannot read this woman? Why not? Is it because you are attracted to her?"

Stanton let out a protesting noise. "Absolutely not. Really, truly, most emphatically not."

Julia looked unsure. "As I recall, she is fairly young and was well brought up before her fall. Surely she isn't that bad. Otherwise you could not plausibly pass her off as your mistress."

Stanton felt his shoulders ache with the strain of further stiffening. "I am hoping Society will buy that I am partial to stout, pudding-faced women with beautiful eyes."

Marcus quirked his lips again. "Beautiful eyes, eh?"

Stanton nodded shortly. "They're green and . . . well, at any rate, with some help and expensive gowns, I'm hoping she'll pass."

Julia folded her arms again. "I don't know whether to worry about you or about her. Is she aware that your intentions are completely businesslike? She could easily get the wrong idea."

Julia was protective of her gender. While his reputation did him no harm with the Three, she obviously did not discount it completely. "Oh, there's nothing wrong with her brains," Stanton said. "Although her manners could use a bit of work."

Marcus laughed out loud at that. "Says the rudest man I've ever met!"

Stanton stiffened. "I am not rude. I am . . . terse."

Even Dane was laughing. "She was rude to the Dark Marquis? I think I'd like to meet this Lady All-three-cia."

Stanton shot him a look. "I think we ought to refer to her as Lady Alicia, at least for the duration. Besides, there is no point in your meeting her. I will accompany her to Cross's fleshpot and she will point out the alleged conspirator. At that point I will ship her back to her hovel, well paid for her assistance."

"An expensive venture, when you're not sure of her veracity."

"It cannot be helped. If any of you have a better plan, I'm ready to hear it."

Julia looked as though she truly wished she did, but even she had to shake her head. "You must pursue this to its conclusion. I assume that if she is lying, she will learn a valuable lesson in consequences?"

Stanton gazed back evenly. "Indeed. An example will be made."

"Are you sure you don't wish for backup on this one?" Marcus grinned. "I've always been curious about Cross's house parties."

Dane laughed. "I have to admit, my curiosity is itching as well."

Stanton gazed at them all in alarm. "I am perfectly capable of handling this on my own."

Julia was the only one not smiling. She was bloody frightening sometimes. "If you are sure you can handle both the Prince Regent and Lady Alicia, then of course you should go alone," she said. "If you are sure."

"As far as I know, I'm the only one George is still speaking to," Nathaniel added. "And that's only because I'm married to his ward. Perhaps Willa and I should drop in on the week's events. She's very good with George."

Dane looked disgruntled. "Olivia is very good with George as well . . . perhaps a bit too good."

Stanton gazed at them all warily. "Don't. Come. To. Sussex."

Julia tilted her head and beamed him a stunning smile. Though she was most assuredly taken, and not Stanton's type in any respect, her beauty was such that no man could think straight when she focused her considerable charms upon him.

"Now why would we do that?" she purred.

Stanton blinked. The room was becoming warm and it had been a very, very long time since a woman had looked at him at all. The back of his neck began to dampen—

He shot a dark glare Julia's way. "Stop that."

Marcus was a puddle in his chair. "Witness to my daily battle," he gasped between chuckles.

Julia bowed her head briefly. "I defer to the master. You are made of stern stuff, Wyndham. I don't think Lady Alicia has a chance in hell of dividing your attention."

It had been a test. Wyndham would have been angry if he hadn't seen the sense of it. If a renowned beauty like Julia couldn't sway him, what chance had poor, disadvantaged Lady Alicia?

6

Later that evening, however, as Stanton undressed for bed, he began to have his doubts.

For the first time in his memory, he was no more astute than the average human, at least where Lady Alicia Lawrence was concerned. For the first time, he had a taste of the awful confusion and morass of doubt that every person about him suffered through on a daily basis, forced to trust blindly or even to mistake real truth for lies, driven to it by their own suspicions.

When he'd been no more than seven, he had watched his father casually accept a ledger from his housekeeper's hand and he had known the nonchalance was a lie. He had continued to watch as his mother greeted his father after arriving home from a shopping trip to London and he had seen that her bright smile and offhand affection for her husband was a lie.

The housekeeper, a statuesque woman named Ilsa, stood between his parents like a fortress wall, her hold on Lord Wyndham complete. It was obvious to Stanton, even at such a young age, yet no one spoke of it. His mother, whether help-less or simply unwilling to combat the woman, spent more and more time away "shopping," although the rumors of her true activities spread to the estate of Wyndham and beyond, while his father fell more and more under Ilsa's spell.

The handsome, dignified lord, his beautiful young wife, Stanton himself playing the part of the sturdy scion, all liv-ing out the roles given them. Meanwhile, beneath that shin-ing façade there lurked hatred and jealousy, obsession and oppression, writhing and growing like the squirming life found beneath a stone.

So young Stanton had observed the lies. He'd seen the way people moved, the way they held themselves, the very manner of their speech, and he had simply known who lied and who did not.

And discovered, of course, that everyone did, in ways that betrayed their very souls to his eyes.

Until now.

The sickening possibility that he might have lost his unique skill caused Stanton to turn to his valet quickly.

"Herbert, I have decided to adopt a goatee."

Herbert, who was well-known for his disdain of facial hair, nodded without a blink. "Very good, my lord. Very dashing."

Lie. Stanton nearly closed his eyes in relief. "Or perhaps not," he said, to provide good Hamersley with a bit of the same. "Rather too devilish, I would think."

"True, my lord. Too true."

So his mysterious skill still worked, only not on Lady Ali-cia.

Why her, of all people? What strange skill did she have, that she could hide from him, yet the world had no doubt of her lies? Why did she affect him so?

She was odd, rude, indelicate, reputedly unchaste, and . . .

well, damn it, she was annoying, from her bare feet to her green-as-first-spring eyes!

Bloody hell. Now she had him waxing poetic about her damned eye color!

Yet his two encounters with her had put none of his doubts to rest. She wasn't lovely, but neither was she stupid. Surely a woman as sharply intelligent as that would not put herself in such a position to be caught sleeping with a stable boy?

Perhaps there was more he ought to know about Lady Alicia Lawrence after all.

To Lady Alicia Lawrence,

While I indeed instructed you to purchase new items as needed for our purposes, I fail to see the necessity of charging the cost of an entire year's wardrobe to my accounts.

Sincerely,
Stanton Horne, Lord Wyndham

To Lord Wyndham,

I don't expect you to understand the necessity. You're a man. You have no idea what a woman of Society requires. You undoubtedly believe we all wake up looking like fashion plates every morning. Pay the bills and let me be.

A.

To Lady Alicia Lawrence,

Why the need to buy a carriage? I will be escorting you to any and all necessary events and I already own several, admittedly not as opulent as the one you attempted to order, but I find them sufficient.

Sincerely,
Stanton Horne, Lord Wyndham

Wyndham,

Oh, very well. Then I shall require the exclusive use of one of your carriages for the duration. You might as well send along a driver, if you can manage to pry his pay from your tight fist.

I have found a suitable house. Here is the address.

A.

To Lady Alicia,

A house? Are you entirely mad? Why in heaven's name would you need to buy a house? Especially one that is larger and more ostentatious than mine? Why do you need a new address? We will be leaving London in a week.

Wyndham

Wyndham,

I realize that the larger part of the brain of most males resides somewhere other than their skull, but do try to think logically for a moment. No one gossips more than a dressmaker. The fact that you allow me to live in a sewer pit will be all over London—and your precious house party—before we even arrive.

A.

To Lady Alicia,

If you insist upon a new residence—and only for the duration!—then I shall rent you a small, respectable house within the confines of Mayfair. I am confident that will suffice.

It had better.

Wyndham

Wyndham,

It was worth a try.

A.

To Lady Alicia,

I promised to pay your expenses, but I should be highly displeased if you beggar me in the process.

W.

Wyndham,

What are you going to do, ruin my reputation? Oh, worry not. I am only doing what is necessary to create your precious illusion. Besides, mistresses are supposed to beggar their paramours. It's practically a law.

P.S. I need jewels.

A.

To Lady Alicia,

You'll buy paste.

W.

Wyndham,

You're not doing your own reputation any good, you know. Every Society lady worth her salt is trained from birth to spot paste ten yards away.

A.

To Lady A.,

I will take care of the jewels. Do not purchase jewels. At all. In any form. Is that understood?

W.

Wyndham,

Yes, milord. Of course, milord. Whatever you say, milord.

However, must you be so stingy with the salaries for my new staff? We need discreet people who value their jobs. Must I think of everything?

A.

To Lady A.,

I will hire your staff. You may choose your own lady's attendant. Do not press me further.

W.

To Lady Alicia Lawrence,

  You have not replied to my letter of yesterday. Did you fully understand my instructions?

W.

W.,

  No jewels. Hire a dresser. Don't press you. Now stop bothering me. You have no idea what a chore all these fittings are. Go take care of some useless male business and let me do my job.

A.

  P.S. I do think we ought to run a practice excursion before we attend Lord Cross's house party. Perhaps you have received a suitable invitation?

To Lady A.,

  I think not. It is one thing to bring your mistress to a gathering of sophisticated adults. It is quite another to flaunt a woman of bad virtue before the innocent young ladies at Almacks.

W.

W.,

  "A woman of bad virtue"?
  Couldn't have put it better myself.

A.

To Lady Alicia Lawrence,

  I assume from your lack of correspondence during the past two days that you are busily preparing for our departure. I will arrive at your new residence tomorrow morning to escort you to Lord Cross's house party. The journey will take less than a day.

W.

To Lady Alicia,

  Did you receive my earlier notice of our departure tomorrow morning? I received no reply.

W.

W.,
   I shall be late.

                                            A.

To Lady Alicia,
   You shall not.

                                            W.

Stanton folded his admittedly terse note and sealed it absently. He ought not to have written that about the "woman of bad virtue." He had slipped into a strangely informal correspondence with Lady Alicia over the last week and had not been taking careful note of his tone.

Well, there was little he could do about it now, although he would make a point to apologize tomorrow. In fact, it would be an opportunity to model some pretty manners for the woman. Hers could do with improvement.

Herbert tapped at the door of Stanton's study. "My lord, Gunther is here to report."

Oh, dread. What was the maddening creature up to now?

Gunther stepped into the room and bowed. "My lord, you wished to be informed whenever her ladyship made plans without you."

Stanton nodded at Gunther with a wry twist to his lips. "So I did." He'd taken Gunther from his own household and installed him at Lady Alicia's on the off chance the man would be useful. It turned out that he'd been vital to keeping Lady Alicia's excesses in check.

"Her ladyship has arranged to attend the final performance of the opera this evening. She has reserved a very prominent box, where she will be sure to be seen."

Stanton narrowed his eyes and considered his options. Lady Alicia had already proven her complete lack of discretion and decorum. There was no telling what mayhem she might ignite in the torridly dramatic setting of the opera.

"Should I try to talk her ladyship out of her plans?"

Stanton eyed the overeager Gunther sourly. "Thank you, no." Then he smiled slightly. "I haven't been to the opera in years."

If Lady Alicia thought he would turn her loose on an unsuspecting London, she was sadly mistaken. He would meet her there and keep her contained. She would accomplish her goal of putting herself on tawdry display and he would be able to keep an eye on her every move.

And you'll be in public, so you'll be safe.

Stanton dismissed that errant thought. Ridiculous. As if he needed protection from one wayward lady!

Although Alicia had vowed never to care what a man thought of her ever again, she found herself wondering what Lord Wyndham would think if he could see her now.

The gown she'd chosen for the opera was an opulent concoction of midnight-blue winter velvet and gold lace.

"I feel rather like a stage curtain," she muttered as she twisted and turned before the mirror. "From a very disreputable stage."

When she'd ordered the gown, she'd been aiming to cause shock and consternation, and possibly to prompt a few ladies to cover their gentlemen's eyes. The skirts of the gown were designed to cling and sway with her figure's movements, with very little in the way of petticoat beneath. The bodice was boned and padded, secretly of course, to lift and expose every legal inch of skin . . . and then a bit more.

Seeing the upper half-moon of her own areola peeking above the neckline proved to be too much for even Alicia's determination. She took the length of gold lace which had been intended to be used in her hair and tucked it into her décolletage.

Much better. Still daring and still shocking, for the fine lace was anything but solid, but at least she now felt able to leave her own dressing room.

Garrett, her lady's maid—whom she'd hired in an impulsive attempt to irritate Lord Wyndham, but who had turned out to be invaluable in her quest to be outrageous—entered the room carrying the fur cape he had been brushing out for the evening. He stopped when he saw the lace alteration she'd made. "Coward," he said accusingly.

"I know. I simply couldn't." Alicia spread her arms and turned for his viewing. "Will it do, d'you think?"

He tilted his head and folded his arms, studying her. "Do what, milady? Scorch their eyeballs? Yes. Put you down in history as the most scandalous lady in all of England? Possibly, although you'd really need a royal affair to truly make your mark."

Alicia considered herself in the mirror. A royal affair? "Hmm."

Garret shook his head. "Don't shoot at the moon, my lady. Prinny has got himself a brand-new lady and he won't tire of her for months, by all accounts. Besides, I believe that copious amounts of giggling is required in that position. You don't giggle."

Alicia shrugged and let it go. "True. Although I should probably learn to, don't you think? Don't all mistresses giggle?"

"Shouldn't worry about it now, milady. Himself doesn't seem the type, anyway. I think he likes you for your mind, scrambled as it is."

Alicia turned to glare at Garrett. "I told you before, I am not trying to win Lord Wyndham. He and I have a business arrangement, that is all."

"Sure, that's all it is now. But he's unmarried and so are you and I'm a lady's maid. It's my job to make matches."

Alicia narrowed her eyes. "You've been a lady's maid for all of a week. I made you and I can break you."

"And where would you find another male lady's maid so perfectly designed to cause scandal and gossip?" He paused to smooth his golden hair in the mirror. "Especially one so handsome and virile and guaranteed to cause prurient speculation in the most pristine of minds?"

"Ha," Alicia groused. "You're a grandstanding tea-leaf actor and half the world knows it."

He smiled and patted her shoulder comfortingly. "But not the half which you are trying to shock. And so I carry on, poof though I am, gazing at you with seething passion when someone else is in the room and dressing you like a wicked man's darkest dream."

He frowned at the lace in her bodice. "Now stop being a marshmallow and strike as if you mean it, which you do—or you will if you'll stop thinking about what Himself 'll think of you."

Alicia toyed with her neckline uncertainly. "I do mean it . . . or at least I did mean it." She pressed her cool fingers over her hot eyes. "I thought I knew what I was after, but now I'm completely turned about."

"Perhaps if you remember what Lord Almont did to you—"

She shook her head. "I don't want to think about Almont right now. Tonight is about my family. Almont's lies were terrible, but what my own flesh and blood did to me . . ."

Hot betrayal rushed anew through her veins and she regarded her neckline with newly heated resolve. With a sharp movement, she yanked the concealing lace away. "There," she said with satisfaction. If only her family could see her now.

You were so ready to believe the worst of me—well, here you are then. Your worst nightmare come to life. Now you'll be the object of gossip and dismay, you'll be rejected by your peers, you'll be the ones sitting in silence day after day, welcome nowhere, no visitors, until you think you might go mad from the ticking of the clock.

She raised hot eyes to meet Garrett's in the mirror. "Now, I'm ready to go to the opera."

7

Stanton leaned back in Lady Alicia Lawrence's viewing box and regarded the ongoing opera with a level of boredom of which he hadn't thought himself capable. Oh, the soprano was very talented and the set was extravagant, as was the pageantry of the cream of London Society that swirled below him—but Lady Alicia was not here.

Apparently she was making a fashionably late appearance. Since the performance was nearly half over, even the unpredictable Lady Alicia must surely arrive shortly.

Not surprisingly, the orchestra had just begun the next movement when the curtains parted behind Stanton and an usher bowed Lady Alicia through. Stanton stood to greet her.

She seemed startled to see him, hanging back in the shadows that overtook the rear of the box. He smiled cordially enough. She did not seem reassured. "What are you doing here?" she hissed.

"Did I not make myself clear? I am to be your escort at all times."

"You were entirely clear. I simply ignored you." She looked behind her as if contemplating a quick escape.

Stanton debated engaging in a bit of timely sarcasm, but unexpectedly felt no need. In fact, he felt inexplicably light-hearted this evening. He smiled easily at her. "You must be warm. Why don't you let me take your cape?"

She tucked the collar of the cape closer to her throat, hesitating. "I—" She pressed her lips together and gazed at him in irritation. "Oh, I simply do not care what you think!"

She abruptly stepped forward, out of the shadows and into the play of light from the stage lanterns. She dropped the cape and raised her chin defiantly.

Stanton felt his mouth go dry.

It wasn't her. It could not be her. Lady Alicia Lawrence was a blotchy, ill-kempt creature, swollen like a grape and not as appetizing.

Before him stood a faultlessly elegant lady, posed with her head high and her shoulders back, showing off a truly prepossessing figure, if one was inclined to prefer a bit of plump abundance with one's morning cup of tea . . .

She wouldn't be elegant in his arms. She would be earthy and untamed and shameless—

Stanton blinked. That thought had flown through his mind like an outlaw's arrow, coming from nowhere.

It wasn't her.

Yet lively cat-green eyes gleamed at him knowingly.

"You seem taken aback, my lord. And rather boring. In the last week I've spent more money than the Prince Regent's new mistress! Have you nothing to say about my accomplishment?"

She looked like a prostitute—a beautiful, opulent, extravagantly endowed prostitute with sexual fire alight in her eyes.

She was the embodiment—oh, dear God, that body!—of every man's most wicked dream.

Whose dream? Theirs . . . or yours?

The air came back into Stanton's lungs in a rush. "What in the seventh level of hell are you wearing?"

He hadn't meant to bellow and he certainly hadn't realized that the orchestra was just finishing the last movement, and he sure as hell hadn't meant for his question to echo through the opera house like a bass crescendo.

"Oh, well done," Alicia murmured to him.

He turned to gape down at her. She patted his arm with a pleased smile tugging at the corner of her mouth. Then she stepped away from him in a dramatic flounce of skirts. "You beast!"

Again, her voice carried over the hall as if she stood on the stage itself. Every neck craned to see. A soggy sob followed, and then she turned back to him, dramatically wiping her eyes. "You horrible, cruel . . . man! First you seduce me, and then you denigrate me for it!"

For a horrified moment, Stanton thought she intended to throw herself to her knees at his feet, but then she seemed to realize she would no longer be visible to the people below.

To catch herself, she staggered melodramatically, then teetered as she raised the back of one hand to her brow. "I cannot go on this way," she wailed. "I love you so, no matter how cruel you are to me—"

Stanton wasn't entirely sure how it happened. Perhaps she became too caught up in her own performance, or perhaps it was the trailing skirts of the elaborate gown, but suddenly Alicia lurched sideways, hit the balustrade with her hip, and then began to tip over the railing of the box.

Still shocked motionless with dismay at her public theatrics, Stanton almost didn't react quickly enough. It was only when she shot a surprised and horrified gaze to his that he realized she was truly about to fall.

The crowd below gasped in delicious horror and several ladies screamed even as Stanton leaped for her. He caught one flailing hand and wrapped his other arm about her waist even as her feet completely left the floor and she began to flip backward.

Stanton almost lost her when the railing began to crack beneath their combined weight. From the corner of his eye, he saw something fall to the crowd below. Wrapping both arms about Alicia, he swung her high and around, pulling them both back from danger as the railing failed completely and fell.

They rolled together across the carpeted box, ending with her beneath him. The sound of the crowd rose about them as the people who had gathered to help catch the falling lady fled the falling bits of balcony railing.

Stanton heard only his own racing heart and the gasping breathing of Alicia against his face. He wrapped her tightly in his arms and tucked his face into her silken neck.

She hadn't fallen. She wasn't broken and bleeding on the floor below. She was safe and warm in his arms, clinging fiercely to him and shaking from reaction.

Or perhaps it was he who shook. That moment when his grip had slipped—he'd never felt fear like that before.

That fact alone was enough to bring him to his senses. He released her smoothly and stood, holding out one hand for her to take.

Alicia gazed up at Lord Wyndham in confusion. He gazed calmly down at her, as if he were merely a stranger helping a lady up a step. She blinked. Less than a second ago he had been holding her so fiercely—

Obviously, her imagination had failed her again, for she now saw no hint of that desperate emotion on his face. Bemused, she took his hand and allowed him to raise her to her feet.

The crowd beneath erupted into cheers, the opera performance forgotten in the drama being enacted above them.

Alicia blinked at the sea of faces now revealed by the lack of railing. They were smiling . . . cheering . . . her!

"So turns the fickle tide of Society," said a deep warm voice in her ear. "It seems our passionate affair has quite caught their fancy."

Alicia snorted. "And why not, when we deliver such entertaining fare?"

It didn't bode well for her mission, however. How in the world was she to enact her vengeance if Society loved her instead of loathed her?

"I'm simply relieved your bodice remained in place, such as it is."

Alicia raised a brow at him. "That should teach you not to disrespect the feminine arts. It takes work to look this scandalous. I've seen ancient battle armor less formidably constructed than this bodice."

He bowed mockingly. "I concede to the mighty bodice— although I insist that this gown go back to the dressmaker. It seems she forgot to finish the neckline."

"Very well." Alicia shrugged. "Its work is done. I could hardly wear it again, lest I diminish its impact."

"Heaven forefend," Stanton replied wearily. "Now, I shall have one of my men escort you home. I have another matter to attend to. That railing was deliberately weakened."

She nodded. "Indeed. I would very much like to know who rigged this box with a trip wire." She bent to hike one side of her skirt to reveal her ankle. "I felt it cut me."

Indeed, there was a fine bloody slice through one stocking.

Stanton clenched his jaw. He'd not suspected a trip mechanism, although now it seemed obvious. Why else tamper with the railing unless one could guarantee someone would fall against it?

What he wasn't prepared for was the fierce jolt of

primeval protectiveness which shot through him at the sight of her bloodied skin. The wound was nothing—a mere scratch—so why did his vision begin to redden at the thought of getting his hands on the perpetrator?

Lady Alicia was eyeing him with some consternation. "Are you ill? Did you strain something when you caught me?" She leaned close to peer into his face. "You must be more careful."

"Someone wanted you dead," he said slowly. "Now why would that be?" No one but the Four knew of their investigation. Then again, a notorious lady might have made a few enemies on the way . . .

Lady Alicia's eyes widened. "I—" She stopped short. Stanton's attention was caught by the abrupt lack of expression on her face. It was rather eerie in fact, for Alicia's lively features were never still.

"What are you thinking?" he asked, more gently than he'd intended.

She exhaled and smiled brightly. "Nothing. Nothing at all. I shall see you in the morning . . . about eleven, if you please."

"I was thinking a bit—" *Earlier.* But she was gone, with nothing but a fluttering of the curtain remaining.

The next morning, Garrett was calmly packing while Alicia was panicking enough for both of them. "Did you remember the gray satin gloves that go with the—"

"I remembered all the gloves, and all the gowns. I even remembered to include a few pairs of the vast collection of shoes that you billed to poor Lord Wyndham."

Alicia paused long enough to sniff indignantly. "Who knows when I'll have another chance to buy shoes," she reminded him.

Garrett folded his arms. "You're dressed. You're packed but for your toiletries. You have plenty of time—"

Even in the bedchamber one could hear the authoritative rapping of the door knocker. "Oh, blast. He's early!" Alicia patted her hair unnecessarily. "Finish quickly. I'll distract him."

She flew from the room and down the stairs, intercepting Gunther before he could open the door. "I'll get that," she told him. "And by the way, you're fired."

That would teach him to rat out his mistress! It had to have been Gunther, for every time she'd sent him on an errand, Wyndham had been able to mysteriously interfere.

Now, to deal with Wyndham himself . . .

She was late when he'd specifically ordered her to be on time. Therefore, Alicia decided upon a preemptive strike. She threw open the door to frown at Stanton. "How dare you show your face here after the way you behaved last evening?"

That outrageously unjust statement had the desired effect. Lord Wyndham stopped short and actually seemed to be casting through his memory for the alleged offense.

The moment was priceless, and far too much for Alicia. She collapsed into laughter and turned away, leaving him fuming on the doorstep.

She wiped at her eyes and looked back to see him still standing there with a deadly glint in his eyes. "Why are you still out there?"

"I have yet to be invited in," he said, biting out each word with precision.

She put her fists on her hips. "That is ridiculous. I think I shall leave you there to ponder the stupidity of clinging to propriety on the doorstep of a house which you, in fact, are paying for. I shall be in the parlor should you come to your senses."

Casting him one last glance that plainly said she found such an event highly doubtful, she turned away.

She'd scarcely taken two steps before his hand came about her elbow. She glanced up at him. "For someone so constrained by propriety, you do seem to lay hands upon me rather often."

He glared down at her. "We have a timetable to adhere to and some basic rules to discuss. I do not have time for your theatrics."

She rolled her eyes and pulled her arm from his grip. "If you came here to spout rules at me, I'd prefer not to waste a moment on such nonsense." She smiled coquettishly at him. "Since we have a timetable, of course."

"We have an agreement, Lady Alicia. You are to assist me in finding this person. You must adhere to certain rules if we are to succeed."

She folded her arms. "You are repeating yourself, Lord Wyndham. Furthermore, I can break my side of the agreement at any time. I have two feet. I merely need to walk out of that door."

"I could make sure you don't leave this house."

She narrowed her eyes at him. "You could try." Then she shrugged and quirked her lips in that way that drove him mad. "That would not help you find your mystery lord, would it?" She smiled fully and batted her eyes in false flirtation. "I declare, I am beginning to forget the sound of his voice!"

Lord Wyndham growled. She blinked at the sound. "Was that you?"

He took a step toward her. "You believe you have nothing to lose by taunting me thus?"

She raised her chin. "I have nothing, therefore I can lose nothing."

He came another step. She had never been so near him—at least not while upright. He truly was a very large man. An icy tingling began in her belly—or was it fiery? Either way, her mouth still went dry at the way his shoulders blocked the light.

"There is always more to lose," he told her, his voice a husky rumble that worked its way beneath her very skin.

That did it. Her knees went fully weak and she staggered back a step. Or rather, she meant to back away. Apparently, her body had something else in mind. She found herself fully pressed to his broad chest.

Startled, she pulled away, but it was too late. His hands came to grip her shoulders and pull her closer.

"Lady Alicia, you continue to surprise me."

"And me," she gasped. She meant to back away, she truly did, but then she had that thought.

It was the thought that had caused the entire mess that was her life. It was the thought that led her to eat too many green apples when she was twelve. It was the thought that led her into the arms of a liar.

Always the same thought—and always followed by the most terrible consequences.

What is the worst that could happen?

Not a bad thought in itself. The fault always seemed to lie in her lack of imagination. The worst was always much, much worse than she'd envisioned.

She quickly ran down the list of terrible things that could ensue from kissing Lord Wyndham.

He might kiss her back. That would not be so bad.

He might not. That would be a pity, yet survivable.

Then again, considering the dark heat she sensed within him at this moment, his passionate response might land her in his bed . . . or rather, her bed, since they were in her house.

Hmm. She had no reputation to shatter and no virtue to lose. What she did have was one very large, very comfortable bed and two very weak knees.

Yes, all in all, she rather thought she might want to kiss Lord Wyndham.

So she closed her eyes and lifted her face to his, lips slightly parted. And waited.

8

Stanton couldn't move. She was too close . . . too real.

This was a mistake.

Alicia continued to wait. Finally opening her eyes, she stepped back. Her eyes narrowed. "Never mind. I've reconsidered helping you. Piss off." She turned to stalk from the room.

Stanton came out of his daze in an instant. His witness was walking off the case. He caught up with her in a few swift steps.

"You cannot reconsider, Lady Alicia."

She turned. "Oh? Can I not? Observe." She moved away from him.

Stanton ignored a lifetime of social training and caught her by the arm, pulling her closer. "You belong to me now."

Startled—and angry, he'd do well not to forget angry— green eyes fixed on his. "I beg your pardon?"

"I paid for a mistress—put her in a house, bought her a new wardrobe, a new staff. I demand that certain services be rendered in return."

She gazed at him for a long moment. "Very well. But only once."

Then she went up on her toes and kissed *him.*

It was a clumsy, untutored kiss—the kiss of a sheltered girl, fervent and hesitant at once. The innocence of her lips on his transported him directly back to his first achingly sweet kiss, to the boy with the shaking hands and the pounding heart, his first taste of female lips on his. Another time and place—indeed, another Stanton entirely.

Except that boy of the past still lived within him. And what had happened next still loomed over his present. He couldn't allow himself to kiss her back . . . but neither did he stop her. He merely went very still, neither advancing nor pulling back.

This gave Alicia a delicious sense of power. She allowed herself to selfishly explore his lips with hers, tantalizing herself with the differing textures and sensations.

There was the heat of him that sank into her flesh through her lips and her hands where they rested upon his hard chest. There was the surprising softness of his mouth and the tickle of shaven skin above and below. She found herself enamored of the corners, where she could taste it all.

She became aware of the racing of his heart as it pounded against her palms. Had she such a power over his very pulse? She tested her theory by slipping the tip of her tongue between his lips.

More heat. More enticing masculine tastes. Coffee. Mint.

Him.

He still did not kiss her back, although his grip on her shoulders was fierce. However, she became aware of a different response as he pulled her closer still.

Based on the evidence presented in the front of his

trousers, Stanton Horne, Lord Wyndham, wanted to bed her, Lady Alicia Lawrence.

And if size and hardness were any indication, he wanted to do it now.

Now. Stanton's thoughts were simple and urgent. *Now. Here. Immediately.*

She was refreshingly sweet when she wasn't speaking—so tentative and yet so willing. There were things he could do to a woman like that, things that would please them both enormously—for a time, anyway.

This one wouldn't shy. She would take it all and ask for more. She could match any amount of lust, if one allowed her to.

If he allowed himself to.

God, if only he dared. Unfortunately, he feared if he truly released his passion upon Alicia, he might never forgive himself.

He felt her fingers fumbling at his neck. She was untying his cravat while she gently ran her tongue over his teeth. Aching need pulsed within him at her eagerness. *Now. Now.*

He took her shoulders and pushed her back from him. Raising his gaze to the ceiling for a moment, he breathed deeply—once, twice, thrice. At last a shred of control returned. He cleared his throat and looked at her. "Not now. We have a—"

"A timetable." She had one hand pressed to her temple as she stared at him with wide eyes. "Right. God forbid we upset the timetable." She backed away, clearing her throat. "I'll just check on my maid's progress then." She scurried from the room, leaving Stanton to let his shoulders drop with sudden deep exhaustion.

Voluptuous, sensual Lady Alicia, alone with him in the carriage all day.

It was going to be a very long drive to Sussex. Hopefully, the chill in the air would cool his heated blood.

A few hours later, Stanton was verging on a slow boil. Lady Alicia Lawrence was continuously getting in his way.

"Must you sprawl?"

She was lolling across the opposite seat, toying idly with the velvet-covered buttons tufting the cushion. Her skirts trailed over the floor of the carriage, forcing him to sit nearly pigeon-toed in order to avoid treading on the silk. She slid her gaze his way, raising a brow at his gruff tone.

"I'm not sprawling on you, so why should you object?"

"You consume more space than any three women."

She looked thoughtful. "Do men take up more space than women?"

He wasn't sure where this was headed. "I suppose. Men are generally larger."

She snorted. "Have you seen some of the ladies of the *ton*?" Then she narrowed her eyes. "Yet even they are expected to 'consume' less space, aren't they? Ladies are not supposed to lean back on a chair, no matter how weary. Are the backs of chairs put there solely for the use of men?"

Stanton closed his eyes. "Yes. The backs of chairs are the sole province of the males. You must not touch your flesh to it or you'll grow copious amounts of hair there."

He opened his eyes to see her staring at him.

She blinked. "You have a sense of the ridiculous. Why did you never mention this? How could you leave out something so important?"

"So sorry," he said wearily. "It won't happen again."

She lifted a corner of her lips. "You're an untapped keg, Stanton. How marvelous. Now I won't be forced to bait you out of boredom."

"Oh, please," he said flatly. "Don't stop on my account."

She tilted her head at him. "Oh, this will be fun."

He sighed. "I preferred you when you were rude."

She grinned. "Too bad. You're my new playfellow."

"Oh, dread."

She laughed delightedly. Stanton had to admit that she had a delicious bubbling laugh—the sort that made one want to laugh along.

If one was the laughing sort.

Unfortunately, there were too many unanswered questions streaming through his mind to spare time for such amusements.

Last night's incident at the opera, for one. As murder attempts went, it had been oddly complicated. There were so many ways in which the sabotage of the opera box might not have worked—if no one had neared the railing, if someone had spotted it before darkness shrouded the opera house, if the perpetrator had been spotted in the complicated act of arranging it . . .

In addition, there was Lady Alicia herself. Surely she had not intentionally deceived him on their first meeting—yet how could he not have seen how attractive she was?

He let his shadowed gaze travel over her soft curves—lingering secretively on her generous bosom. Those breasts! He didn't consider himself a weak-willed man, but those succulent temptations would stir a saint to sin!

Would he have proposed this particular ruse had he known she possessed more than simply a pair of beautiful eyes?

Probably not. She was precisely the type of woman he usually avoided—voluptuous, witty and bold. Being in the presence of such a female usually left him feeling on bumpy ground, prompting him to become even more stolid and reserved than normal—which was saying a great deal.

Instead, he found himself stimulated by her wit and set at ease by her forthright manner—or at least what passed for ease with him.

Except, of course, for when she had kissed him.

You should have kissed her back, you fool. No. On the contrary, he ought to feel relief that he had not crossed that boundary. This was a mission and she was by no means a trusted comrade in arms.

And he was no light-hearted lover, free to make pleasure with the town trollop.

Yet those lips on his—like warm fire-glow on chilled skin . . .

Alicia inhaled deeply, watching Lord Wyndham through dropped lashes. Yes, he was most definitely looking at her bosom.

Interesting and flattering, but it signified little. It was her experience that most men—except Garrett, of course—were much preoccupied with bosoms in general and large bosoms in particular.

Well, then, there was nothing to do but return the compliment. She let her veiled gaze wander over him slowly, enjoying the intimate theft to the fullest. He was so very ornamental, wasn't he? Those wide shoulders, the way his weskit lay so flat over his hard stomach, the bulk of his muscular thighs in his snug-fitting breeches . . .

She caught herself from flicking the tip of her tongue over her lips. Shocking, but understandable. There were few men on earth like Lord Wyndham. A woman would be a fool not to fill her eyes while she could.

Her eyes, her arms, her body . . .

Alicia swallowed, hard—then licked her lips after all. She still tasted him there, faint and tantalizing. She'd been mad to kiss him.

Thank heaven for that sort of madness. To think she might have lived out her life without kissing a man like Wyndham!

Not that she'd kissed many men. There'd been that handsome young dancing master who had stolen the briefest touch of her lips. What had his name been? She'd promptly developed a mad passion for the fellow, then forgotten him just as quickly when he'd moved on. There had been Almont's skillful, heated kisses—which did not bear thinking about. Ever.

And now, Lord Wyndham. Unlike Almont, Wyndham managed to fire her passions with no effort whatsoever. In fact, he'd seemed bloody dismayed.

She couldn't wait to dismay him again.

Wyndham cleared his throat. "We're here."

Alicia rested her arms on the window frame and gazed out, letting the damp air cool her heated cheeks. The graveled drive up to Cross's manor house gave one ample time to contemplate the grand exterior. Lord Wyndham seemed unimpressed, as well he might. She'd never heard much about his estate of Wyndham, but she imagined its opulence equaled or surpassed anything in Sussex.

The sky was bluing into night as their carriage pulled to an unhurried stop before the grand steps of the house. Footmen and maids and piles of luggage abounded. Even as Lord Wyndham's man lowered the carriage steps for them, another elegant transport drew up behind them.

The party had begun, it seemed.

Stanton wasn't looking forward to any of it. There would be loud music and drunken, immoral behavior—and that was only the morning activities. Such self-indulgent chaos would reign until dinner each night, when the real bacchanalia would begin. He had seen it many times before, from the viewpoint of someone who did not want to be there.

I do not want to be here.

Lady Alicia, on the other hand, seemed most eager. She practically tugged him from the carriage, exiting as soon the footman could lower the step.

Stanton followed with pointed dignity. "I believe the party will still be here if we take our time."

"Shh." She wrapped her hand about his arm, her grip like a vise. "It has already begun."

And it had. Every eye was turned their way. Even at the top of the steps, people were appearing at the double doors simply to gape at them.

For the first time, Stanton felt a bit guilty for exposing her in this way. It could not be easy to face down her notoriety. He laid his hand over hers. "Fear not, Lady Alicia—"

She turned to look up at him, the light of battle in her eyes. "They ought to be afraid of me."

"They" weren't the only ones. As Stanton allowed her to haul him forward, he had the terrible sensation of losing his grip on the situation.

Lady Alicia was back in Society with a vengeance—and apparently there was going to be hell to pay.

Up the grand steps and through the door, they were led into a large, welcoming entrance hall. Small groups of other guests clustered about them, close enough to observe but not so close as to be required to greet them.

Lord Cross's mistress, a well-born widow was acting as his lordship's hostess. Alicia watched the woman, who was perhaps a few years older than Stanton, gravitate toward him with a smile. Then the woman recognized Alicia and hesitated.

It was obvious that the woman desperately wanted to cut her or snub her in some way. Alicia smiled even more brightly, for it would not happen. With Lord Wyndham at her side, no one would dare, no matter how badly she behaved.

A theory she meant to test to its limits.

"Lord Cross," Alicia purred to their host, a stout, graying man with a face like a bloodhound's. "You are looking extremely well this evening."

Lord Cross's eyes widened, then dropped to Alicia's bosom. She inhaled invitingly.

"Hmm. Well . . . yes, my dear. Thank you. Er—"

Cross's mistress had her hand on her paramour's arm

now, and by the look of her whitened knuckles, he was feeling the nip of her nails through his sleeve.

Alicia bent forward and delivered a catlike smile of invitation. "Perhaps, my lord, we shall encounter each other on the dance floor . . ."

She turned away, leaving Cross red-faced and distracted and his lady friend white with fury.

Such a lovely beginning to what promised to be a truly magical evening.

"You are criminally insane."

Alicia smiled up at Lord Wyndham. "You wanted me here. I'm here." She adjusted his already perfect cravat in an intimate gesture sure to be seen by everyone in the hall. "I will find your mystery lord. But first, I am going to have a bit of fun."

A footman stepped forward. "My lord, my lady." He bowed deeply, taking no chances on Alicia's supposed loss of status. "If you'll follow me to your chamber?"

Alicia blinked. *Chamber?* A few moments later, Alicia stood in a mint green and ivory papered bedroom looking at a pile of shared luggage.

She was indeed sharing a chamber.

With Wyndham.

9

Alicia turned to Lord Wyndham, protest on her lips. He tossed his writing case on the petite, feminine escritoire and glared at her defensively. Obviously, he was no happier with the situation than she was.

"What did you expect, Lady Alicia? There were apparently some last-minute additions to the guest list, this house is packed to the rafters, and we are known to be lovers, are we not?"

Alicia chewed her lip. "True, but—"

"I thought you wished to scandalize the stuffing from your family. Isn't that your master plan?"

She folded her arms and glared back at him. "Don't interrupt me when I'm trying to adjust to something unexpected. It doesn't help."

Turning her back on yet another annoyingly true comment, Alicia regarded the giant—only!—bed. At least there was plenty of room for two.

She was being ridiculous. She was no virgin maiden, nor was she so spoiled that she'd never doubled up with her sisters.

She inhaled deeply and let her breath out slowly. Then she let her arms drop and turned back to Wyndham with a smile. "There. I've adjusted. We can share the bed."

He raised a brow. "Such resilience, my lady. One can only admire your . . . adaptability. However, I intend to sleep in a chair."

She looked around. "Which chair?" There was only one upholstered chair in the room, a rigid wingback before the fire. "That one?" She gazed at it doubtfully. "You'll ravage your spine in that."

Wyndham didn't look any too pleased about it either. "Nevertheless, I shall sleep there."

Having eased her mind either way about the sleeping arrangements, Alicia left the topic with a shrug. "Very well. Now, I must dress for the afternoon's amusements."

After a muted knock on the chamber door, Garrett entered with his hands full of hatboxes and accessory cases. He gazed at them brightly. "Good afternoon, milord. Herbert was on his way, but I thought milady needed me first."

Wyndham sighed. "I can see that changing is going to constitute a logistical nightmare."

"I could seek out another screen, milord," Garrett suggested a little too helpfully.

Alicia shot him a quelling glare. "That won't be necessary, Garrett."

"Forgive me, milady, but his lordship is correct. We'll not be able to avoid dressing you both several times a day." Garrett's expression was innocent, but the twinkle in his eye was anything but.

Alicia already felt guilty enough that Wyndham was going to sleep in the chair—how could she banish him to loiter in the hall while she changed for every event of the week?

"Very well, Garrett," she said. "Find a very large screen, if you please."

Wyndham brightened slightly at the change in plans, so Alicia resolved to be gracious about it.

He bowed shortly. "In the meantime, I shall leave you to freshen your toilette." He left quickly, which Alicia had no doubt was related to the vast pile of unpacking that needed doing.

"Oh, milady!" Garrett dug into the work with a smile. "The gossip here is fabulous. I should have become a lady's maid years ago. Now, I shall be able to bring in your breakfast every morning myself," Garrett said. "So you needn't panic at every knock on the door."

"Well, that's a mercy." She could just imagine his lordship leaping into bed with her every time someone came to the door.

Unexpected heat crept up the back of her neck at the image of a lean, naked Stanton throwing himself upon her. She pressed a cooling hand to her cheeks, but not before Garrett saw her blush. He leaned forward.

"Ha," he said in her ear. "I knew it."

Alicia pressed both hands to her face, but it didn't help. "Oh, why did I have to kiss him?"

"What?" Garrett pulled her hands down to peer into her eyes. "You kissed him? Why don't I know about this? Why must I drag all this out of you with a fishhook?" He dragged her to sit with him on the edge of the bed. "Am I not your lady's maid, your personal attendant, your most personal confidant? Tell, tell!"

Alicia sighed. "I kissed him this morning. And it was more than once . . . or at least, it was a very long kiss. He didn't like it, not really. At least, he didn't kiss me back. He just stood there and . . . sort of *allowed* it."

Garret narrowed his eyes. "Allowed it? For how long, precisely?"

Alicia thought about it. "Six minutes? Seven, perhaps?"

A slow grin lit Garret's handsome features. "Milady, if a man takes anything for seven minutes without rejecting it, you may trust that he liked it. He simply didn't want you to know how much he liked it."

Alicia's lips twitched. "Well, he could hardly hide *that,* now could he?"

Garret clapped his hands. "Better and better! How was it? Was it of lordly proportions?"

Alicia laughed and shut her eyes in embarrassed memory. "Royal proportions, I'd say, although I have little experience to go on."

Garrett, who knew everything about everything, snorted dismissively. "I would hardly think Almont could compare to Lord Wyndham! I'd say 'little' is the appropriate term indeed."

Alicia shook off the memories prompted by Garrett's words. "I cannot think on Almont right now. What am I going to do, sharing a room with Wyndham?"

"Sleep with him? Drag him into that obscenely large bed and make him never want to leave it?"

"That's ridiculous." Although it wasn't.

"All right then. Marry him and bear him lots of strapping sons. I would, if I could. The man is a god."

A god. An obscenely large bed. Strapping sons. Alicia took a deep breath and calmed her sizzling nerves. This week was going to be strain enough without Garrett's persistent matchmaking.

"Garrett, you're fired," she said flatly.

He grinned at her. "Better and better, for Himself will be doing up the buttons then."

Oh, bother. The blush was back. "Garrett, you're hired again."

He patted her hand. "Trust Brother Garrett, darling. His lordship likes you, somewhere beneath that steel-jawed composure. Now, I'm off to find out the bathing arrangements. You'll be wanting to wash off the travel dust." He opened to door to reveal Wyndham outside, about to knock. Garrett batted his lashes at Wyndham, then grinned at Alicia over his shoulder. "Remember, seven minutes!"

Garrett tripped off to find another screen. The door closed on him, leaving Alicia alone with Wyndham once more.

"Well!" she said brightly. "You see, everything's working out just fine."

He was gazing at her, his dark eyes impenetrable. "Seven minutes of what?"

Oh, dear. Alicia wished Garrett to the deepest level of hell. She dashed to the wardrobe and pulled out the first thing she touched. "I think I shall wear this one to dinner. What do you think?"

"I think you'll feel a bit conspicuous while everyone else is in evening gowns."

Alicia looked down to see that she was holding a forest-green riding habit. "Ah . . . yes, well . . ." She shoved it back.

"Seven minutes of what?"

She turned to see his assessing gaze. She stepped back from his intensity. It was almost as if he were trying to look inside her.

Edgy from her own thoughts regarding the giant bed and Garrett's decidedly unhelpful help, she failed to come up with anything useful. She gave in. "I told him about the kiss. Now he's . . . well, he's Garrett."

Wyndham's gaze went to the door briefly. "He is that." Then it swung back to her. "About that kiss—"

Alicia let out her breath in a great gust. "I know. Our arrangement is strictly business, you are not interested in me in that manner, and the sky might fall if you ever unbent enough to kiss me back, so let's just avoid worldwide catastrophe and never mention it again. All right?"

Stanton bit back a tendency to smile and merely bowed neatly. "As you wish, my lady."

He seated himself in the chair by the fire—it was every bit as stiff as it looked—and contemplated her unexpected practicality. He hadn't intended to be quite so blunt, but she'd covered every point he'd been about to make.

He wasn't used to being so easily read. Disturbing. Then again, it did save time.

She busied herself with distributing her things in the bureau drawers. He watched the swing of her hips as she moved rapidly about the room.

It had been a very long time since he had been alone with a woman in a bedchamber. And even then, it had not been so very often. Even lovers for hire took pause at sharing a bed with the Dark Marquis.

Stanton felt himself well out of it and quelled his rather alarming passions with an iron hand. He burned too hot—or so he'd been told.

He felt that heat now, awakened by the kiss this morning—or perhaps by the sight of Lady Alicia in that wicked gown last night, or the feeling of her softness beneath him when he'd caught her.

So soft, so full—

He doused the heat in icy self-control. Decisions forged in such a flame would not hold the weight of reality in the end.

She glanced at him warily now and then as she carried out her mundane tasks. She was obviously uncomfortable, but he could not tell if it was because she was finding it difficult to share a bedchamber or if there was something else that made her nervous.

Damn this lapse of his skill. He felt like a three-legged table, unsteady and liable to tip unexpectedly. The one thing he was sure of in his world had failed him. Even as a small boy, he'd known when those about him uttered those easy untruths.

If he had been a watchful, wary child, then it was his disbelief that had turned him so. That careful distance, unfortunately, did nothing to encourage any sort of intimacy or honesty from those in his life.

Alas, he could not prove his certainty. His "talent" was more of a warning bell than a forecast. He could see the lie, but that didn't necessarily give him the truth. Accused of losing his valuable texts, he had no evidence to convince his mother that his tutor was selling them for the opium Stanton smelled on the man's clothing every morning.

So he began to learn to observe, to take note, to collect seemingly unrelated facts and events so that when he caught someone in a lie, he could prove it.

The fact that he was never wrong reinforced his belief in his own mysterious instinct even as it alienated everyone he came to know.

One fact came clearer and clearer through the years.

Everyone lied. From the king himself to the nightman emptying the privies, every human soul was a web of tangled untruths.

When Stanton had finished his education he turned to the government service to occupy his talents, thinking that his unique ability might be of some use to England. He took a position as an assistant to the War Office, only to find that the easy faithlessness of the general population had distilled to a simmering pit of deceit within those walls.

Shortly thereafter, he'd been tapped by the previous Falcon—a man with secrets swimming behind his eyes like fish schooling in the sea, who spoke so seldom he had little need to lie.

Stanton took the life offered him with profound gratitude and the understanding that the Royal Four were a better lot than most. So far, he'd not been disappointed in the other three.

They were not friends. They were . . . well, perhaps soldiers under fire shared a similar bond, but in its way it was as satisfying as any Stanton had ever experienced. His distance did not alarm them. His eerie skill was found valuable, not invasive. He could turn his misfit nature to the service of England herself.

At least, he could until Lady Alicia.

What should he do about Alicia? He couldn't invest much faith in her story, yet here he was. With her history of inconstancy, how long could he truly trust that she would continue her current honesty?

Was she merely indulging in honesty because she need not bother to lie? When a moment of true conflict arose, which way would Alicia turn?

It was not his practice to use subterfuge, since his talent did not require him to use guile to discover the truth. This woman, however, had confounded him on every turn. When he looked at her, he saw only her—not her secrets, not her lies, not the dark underbelly of her soul.

Her glances lingered on him now. He stretched slightly in the chair, extending his legs and crossing his booted ankles. Her eyes were drawn to his flat stomach and below. Her cheeks pinkened and she looked away, suddenly finding great fascination in the arrangement of the brushes on the vanity table.

Her interest in him seemed real enough. It occurred to Stanton that he might have some advantage there, for he well knew that a woman was never closer to true honesty than when her deepest sexual nature was revealed.

A dangerous game and not one he was willing to stoop to. Yet.

* * *

That evening, as he took her arm to escort her into dinner, Lord Wyndham bent close to her ear.

"Now, I should prepare you for the worst. These sort of affairs are almost always—"

Alicia walked away from his warning, gazing about her with open enjoyment. This was a glittering world she'd never seen. This was no carefully orchestrated mingling of the sexes such as the assemblies at Almack's.

This was a world of music and dancing and passion—a place where the strict and heavy rules of her upbringing were scoffed at and mocked.

Women lounged in the arms of lovers on luxurious couches, drinking spirits and indulging in sweetmeats and kisses. Men smoked and shouted terrible language that made her laugh with the freedom of it all.

Not at all the world she'd been accustomed to—not the environment of propriety and respectability she'd been raised in and rebelling against since her earliest memory.

How delightful.

No longer restricted by her father's heavy hand, or oppressed by her previous poverty, Alicia now felt as light as a bird. She closed her eyes and listened to the laughter and the music, letting the weight of years fall from her shoulders. She could fly up through this magnificent ballroom right now.

She opened her eyes to see Stanton gazing at the scene around them with distaste. She grinned. "Isn't this wonderful?"

He looked askance at her. "Wonderful? No, unless it is that I am wondering how soon we can leave."

"Oh, don't be such a bear." She wrapped her hand over his arm and tugged him farther into the room. "We're supposed to look as though we want to be here, remember?"

"You seem to be having enough fun for both of us." He flicked his dark gaze about the room. "I think I shall play the part of the man so smitten by your charms that I indulge you in ways ordinarily distasteful to me."

She pressed her bosom to his arm and batted her eyes at him. "Oh, Wyndham," she cooed loudly. "You say the sweetest things!"

Several people turned their heads at her shrill declaration. She could see the speculation in their eyes.

"Kiss me," she hissed at Wyndham.

He gazed down at her with something akin to horror. "I will not! Everyone is looking!"

Idiot. "Then grope my bottom or some such thing, quickly. If you want to establish your torrid addiction to my charms, now is your moment!"

He hesitated, his gaze faltering slightly. Good lord, was the mighty Wyndham *shy*?

Then he raised his gaze to hers, focusing on her so intently that for a moment Alicia felt the furor fade and the crowd disappear. *Oh, my.* She swallowed, hard.

"I am not the sort to grope bottoms," he said softly. Then he slowly raised one hand to her face and let his fingers trace through the tiny curls at her temple. Alicia felt his touch all the way to her toes. She closed her eyes to feel it better still.

"Is that enough?" he murmured.

She gave her head a tiny, mute shake. Then she felt him trail his knuckles gently down her cheek. She opened her eyes to see that his gaze had turned inexplicably black as he looked down at her with intensity.

"How about now?" he asked, with his warm fingers still hovering at her jaw.

She was trembling, aching—and all from the merest caress. Good God. If Wyndham ever truly cut loose with a woman, she would be fortunate to come out alive!

Fortunate, fortunate woman.

She cleared her throat, for he'd asked a question. "I think

it would be more convincing if you went a bit farther." She arched her neck.

One corner of his lips tilted. He kept his gaze locked to hers as his fingers trailed down her throat to linger at her collarbone. "There?"

She was forced to let stillness and silence answer for her, since she was trembling too much to trust her voice.

"More then?"

If she didn't know better, she might have thought Wyndham was teasing her.

Then again, Wyndham wasn't really the teasing sort, was he?

She felt his touch heat a trail downward to the revealed fullness of the top of her breast. His gaze fell to where his hand lingered. "My apologies, Lady Alicia," he whispered. "It seems I'm taking liberties."

Lower. Go lower. Now. Alicia swallowed. "I haven't the faintest idea what you're speaking of, Lord Wyndham."

"I see. Well then, not to worry." He lifted his hand and dropped it to his side once more. "No harm done."

No harm done, unless one counted the jellied condition of her knees and the throbbing condition of her—well, suffice to say that harm had been done. Garrett was right. She ought to take this man into that obscenely large bed and make him never want to leave it.

If she could. She talked a brave game, but truly, what did she know? She'd given in to passion only once and frankly there'd been no opportunity to question her partner as to her performance.

Wanting . . . that was an entirely different matter than having, wasn't it? What would she do with Wyndham if she had him?

Marry him and bear him lots of strapping sons.

Oh, dear. Best not think on such fruitless things. She was

here for a reason—two reasons, actually. To earn her reward by finding the traitor lord and to cause her family the maximum embarrassment possible.

It was good to have goals. It kept one's feet firmly on the ground. Handy that.

Especially when one threatened to float away on impossible dreams.

10

Cross's opening dinner was a lavish, fashionable feast in the manner of the desert nomads, cleverly served buffet style to maximize the intermingling—in more ways than one—of his guests. Lush, ornate platters of venison, gamecocks, and suckling pigs ringed the hall like a fantastical barnyard. In the center, an array of luxurious couches and sofas and piles of pillows supported various acts of overindulgence, a few of which actually involved eating the food.

It was a very pretty picture. It was only too bad Stanton couldn't enjoy it.

He was beginning to feel an emotion he'd not encountered since his hotheaded youth. He was furious.

Lady Alicia Lawrence was cutting a swath of chaos and dismay through the fascinated crowd. All eyes followed her—the female ones with assessing curiosity and a good amount of jealousy, the male ones with a predatory appreciation that bode no good for what remained of Lady Alicia's dubious virtue.

Then those eyes flicked toward him—*him!*—with envy and

approbation and flickers of calculation. He could almost hear their thoughts.

Will he tire of her soon?

What would it take to attach such a woman as a mistress?

The man loitering next to Stanton was giving him just such a considering look. Stanton folded his arms. "Don't strain yourself. She'd ruin you."

The fellow blinked. Then his gaze slid helplessly back to Alicia. "It might be worth it."

Stanton scowled. Moron. "Then let me make myself clear. If she didn't, I would."

The man held up a fending hand and grinned. "I'm innocent, I vow."

Stanton turned away. The fury within him seethed and roiled. He fought the deep desire to lay out every man in the room who couldn't take his eyes from Lady Alicia.

He didn't dare contemplate what he wanted to do with Lady Alicia herself. The thought of taking her over his knee crossed his mind, leading him into dangerous territory occupied by lingering thoughts of a soft womanly bottom bare to his touch . . .

He jerked his mind back to simple seething fury.

Just look at her. Even now she stood in a circle of admiring men who jostled for the center of her attention, flirting madly with each without regard to looks or status or even girth! If she didn't watch it, there would be a dozen duels before sunrise!

Stanton found himself at her side with no memory of crossing the room. He slid a possessive hand about her elbow. "My lady, I believe these gentlemen have their own ladies to attend to."

He sent a pointed glare about the circle. Most of them had enough sense to disappear, although the man Stanton had spoken to earlier lingered a moment longer.

"I have no lady," the man told Alicia, with a heavy sigh. "Not a single, solitary one. No place to be, no one to talk to."

Alicia bent toward the bloke. Stanton had to give the man points for not letting his gaze drop.

"Lord Farrington, if you wanted, you could have any woman in this room."

Lord Farrington smiled slowly at her. Stanton felt his other hand form a fist.

"Any woman? Now there's a happy thought."

Stanton pulled Alicia back upright. "Then go think it elsewhere, Farrington. My lady is quite unavailable."

Farrington glanced at Stanton. "It's your own fault, Wyndham. None of us ever thought *you'd* play the rooster so. You've piqued our curiosity."

Alicia turned to Stanton. "Rooster?"

Stanton continued to glare at the interloper. "Good evening, Farrington. Enjoy the party. Over there."

Farrington's grin widened. Cocksure bastard.

"I shall be seeing you, my lady," he said with a bow over Alicia's hand.

She curtsied deeply, and this time neither man could resist a glance down. God help them all.

Farrington left, looking a bit bemused. Stanton didn't blame him. "That gown is going into the fireplace the moment you return to our chamber."

Alicia patted his hand. "That's fine. Garrett ordered variations on it in several colors. All billed to you, of course. None as demure as this one, unfortunately—"

Stanton grabbed Alicia's hand and pulled her into an alcove where they were partially concealed by a potted palm.

"Why, Wyndham," she said with a laughing gasp. "I didn't know you cared."

He pulled her closer for better concealment and glared

down at her teasing smile. "You cannot arrange assignations while under my protection!"

She lifted a brow, still smiling. "What is the difficulty? Don't worry. I won't tell them you aren't capable."

His eyes narrowed. "My 'capabilities' are not as questionable as your judgment. Lord Farrington is not known for his ability to hold on to a guinea, or a decent hand of cards. His fortunes depend on the prospect of inheriting from his uncle, who is one of the healthiest men in England. He'll be old and gray before he can afford you, if ever!"

She blinked at him. "You've clearly put a lot of thought into this."

Stanton had to repress a growl. "I don't. It's simply that you're making a cake of yourself."

She smiled with satisfaction. "Oh, yes. A fondant cake with candied roses on top."

Stanton couldn't bear the image that exploded in his mind. Creamy icing, silky pink petals . . .

"But why?" God, was that his voice? He almost sounded as though he were begging!

Even Alicia seemed startled at his tone. She studied him for a long moment. "You like me, too?" She frowned. "Really, Lord Wyndham. I never thought you'd fall for such obvious gambits."

She leaned closer. It was torture designed by the devil himself. "If it helps, I shall let you in on a bit of secret," she whispered. "It's all corset and stuffing."

Stanton closed his eyes. What a relief. Not the devil then. Simply more of Lady Alicia unleashed. "All of it?"

She lifted a corner of her lips. "Well . . . some of it."

Stanton gritted his teeth. That didn't help, not at all. Now he'd be up all night wondering what was real and what wasn't.

"You have yet to explain why. If we find our man, you'll never want for anything. Why fish for a protector?"

She tilted her head. "I'll show you mine if you show me yours."

His control shivered. He was never going to survive this madwoman. "What?"

"I'll tell you why I'm doing this if you tell me why you're doing this."

"That is not your concern."

"Well, then, I'll be the bigger man and tell you part of my reason." She leaned closer.

Corset and stuffing. Corset and stuffing. As false as she was.

"I'm not fishing. I'm making sure I speak to every single man."

The worst of it was, she made sense. Putting herself on display like a fat lamb before the butcher shop would indeed give her plausible reason to speak to many men. A high-priced mistress would most assuredly want to scout her potential protector list, after all. No one would ever suspect she was on a mission, searching for a certain voice. It was a good plan, perhaps even brilliant.

Damn it.

The worst of it was, he didn't know why he was angry and that only made him angrier. He ought to be above this territorial behavior—especially over a territory he didn't want!

Right. You don't want her. That's why you're sporting a rod the size of St. Paul's spire.

He wanted, it was that simple. It had been a long time for him and this place reeked of sin and sex and willing, wet, soft places . . .

Oh, wait. That was Lady Alicia, pressed next to him in the tight space. She was aroused.

By you or by Farrington, or any of the other ten men she's flirted with this evening?

"Of course, Lord Farrington is a very handsome man. Still, handsome is as handsome does," Lady Alicia said wistfully. "Al—someone else seemed fine and noble and perfect to me once. Now I find him as ugly as a toad. Uglier, for it is not the toad's fault."

She tilted her head back to glare at him. "So the fact that you are divinely handsome shouldn't even enter into my opinion of you."

He was staring at her with open surprise on his face. She laughed. "Oh, Wyndham, don't tell me that you don't know you are a veritable god among men. You've the entire combination of classical male beauty in your pocket and I'm not in the mood to hear false modesty at the moment." She put her hands on her hips and glared at him. "Your behavior, on the other hand—"

"I do not suffer fools," he said with his usual grimness.

She rolled her eyes. "Pity the world, then, because next to you, most men are fools!" She shook a scolding finger at him. "Being superior does not mean that you should act superior. In fact, it means that you should be even more aware of the limitations of others, and more forgiving of them, for they have not your advantages."

"There isn't a man in there who does not possess the same advantages as I."

She folded her arms. "All at once? Is there another man in that ballroom who is as wealthy as a king *and* highly intelligent *and* of very nearly royal lineage *and* would put Adonis to shame?"

He scowled. "There is the Prince Regent."

She flapped a hand, dismissing his suggestion. "As much as I respect my ruler, I gather that he has destroyed his looks with his indulgences. And while he might yet win out on pleasant personality, rumor has it that he loses points on character."

Stanton nearly strangled on the concept that his mercurial, childish tempered ruler might have a more pleasant personality than himself—but took secret pleasure in the fact that Lady Alicia found him attractive.

Too much secret pleasure, in fact.

All the better reason to keep this conversation on philosophical ground. "So I am to forgive my fellow man for his inadequacies—most of which are self-inflicted, I might add—and be tolerant of bad judgment, laziness, and poor ethics?"

She nodded briskly. "Absolutely."

"Must I also forgive gambling, drunkenness, and lime-green waistcoats?"

Her lips twitched. "Perhaps on a case-by-case basis."

"Am I also to overlook bad hygiene, a tendency toward spittle-spraying, and the passing of wind?"

She had to press her lips thin to suppress her laughter, but her shaking shoulders betrayed her. She nodded again. "Mm-hmm."

He folded his arms, mocking her stern stance. "Very well, it is agreed. But I draw the line at the scratching of personal parts. Offenders must die."

"I cannot argue there." She stuck out her hand. "Done."

Her hand felt very small in his larger one, yet he felt he could barely contain her there. She was like a bird in his grasp, difficult to hold securely without harm.

Her eyes were wide and deep as the forest as she gazed up at him. "When you look at me like that, I want to bed you," she said.

He choked. "What?"

She tilted her head, considering him closely. "I would think it advisable to limit ourselves to one night, in case it's unpleasant."

"Unpleasant." God, no. That's the last thing it would be . . . at least at first. Later perhaps matters might turn, but never, ever "unpleasant."

Thankfully, they were interrupted by a great fanfare from the hall. Stanton pulled Lady Alicia from behind the plant to see a familiar robust figure step grandly into the party.

"Oh, heavens," Alicia whispered. "Is that—"

"Oh, yes," Stanton said grimly. "The Prince Regent himself has arrived."

Prince George IV turned from greeting his host to see Stanton beside him. He frowned.

"Bloody hell, Wyndham. Can't I escape you lot? Are you planning to follow me to the privy?"

"You don't use the privy," Stanton pointed out. "You have minions to carry your piss." Titled minions, at that. It was supposed to be an honor to be Lord of the Royal Commode, or whatever it was called, but Stanton was deeply thankful he didn't have to tote anyone's offal.

George clasped his hands behind his back and glared. "Typically literal. What are you doing here?"

"I am enjoying Lord Cross's hospitality. I brought along my mistress, just as you did."

George blinked. "You have a mistress? I shudder to think on it. Where is she?"

Oh, hell. Perhaps he ought not to have brought Alicia to George's attention. Buxom and lively, she was just the sort of woman to attract the Prince Regent. Although his highness's current mistress was still quite new, lusty George had been known to keep more than one at a time. The ladies never complained.

George was waiting, so rather than call any more attention than necessary, Stanton gestured offhandedly in Alicia's general direction. "There, in the green gown."

George gazed curiously across the room. "The zesty redhead with the astounding figure?"

"Er . . . yes."

George gazed at Alicia with continued appreciation. "Well, damn it, man, perhaps you do have blood running through those veins! I'd have wagered the kingdom on its being icy water." He slid his gaze back to Stanton. "So that's the woman who brought you to a boil, eh? Shall I beg an introduction?"

Stanton reached for any distraction. "Your highness, about your presence here—" It might be throwing oil on the fire, but anything to get George's greedy gaze off Alicia. "With our enemy loose and possibly still nearby, you are not safe enough here."

The warning did the trick. George's eyes narrowed. "You think the Four have me well leashed, but you forget. There is nothing you can do to me. Steal my crown as you did my father's? My little Charlotte is overyoung, but I'm sure my brothers can regent for her. You'll likely have better luck with one of those puppets on your strings anyway."

He turned slightly to bow to a nearby lady, then turned back to Stanton. "I will not be caged, Wyndham."

A footman approached one of George's entourage, who then whispered to another person in blinding gold braid, who then whispered to another, finally moving up the chain of command to the man allowed to whisper in the royal ear. George listened impatiently. "Very well," he told the man, who sent the message back down the chain to Cross's footman once more.

The musicians paused and everyone's gaze turned to the dais at one end of the room.

Cross stood there, hands outstretched. "Esteemed guests, I am very proud to present to you our master of ceremonies, our very own Prince Regent, Prince George the Fourth—this week's Lord of Misrule!"

Rapturous excited murmurs moved in waves about the hall. Stanton closed his eyes briefly. Bloody hell. Not only was this a week-long orgy of food and sin, but Cross had resurrected the ancient rite of Saturnalia—albeit a few weeks early.

George took the dais.

"In the finest of ancient pagan Saturnalia tradition, and in accordance with our own amusement, we must have a Lord of Misrule—one man who will set the tone of the festivities. Our king for a week—whom we must obey. One man who will embody every wicked thought, every scandalous deed—every lascivious wink!" He accompanied that with a broad and gleeful wink of his own. The gentlemen guffawed. The ladies winked back.

Stanton folded his arms, feeling ever more uncomfortable and out of his element. He longed for his quiet house, or even the cramped Chamber of the Four. Give him an international incident to resolve and he was fine, sharp and incisive. However, surround him with vivid social intercourse and his quick mind slowed and his voice had to fight past a bog of wary distance.

He tried to relax his brooding scowl, for it was imperative that he seem to be one of the mob, but those near him tended to sidle away despite his best effort.

George clasped his hands over his belly and looked benignly upon them all. "I have a surprise for you, my darlings."

The Prince Regent slid his gaze in Stanton's direction and smiled. It was not a friendly smile.

Oh, damn.

"As your ruler," George pronounced, "I promise to always care for your pleasure and prosperity. That said, I fear I cannot go on. I declare that I shall abdicate my throne!"

A moment of shocked stillness followed. Stanton moved closer to George, just in case the capricious and unhappy prince meant to do something dangerous. The crowd of guests began a worried murmuring.

George raised both hands to quiet the growing hum. "Do not worry, for I have decided upon a better man to lead you all."

Stanton stepped up on the dais, ready to stop George with physical force if necessary. He could not be allowed to toss such a torch into the current political climate. England might never recover!

Unfortunately, George seemed all too resolute. "As my last act as your ruler, I declare . . ."

Stanton was only a few yards away. Five more steps and he would be at the Prince Regent's side.

Even as George watched Stanton's approach from the corner of his eyes, the prince threw his hands wide. ". . . that Lord Wyndham shall be crowned your new Lord of Misrule!"

Oh, no.

11

It was Stanton's own personal hell on earth. That was truly the only way to describe it. Stanton stood on the dais with all eyes upon him, the Prince Regent's arm slung across his shoulders, while everyone present waited for his reaction.

It seemed like an hour, but was likely only seconds—yet Stanton was able to fully calculate the result of various futures based on his possible reactions.

He could shrug off his prince and ruler and stalk from the room. Tempting, but what would that do to his mission? He did not wish for a certain mysterious gentleman to wonder too hard upon why Wyndham might come to this event if he wasn't intending to take part.

He could politely try to put the crown back on George's head.

"It's done. You're entirely stuck, Wyndham," George whispered in his ear. "You might as well enjoy it."

Close your eyes and think of England.

George was right. He was stuck. However, he absolutely refused to enjoy it.

He stepped forward, out from the unwanted embrace of

the prince, and cleared his throat. He need not have bothered, for every eye in the room was fixed upon him.

"As your new Lord of Misrule, I declare the first law of Saturnalia to be . . ."

He caught sight of Alicia, who stood with one hand pressed over her mouth, her eyes wide above it. She was either trying very hard not to scream, or failing rather badly not to laugh.

Very well then. If he must, then he would serve his own purposes as well.

"I declare that until midnight tonight, everyone here must tell the absolute truth!"

He saw frowns cross several brows in the sea of faces before him. The silence grew. He'd bungled it, he feared. He wasn't accustomed to playing this sort of game.

Then Alicia leaned forward to cup her hands about her mouth.

"Then I shall go first!" Her voice carried through the nearly silent hall perfectly. "My lord prince, I fancy your very large . . . hands!"

Laughter erupted around her. "And I, your highness!"

"I too!"

"I fancy Lord Wyndham's superior shoulders!"

The laughter and cries increased as people became more enamored of this game of bawdy confession.

Which, of course, was not quite what Stanton had in mind.

As soon as possible, Stanton slipped from the dais to stalk across the hall to where Lady Alicia stood. She was grinning at him, clearly enjoying the moment of his downfall.

"You were quite correct," she teased. "You are indeed a complicated fellow."

He gazed at her without expression. "You aren't helping matters."

She flapped a hand at him. "Oh, pish and tosh. You wanted to blend in. Now you're blending."

"Ruling this madness is blending in?"

"It is if everyone thinks you are playing a part instead of being your own annoying poker-up-your-arse self."

"I don't have a poker up my—" He shut his mouth, clenching his jaw against such a childish denial.

She patted his arm with mock sympathy. "Now, now. You wanted to pass as one of us. Now, no matter how you go on about honor and duty and all that, everyone will think it the height of irony and the party will go on."

He gazed at her now with his head tilted. " 'One of us'?"

She blinked at him. "What?"

"You said, 'You wanted to pass as one of us.' " He narrowed his eyes slightly. "You cannot truly think you are anything like these people?"

She looked startled, then seemed to consider the matter. "I suppose I do. After all, everyone here is wellborn or wealthy, yet lives outside the general rules of Society."

He folded his arms. "Nonsense. Having a mind of one's own is not synonymous with being as amoral as a cat."

She gave him a startled look. "I . . . that is . . ." She shrugged, obviously frustrated. "Oh, bother. Just when I believe I have my own mind sorted out, you grow annoyingly perceptive!" She threw out her hands. "Then I have no recourse but to go out and prove you wrong!"

Ha. Victory stole through Stanton's veins as he watched her stalk away, her skirts atwitch with irritation. He was taking far too much pleasure in baiting her, but the rush of triumph when he bested her was sweet indeed—

Prove him wrong?

He cast his gaze about the room urgently. She wouldn't.

He found her in intimate conversation with that willow twig of a green boy, Lord Farrington. Her hand rested on the fellow's lapel as she stood on tiptoe, leaning far, far too close. Farrington's gaze fell blissfully to her bodice as he nodded eagerly to what she whispered in his ear.

Bloody, bloody hell.

He could drag her aside again, but it wouldn't stop her. It seemed nothing short of an iceberg would stop the H.M.S. *Alicia*. He would do better to hang back and guard—er, observe. After all, she had made it clear she meant to speak to every gentleman on the guest list.

Every damn, bloody one.

"My dear, if I could have but a moment?" A deep fruity voice interrupted Alicia's conversation with yet another clump of admiring men.

She turned to see the face on the coins, the figure in every newssheet and gossip rag, the head of the parade, the man who was king in all but name. Oh . . . *criminy*.

She dropped to a deep curtsy, but could not find her voice to greet him properly. A beringed hand moved into her vision. "Don't be boring, dear lady. Walk with me."

She took that hand and straightened, entirely numb with shock. She was hand in hand with the *prince*!

Mama, if you could see me now.

The Prince Regent regarded her closely. "We have not been introduced, but I'll be blamed if you're not familiar to me for some reason."

Alicia curtsied deeply. "Lady Alicia Lawrence, your highness, infamous tart and liar," she said. "But that was a few years ago."

His eyes glinted. "Are you still a tart, then?"

Alicia blinked, then grinned. "I'm currently under a certain gentleman's protection, your highness, and I do cleave only to him . . . so far. Does that make me a tart in your eyes?"

"Heavens, no." George blinked. "Though I've nothing against tarts, myself. Are you still a liar?"

Oh, he was marvelous. "Truth is more or less a matter of opinion, it seems to me, your highness, but I have never really been the liar I am reputed to be."

He waved a hand carelessly. "Me either." Then he grinned at her. "So tell me about this 'certain gentleman.' Is he taking proper care of such a treasure as more or less honest woman?"

Alicia hesitated, but then it wasn't a secret, of course. "I am with the Marquis of Wyndham, your highness."

The Prince Regent's air of lazy near-boredom slipped away to be replaced by sharp-eyed interest. "Yes, I'd heard. Wyndham is with you? Truly?"

Oh, dear. Had she shed doubt with her hesitation? "We are sharing a chamber on the third floor," she affirmed hurriedly. "Wyndham is a most generous man."

So far everything she'd said was entirely true.

Yet the prince's interest only sharpened. "And he treats you well? Not too . . . demanding?"

Alicia's eyes widened. "Demanding? Er . . . no, I do not find his demands overwhelming, your highness." Again, all true.

George shook his head, respect glinting in his eyes. "You are quite the good sport, then, Lady Alicia. You must remember to come to me should you ever regret . . ."

Alicia was panting to ask the prince what he meant, but how could she when she was supposed to already know? And what could Wyndham's demands consist of, that they would put such urgency in the voice of a libertine like the Prince Regent?

Good heavens, was Wyndham a participant in strange acts and perversions? Anything was possible. She scarcely knew the man, after all—and she already knew she was prone to trust the untrustworthy.

Demands. Just thinking about the possibilities made Alicia's breath begin to come faster and her pulse to pound.

She ought to be alarmed and fearful, not titillated! She ought to ask Garrett to sleep in the room with them tonight. She ought to run screaming into the night—

An image popped into her mind of Wyndham dressed in

highwayman's black, his hands full of vaguely obscene instruments of pleasure, dark eyes gazing at her with hunger and fire and evil intentions . . .

"Lady Alicia?"

She put a hand up to cool her cheeks. "Yes, your highness?"

George was watching her with knowing eyes. "Hmm. I can see that you are well able to handle Wyndham. Still, do call upon me should you ever tire of him." This time it was not an offer of rescue, but an invitation.

Alicia smiled warmly at him. "Your highness, if I tire of Wyndham, you will be the first to know."

"Know what, my lady?" It was Wyndham, standing directly behind her.

His deep voice was a spark to the embers already glowing deep in Alicia's belly. She shivered slightly, her cheeks heating again, then realized that George was watching her reaction with genial curiosity.

"You're a lucky bastard, Wyndham," the prince stated with evident envy.

"So I hear," Wyndham replied dryly. "My lady, have you yet tired of the revels? I am most eager to return to our room."

Alicia watched the flicker in George's eyes. Did Wyndham even realize that his statement made him sound like an overeager lover, or was he merely bored with the evening?

Either way, it had sealed the Prince Regent's opinion of their affair.

"Perhaps . . . in a while, my lord." Alicia allowed herself to lean back against Wyndham. He stiffened almost imperceptibly but didn't move away. Instead, she felt his fingers toy with her hair.

Lovers, such behavior stated. Trembling, passionate, cannot-wait-to-be-alone lovers. At least, she was quite sure her own performance was convincing, for it was no perfor-

mance at all. She was abruptly and completely on fire for
Wyndham's slightest touch. If he'd made those mysterious
demands on her at that moment, she might very well have
performed them in public.

Danger.

Oh, yes. Hot, physical, aching danger—yet she felt no
fear. All she felt was a mad need for him to be naked behind
her, and for her to be naked before him. Would his skin be as
hot as it seemed? Would his touch scald her? Would she burn
alive? Would she care?

She felt his hand slip down over her bare shoulder scarcely
touching—yet scorching her skin all the same!—until his
gloved hand took hers.

"If you will excuse us, your highness?"

Alicia curtsied blindly and turned with Wyndham, allowing him to lead her away from the Prince Regent. He continued to cradle her hand in his until they had reached the
other side of the hall.

Once there, however, he dropped her hand and stepped
away. "That was quite convincing, I'd say," he said coolly. "I
do think it might behoove you to stay far from the Prince
Regent's attention."

"He—" Words wouldn't come. She couldn't seem to think
past the thrumming in her body. Her very bones ached to feel
his heat again. She swallowed. "He came to me," she managed. "He recognized me from . . . before."

"Ah. Trust George to keep tabs on every fallen woman in
town."

Fallen woman. The words were true. She'd heard them before, said more cuttingly. So why did it slice directly through
her heart when Wyndham called her that?

"I'm thirsty," she said abruptly and turned away.

Stanton watched her go, aware that his terse words had hurt
her. He hadn't meant to, but his control was unraveling as the

evening waned. When she'd pressed back against him just then, he'd fought back a rush of mingled black lust and panic that had threatened to dim his vision.

He wanted her. He wanted her helpless and quivering, his to kindle, to stimulate and satisfy—to give in and dissolve into his hands.

He swallowed, reaching for the still, cold center that had sustained him in the years since he'd turned away from that part of himself.

There was only a hot, darkly burning core, like the one within a volcano. He knew precisely who he wanted—and how he wanted her.

It had been years since he'd allowed himself to want a woman this way.

Allowed? You've no defenses against her at all. She's got you wound like a spring.

Indeed, it seemed he must double his resistance. It ought to be easy, for he'd years of practice behind him.

It hadn't always been thus. Once he had been a normal enough young man—a bit on the watchful side, wary of lies and liars, but not so much so that others avoided him as they did now.

One person ventured easily past the barrier of Stanton's reserve. Miss Melinda Petrie had bright blue eyes, golden hair and a smile that had more fellows than Stanton alone thinking thoughts of coming home to such a creature every night.

She came to nearly every party that season, tireless in her pursuit of the perfect match. She would dance into each room in a flutter of muslin, her breathless chaperone at her heels. Stanton watched her flirt, openly and sweetly, with every man in sight, although she seemed to let her eyes rest on him the longest though he spoke little.

He was a good catch, for his prospects were very good if

his uncle died without a son, and he was aware that he'd grown into his height and that he wore his somewhat stern version of the Horne features well. There was nothing unusual in being gazed at with such consideration by marriageable young ladies.

Melinda, however, had caught his attention with more than shining eyes and hair and a rather splendid bosom. Melinda didn't lie.

Not once did he catch her in even the tiniest untruth. If she was late, she blithely blamed her own tendency to oversleep. If a fellow asked her what her plans were for the following day, she felt no shame in informing him, with a careless laugh, that she meant to shop for unmentionables all afternoon.

Stanton was so impressed that he began to test her himself.

"What did I think of Prince George's attire at the Smithson's ball? La, I do think his highness ought to stay away from that particular shade of puce, don't you?"

"Reading? Oh, heavens, no. You'll think me a ninny, I'm sure, but I cannot for the life of me finish a book once started."

Greatly encouraged, Stanton began to allow himself to relax in Melinda's presence. He was rewarded by easy smiles and encouraging laughter and her father's indulgent approval. Melinda was not a complicated sort, but Stanton began to believe that for the best. She had more than enough physical attractiveness to keep his interest, and she was not stupid, merely happily shallow.

He began to call upon her at her home. Her mother found many reasons to leave them shockingly alone and her father looked on with comfortable greed glittering in his eyes.

After one particularly heady session of kissing Melinda's hand repeatedly while gazing down her temptingly low décolletage, he felt the bonds of his passion break. He pulled her into his arms and rolled her flat onto the sofa. She went willingly, opening her lips for his hungry kiss, allowing his hands to roam without protest.

Stanton set his need free with profound relief. He would marry this girl, he would take care of such a precious honest female for the rest of his life, he would never forget what a gift he'd been given.

She quivered in his arms. Her breath came faster. She was pliant and willing, making no objection as he fed hungrily on her lips, her neck, her breast. Time stopped and his heart pounded. He was lost in sweet skin and fragrant hair and Melinda was—

Melinda was terrified. Her heart raced in panic, not lust.

He froze. "Do you not wish me to touch you?"

She buried her hands in his hair. "Oh yes, Stanton, I cannot wait to be your wife. I love you so."

His gut went cold. He went very still, his face buried in her neck, his hand buried in her bodice.

Every word she'd just uttered was a lie.

There were tears. There was disapproval and condemnation. There were threats. Through it all, Stanton remained unmoved.

"I do not want her. She does not want me. You cannot accuse me of ruining your daughter without bringing her virtue and your own careless chaperonage into question. Since I will not wed her, no matter the consequences, you might reconsider staining her name in such a way that no man ever will."

There had been no more threats and no more tears. Stanton had left the Petrie's house with the knowledge that he had saved himself from a long and horrifying future with a woman who was not as truthful as she was too entirely spoiled to bother making excuses.

Furthermore, there had been no denying the relief glinting from Melinda's reddened eyes. She'd gone on to marry some charming younger son and doubtless drove him alternately rapturous and insane with her bountiful figure and her thoughtless chatter.

Unfortunately however, not before she informed the world that she had broken the engagement herself. It seemed the next Marquis of Wyndham was something of a cruel and rapacious monster.

After that, there was no squashing the rumors. His displeasure only fanned them. So did withdrawing from Society, of course, but at least then he wouldn't have to hear the hushed whispers and see the pointing fingers.

Over time, the stories grew. He was a violent master, he was a brutal horseman and, his particular favorite, he was a sexual deviant, the likes of whom the world had never seen!

Too bad that one wasn't true. Unfortunately, one needed a partner if one were to be truly deviant, and Stanton lacked the powers of persuasion to cajole any attractive widows to his bed.

If he couldn't obtain it for himself, and he wouldn't pay for it, there was only his own icy control to depend upon.

So he bound that part of himself tightly and stowed it deeply away. He could kill that man by simply abstaining from women for the rest of his life.

For the past ten years he had not touched a woman, nor taken spirits, nor so much as removed his jacket in the company of anyone but his valet.

In this one evening, he had done all of the above.

No matter. He must expect to make concessions when in the field. It wasn't as if he didn't remember how to operate covertly. He might be a bit out of practice, but he had once been very active at the behest of the previous Falcon.

It wasn't as though he were about to lose himself in one brandy and the merest touch of a woman's cheek.

12

On her way to the table where servants filled glasses of spirits, Alicia saw many people she knew by sight or reputation. She waved gaily at the women and smiled tauntingly at the men. She had spoken to every man present this evening, ignoring most of the words while she listened to the voices.

Now she had to confess that the mystery lord was not here tonight. In addition, she was finding that being the center of such attention was rather wearing. Although she still stung from Wyndham's comment, and the sharing of the bedchamber loomed large in her mind, she began to long for the night to end.

She took a glass of something chilled, then slipped around a column, out of sight of the rest of the hall.

A trio of ladies approached her indirectly, as if they could not decide whether to intercept her or to cut her.

Alicia knew who they were, although she'd never met them personally. These three studded the gossip sheets the way the heads of state studded the news. They were all married and had been for some time, evidently long enough to bear their husbands heirs and to seek their pleasure elsewhere. They had status and wealth aplenty and reigned comfortably in this world of intrigue and illicit drama.

Yet, for all their style and self-assurance, they seemed to hunger for something. Alicia had an abrupt vision of the girls they had been, girls like her sisters and herself—willing to do their duty, aware of the realities of Society marriage, yet still hoping for that elusive dream known as a "love match."

Holding out that hope that somehow, by some chance, the men who courted them and signed the marriage contracts and received the dowries and the influence of the family connections—that those men did it all for love.

And what were the odds of that?

Sadness overwhelmed Alicia for a moment. She would rather be the unfettered outcast than to be trapped in that glittering, restless world of unfulfilled dreams.

At the last moment, the ladies seemed to come to some sort of unspoken agreement and veered toward Alicia like a small flock of colorful birds moving as one.

Alicia braced herself. This would prove interesting—although possibly difficult.

The foremost lady, the one at the vee of the flock, came to a stop before Alicia.

"You are with Wyndham."

Despite the purposeful lack of courtesy, for she was being addressed like a servant, Alicia dipped a carefully nonobeisant curtsy. "I am indeed, Lady Davenport."

The woman's eyes flickered with irritation, for now she need not introduce herself with loaded consequence.

Lady Davenport was the third wife of Lord Henry Davenport, who was more wealthy than landed, the second son of a second son. Lady Davenport had borne her much older husband the only heir and so secured her position with him no matter her subsequent behavior.

The other two, Mrs. Cassidy and Mrs. Abbot, were in much the same position, although their husbands were not so highly connected. Lady Davenport was rumored to have been a favorite of the Prince Regent's at some point—then again, most ladies cultivated that rumor, didn't they?

The three were the ruling tigresses of this particular jungle, so Alicia adopted an inquiring expression and prepared herself for the worst. She had one simple advantage here—she cared absolutely nothing for the good opinion of these glacially elegant, brittle brilliants.

Her mouth widened into an insouciant grin.

Lady Davenport narrowed her eyes, obviously not pleased with Alicia's lack of toadying. "How charitable of Wyndham, to raise you from your sad position."

"Charitable?" Alicia smiled at the idea. "On the contrary. I made him pay through the nose."

Lady Davenport soured further. "And he did so willingly?"

"Nay, I would say eagerly or . . ." Alicia smiled as if in fond recollection. "Perhaps a better word would be 'urgently.'"

All of which was quite delightfully true, if not precisely as Lady Davenport might think.

Alicia tilted her head. "And my sad position? Do you mean the position of freely choosing the man with whom I wish to share my bed and my time? Do you mean the position of being in charge of my own finances, or of not caring a whit if I am accepted or shunned by angry women who despise their own husbands and who long for a single day of my lack of restrictions?"

Lady Davenport choked on her surprise and Cassidy and Abbot both blinked in confusion and—if Alicia was not sorely mistaken—flaring envy.

Yet Alicia could not allow the truth to pass unspoken. "Yes, I am free but I am alone, independent but unsecured.

Even if I do grow fond of Wyndham, he will eventually leave. So despise me or pity me, I care not." She shrugged, abruptly tired of the exchange. "We are all of us none too free."

She turned to walk away, only to find her way blocked by a broad expanse of manly waistcoat. She looked up. "Oh, hello, Wyndham," she said wearily. "Remind me to bell your neck. Did you hear all of that, or need I recount anything you missed?"

Wyndham looked down at her, then raised his gaze to the ladies still standing behind her. Alicia was surprised to see a flash of dark anger cross his features.

He was angry on her behalf? Pleasure rippled through her at the thought. Yet, as tempting as it would be to believe that he cared so for her feelings, there was no denying that Wyndham was a territorial sort. He'd likely get as upset about a dirty handprint on his gleaming carriage.

"Lady Davenport, Mrs. Cassidy, Mrs. Abbot." Wyndham's scant bow was just short of insulting. "I trust you have enjoyed your evening?"

Lady Davenport opened her mouth to reply, a strangely avid expression upon her features, but Wyndham rode over her.

"If you will excuse us—so kind of you to welcome Lady Alicia to the party. I trust you were not too shy to approach her? She is not at all self-conscious of her proper rank, is she?"

Lady Davenport twitched with fury, but the other two ladies looked frankly alarmed. Lady Alicia, daughter of the Earl of Sutherland, was once indeed too high to speak to without introduction . . . in actual Society.

Obviously confused, the three ladies curtsied quickly—although Lady Davenport seemed about to strangle on the courtesy—and murmured their departing courtesies.

When they were gone, Alicia looked up at Stanton. "You made them curtsy to me!" She shook her head. "I'll only pay for that later, you realize. You should have let me handle them."

"By allowing their dissatisfaction to infect you with melancholy? I heard what you said, and I saw your expression when you turned away. I have never seen you sad before."

She blinked up at him. "I am occasionally sad, Wyndham, as is everyone. Furthermore, why on earth would you care?"

And just like that, he withdrew from her completely. His dark eyes returned to their previous sharp unconcern and his posture stiffened. "Of course. You are quite correct. It won't happen again."

Stanton stepped back once more, turning Lady Alicia loose on the men of the group. The couches had been removed and there was now dancing. He positioned himself with his back against a column and watched.

Like the others, Alicia was dancing—but she danced like none other. The music was a country reel, played with full lack of restraint. The guests were all shedding their social reserve with glee, but none more than Alicia. Her shoes were off and she kicked out in stocking feet, with her hair coming down further with every spin.

She was mesmerizing. Stanton couldn't take his eyes off her free-spirited grin as she dragged more gentlemen into the dance, towing them by the hand with the blissful assurance of a child, then turning them loose to dance as a seductress might dance if she were alone.

There were more graceful dancers, and there were more beautiful women in the room, but Stanton couldn't see them. To him, Lady Alicia shone like a bright parakeet in a roomful of hens.

However, Stanton could still see the gentlemen and he wasn't the only one gazing at Lady Alicia with longing, lust, and ill intent.

Not that his intentions were ill—and longing certainly

didn't enter into it—but he was more than willing to admit to the lust. He was a man after all.

And Lady Alicia was very much a woman, her pagan wild-child behavior aside.

"Wherever did you find her, Wyndham?"

If the voice at his shoulder had belonged to anyone else, Stanton would have cut the speaker off at the knees. He was in no mood either to defend his territory or to excuse his choices.

However, since it was the Prince Regent who stood beside him, a bit of social politeness was required—but only a bit.

"In the gutter, your highness," he replied shortly. "I found her in the gutter."

George gave a short laugh of surprise. "I had no idea you frequented the gutter, Wyndham." He turned back to watch Alicia dance. "Still, while you're down there, find me one of those, will you?"

Alicia's hairstyle gave up the fight and now her sunset locks flared brightly about her with every turn of her pretty ankles. She was entirely delicious, all flashing green eyes and bouncing bosom and lively sensuality. Stanton's mouth went quite dry.

"There was only one, your highness," he murmured slowly.

He was dimly aware that George had turned to gaze closely at him. "Hmm." The prince moved in front of him, blocking Stanton's view of the dancers. "Snap out of it, Wyndham."

Stanton blinked, shock chilling his spine. What was he doing? He had no business losing himself in a woman, especially not *this* woman!

She was not the simple free spirit she pretended to be, he was becoming sure of that. For all her gaiety and verve, he detected sadness beneath the perpetual moving of her full, lovely lips.

She might truly mourn the loss of her family and the loss of her place in the world.

She was rather brave, now that he thought about it. To come to this house party on his arm, with all the worst shadows of her past thrown into the bright light of public attention once more—he wasn't sure he'd want to face such exposure.

And the way she'd handled those harpies this evening? His punishment had been almost unnecessary, after the way she'd cut them off at the knees with the simple truth.

The simple truth.

God, if only he could be sure.

He was forced to rely upon observation alone. She showed no telltale signs of lying, but not everyone did. Some few had fully mastered the control of their facial muscles and the tendency of the gaze to either wander sheepishly or to fix earnestly upon the recipient of the lie.

Her hands gave nothing away, for they were constantly in motion, no matter the topic. She gestured quickly and gracefully, as natural as the motion of a bird's wings.

If she was lying, she was very, very good at it, which was far more disturbing than if she'd been clumsy. Such professional ability spoke of either training or natural deviousness of an alarming depth.

Or she was simply telling the truth—every moment of every day. Which was impossible, of course.

He rubbed a hand over his face. She was driving him mad with not knowing. Sometimes he wanted to grab her and shake the truth from her—or else kiss it from her.

He shut his eyes tightly. He was losing his grip. She was nothing but a very ordinary woman. Not actually beautiful. Not terribly well behaved. Rather more intelligent than some, perhaps. And wiser, if she had truly meant the things she'd told Lady Davenport tonight.

And braver.

You're doing it again.

He shook himself slightly, trying to dislodge this strange sensation that was forming. She was a mouthy, bloody-minded female with a blackened reputation and vengeful heart. He could not possible admire such a woman.

Yet he could not forget the bleak sadness in her eyes as she'd turned his way tonight—nor could he deny that it had sliced right through him to see her thus. Her bright smile had been doused, her light dimmed, her lovely eyes lost.

Still, she'd held her head high and won the day. If he could not admire her, he could at least stop denying that there was more to her than he'd first believed.

Except that he had no idea what to believe.

He found himself unable to take his eyes off her. He watched her constantly, perhaps afraid that the one moment he wasn't watching would be the moment when she showed the truth—or lies—within her.

Or perhaps it was because she was so very pleasing to look upon. He watched her dance.

She certainly appeared to be enjoying herself. Perhaps she truly was, or perhaps she was only projecting the illusion of enjoyment so as to appear as charming and adorable as possible.

Or perhaps she was truly enjoying projecting the illusion—

Stanton closed his eyes again in self-induced exhaustion. He felt very much like plowing his fist into his own head if it would only stop the circling and second-guessing going on within.

How did others do it? How did they survive the lifetime of never truly knowing what another's intentions might be? The spinning doubt that one woman could cause was nearly enough to send Wyndham to Bedlam—how much worse would it be to exist blind and oblivious to the rest of the world?

She was mad—entirely, completely, and utterly mad. He very much feared he was going to go mad from sheer proximity to her insanity.

Because he liked her. More than once over the last few days, he'd found himself smiling when thinking of some outlandish thing she'd said or done.

Hence the contagion. He pressed his fingertips to his temples, forcing away the invasive influence of Lady Alicia Lawrence and her rebellion.

Rebellion? 'Twas more of a revolution! She was determined to flout every convention and grind every social standard beneath the toe of her tiny slipper.

He realized he was smiling again.

Mad. Stark, staring mad . . .

The ballroom was draped with lengths of rich fabrics, arranged to provide several nooks of semi-privacy, most filled with cushions and the odd fainting couch.

Weary and breathless, Alicia fled to one of these to repair her fallen hair, hoping to catch her breath. It had been a very long time since she had been around so many people. The constant noise and the feeling of being watched and judged had scraped her nerves a bit raw.

Not that she wasn't having the time of her life, of course. It was precisely what she had wanted—to be in the center of things, to feel the excitement of the crowd, to dance and be· danced with.

At the moment, however, her feet ached and her head pounded. She'd had more wine in the last hours than she'd had in five years altogether. She pressed her fingertips to her temples as she relaxed slowly onto a luridly violet fainting couch. Just a moment of quiet, even if the noise had not truly abated and the little enclosure was no cooler than the overheated ballroom itself.

Or perhaps it is Wyndham who is overheating you?

Not that she cared one little bit what the mighty Lord Wyndham thought, of course. He was being an idiot, standing out there watching her every move with those eagle eyes, looming threateningly on the outskirts of her vicinity, probably frightening away the very man he sought.

Didn't he look smashing in his evening coat and tails, though? He made every other man in the room, even handsome Lord Farrington, look like badly put together copies of the original. She still found herself surprised to find herself in the company of a man like that.

You mean sharing a chamber with a man like that?

That, too.

Suddenly she was no longer weary. No, really, she had hours left in her—hours before she would be alone with him in that dark room, pretending to sleep—

She stood to leave, determined to spend as gay an evening as possible, even until dawn if necessary. Just as she reached for the drape over the "entry," it was swept back before her. She moved back, startled. Two bodies, entangled in each other, stumbled past her to land upon the small chaise. Alicia took three steps aside to avoid them, then found herself in the corner—the real corner, with real walls—as clothing flew and cries of passion escalated before her.

She held up one hand. "Ah—"

Something white and linen and warm landed in her hand. She dropped it quickly. "Ew."

The gentleman—for it was a lady and a gentleman, which she could see quite well now—was making heated, heartfelt demands. "More, darling, oh yes, my love, that's it, that's so good—"

Well, it certainly looked good. He was a firm, handsome specimen and his "darling" was a curvaceous person herself. As the clothing diminished, Alicia's fascination grew. Would they really become naked here, in the ballroom, right in front of her?

Would they truly go so far as to—

She shut her eyes tight. Oh, my. Apparently, they would.

She opened one eye—just to find her way out!—and caught sight of something she'd no idea existed. The lady was on her knees, clad in nothing but a lacy pair of pantaloons, while the gentleman stood before her, clad in boots with the remains of his breeches and drawers still tangled about his ankles.

He really was a handsome fellow, nearly as ornamental as Lord Farrington. She hadn't met him earlier, but she was quite able to disqualify him from Wyndham's search on the basis of his cries of rapture as the lady took his rigid organ into her mouth.

This was new. Almont hadn't mentioned it and it wasn't the sort of thing one ran across in one's reading . . .

Alicia tilted her head, trying to figure out how the lady was managing to encompass the entire . . . matter. Her interest was purely curious, until the gentleman buried his large hands in his lady's fallen hair and threw back his head, letting out such a visceral groan that Alicia felt it resonate deep inside her.

If she did *that,* could she make Wyndham surrender so?

Wyndham standing before her, the tip of his thickened rod at her lips.

Wyndham with his hands buried in her hair, lost in ecstasy while she—

Arousal swept her, drowning out her embarrassment, or feeding on it, she wasn't truly sure.

She was watching something she shouldn't—and that made it all the more exciting. Like this ball, she shouldn't be here. She shouldn't be standing here, half-hidden in the purple draperies, watching this woman pleasure this man.

I could do that. I could make him quiver and moan like that . . .

Then the gentleman pushed his lover away and breathlessly swept her up to lie on the sofa, then knelt to . . . ah, return the favor.

Oh, my.

This, Alicia remembered well. This was what had led her to her ruined state, this was what had made her throw caution to the wind, this was what she thought of when she found her gaze lingering on Wyndham's expressive mouth—

This was what had made the whole thing very nearly worthwhile.

She stood there, frozen in memory and tantalized arousal, as the man drew his tongue through the lady's dark nether curls. To watch these two attractive bodies, people she didn't know, strangers who embodied nothing but passion and reckless abandon—she felt as if she stole from them. Oh, she was wicked!

Then the woman rolled her head in Alicia's direction and opened her eyes. Alicia froze. For a moment, the lady's passion-glazed eyes registered nothing. Then, with a slight surprised widening, she focused on Alicia.

Alicia was horrified. She'd not meant to intrude—not meant to steal—

"I'm sorry—"

The woman smiled slowly, her eyes glinting wickedly. She reached one hand upward to Alicia. "Won't you join us, pretty one?"

Eek! Alicia sidled quickly out of reach. "Ah . . . thank you, really, but . . ."

She fled, pushing aside the drape so violently she heard threads pop. The party raged on outside, and the stench of mingled perfumes and overheated bodies struck her in the face. Blushing furiously, although no one had noticed her, she pushed through the crowd toward the hall doors.

She wasn't simply shocked and dismayed. She was wicked—bad and wicked and out of control. One scalding thought raged through her brain as she scurried far from the wild throng.

If that man had been Wyndham, what would my answer have been?

Across the ballroom, Stanton opened his eyes to spot Lady Alicia making her way from the hall at great speed.

Lady Alicia, turned loose upon the house where every room would be occupied by half-dressed couples—and not a few trios as well?

God help them all.

13

Stanton caught up with Lady Alicia as she passed from the great hall to the passageway beyond. She was leaving the room at great speed, her skirts fluttering about her ankles.

"Are you perhaps fleeing the scene of a crime?" he asked dryly.

She grabbed his hand. "Absolutely. Come quickly."

He went willingly, for now he was curious. "And whom have we sinned against this time? Our host? Our hostess? The Prince Regent?"

"I don't know them." She glanced up at him. "They'll recover."

That boded ill for them all. Unfortunately, Stanton couldn't bring himself to care. "Will they recover? I wonder. The rest of us are still a bit bemused by you."

Alicia entwined her fingers with his as she tugged him along the hall. Did she realize how perfectly their gloved hands fit together? She made no sign of it.

"The rest of you are entirely flummoxed by me, you mean." She sighed without much real regret. "It is always thus."

"Always that you are fleeing certain retribution, or always that you remain misunderstood?"

She glanced over her shoulder at him admonishingly. "Is now really the time to consider my inner clockworks?"

"That depends. Do we face a lynching, or mere arrest and trial?"

She stopped, cast a worried glance back toward the thankfully inactive door to the ballroom, then crossed her arms and glared up at him.

"I didn't do anything illegal. I never do."

He thought about that for a moment. "That's true. Very well, then. What sort of doom is it that we're fleeing like a pair of parlor thieves on the run?"

She glanced away. "You weren't entirely wrong about the people here."

Stanton crossed his own arms, mocking her stance. "So you teased the lion and the lion didn't like it?"

A tiny curl appeared at the corner of her mouth. "Oh, they liked it all right."

Stanton resisted the urge to clench his fists. "You're fleeing an *amorous* 'they'?"

She dropped her hands in a helpless shrug.

"They . . . it wasn't . . ." She threw out her hands in frustration. "They . . . they propositioned me!"

A bark of rusty laughter erupted from Stanton's throat. Astonishingly, it was followed by another, and another. At last he was forced to lean against the wall as he was made helpless with it.

Finally it subsided. About bloody time. Still chuckling, he dabbed at his eyes before raising his gaze to see Alicia standing before him with her eyes wide.

"Are you unwell?"

He heaved a great sigh. For some reason, he felt lighter, as if he'd given up some burden. "I am quite well, thank you."

She still gazed at him warily. "The reason I asked is that I thought you didn't have the capacity for gaiety. Are you sure you aren't suffering a fever?"

He took her hand and stripped the glove from it in one motion. Then he placed it on his forehead. "I am quite without fever, as you can see."

His grin faded as he watched a transformation come over her. Her eyes went wide. Two pink spots appeared on her cheeks. Her fingers began to tremble on his brow and the tip of her tongue flicked over her lower lip.

Stanton was about to remark on that when he found himself caught by the hungry golden gleam in her green eyes. He went very still under her touch. Had she ever been so lovely?

Her hand slipped down slightly as her fingertips began to trace the arch of his brow, ending at the pulse point of his temple. Then her fingers curled and it was the back of her knuckles that brushed down over his cheekbone.

She was mimicking the way he'd touched her earlier. A strange sensation was seeping through Stanton. The thought that she'd so perfectly recall a mere touch sent a jolt of something unfamiliar through him.

She let her hand trail down until she traced his jaw to the point of his chin. Only then did she depart from their earlier encounter.

She let her index finger uncurl to lightly brush its tip along the corner of his mouth, then inward to outline his lower lip.

Stanton couldn't believe the amount of sensation a single fingertip could generate within a man. From that one point of skin-to-skin heat, it was as if lava poured through his veins. His heart began to pound even as his breath seemed to leave him.

Her gaze was intent upon his mouth and he was free to look at her, to see the hungry shimmer in her eyes, to drink in the beauty of the way her opulent breasts threatened the safety of her décolletage, to see the way the tip of her tongue followed the path of her finger upon her own lips.

She was flame and cream and wicked shimmering wood-goddess green and hot enveloping silk, all at once.

To top it all off—and for him it very nearly did, as he'd been celibate for most of his life—she smelled like spice and roses and warmly aroused woman.

He felt himself begin to fall, slipping freely and unresistingly, even longingly, from his lonely, watchful aerie. This woman was more than intriguing, more than desirable, more than a mere sexual distraction. No, he was becoming increasingly aware that Alicia was the answer. She was the fiery, delightful, contagious cure for the chill of isolation that had always lived within him.

And as such, she was entirely dangerous.

He cleared his dry throat, desperate to break the spell before it broke him. "Alicia, what are you doing?"

To his dismay, his words didn't jolt her out of her fascinated exploration. "What?" she said, her tone distant. "Did you say something?"

He raised his hands to her shoulders, intending to move her away, to put some space and chill air between them. All that resulted was that he felt the heat of her pale, bare skin sear right through his gray silk gloves.

As if in a dream, he saw his hands leave her flesh to move together. One hand stripped the other in a motion as automatic as breathing—not that his breath was altogether automatic at the moment.

Then his mutinous hands returned to her bare shoulders, where his fingers sank into the soft, sweet creamy flesh there like a parched man who has finally reached an oasis. Her heat pierced through him, melting away the ice.

He watched his fingers slide over her smooth silken warmth with betrayed disbelief and anticipation. They spread across her bare back, then slid upward to bury themselves in her hair.

Pins plinked to the floor and the heavy mass of fiery silk fell into his wayward hands, a fitting reward for such rebellion.

She let her head fall back, shutting her eyes and exposing her throat for him to devour should he so choose. The soft sound that left her parted lips struck him as hard and sharply as a sword. He willed himself to ignore the blow.

Thankfully, it seemed the only part of him that outpaced his control were his hands.

Well, perhaps not the only parts. His erection swelled painfully against the restriction of his trousers. He welcomed the pain, welcomed the throbbing beat of trapped arousal, like drums in the jungle, for it would lead him out of the tangle, back to sanity.

Then she moved into him, pressing her soft breasts to his chest, her rounded belly to his throbbing, barely restrained cock.

Then she whispered his name. "Stanton."

Never had he heard it uttered thus. He was Wyndham to everyone who mattered, and Lord Wyndham to everyone else. Even his mother called him Wyndham.

Her husky, hot-buttered voice called to another man altogether—one who was not as disciplined as Wyndham. That man welled up from beneath, answering her siren's summons, tearing through Wyndham's legendary control like paper before talons.

Stanton's hands clenched in her hair and brought her mouth to his, raising her cruelly to her tiptoes to meet the eruption of his dark and voracious need.

She came easily and willingly, wrapping her arms about his neck in equal urgency.

Her eager generosity was the end for Stanton. He was quite completely and thoroughly lost at that moment.

And by God, he hoped never to be found!

Alicia struggled in the midst of a whirlwind. Cross's house and guests disappeared from her awareness, obscured by the storm of this unpredictable man. Wyndham's mouth was hot and angry and achingly hungry on hers. She felt herself absorbing his heat and fury and need like a sponge. This man—this hard, cold, solitary man needed her, she could feel it.

He needed *her*.

So she gave over to his hard hands and punishing mouth, pressing herself to him, offering her softness and herself in a primeval answer to the howling, spiraling solitude she felt in his kiss.

His fists pulled at her hair, but she willed the pain away, only allowing a slight sting past her guard to add to the pleasure of being caught up so urgently in his arms.

The more she gave, the more avidly he took. His mouth moved from hers to suck urgently on her neck, to scrape teeth over her shoulder, to explore her ear with a hot tongue.

One hand slipped from her hair to pull urgently at her bodice. Before she could realize what he was about, he'd tugged her tiny cap sleeve down to her elbow and released her bare breast to his voracious mouth.

"Oh—"

Her squeak of protest was lost as he whirled her about to press her to the wall, lifting her high to gain better access to her bosom. The plaster was cold against her back and his mouth was hot and wet on her nipple. He sucked hard and she forgot to protest, instead burying her hands in his hair to press him closer.

He pushed his body hard to hers, keeping her pinned to the wall. She felt his hand lift her skirts to scorch a path up her thigh and forge past the gossamer drawers she'd thought would be her own private secret.

He found her with urgent surety, cupping and claiming

her with his big hand. A long hard finger pushed inside her without preamble. It was a crude and wicked invasion. In some corner of her mind she knew she ought to care, but all she could do was to hang there in his grasp, allowing his rough, nearly cruel caresses.

The finger thrust deeper, then withdrew to begin a merciless, plunging rhythm. She took the carnal ferocity with utter lack of will, controlled only by the heat of him rushing through her body, claiming her, robbing her of self and self-protection.

His mouth moved to her other breast, leaving the first sore and damp and bare to the chill air. Her sleeves were now both down to her elbows, trapping her arms to her sides. Her hands were lost in his thick hair, grasping and fisting in it as he continued his rough rhythm deep inside her.

She felt impaled and imprisoned and wickedly, erotically violated—and entirely, exquisitely alive in his hands.

He found a way to penetrate her, a new angle or pressure, that suddenly caused her to cry out. She felt another large finger join the first, pressing hard into her tightness, forcing her to open her thighs wider to accommodate. She had a sudden impression of how she must look, half-naked and roughly handled, with her skirts hiked to her knees while a man sucked at her nipples and forcibly violated her vagina.

Part of her was horrified at the fact that she wasn't . . . well, horrified. The rest of her exploded in a spinning burst of pleasure that swept her last conscious thought away. She didn't care that she cried out shrilly. She didn't care that Wyndham's fingers were well slicked with her wetness. She didn't care that he'd left stubble-reddened patches and teeth scrapes on her breasts or that her nipples were hard and swollen and sore from his hungry mouth.

There was nothing left of her but white-hot pleasure and freedom and him.

Then she came back to herself, became aware that her

breath still sobbed from her throat, that he had removed his hand from beneath her skirt and now held her by the waist, his forehead dropped to rest upon her neck.

She could feel his hot breath gasping against the tops of her breasts and knew he'd not reached the same release.

She lifted her hands from where they'd somehow moved to clutch at his shoulders and softly stroked them through his hair. "Stant—"

"Lady Alicia," he interrupted, his voice a rasping grate. "I must beg you to accept my deepest apology. I had no right to use you so cruelly."

"Oh, dear heavens," she said with a nervous, breathless laugh. "I hope you never show me kindness, then. It might very well kill me."

Stanton didn't hear her. He was consumed by the magnitude of his error. He'd completely lost control. It had not been until he'd heard the keening sound of her orgasm echoing through the marble halls that he'd come back to himself, to who and where he was.

Now, with his trousers still trapping a mountainous erection and his fingers still wet with her juices and his arms still full of shivering, satisfied woman, he forced himself to consider the situation coldly.

He'd always secretly hoped that if he ever did someday find that one woman who could penetrate his reserve, if he ever found someone whom he craved more than control and duty, she would his and only his, forever.

Someday.

But now was not the time. This worldly bacchanal was not the place—God, no! Not with a conspirator on the loose.

Moreover, notoriously immoral Lady Alicia was most assuredly not the woman.

14

After Wyndham waited for her to pull herself and her gown together—turned half away with his gaze on the floor, mind you—he led her to the first step of the sweeping staircase that led up to their room.

He bowed shortly. "My thanks, my lady, for a most enjoyable . . . evening."

She hesitated, then nodded in return. "It was my pleasure, my lord. Shall I see you tomorrow . . . ah, later today?"

He spent a moment adjusting his cravat. "Of course," he said without looking at her. "We have the Masque to attend."

"Ah, yes," she said softly. "The Masque. Lord Cross spares no imagination in his entertainments. I shall see you then." She turned away and began to climb the stairs. Three steps up she halted and turned back. "This was a terrible mistake, wasn't it?"

Stanton took a deep breath, then lifted his head to meet her eyes. "It was."

She nodded slowly. "My best ideas usually are." She frowned slightly. "I have no idea what to say to you. Am I supposed to reassure you and make you feel unobligated and all that rot?"

His lips twitched. She was unsinkable. "Consider me adequately reassured."

She let out a breath. "Very well then. Have a pleasant morning then." She turned and lifted her hem to trot briskly up the stairs.

Stanton watched her go. It had been a capital error, all around. She seemed to be taking it well—although the look in her lovely eyes afterward . . .

He feared he would be haunted by that flash of desolation for some time. He ought to have realized how vulnerable she was beneath her façade of the social rebel. She was all that was free-spirited and capricious, but she was still a lady behind all the rash behavior—a lady who deserved better from him than to be ravaged in a hallway.

Alicia returned to their bedchamber. The room seemed dark and unknown now, treacherous with unfamiliar furnishings. Objects loomed in the shadows and the bed curtains swung menacingly as she brushed by them, the hooks above creaking on their rods.

She felt her way to the hearth to find the box of candles on the mantel but didn't bother to light one once there. She didn't want to see Wyndham's presence about her, to feel his absence in the very existence of his horn hairbrush next to her silver one on the dressing table.

Wrapping her hands over the edge of the finely carved stone, she dropped her forehead to rest on her knuckles.

She'd nearly been very, very foolish.

The rug beneath her bare feet was soft and warm, the glow of the coals against the fabric of her fine-spun gown warming as well. Too warm. The heat of their bodies might have long faded, but she imagined she could still feel the scorching of their sudden, flaring passion.

A mistake, she'd offered, and he'd agreed. She hadn't wanted him to. She'd hoped he would deny any such thing. She'd hoped he would kiss her softly and walk her upstairs and help her quiet the shimmering reverberations that still rippled through her body. Instead, he'd bowed and walked away, as if they'd shared nothing more than a not-very-enjoyable waltz.

Fortunately she'd kept her head enough to remain lightly unconcerned. Her heart was not subject to girlish fantasies of love everlasting.

He had been—and still was—very arousing to her senses and her animal nature. She'd talked herself into believing that giving in to those stimuli was a good idea.

"So sorry," she whispered. "My mistake."

Luckily—she could hardly believe her good fortune—her heart was supremely uninvolved.

Good thing, too, or otherwise she very much feared it would be breaking even now.

Lady Alicia slept much the way she lived—largely, taking up an astonishing amount of the giant bed with far-flung, deliciously rounded limbs. The bedchamber was nearly dark, giving Stanton the privacy to look his fill. Her hair, never much restrained, curled over the pillow like copper on silk, the discipline of her bedtime braid long lost in her restless sleep.

Her sleeping garments were sheer and inclined to make men drool. Even in the dim glow of the coals, Stanton could see her rosy nipples and the dark shadow of her pubic hair between her parted legs. He could imagine tearing directly through the spiderweb batiste to reach such delicacies.

Then it occurred to him that the gown was expensive as well, which meant she'd purchased it with his money. Why had she chosen such provocative nightgowns? He was fairly sure she never expected to share a room. Her dismay earlier had not been feigned . . . at least, he didn't think so.

For reputation's sake? A smile crept over his lips as he imagined her in the unmentionables shop, boldly ordering a dozen brazen nightdresses, relishing the gossip that would surely follow.

His smile faded. Why was she so bent on destroying what shreds of virtue she had left? What had her family done to her that made her hate them so? Should he pity or revile her for her estrangement from them?

She'd left him behind again, confused by the mere purchase of a negligee. Damn the woman! Her mercurial nature defied even the most basic reading of her purpose!

The only surely true thing Stanton could say about Lady Alicia Lawrence was that she was never, ever dull.

And that her luxurious body haunted his dreams, both sleeping and waking.

He turned away from that sweet body sprawled invitingly on the great bed and ran a shaking hand over his face.

No.

He'd vowed years ago that no matter how he ached for it, he would never subject another woman to his dark passions. His bleak search for the truth brought out the worst—and the best, apparently—in his lovemaking.

For never was a woman more honest and true than when she writhed in orgasm, insensible with pleasure, raw and open to him. He craved that moment, needed it, grew addicted to it, putting off his own pleasure until women fled his bed from exhaustion and fear of his torturous self-control.

If you can't read her now, perhaps you could read her then.

Bloody hell.

It might work. Perhaps seducing Alicia to that point would break down the walls of her mysterious resistance to his powers.

Take her. Own her. Send her to that shadowy place with your hands and your mouth, over and over again, until the

truth is in her cries and her damp, sweating face and the
taste of her secrets is on your tongue.

Stanton turned blind eyes to the fire, his gaze wide and
absent as he pictured her in his hands, victim to his search
for truth, wet and gasping and trembling in his control.

He wouldn't let need catch him by surprise again. He
would control the moment, the pursuit, the capture.

The climax.

Do it. She's a wild, succulent creature, more freely passion-
ate than any woman you've ever known. Take advantage of her
nature, use her sensuality to prevail over her. She'll be willing,
warm clay in your hands. Take her. Make her let you in.

He threw himself down onto his bed for the night, the
chair by the fire. It was even less comfortable than it looked,
but that was nothing compared to the state of his soul. Mind
wrestled with body, logic battled with lust.

Their surroundings didn't help his struggle. Passion siz-
zled all about them, digging beneath the walls of his self-
control like Normans in the night.

Where Lady Alicia saw freedom, Stanton saw a siege. He
could feel his darker nature coming forcefully alert, waking
from a decade of frozen sleep. The moans sounding all about
them, the rhythmic rattle of bed frames and the muffled,
wicked laughter in the halls insinuated into his mind dark,
hungry thoughts of plump pale thighs and jutting ruby nipples and slick, wet, hot places that tasted of the sea.

He stared at the ornately plastered ceiling of the bedchamber with aching, unseeing eyes. He could not go out
there, yet staying here was endangering him as well. The
soft, sweet breathing of a perfectly willing woman whispered rhythmically just across the room.

It was going to be a very long night.

The next morning, Alicia woke suddenly, with the startled
feeling that she was being watched.

The room was empty. Lord Wyndham was dressed and gone, the fire had warmed the room, and a covered plate on a tray was emitting tempting steam on a side table.

"Food!" That was always worth getting up for. Alicia slipped from beneath the covers and padded over to the table without bothering with a wrapper. The lifting of the lid rewarded her with eggs and sausage and pretty little toast corners. The small silver jam pot on the side contained nothing more dangerous than a bit of honey. She smiled. Dear Garrett.

Having the breakfast took less time than admiring it had. Alicia busied herself with a freshening wash in the basin. Then she brushed out her hair. Then, out of sheer boredom, she made the bed and fluffed the pillows and removed any sign that Wyndham had slept in the chair.

At last Garrett appeared. Alicia fell on him like a starving hound on a bone. "Thank heaven! It's been *hours.*"

Garrett gazed at her doubtfully. "I left you sleeping not a half hour past. What are you so eager for today?"

Wyndham.

Alicia blinked. "Oh, no."

Garrett smirked. "Didn't like the answer to that one, did you?"

She sat in the chair as her knees threatened to quit her completely. "I'm perishing to see him. What does that mean?"

Garrett rolled his eyes as he pulled a fetching green woolen day gown from the wardrobe. "It means you're perishing to see him. What of it? He's a handsome eyeful. A lady needn't be ashamed of wanting to rest her eyes on an ornamental bloke like him."

She sighed. "He is quite attractive. And I haven't been around many attractive men lately."

Garrett cleared his throat. She patted his hand. "You know what I mean. Besides, you aren't attractive. You're insanely beautiful."

He nodded matter-of-factly. "Quite right." Then he helped her into the gown and sat her down on the stool before the dressing table to fix her hair. "Now, are we aiming for coy vixen or are you going all out this morning and aspiring to shameless hussy?"

She squinted at her image in the mirror. "I'd say shameless vixen. Much more appropriate for daytime, don't you think?"

This resulted in her hair being a rather mussed version of what the other ladies were wearing, with a few long strands pulled loose "as if some man just couldn't keep his hands off you in the linen closet" and allowed to dangle into her cleavage.

"It'll drive the gents mad," Garrett insisted. "They'll be wishing they could pull it free for you and not daring to be so bold."

The deceptively demure day gown was anything but, for it was constructed with all the floating bosom that whalebone and buckram could provide her—which was a considerable expanse of plump, ivory skin.

"Oy," Garrett breathed worshipfully when she was dressed. "It's almost enough to make a tea leaf turn to women."

"I wish you would," Alicia grumbled. "For I'd much rather run away with you than to go back into that writhing brothel downstairs."

Garrett pinched her arm. "Nonsense. I'm entirely out of your reach anyway."

"Humility is a virtue, Garrett."

"So say ugly people." He fetched her gloves and a lacy lambswool shawl. "Now, remember to lean toward the men and to lean away from the ladies." He fiddled with a stray lock of hair. "And don't spend all your time staring wistfully at Wyndham today. You don't want him to know you prefer him above all others."

"I don't stare wistfully at Wyndham!"

"No, you're right. It's rather more ravenous than wistful. Either way, ignore him a little at least. He'll hate it."

"Oh. All right then." Dressed and ready to make her appearance, Alicia turned one last circle before Garrett. "Am I properly armed?"

"You're entirely deadly and you're decidedly late. Everyone else has been up for hours."

She whirled at the sound of Wyndham's rumbling voice. He was standing in the doorway of their bedchamber as if he'd been there some while.

Oh, bother. She only hoped he hadn't been there long enough to hear the "wistful" remark.

"Well, then. I had best be on my way then." She excused herself quickly, ducking past Wyndham with a nod, fleeing the room and the lingering heat that threatened to melt her away.

Once downstairs, she was told by a footman that the ladies had gathered in the east morning room. She heard them before she found the room, as the gay chatter penetrated past the door with ease.

Her steps slowed. She ought to spend the day with the ladies, as the gentlemen would be pursuing shooting or gaming all day. Custom dictated that she do so.

Then again . . .

She smiled and turned on her heel, nearly running as she made for the front door. Garrett was waiting for her there, her bonnet and coat in his hands.

He smirked. "Took you that long to remember that you never do as you're told?"

She grabbed up her things and bestowed a quick kiss on Garrett's sculpted jaw. "Silly me." She ran for the crisp, chill day as if it would save her life—or at least her sanity.

She knew Cross's estate fairly well . . . and she could feel Sutherland tugging at her through the wood.

The path was overgrown now, barely visible through the spiderwort and feverfew that had sprung up since last she'd come this way to spy on the extravagant parties given here.

Her parents must be holding a tighter rein on Alberta and Antonia since then, for they had once been known to trail after her, protesting all the way but just as determined to see.

"I'll just go to the hill, just to see the house," she told herself. "There is a pretty aspect there." She started out briskly enough, striding through the brush with her skirts lifted. Then, as the way became more and more the playground of her childhood, she began to slow.

She'd never expected to set foot on Sutherland soil again, yet there was the tree where Alberta had fallen and turned her ankle. Alicia and Antonia had run her errands for weeks, hiding the injury from their mother for fear of being forbidden to climb.

And there was the pool where Alicia had learned that falling in the water fully dressed was nothing at all like taking a dip in a shift and that pinchpenny fathers took a dim view of careless daughters who ruined nearly new frocks that were supposed to last through three girls.

Forgetting entirely her plan to stop at the hilltop, Alicia let memories pull her from one spot to the next. A favorite picnic spot, the thicket with the best berries in summer, the stile by the dairy pasture where Antonia had torn her petticoat.

Her entire life had been spent in these grassy hills. She topped the last rise and looked down upon Sutherland itself.

It was even shabbier than she remembered. The drive needed graveling and the gardens languished, the long neglect visible even in winter.

The house itself looked smaller. Those elderly stone walls had been too small to hold her then. She would surely burst them now, should she ever be allowed within again.

Which she wouldn't.

She ought to leave before someone spotted her... although there were precious few servants about. She heard someone pounding nails in the stable and a scullery boy she did not recognize came out to dump dirty water in the yard, but where was the bustle she recalled from her childhood?

Could it be that her family hadn't come home for the winter yet? Emboldened by the deserted state of the scene below, she let the ache in her heart draw her nearer.

She kept to the outer garden, stepping carefully through the fallen limbs and leaves that had yet to be cleared from autumn. There was a small garden structure nearby where she used to lie on the bench for hours, dreaming of the life her mother told her she could live—a life with a wealthy handsome man who would adore her and who would be happy to spill his pounds into Sutherland, allowing her parents to live in security and comfort and providing high connections for her sisters' marriages to boot.

All of which Alicia had very properly wanted for herself—but it was the part about the handsome man who adored her that kept her dreaming her youth away.

The small Greek-styled temple was full of garden debris and creature scat, the stone bench that had played as Ophelia's couch now caked in bird droppings.

"Of course," Alicia whispered to herself. "Isn't that the way of dreams?"

"Yours perhaps," snapped a high voice behind her. "But then you never bothered to care about anyone's dreams but your own."

15

Alicia turned to see a tall girl with telltale auburn hair. The angry eyes took five years away and left only one answer. "Antonia?"

Alicia took an automatic step forward to embrace her youngest sister. Antonia drew back as if a serpent threatened her.

"What are you doing here?" Antonia wrapped her shawl more tightly and glanced over her shoulder. "Papa told you never to set foot on Sutherland again. I heard him."

Alicia drew herself up. "I don't have a father anymore, remember? Therefore, I need not obey one."

A flash of envy crossed Antonia's expression. Then her furious gaze turned fearful with the sound of a footfall on the garden path. She drew back, as if to be spotted a distance from Alicia would be less blameworthy than to be found too close.

Which, of course, was entirely sensible. As the footsteps neared, Alicia looked about her for an exit or a place to hide, but since she didn't care to drop to her knees behind the filthy bench, she resigned herself to dealing with an ugly scene.

It wasn't as though anyone here would physically harm . . . at least, she was fairly sure of that, sabotaged opera box or no.

Alberta rounded the corner of the building. "Tonia, Mama is looking for y—"

Alberta had changed as well. Always cheerfully plump, now Alberta was divinely curvaceous, even more so than Alicia, with a large bosom and a tiny waist. Alicia hoped her middle sister stayed out of the Prince Regent's path.

Alberta's eyes widened. "A-Alicia?"

Resigned to more accusations, Alicia folded her hands before her. "How have you been, Bertie?"

Alberta's rushing embrace nearly knocked Alicia from her feet. She let her arms come about her sister, closing her eyes against the rush of gratitude that swept her.

Alberta's emotional babble continued for several long minutes—not that Alicia minded, of course—until a sharp word from Antonia prompted Alberta to let go.

Still, she kept hold of Alicia's hand as she turned on Antonia. "Do not admonish me, Antonia. You are not the elder!"

"And yet I am the wiser," Antonia shot back. "We cannot behave as though nothing has changed!"

As she moved between them, Alicia was reminded of how she had always been the peacekeeper between these two very different girls.

Now it seemed that she was the bone of contention as well.

"Antonia, Alberta has not done anything but greet me. However, Alberta, Antonia is quite correct. We must not forget how very much has changed. I would not hurt either of you for the world—"

"It's a bit late for that, isn't it?" Bright fury flashed in Antonia's eyes. "You have no idea what your wanton behavior has cost us—all of us!"

Alicia looked from one sister to the other. It was true that they both looked rather pale and she had certainly never seen the temperamental Antonia so tightly strung.

Antonia's accusations hurt, but did not surprise. However, Alberta's defense did.

Her more sanguine sister rounded on the younger one with red-hot anger. "Shut it, Tonia! You know nothing of the real world—you know nothing of what caused Licia to do what she did—not that I believe more than half of those stories, and neither should you!"

Alicia looked at Alberta in surprise. "You don't believe I spent the night with Almont's stable boy?"

Alberta flapped a scornful hand. "Of course not. What a mad idea. You were ever notional, Licia, but you were never cruel. You might have sneaked the lad some cake in a napkin, but you wouldn't use him so poorly for the world."

The perfectly Alberta-esque logic of that made Alicia smile. "Thank you, dear."

Antonia was not so easily convinced. "The fact of your ruination does not change. It makes no difference who you allowed yourself to be seduced by."

Alicia opened her mouth to point out that it made all the difference in the world to Society's eyes, but it was Alberta who leaped to her defense once more. "Oh, shut your silly trap, Tonia. She cannot help it now."

"No one can help us," Antonia said sourly. "Bertie's beau won't ask for her hand until his father gives permission, and he won't do that unless I marry very well, for he says that one might cancel out the other. And no one will court me until they've seen Bertie make a good match."

Her sisters were lost in limbo, cast there by her own actions. Alicia felt sick, and doubly furious at her parents. She'd been a fool, it was true, but she'd been a sheltered child. The entire matter could have been covered up, made to go away, had they only stopped to think before exposing her situation to all of Society.

"Antoniiiiaaa!"

Their mother's voice came from the direction of the house.

Lifelong habit kicked in. The three of them ducked quickly behind the temple and pressed their backs to the wall.

"What does she want?" Antonia asked Alberta.

Alberta grimaced. "She wants you to retrim her gowns again. She says you have the better knack."

Alicia looked at her sister. "Why doesn't she have Pitt do it, as always?"

Antonia slid a filthy glance her way. "Because Pitt is gone, like the others. We've almost no staff at all now."

Alicia looked to Alberta for confirmation. Bertie shrugged reluctantly. "It's true. But it isn't your fault, Licia—"

"The devil it isn't!" Antonia pushed away from the wall. "We were ever poor, Alicia, but not destitute. If you'd managed even the most mediocre of matches, Papa could have obtained some sort of loan from the family, enough to keep Sutherland going a bit longer!"

Alicia straightened. "I didn't send Sutherland into ruin, Antonia. I didn't cause Papa's gambling or Mama's spending. And another loan would only mean another debt, for it would be gone as quickly as the others."

Antonia flushed. "At least we would not be eating poultry every night for a year!"

Alicia raised a brow coolly. "I would have adored having poultry more than once a month in the last five years. As it was, I could scarcely afford bread."

Alberta flounced between them. "Oh, stop it. I don't want to play 'who is suffering more' right now."

Alicia let out a breath. "Nor do I." She was getting angry at the wrong party, anyway. Her sisters were caught in a terrible trap.

Bertie's young man would wait until Antonia married, and Antonia's beau would wait until Bertie married—and her sisters would wait their lives away.

Money had the marvelous ability to wash away any sort of family stain—but the Lawrences had no money.

Until now.

Alicia turned pleading eyes toward both girls. "I know it seems hard that I ask you this, but trust me. I can help. I just need time."

Time to find Wyndham's mystery lord. Time to undo some of the damage she had been so hell-bent on creating only yesterday.

Time to make sure that her parents didn't ruin another Lawrence sister in their desperation.

Stanton had little to do that morning but wait for the descent of the Prince Regent—and mull over his dilemma with Lady Alicia—so he stationed himself by the front door of the great house in order to learn as much as possible about the other guests.

Despite Stanton's efforts to investigate before he left London, it seemed that the guest list to Lord Cross's parties was one of the best-kept secrets in Society. Apparently every one involved was quite determined to make sure it stayed thus. How reassuring it must be to know that what happened on Cross's estate never left its borders.

There were quite a number of guests lingering in the hall already, mostly ladies and, well, women who weren't ladies. Stanton felt like a crow among the flowers in his classic black, while the women swirled about him in their brightly colored morning gowns.

It was a superior place to hear the latest gossip, however. Stanton listened carefully even as he tried to portray an air of indolent boredom. He must not have been terribly successful, for the ladies nearest him gazed at him warily and spoke in low tones.

Still, they found him less interesting than the new arrivals. It looked as though this were by far the most popular party of the early winter Season.

Lords, gamblers, and a few men of the church came through with their companions, each arrival renewing a storm of gossip. Stanton learned more than he'd ever wanted to know about the various gentlemen's sexual practices, but not much more.

Then the front door opened to reveal a large, vaguely barbaric silhouette, one that was entirely familiar to Stanton.

Bloody hell, what was Greenleigh doing here? Dane was followed by the buxom Valkyrie form of his lady, Olivia. Stanton was stunned that Dane would bring his lady wife to such a gathering, but Olivia seemed anything but offended. She gazed about with eager curiosity, then spotted him and smiled very briefly before continuing her examination of the grand entrance hall.

Stanton decided that nothing forbade him from casually greeting another man of nearly equal social status and strode forward to castigate Greenleigh.

Dane saw him coming and grinned. "Don't charge at me like that, Wyndham. People will think we have a history."

Stanton forced his demeanor to one more relaxed. "Why are you here?" Well, *almost* relaxed.

Dane folded massive arms. "The same reason you are."

"But you brought your lady!" If Stanton could have, he would have swept the intrepid Olivia right back out the door and into her carriage.

"Olivia adores fireworks." Dane lifted a corner of his lips. "To be truthful, she brought me. I wasn't convinced that you needed help." He rubbed the back of his neck ruefully. "Unfortunately, Lady Dryden has a most unique method of gaining the cooperation of Reardon and myself."

"She set your wives upon you, didn't she?" Damn. It was a very good thing he was immune to such influence. Someone had to rein Lady Dryden in before she disturbed the careful balance of the Four. "Well, at least Reardon had the sense to—"

Dane was looking over Stanton's shoulder. "Ah, yes . . . about that—"

Stanton turned to see Lord and Lady Reardon entering the house. Nathaniel was immediately deserted with no more than a fond kiss on the cheek as his lady, Willa, spotted Lady Greenleigh in the hall.

Lady Reardon was small, dark, and curvaceous next to the statuesque Lady Greenleigh, but the two were obviously thick as thieves.

Stanton turned back to Dane with a frown. "I had—have—a plan," he said grimly. "My plan is simple, unproblematic, and requires no assistance from the other Three. Is that clear?"

Dane shrugged. "Wyndham, I'm here for the food. If Lady Dryden has any purpose other than to keep a few extra pairs of eyes on the Prince Regent, I know nothing about it."

"Hmm." Stanton gazed at him sourly, then across the grand hall to where Reardon stood with the two ladies. "I suppose we should expect Lord and Lady Dryden as well?"

Dane grinned. "I'm surprised they are not here already."

Stanton fought the urge to sigh in resignation. "This certainly explains the last-minute additions to the guest list." He refrained from complaining about being forced to share a chamber with Lady Alicia—what the Three didn't know wouldn't do Stanton any harm.

"So, where is the infamous Lady Alicia?" Dane asked genially. "Olivia is positively panting to have a look at her."

Sleeping in our bed. Of course, Stanton couldn't say that out loud, no matter that it gave him a tiny, unwanted sense of satisfaction to think it.

Then again, it was getting rather late. Surely she had risen by now?

"I'll have a go at finding her, shall I?" Stanton smiled casually.

He must not have been very good at it, for Dane looked askance at him. "You do that," he said. "I'll try to keep the ladies at bay for the moment."

Unfortunately, Lady Alicia was nowhere to be found. Where could she have gotten herself to this time?

Stanton cursed wearily. This was beginning to cost him his habitual composure.

At last he thought to check the stables. The weather wasn't encouraging for a ride, but one never knew with Alicia.

When Cross's groom told Stanton that he'd seen Lady Alicia walking into the east wood, Stanton's first thought was that she was disobeying him again.

His second thought was that she was meeting a new lover.

His third, much worse, thought turned out to be the right one. She was headed home.

Damn. When he'd made this devil's bargain with Alicia, he'd sworn to himself not to inflict her upon any sort of decent society. Now here she was, flinging herself into the very den of the upright.

To be truthful, he didn't know who he was more worried about—Sutherland or Alicia herself.

It wasn't difficult to track someone who wasn't particularly inclined to hide their passage, so he was able to follow her meandering path easily. He ought to be able to catch up to her before she—

Cresting the last hill and looking down on what must be Sutherland, Stanton cursed. He'd never been much of a curser before, but he was becoming rather proficient, if he did say so himself. And who wouldn't curse if they were saddled with the willful and outrageous Lady Alicia? Stanton permitted himself a moment of sympathy for the parents of what must have been a truly trying child.

There was no sign of her, but there was no sign of a ruckus either. Her trail led into the rear gardens. Perhaps no one had yet detected her presence.

Following her on foot now, Stanton led his horse through the neglected gardens until he approached the rear of a battered garden structure. There was a heated argument coming from within.

Stanton blinked. It sounded very much as if Alicia were holding a fierce, mad three-way argument with herself!

Turning the corner, Stanton spied a trio of Titian beauties with tempers at least as bright as their hair. Two stood toe to toe, their voices growing more shrill by the moment. Alicia— Good God, could it be true?—appeared to be the voice of reason, her tone more one of mediation. Stanton felt an insane chuckle rising in his chest at the very thought of a world where Alicia was the rational one.

Alicia's sisters, for who else could they be, were very nearly as pretty as Alicia herself. There was a plump, buxom sister and a slim, elegant sister. Three passionate, tempestuous flame-haired young women in one place? The mind boggled.

"Alicia was only doing what she had to do to get out of this awful valley!" The bosomy one said. "You hate it here as much as she ever did, Antonia, don't deny it! At least she lives in London now, and chooses her own lovers, and goes to the opera in beautiful gowns—"

He saw Alicia put a hand on her sister's arm. "Alberta, you mustn't think it. My life is nothing to envy!"

The slender one, who was Antonia—he was going to figure this out if it killed him—shook Alicia off like an insect and turned on her. "You come here, after all these years, and put such thoughts into her head! If she follows your path, I am doomed!" Antonia threw out her hands. "Do you realize that even by talking to you today we are putting our fragile reputations in danger? What if someone has seen us? What if—" Antonia froze as she saw Stanton standing at the corner of the temple. "Oh, no."

Alicia turned and saw him there. Several expressions flashed across her lively features, but the one that caught his attention was pride. Possessive satisfaction, the sort of thing one might feel about having a fine family home or a beautiful horse.

The fact that she felt that way about him was a bit disturbing, but he would have to address that later. At the moment, it seemed as though Antonia were planning to faint.

Alicia caught her sister. "Antonia, do not distress yourself," she urged. "This is Lord Wyndham, my—" Her gaze flickered up at him again with that odd tinge of pride. "My very good friend. He will not tell anyone you were speaking to me."

Alberta was gazing at him in fascinated awe, Antonia's fainting fit bedamned, apparently. "This is your lover? But he's so handsome and fine! Why must he pay for—" Alberta halted, hearing her own tasteless words. She looked at him with horror. "Oh! I'm s-sorry, my lord! I—"

Alicia pressed her twitching lips together as she looked at him. "Oh, he looks well enough on the outside, Alberta, but he has dastardly proclivities aplenty."

Alberta only seemed further fascinated. "Really? Like what?"

"I eat tabby kittens for breakfast," Stanton said dryly. "Fortunately, I'm not hungry at the moment."

Antonia sprang upright like a jack-in-the-box to glare at him. Stanton stepped back. Really, they were the most alarming trio.

Her eyes still fixed on Stanton, Antonia grabbed Alberta

by the arm. "I cannot believe you would stand here talking to a rake and his leman!"

Leman? Stanton slid a glance toward Alicia. "Did she actually say 'leman'?"

"I fear so." Alicia came to stand at his side, her arms folded. "And she wasn't even embarrassed."

Antonia reddened and yanked furiously on Alberta's arm. "Papa!" she shouted back over her shoulder. "Papa, there's an intruder on the grounds!"

Alicia sighed. "Oh, Antonia." Then she took Stanton's hand. "We'd better run for it. Papa is likely to lead with his flintlock and ask for names after."

Stanton stood fast. "I don't run for it. Ever." His tone was grim. "Lady Antonia! Stop this ridiculous behavior at once!"

Antonia stumbled to a halt, a lifetime of obedience betraying her, as he'd known it would. He approached her slowly, Alicia's hand still wrapped in his.

He bowed. "Lady Antonia, my deepest apologies for mocking you. It is true, I was not invited here today. It is also true that as the Marquis of Wyndham, I have been welcomed into your home before, so it is arguable that I am not quite the 'intruder' you claim."

Antonia visibly deflated at that. Now her worried gaze was fixed on his, for offending a powerful acquaintance of her father's might very well surpass the crime of speaking to her wayward sister in the garden.

Alicia squeezed his fingers. "Don't frighten her, Stanton. She's only doing the best she can. It isn't easy being a daughter of Sutherland."

Antonia's gaze flickered to Alicia for a moment, and Stanton saw fury and envy and, beneath it all, longing. For the first time it occurred to him that Alicia, even in her disgrace, seemed more contented and more self-assured than either of her more well-behaved sisters.

Voices neared. Alicia tugged at him.

"We ought to go. It will not be good for Alberta and Antonia if we are found here."

Stanton allowed himself to be pulled into the concealment of the wood like a common thief for the sake of Alicia's sisters, but he found the entire encounter disturbing.

What sort of house was this, where ruin was preferable to respectability?

16.

Wyndham said little to her as they walked back through the wood to the Cross estate. Alicia tolerated it for a while, for her thoughts were filled with her sisters' situation.

She'd been so wrong not to realize what they were going through as a result of her ruin. Oh, she'd known they would be embarrassed, and that the entire family might lie low for a Season—which indeed they had. Five Seasons, to be precise.

But her father was an earl! Surely such connections outweighed one blot on the ledger of such an old and respectable title.

She said as much to Wyndham, who stopped to turn and stare at her in disbelief.

"Do you not realize that your father is the last of his line?" He sent a sympathetic gaze back toward the house. "Had he a direct heir," he explained, "or if there was a young and viable Earl of Sutherland on the horizon, then of course Society would turn a much blinder eye to one young lady's indiscretions. But why should anyone try to stay in the good graces of a family who is already on their way out?"

"Out?" Alicia stumbled. Wyndham's hand came out to support her, then was immediately withdrawn.

She stayed where she was, stricken. "Out?

Wyndham frowned at her. "Of course. Do you not see what is right before your eyes? This estate is nearly abandoned, the house a ruin. Sutherland is many thousands of pounds past destitute. I would be surprised if the Crown didn't seize it eventually."

"I—I never realized." Alicia sat abruptly on a fallen log. "I knew we had less than others . . . and I knew my father wanted us to wed wealthy . . ."

"Hell, yes." Wyndham shook his head. "I feel for your father. A hundred years of debt and the burden of three daughters to boot. Poor bloke."

Alicia jerked her head up at that. "Our sex is not our offense to apologize for."

Wyndham gazed back at her. "I mean no disrespect to your sisters. I'm sure they are doing their best to be good daughters."

The shot went deep, whether he meant it to or not. "Unlike me, you mean."

He did not drop his gaze. "You made your choices. Everyone in this world must bear the consequences of their actions."

Alicia felt her fingers dig into the punky wood of the log. "Not everyone, Wyndham. Not by far."

He folded his arms. "You still make no apology for the position in which you have placed your family? You must realize what you did to them."

His eyes were dark and unreadable, his face stern. He disapproved of her still, last night notwithstanding.

And what about last night would have convinced him that you are anything but precisely what he thinks you?

Alicia wanted to shout at him, wanted to fling sticks and

stones and dead leaves at him, wanted to scream at the top of her lungs that *it wasn't her fault*!

Then again, she'd tried that before, many times, minus the dead leaves of course, and it had never made the slightest difference. Nothing would erase that stain, nothing but her death, and even then it was likely that her family would bear the tinge of it for generations.

So instead of pelting his blasted face with woodsy detritus, she unclenched her hands slowly, brushed them together with studied care and stood.

"I've caused you to miss the morning activities Lord Cross had planned for the gentlemen," she said coolly. "How careless of me."

She walked past him, striding down the path, away from Sutherland and all the black doubts and blame it held. "Come along," she called over her shoulder. "I heard there will be shooting along the river. Gentlemen love shooting, do they not?"

Stanton followed her more slowly. Perhaps he ought not to have taunted her so about the past, but he'd hoped to break through to her some way, any way—

Any way that didn't involve breaking the habit he'd so severely bent last night. One more strain on his control and he didn't think it would hold—and once unleashed, he didn't know that it was possible to bind that other man ever again.

He wasn't sure it was possible even now.

Once back at the manor house, Alicia made the barest of courtesies to Wyndham for his escort home and escaped into the very place she'd fled earlier that morning—the ladies' parlor.

As she'd expected, the room was too warm and close with assorted perfumes that stifled the fresh air so recently in her lungs. Alicia engaged another woman in conversation, not caring if she was lady or mistress or serving help, so desperate was she to escape the circling thoughts brought on by her journey home.

"Oh, heavens! What are they doing here?"

Alicia turned at the shocked comment from the woman behind her. Entering the parlor were three ladies who should have been anywhere else but here.

"That's Lady Reardon!" Alicia's neighbor continued. "And Lady Greenleigh—so that must be Lady Dryden!"

Well, at least Lady Dryden was a bit scandalous, unlike the first two unimpeachable social goddesses. Lady Dryden had buried her first husband only weeks before her second marriage—although Alicia thought it was silly to blame her when her elderly Lord Barrowby had been bedridden for years. She must be quite eager to live her life once more.

Apparently, no one else made much of it, for there Lady Dryden stood in the company of two of the highest of the high.

And those two were looking directly at Alicia.

She took a breath, for this had always been a common occurrence. Red hair did make it rather hard to disappear in a crowd. They would soon recall her identity, and then they would look away, intently pretending they had never been the slightest bit interested in a nonpersonage such as she.

Except they were still staring at her. A tremor of alarm went through Alicia. The social opinion of ladies like these could make her purpose here much more difficult, not to mention painful. Would they take after Lady Davenport, who was even now arrowing across the room as if the three newcomers were her nearest and dearest friends? For all Alicia knew, they might be.

Although somehow they didn't look the type. Lady Reardon was a rounded brunette with a bold manner and bright blue eyes that glimmered with mischief. She appeared to be on the short side, but that might be simply in comparison to her companion, Lady Greenleigh, who towered over her two friends in voluptuous grandeur. Her hair was a dark blond that picked up the light from the windows in sleek shine. She surveyed the room with a half-smile already in place, as if she were sure to find something amusing.

Both ladies were lovely in their way, but the scandalous Lady Dryden was beautiful in every way. Alicia found herself dismayingly fascinated by the woman's perfection. Then she saw that a few strands of unruly blond curls had escaped Lady Dryden's severe hairstyle. Knowing that such a woman still had difficulty with her hair made her more human. Alicia found herself smiling at Lady Dryden in a friendly way.

Lady Dryden's gaze caught on hers and Alicia nearly took a step back from the sharp inquiry there. This was no vague and insipid beauty!

Lady Davenport descended upon the trio at last. Now Alicia wished she were close enough to hear the exchange of greetings, for she didn't think those three women were the sort to suffer fools lightly.

Yet even as they greeted Lady Davenport with no visible sign of enjoyment, their gazes still continued to flick back to Alicia. She had the uncanny impression that they were here to see *her*.

Which was ridiculous and more than a little alarming. She wasn't sure she wanted to come to such attention.

Then again, that was why she was here, wasn't it? To do battle with Society? Well, Society—true Society, not just these decadent hangers-on—had arrived on the field.

Right. Headfirst then. Alicia took a deep breath, pasted on an irreverent smile, and sailed closer to the door.

Lady Davenport shot her a look full of venom as she approached.

"Oh, yes. Here we have Lady Alicia herself." Lady Davenport sneered a barely legitimate smile at Alicia. "We were just speaking of you."

Alicia smiled widely. "I'll wager you were." She turned to Lady Dryden. "Hello."

By not waiting to be introduced, Alicia had crossed that shady boundary of her social limbo. She was as highborn as any of these ladies—or nearly so—and as such would normally have been their equal.

Or they could legitimately cut her, for she was in her way worse than the lowest street whore, who could be but pitied for her predicament.

The tall Lady Greenleigh bent to whisper in the smaller Lady Reardon's ear. "She's quite pretty."

Lady Reardon sedately stepped upon her friend's foot. "She can hear you," she said, her voice normal.

Lady Greenleigh sighed and straightened. "I never could whisper properly."

Lady Dryden, who was obviously in charge, sent a repressive glare over her shoulder at her friends. "You'll have to excuse them, Lady Alicia," she said coolly. Ignoring Lady Davenport's indignant sniff—which immediately endeared the beauty further to Alicia—she held out her hand. "I am Julia."

The other two ladies surged forward. They flanked the exquisite Lady Dryden like a pair of Valkyrie guards.

Alicia eyed the diminutive Lady Reardon. Perhaps a Valkyrie and a half.

"I am Willa," the curvaceous brunette declared.

"Call me Olivia," the taller woman offered.

Lady Davenport, apparently offended that she had not received a similar welcome, drew herself up. "I fear I'm needed elsewhere." With a sharp, angry dip of a curtsy, she flounced off.

"Oh, God, I thought she'd never leave," Olivia said, inviting Alicia to join her in a smile.

Alicia was not entirely gullible. She folded her arms and gazed at them warily. "That's very nice, I'm sure, but why do I have the distinct feeling that you came in here looking for me?"

Lady Dryden sighed. "You two are about as subtle as Huns," she said to her companions.

"Subtlety is a blooming waste of time sometimes, Julia, and you know it." Lady Willa smiled at Alicia with satisfaction. "Something I think Lady Alicia understands very well."

"She's really very pretty," Olivia insisted. "Do you think Wyndham notices?"

"Wyndham isn't blind," Alicia said wryly. "Whether or not he wishes to do more than look is still in doubt."

Olivia's eyes lighted. "Oh, good. Tell us *everything.*"

"Yes," Julia said, although her tone implied she wanted more than good gossip. "Come to my room in ten minutes. Left at the top of the stairs, seventh door on the right. Do try not to make a fanfare, if you please." She turned to the other two. "Let us make our escape before Davenport comes back. That woman gives me hives." She cast a look back at Alicia. "Do not keep us waiting, Lady Alicia."

The three beauties strode from the room, taking with them the greater portion of class and elegance present. Alicia was torn between running after them and fleeing them for her life. Willa and Olivia seemed kind, even friendly, but Julia—

Alicia shivered. Lady Dryden reminded her of someone. She couldn't think who, but it was someone else with that sharp watchfulness and that assessing gaze that made one constantly wonder if there was a crumb on one's chin.

Someone like . . .

Wyndham.

She blinked. Well, now. That was an arresting thought.

Now what could Lady Dryden and Lord Wyndham have in common?

She glanced at the standing clock in the corner of the parlor. She still had eight minutes.

Wyndham wasn't in their bedchamber, although Herbert was present, tending to his lordship's wardrobe.

"Lord Wyndham is playing billiards, I believe, my lady," he told her when asked.

The door opened and Garret strolled in with yesterday's gown over his arm. "Oh, hullo, love!" he caroled to Alicia.

Herbert went into paroxysms—which for Herbert meant quivering and twitching his sideburns—at Garrett's impertinence. Garrett grinned at Alicia.

"Sorry, milady, but I cannot help myself. He's such a monstrous stick about everything. Do you know he waits until the minute hand is precisely on the hour before he'll pick up his breakfast fork?"

Herbert twitched with more ferocity. Alicia gazed at him worriedly. "Garrett, I think he might be having an attack of some kind."

Garrett threw a pillow at Herbert. "You there! Calm down. You're alarming her ladyship."

Herbert stiffened, his wild gaze traveling between Garrett and Alicia at great speed. "If—if you'll excuse me, my lady—" He left the room in strangled haste, leaving Wyndham's shirt on the bed.

Garrett took it and held it up to himself. "Would you look at these shoulders, lover? I'm telling you, your man is a god among men!"

"He isn't," Alicia denied with a sigh.

Garrett slid her a knowing look. "Isn't a god or isn't your man?"

Alicia shook her head. "Not now, darling. I need your help. I need to know everything you can find out about Lady Dryden, Lady Reardon, and Lady Greenleigh. They just cornered me downstairs and they are far too interested for my comfort."

Garret blinked and dropped the shirt on the bed. "The Sirens? What are they doing here?"

Remembering the cool glint in Lady Dryden's gaze, Alicia shook her head at the nickname. "More the Fates than the Sirens, I'd think. Julia's on the scary side, to be truthful."

Garrett narrowed his eyes. "The Sirens cornered you, eh?"

Alicia pressed fingers to her aching temples. She had already had a rather trying day, and now had only four minutes left. "I've been summoned to Dryden's room. Quickly, tell me anything you know."

Garrett folded his arms, thinking. "Lady Reardon married Reardon while he was still in disgrace. They called her his 'broomstick' bride, for he compromised her while passing through the village where she lived. I heard she stood up for him when everyone told her wedding him was a mistake. Then of course, the whole truth came out about his scandal and he was a hero and she was his heroine."

"That's a nice tale."

Garrett was merely warming up. "Lady Greenleigh got her man by falling into the Thames and letting him rescue her. There was a spot of trouble after the wedding, something about the Prince Regent taking her as his mistress and Greenleigh kidnapping her back, right out from under his highness's nose. I heard there was a duel or some such, and she was accidentally shot."

"Goodness. Another epic story."

Garrett grinned. "These are only the high moments, you understand. Then there's Lady Dryden. She was Lord Barrowby's widow for less than a month before she wed Dryden. First, I heard she disappeared for a bit, was kidnapped or fled or some such, and nearly died before she was found. Some say she killed a man."

Alicia shivered. "Now that I can quite believe." Two minutes left. "Thank you, Garrett. Continue to look into their stories, if you please." She took a breath. "Now, I must go face the lionesses."

17

Once in Lady Dryden's room, seated in a circle about the warming fire, with a tray of tea and cakes at the ready, Alicia found it wasn't as bad as she had dreaded.

It was much, much worse.

"So Lady Alicia," Julia began without preamble. "You're ruined, I hear. Are the stories true?"

Alicia put her teacup down carefully. "Oh, there is no mistake, my lady. My own parents discovered me in bed with the stable boy. At a house party, of course, so it was all very public, very . . . irrefutable."

Julia's beautiful eyes narrowed. "And yet you tried very hard to refute it, didn't you?"

Alicia narrowed her own eyes right back. "Well, one must always try, mustn't one?"

Lady Greenleigh leaned forward, breaking into the staring contest. "How did you and Wyndham meet?"

Alicia blinked, hesitating. "We—there's little to tell. Our meeting wasn't terribly romantic, I'm afraid. It was . . . highly irregular and I'm sure not something you wish to hear about."

Olivia laughed. "I doubt it was more irregular than the ways we met our husbands."

"No, really . . ."

Lady Reardon dimpled. "More irregular than shooting his horse out from beneath him with a slingshot and then spending the night beside his unconscious body?"

Alicia's eyes widened. "Er—"

Lady Greenleigh laughed aloud. "More irregular than being thrown off a bridge and having him leap in after me, only to require me to rescue him?"

Alicia considered that. "I suppose that's rather romantic."

Olivia made a face. "It was the Thames."

"Oh right." Alicia shuddered. "Ew. Perhaps not, then."

Lady Julia was watching her. "More irregular than having him read my diary and use all my secret fancies to seduce me?"

Alicia's jaw dropped. *And all I did was overhear a plot against the Crown and then become his mistress to help find the traitor.*

She became aware that the other three ladies were staring at her with eyebrows raised and teacups poised in mid-sip.

She swallowed. "Ah . . . did I just say that out loud?"

Julia put her cup and saucer down quickly. "Yes, and you must be very careful not to do that again."

The other two were nodding sagely. Alicia looked from one to the next. She saw concern and interest, but that was all.

"You aren't surprised," she said slowly. "Why are you not shocked, or appalled, or even a little bit taken aback—by the conspiracy if not the immorality?"

Willa flapped a hand. "Oh, we know all about the conspiracy—"

Julia looked at her sharply. "Willa."

Willa made a face. "Oh, Julia, leave off. Alicia isn't anything like you thought she would be, admit it."

Olivia nodded. "Alicia's one of us, Julia."

Julia looked frustrated. "You cannot operate solely on your feelings, Willa—"

"Oh, pooh." Willa turned her brilliant smile on Alicia. "Alicia's a peregrine."

"Oh!" Olivia turned a delighted gaze on Alicia. "A falcon lady for the Falcon lord! How perfectly wonderful!"

Julia dropped her face into her hands. "Olivia," she muttered in muffled agony. "You're going to be the death of me."

Olivia picked up her tea. "Dane says that all the time."

Alicia was looking from one beautiful, surprising, exalted lady to another. "You knew about the conspiracy. You knew about me. You ought not to even be speaking to someone like me, yet you are."

She narrowed her eyes. "It's some sort of club, isn't it? Your husbands and Wyndham . . . they likely even have some sort of silly male name for themselves, like the Four Horsemen or something—"

Olivia laughed into her tea and choked. Julia passed her a linen napkin without taking her gaze from Alicia.

"You're half right," she said slowly.

"You mean three-quarters," Willa said with a grin.

"Hush, Willa." Julia leaned forward, pinning Alicia with her gaze.

Alicia leaned back. "You're rather alarming, Lady Dryden. I'll wager your servants are terrified of you."

Willa snickered. "They pat her on the head and call her Jilly."

Alicia slid her gaze from Julia's intense scrutiny to the way the other two watched them calmly, albeit with great interest.

"Three-quarters . . ." She looked back at Julia. "Perhaps I shouldn't have said 'Horsemen.' "

Julia didn't avert her gaze. "Hmm."

Having recovered from a losing round with her tea, Olivia leaned into the path of Julia's gaze to capture her friend's attention. "Julia, she's not going to leap up and tell the French. If Willa says she's a peregrine, then she will be as fierce and loyal as the small beautiful falcon herself. Willa knows these things, you understand. Besides . . ."

She turned her head to gaze at Alicia with mischief in her eyes. "I'm perishing to know what Wyndham's really like!"

Willa leaned forward. "Oh, yes! Tell, tell!"

Even Julia seemed willing to be distracted by the topic of Stanton Horne, Lord Wyndham. "I've known him for years, but only through correspondence," she said slowly, watching Alicia. "I would be interested in hearing your thoughts on the . . . inner man."

Olivia performed a mock swoon, nearly landing in Willa's lap. "The inner man! Be still, my heart!"

Willa pushed her away with a laugh. "Oh, shut it, Livvie. You have your own personal Viking! You're not pining after Wyndham!"

Olivia sat up with a grin. "No, but I am bloody curious about him."

Alicia felt cornered once more when the three of them turned questioning gazes her way. "I . . . I fear I don't know very much about Wyndham," she said slowly, realizing the depth of her ignorance even as she spoke. "I think I've learned more about him in the last five minutes than I knew before."

Willa nodded. "Inscrutable."

Olivia sighed. "His cousin Jane told me that when he rescued her and her mother from poverty, he carried her ill, mindless mother in his own arms."

Of course he did. The fact that she didn't doubt that act for a moment made Alicia feel a bit better. Wyndham might yet be a mystery, but she knew enough to believe that he would always behave in the best of character.

"He aided me when I did not expect him to," added Julia, although she seemed reluctant to give information when she obviously thought she ought to be receiving it.

Alicia studied her three interrogators. Friendly or no, she was under no illusions that this was a friendly conversation.

"Wyndham has never been less than chivalrous and—" Well, "pleasant" might be stretching the truth a bit. "He is an honorable man," she finished weakly. "Although a bit stiff-necked and entirely too suspicious and I don't think he has any clue the effect his eyes have on a woman, or he wouldn't gaze so intensely . . ."

She became aware of three pairs of riveted eyes. "Ah." She held up one hand, palm out. "Do not take me ill, for I have no issue with the man. He has been very good to me."

"Why, I wonder?" Olivia laced her hands over one knee and screwed up her expression pensively. "I mean, of course he wishes to find the Ch—ow!—the conspirator," she finished, surreptitiously rubbing her ribs. Beside her, Willa hadn't moved, Alicia would have sworn it.

Now, of course, she pined to know who the "Ch—" was. She frowned. "I find all these mysteries terribly frustrating, you realize. I cannot be held responsible for the results of that frustration."

Willa grinned impishly. "I know precisely what you mean. I tend to accidentally injure people."

"Men," Olivia corrected her. "You tend to accidentally injure men. I, on the other hand, tend to injure myself."

Even Julia smiled at that. "I myself dislike frustration."

Alicia tilted her head. "And whom do you injure?"

Julia's smile went a bit chilly. "Whosoever is frustrating me, of course."

Some say she killed a man.

"Did you?" Alicia couldn't believe she was challenging the intimidating Julia, but the words wouldn't stay inside. "Did you kill a man?"

Julia didn't so much as blink. "I tried. He escaped, but somewhat the worse for wear, I assure you."

"She tore him to bits," Willa said with satisfaction. "Slashed his face beyond recognition."

"Bastard." Olivia resembled the Valkyrie once more. "I wish I'd been there."

Abruptly, Alicia found herself back in Cheapside, crouching behind the privy of the White Sow. "The scarred man," she said slowly. She raised her gaze to meet Julia's. "That's who they spoke of, the conspirators. You did that."

Julia nodded serenely. "I did."

There was more to the story, but Alicia knew she wasn't going to hear it. She was not one of them. The sensation of being examined had not left.

She stood. "This has been lovely . . . well, not actually, but it has been interesting. That is considerably more than an afternoon spent in the parlor would have been." She curtsied to the three of them. "But, all courtesies aside, I don't especially feel like exposing any more of myself for your edification today."

She turned to leave the room.

"Lady Alicia." Julia's tone did not allow her to walk out entirely. Alicia turned with very ill grace.

"What is it? Do you wish to know what I had for breakfast? Eggs and ham. How about my sleeping arrangements with Wyndham? He takes the chair, I take the bed. My lady's maid is Garrett, my companion is Millie. I have three freckles on my left shoulder that make a perfect triangle." She crossed her arms and scowled. "Will that do?"

Lady Dryden was standing by now, flanked by her friends. "I was only going to add," she said mildly, "that you should take great care not to walk off on your own again. There are dangerous criminals afoot here."

Still frowning, Alicia let out a breath. "Thank you. I'll make note of that." She turned to leave, then turned back. "If you want to talk to me again . . . well, don't. I'm annoyed with you all."

Julia nodded. "Thank you. I'll make note of that," she said calmly, apparently not at all offended by Alicia's brusqueness.

Unflappable. Alicia couldn't bear unflappable people. Especially when she herself was rather . . . flappable. She turned her back on them and left the room, fuming anew.

What upset you more, that you were interrogated, or that you were not included?

"Both," she muttered to herself. "And to hell with the contradiction!"

At the top of the stairs leading down to the front hall, she paused. She didn't want to go back down to the parlor—God forbid! She didn't particularly want to hole up in her—and Wyndham's!—bedchamber for the rest of the day. And despite her dismissal of the Sirens, she did believe them about the dangers of walking about on her own.

Abruptly she sat on the top stair and dangled her hands off her knees. She likely looked the child, but she needed a moment to think about her current state of indecision.

She was never indecisive. She always knew precisely what she wanted—and who, if one were to be completely honest—and had spent her life figuring out how to get around the obstacles to her desires. There were only two rules that she felt compelled to follow.

Don't hurt anyone.

Don't get caught.

The pain in her sisters' eyes came back to mock her first rule. The disapproval in Wyndham's mocked the second.

Without those constants, without the restrictions of convention or the constraints of poverty, without someone to please or to rebel against—well, she simply felt lost, that was all.

She had wealth aplenty now, due to Wyndham's reward. She had lost the taste for vengeance this morning. She wanted to help Wyndham, but it was his quest, not hers. Without the rudder of necessity and the fantasy of revenge, she felt entirely and absolutely . . .

Lost.

She took a deep breath and dropped her chin atop her knees. Lady Alicia Lawrence was never at a loss! She hated this feeling and refused to leave this stair until she'd re-solved herself.

Below, the front door opened to admit yet another guest. Goodness, no wonder she and Wyndham had been forced to double up. Apparently no one wanted to miss Lord Cross's Saturnalia.

A stream of piled luggage with liveried legs staggered through the door, followed by a very stylish bonnet. One as-sumed there was an equally stylish lady beneath it. Several footmen rushed forward with fawning expressions to take said bonnet, so one might also assume that said lady was very attractive.

"My lady, we have reserved the garden suite for you," the butler said to the newcomer with an actual smidgen of warmth in his voice.

Absolutely twitching with curiosity now, Alicia leaned precariously to one side—she couldn't stand, for she hadn't yet resolved herself, of course—to see beneath the brim of the aforementioned bonnet.

"Blasted peacock plumes," she muttered. She pressed as close to the stair spindles as she could without impressing them into her face—for she hadn't lost all sense of decorum—but she could not see the new lady. Was it the Prince Regent's famous mistress, Lady Halswick?

At last the bonnet came off, to reveal a head of shimmer-ing white-blond hair twisted into a flawless construction that even the extremely stylish bonnet had not managed to disarrange.

Alicia leaned a bit farther, but all she could see was a smooth ivory brow and the tip of an unobjectionable nose. The woman must be stunning, however, for the butler and footmen stood in a circle of adoration, their faces lifted as if to the sun.

"Thank you," came a melodious voice from beneath the pile of shimmering hair. "Tell me . . . has Lord Wyndham yet arrived?"

Wyndham?

My Wyndham? But he wasn't, not really, was he? Alicia felt her stomach flip uncomfortably, reminded once again how very little she knew about Wyndham.

"Yes, my lady. He arrived yesterday." The butler bowed excessively low. Alicia hated the lady already. "Shall I inform him you have arrived?"

"Ah . . . no. I believe I shall let it be a surprise."

Alicia felt her fists clench. The bright beauty below her would be surprised, indeed, if Alicia flung her woods-soiled shoe into that perfect coif!

The butler seemed to recover himself enough to realize that the footmen were ogling rather than working. He clapped his hands sharply. "Come now! Carry these things to the garden suite! Lady Wyndham hasn't all day!"

Alicia slowly leaned back from the railing. Her breath had left in startled exhale and didn't seem to want to come back.

Lady Wyndham.

Was that what the Sirens had been trying to find out—if Alicia knew that Wyndham was *married*?

Married. Wyndham. Bloody hell.

Like a ball from a cannon, Alicia was up off the stair and in pursuit, for she had just remembered what she wanted out of life.

Wyndham, of course.

Sans beautiful wife, if she could manage it.

Wyndham strode through the great house, tugging on his riding gloves as he went. Lady Dryden had proposed that he, Greenleigh, Reardon, and Lord Dryden take a gentlemen's excursion—meaning riding out to confer in privacy out-of-doors—with Marcus acting as his wife's second for the purposes of discretion. The usual division of the sexes during a house party was playing hell with any sort of strategizing, or it would if Marcus and Julia weren't such superior partners.

Julia was the first woman in the history of the Four, and as the Falcon, the watchful eye above them all, Stanton was glad to find that she was also the most effective Fox in generations.

Considering it was the Fox's role to chart the fates of nations, he personally considered them all very fortunate that Julia, Lady Dryden, was indeed on their side.

"*Dar*ling!"

That all too familiar intonation stopped him in his tracks.

No. It couldn't be. Not here. Not now.

Yet, this was a decadent party for the fast set, where the wildly wealthy played with the madly inappropriate. And those who were both came to wallow as deeply as they dared.

For a certain classic beauty, who cared not for convention or for censure, nor apparently for Stanton's good opinion, a party such as this would be a playground indeed.

He raised his gaze to the tall, lovely woman standing silhouetted against the diffused light from the front windows. There she was, the only woman he had ever loved, albeit desperately and uselessly. He sighed, giving in to the cruel humor of Fate, and he smiled.

"Hello, Mother."

She smiled and stepped forward, her hands outstretched. "I had meant to surprise you, darling. Instead I've likely frightened you, looking a sight from traveling as I do." She patted at her sleeve with a frown. "I'm an absolute mess."

Stanton took his cue. "Of course you aren't. You look lovely, as usual."

She smiled, satisfied for the time being. Later, he'd have to make up for the brevity of his praise. Catherine, the Marchioness of Wyndham, required the most diligent of attention from every male within the range of her costly jasmine perfume. Most men seemed not to mind.

"I'll just pop on up to my little room then and change. I assume you will be my escort for the ball tonight? We have so much to catch up on."

Hmm. Stanton felt his color rise. He'd never faced this rather sticky situation before. How to explain Alicia? "I . . . I fear I will not. I am . . . that is to say—I must—"

"You are here with someone." Her eyes had narrowed. "You're having an affair."

Stanton opened his mouth to deny it. He wasn't, of course. Or was he? The house grew far too warm. Must Herbert always tie his cravat so tight?

Oh, bugger all. "I am here with a lady, yes."

The marchioness threw her arms about him. "Thank heavens!" She planted several kisses in the air next to his ear. "That's wonderful, darling! Are you madly in love? Or simply crazed with passion? Is she fabulous? Who is she?" She leaned back to gaze at him. "An actress, I'll bet. Some divine goddess of the stage? You always did have exquisite taste, my love."

She pinched his cheek. Stanton maintained his composure by a thread, reminding himself that there was no one in sight—not that the marchioness would have cared a whit. His effusive, melodramatic, outrageous mother had ever been a mystery to him.

"She's not an actress," he said when the sensation had returned to his face. "Her name is Lady Alicia Lawrence."

The marchioness went very still. "Sutherland's daughter? Not the one who—of course, there are three of them, I believe—yet you wouldn't be *here* with anyone but—"

"I believe you are trying to ask if she is the notorious Lady All-three-cia."

She straightened, dropping the arms that had been laced round his neck, and raised a brow. "I would never use that awful name. That poor girl! Nasty, common gossip!"

As opposed to excellent, uncommon gossip, he supposed, which the marchioness was known to devour. Still, her defense of Alicia warmed him. "I was simply saying what you were thinking."

"Well, thinking it isn't the same as saying it! I should think you would know that better than anyone."

Stanton blinked. That was the first time that his mother had made even an oblique reference to his ability. He'd assumed her to be blithely unaware of it, for she lied to him freely and frequently. She always had.

She stepped back and tidied her perfect hair again. "Now, I simply must go repair myself. Goodness, if anyone should see me like this!"

Stanton took her hand and bowed over it. "You are a treasure to anyone's eyes, Mother."

When he straightened, she almost seemed misty-eyed in response. Then she slapped at his shoulder with her gloves. "Heavens, darling, don't call me 'Mother' in public! People will think me positively ancient!"

Stanton smiled at her. She truly was a masterwork of her very own. "I shall break convention and walk you both into the ball."

Her eyes widened in scandalized pleasure. "Oh, *do*! It

will be perfectly shocking! Everyone will feed on it for simply *hours*."

With another kiss in the vicinity of his cheek, she waved gaily as she tripped lightly off toward the stairs.

Alicia ducked aside as Lady Wyndham passed her, pretending to examine a Chinese vase as if her life depended on it. She glanced up after the lady passed, only to have her gaze caught as the marchioness cast a curious look back at her.

Would it be too much to fling herself upon the woman in fervent thanks that she was Wyndham's unbelievably young and beautiful mother and not his unbelievably beautiful wife?

Lady Wyndham's eyes narrowed slightly and a tiny dimple appeared at the corner of her mouth. Then she turned and continued on her way, leaving Alicia alone in the hall with Wyndham, who was gazing at her curiously.

"Where did you come from?"

This from the man who constantly imitated a windup jack-in-the-box. Nonetheless, his visible affection for his outrageous—even by Alicia's lenient standards—mother was thoroughly charming.

Still, there was no point in letting him get the better of her just because of her new and exhilarating infatuation with him. Alicia blinked innocently. "I had tea with Lady Dryden." Entirely true, and likely to throw him off the scent.

It did. His expression became stormy. "You have no permission to socialize with Lady Dryden! What possessed you to visit her?"

"No *permission*?" It was a good thing she was in the throes of recently finding him adorable. Alicia folded her arms. "Well, let me see. Perhaps it was her firm and rather frightening summons. Or perhaps it was the fact that I was outclassed and outnumbered by the Sirens of Society. Or perhaps it was because spending one more moment in the ladies' parlor would have driven me to the justifiable murder of Lady Davenport."

"Lady Davenport's much deserved end notwithstanding," he said, his lips thinned, "in the future, I would appreciate it if you would avoid any further contact with—what did you call them? The Sirens?"

"Yes, the Sirens—as in 'divinely beautiful'? As in 'so socially prominent that one must come when they call'?"

He frowned slightly at her aggrieved tone. "*You* certainly needn't envy their beauty."

Alicia smiled widely and dropped a curtsy. "I wasn't fishing, but thank you anyway, kind sir."

He continued to gaze at her. "You truly weren't fishing, were you?"

"Why would I? Any compliment thus gained would be without value, would it not?" Too late she remembered the marchioness's flagrant maneuverings for praise. Oops.

Well, she couldn't very well take back what she just said without him realizing she'd been eavesdropping, and besides, she truly had no patience for such coy pretensions.

Wyndham continued to gaze at her intently. "Hmm."

Alicia couldn't force herself to look away. His dark eyes were performing their usual cookery action upon the base of her belly and she wasn't currently inclined to break the connection.

Abruptly, she felt the wild excitement of last night's hallway escapade, the one they'd both called a mistake.

It was a mistake that Alicia would very much like to make again.

His hand rose slowly, moving toward her face. Alicia waited, although such patience cost her when she'd rather have climbed him like an apple tree. His fingertips paused just before touching her cheek.

"You're flushed." His voice was a husky whisper. "Did you take too much sun this morning?"

Oh, no you don't. She wasn't going to let him label her good, honest lust as some sort of overexertion from hours ago. "There was no sun this morning, Stanton," she replied softly. Then the devil within awoke. "Perhaps there is some remaining chafe from your beard last evening."

His eyes went entirely black then and his jaw hardened. *Unseemly demands,* the prince had said. A thrill of fear went through Alicia. This was no ordinary man. This was a powerful, mysterious lord known for—oh, heavens, she loved to think it—"unseemly demands"!

She was toying with forces beyond anything she'd ever known. What dark impulses might she have unleashed?

She absolutely couldn't *wait* to find out!

As if he'd read her mind, he stepped back and let the dark fire in his eyes cool to an ember. "I must go," he said roughly. Then he turned on his heel and strode from the hall, slapping his riding crop against his leg as he stalked away.

Left standing alone and suddenly chilled in the front hall, Alicia put both hands to her hot cheeks. He hadn't even touched her and she was vibrating like a drum.

Good heavens, what a man!

"I want *that* one," she whispered to no one but herself.

She smiled and went in search of Garrett. If she was going to launch a full offensive tonight, she was going to need all the firepower she could muster.

Once outside, Stanton paused for a moment in the center of the gravel drive, oblivious to the stares of the Cross staff.

Walking away was getting harder. She was simply so . . .

Warm. Lovely. Real.

Inexplicable.

Wasn't that really the reason for his obsession? Wasn't her resistance to his ability the source of his fascination? She was a novelty and a danger, two things guaranteed to get one's attention.

It wasn't the glow of her bright hair, or the shine in her eyes when she looked at him, or the curve of her cheek or the way she melted at his merest touch. His arousal could be excused due to his long abstinence. His absorption could be explained by the unique challenge of reading her.

How do you explain away your longing?

Stanton shut that door before it could open completely. He was alone by choice. Solitude was necessary for his sanity, being much preferable to the constant decoding of lies told by the people around him. If his house could be managed without staff, he would do so. As it was, he encouraged them to speak to him as little as possible.

So there was no point in thinking along the lines of keeping company with Lady Alicia Lawrence. Besides, all her wide-eyed passion could well be false, along with her story of treason. He had no way to be sure.

Yes you do.

No.

He saw the other three gentlemen awaiting him as he neared the stables. The cool air should have done its work by now, but his blood still ran hot and his groin still throbbed. A bracing ride over the grounds was precisely what he needed.

He only hoped that by the time he took the reins he could mount the horse!

18

Alicia flung herself across the bed and let her slippers dangle from her toes. "I like the green gown."

Garrett rolled his eyes. "How did you manage to live so long without the least clue how to dress? The green gown is to shock and surprise." He pulled shimmering gold from the wardrobe. "This one is to stun."

Alicia popped a chocolate into her mouth as she gazed uncertainly at the gown. "It's beautiful, but it's too grand for me. I ought not to have let you persuade me to spend so much. Perhaps if I were ever to go to Court . . ."

Garrett tapped her on the top of her head with an impatient fingertip. "Great house. Prince Regent. Lord Wyndham's attention." He glared at her. "This is as 'Court' as you will ever see, lover." He shook the gown at her. "Remember the Sirens? You must outshine *Lady Dryden*."

Alicia dropped her head to hide her face in the bed. "Oh, blast," she muttered into the coverlet. "Better try to outshine the sun."

"Precisely. Which is why you will wear the gold."

"Yes, Mummy," Alicia said resentfully. Then another thought struck her. "Won't Lady Dryden be dressing to stun?"

Garrett shook his head. "Not here. In fact, I wouldn't be surprised if she appears almost sedate tonight. She won't want to stand out, as if she could help it. I don't know why those three came, but they aren't here for the orgy."

"Well, neither am I," Alicia said stoutly. "I'm here to save England from traitors . . . or at least, I was." She rolled over onto her back and stared up at the draped cornice above her head. "Wyndham won't so much as touch my hand."

Garrett fluffed the shimmering gown. "That means he doesn't dare get too close. An excellent sign." He cast her a sideways glance. "You never did tell me precisely what happened between you two last night."

Alicia moaned and covered her face with her hands. *Never. Not even to Garrett.* "Let us simply say that he dared get too close."

"Well, if you're going to be stingy with details, I'll simply have to let my very extensive imagination take over."

"Oh, spare me your extensive imagination. I've a quite elaborate one of my own, thank you." She let her hands fall but kept her eyes closed. "For five minutes this afternoon, I thought he was married. It was the longest five minutes of my life."

She felt Garrett's weight settle onto the bed beside her. "Sweeting . . ." His voice was gentle, all sharp parading set aside. "My pretty one, you know he will never . . ."

Alicia opened her eyes and smiled up at Garrett. "He would never wed me. I know. I'm not the sort of woman a man like him would wed. I'm not the sort of woman that any man would wed, I think."

Garrett smoothed her hair. "I'll marry you, pet. We'll take Wyndham's money and live a scandalous bohemian Montmartre sort of life, only in London instead of Paris. I'll have a hundred beaus and you'll have more. You'll go down in history as the scandal of the century."

Alicia reached for his hand. "And you'll be remembered as the best dressed."

He dropped a kiss on her forehead. "Absolutely. Beau Brummell who?" He stood. "In the meantime, there is no reason in the world why you cannot have a wild, passionate affair with the mighty Lord Wyndham." He picked up the gold gown again. "Wearing *this.*"

An affair. It was a lovely, terrifying, delicious thought.

The truth of the matter was that she might as well. The world thought her a most wicked individual already. In their eyes she was little better than a trollop—or perhaps worse than one, for she'd been born with what most considered to be great advantage.

An affair . . .

Better still, an affair with Wyndham.

If she were going to go to the devil, she might as well enjoy the ride. She might as well partake of the well of heady passion that bubbled deeply within that beautiful man. How could she have been so blind to the passion lurking under Wyndham's cool control? How could such volcanic heat go undetected when it burned so close to the surface? No one else seemed to be aware of it, which made it her very own wicked, wonderful secret.

Wyndham's naked skin beneath her hands. Wyndham's big hard body against hers. Wyndham moving above her, inside her.

What would it be like, when his hasty, rough caresses in the hall had been enough to shatter everything she thought she knew about lovemaking?

An affair with Wyndham.

What a delightful idea.

Alicia reached out to stroke the liquid light and shadow of the silk. "The scandal of the century . . ." She raised her gaze to Garrett's and pursed her lips wryly. "So . . . how are we doing my hair?"

"That's the spirit, lover."

A knock came at the door. Garrett answered while Alicia held the gold gown up to herself and examined her reflection in the mirror. The exquisite shimmer of the fabric made her hair all the brighter and her skin turn to smooth ivory with a blush of rose.

She would look like a princess, but for the outrageously low décolletage. "The princess trollop," she whispered to herself. "Well, it certainly beats the spinster whore."

Garrett returned, an opened note in his hand. "It's an invitation for you to take tea with the Marchioness of Wyndham."

The paper was thick and heavy, dyed a pretty lavender. Alicia tipped it toward her nose to catch the heady scent of jasmine.

"Lady Alicia, I beg of you to do me the great honor of joining me for tea in my room in a quarter of an hour. We have much to discuss."

It was signed *"Lady W."*

Even Garrett seemed impressed, and that wasn't easy to do. "You're moving in high circles today."

"Wyndham's circles," Alicia corrected. "Everyone wants to make sure I'm not going to do him some obscure harm. Seeing as my disgrace is thoroughly contagious, you understand."

Still, she was panting to meet Lady Wyndham. How could such an impulsive, lively woman have produced such a controlled, dark man as Stanton?

Oh, heavens. Wyndham would not be happy about her visiting with the marchioness. If he knew about the invitation he'd issue some ridiculous mandate—like the Lord of

Misrule!—and declare that she was not to speak to his mother.

Alicia suddenly remembered rule number three.

Contrition is easier than persuasion.

Precisely a quarter of an hour later, Alicia sat across from Stanton's mother in a grand bedchamber that looked out over the elaborate gardens to the east of the great house.

Lady Wyndham took a sip of tea then set her cup and saucer down with delicate deliberation.

"You claim to be in love with my son."

"Ah." Alicia gazed intently at her hands. "I like him. He's handsome and honorable."

"And rich."

"And rich, of course." Alicia thought about it for a moment. "But those aren't my reasons for liking him."

"And your reasons are?"

"He doesn't lie." Now where had that come from? Still, it was true, wasn't it?

Lady Wyndham was looking at her. "You are perceptive. Most are too involved with their own lies to see that about Wyndham." She tilted her head, her bright blue eyes fixed on Alicia. "Do you lie?"

"Of course." Alicia shrugged. "But I am not as good as Wyndham. I am merely human."

Lady Wyndham sighed. "Aren't we all?" She picked up her tea again. "Wyndham isn't very forgiving of mere humanity."

Alicia leaned forward. "Why? Why is he the way he is? If anyone knows, it must be you."

Lady Wyndham blinked. "Goodness, you are forward, aren't you? You wish the subject changed, so you change it."

Alicia dismissed the accusation with a wave of her hand. "I have no wish to discuss my flaws. It would take far too long, anyway. Besides, I came here to find out about Wyndham."

Lady Wyndham raised a perfect brow. "You came here because I summoned you."

Alicia leaned back in her seat and folded her arms. "Do you truly think I come at anyone's summons? I am far too bloodyminded for that. Ask Wyndham."

Lady Wyndham gazed at her for a long moment, apparently speechless. Then she bestowed a brilliant smile upon Alicia. "My dear, I think you'll do nicely."

Alicia smiled wryly. "Thank you. I feel so much better being your son's mistress now that I have your approval."

Lady Wyndham smiled behind her cup. "Is that your only goal? Mistress?" She took a small sip and murmured something as if to herself. Something that sounded very much like "we'll have to see about that, won't we?"

Alicia had other priorities. "Now that you've established my complete lack of character, tell me about Wyndham or I'll go play somewhere else."

Lady Wyndham gazed at her thoughtfully, then nodded shortly, almost as if she'd come to some agreement with herself. "Wyndham wasn't always so cold. He was a sensitive boy. Beautiful and brilliant, and much too observant. He did not have the oblivious self-absorption which many children have. It might have gone better for him if he had. It was as if he could see inside people, as if he had a special sense for liars."

"He is angry at you," Alicia said quietly. "Or on your behalf. I cannot be sure."

Lady Wyndham blinked. "Oh, dear. I can understand if he is angry with me. I was a very poor mother. I was no more than a girl, an unhappy girl at that, wed and bred too young. And I have ever enjoyed the social whirl—although in those days I suppose I tried to lose myself too much within it." She frowned, delicate brows drawn together in a charming manner that Alicia despaired of ever mastering.

"However, if he is angry on my behalf—well, there would only be one reason for that! I have comforted myself for years that he knew nothing of that particular situation . . ."

She glanced hesitantly up at Alicia through her lashes. Again, delectable, and somehow not the least inappropriate on a woman her age.

"I suppose it doesn't matter anymore," she said slowly. "I suppose it truly wasn't as great a secret as I thought either."

She straightened and looked Alicia in the eye, apparently having had decided something. "My husband had a mistress, as many men do. Unfortunately, she was situated long before I arrived. Inside of a week after my vows, I was put thoroughly in my place. I was to bear the heir. She was to share my husband's bed before my very nose."

Alicia's eyes widened. "She was in your house?" She hadn't meant to interrupt, for she was fairly sure Lady Wyndham shouldn't be telling her anything so personal—although she was absolutely perishing to know!

But Lady Wyndham only nodded miserably. "In my house. In charge of my house. Choosing my meals, directing my staff, even selecting the nurses and tutors for Stanton, when that time came. She was our housekeeper, you see."

Her tone was so miserable with remembered pain that Alicia reached for her hand without thinking. Lady Wyndham gripped her fingers tightly in her own as she continued.

"All of which was bad enough, to be true, but to make matters worse, she was of a resentful nature despite her privileges. She wanted to be his wife, but his lordship was not a man to throw aside generations of Wyndham tradition to marry someone so far beneath him. He merely wanted it all—the woman of common birth he loved in his bed, the woman of high birth giving him his well-bred Wyndham heir.

"Consequently, she hated me and she hated Stanton more—for he was the reason I was there. Except I wasn't, was I?"

"What do you mean?"

Lady Wyndham sighed. "If I had paid attention, I might have realized that Ilsa hired only those she could control and influence against myself and Stanton. His tutors were sots, his nurses ignorant and unkind. I have no idea what he must have endured in that prison of a house. All I saw was that he grew more silent every day, losing himself in his books, or in long rides about the country. He would be out of the house from dawn to dusk, while the people who were supposed to tend him were drunk or carousing or both."

Alicia swallowed. She knew a little something about living in a place that felt like an iron cage. She would have given much for a boy's freedom to ride away—although she escaped often enough to run wild through the very wood she'd traversed this morning.

"As I said, I make no excuses. I am entirely at fault. I was much too lost in my own unhappiness. I had affairs of my own in retaliation, the more public the better. I thought Wyndham far too young and too isolated to have any idea. But Ilsa—Ilsa made sure that my lonely little son heard every story, read every word in the gossip sheets." She closed her eyes. "My husband never noticed, nor cared about my behavior. If only I had known who I was truly hurting." A barely perceptible tremor went through her.

"You must realize what you did to them."

Alicia sat back in her chair, deep dismay coursing through her. Was she any different than the marchioness?

Not in Wyndham's eyes, it was obvious. If she had known of his history . . . but would that have stopped her need for her petty vengeance?

Vengeance, or validation? Had she actually wanted to hurt her family? Hadn't she truly been crying out for them to *see* her?

Just like the marchioness. Alicia covered the woman's hand with her own. "I understand."

The marchioness opened her eyes. "I know you do, my dear. Unfortunately, that is the very reason Wyndham might rebuff you in the end." Then she brightened. "On the other hand, he has not let your history diminish his passion for you so far. It might be that you have finally healed those old wounds!"

Sorrow laced through Alicia. It wasn't true . . . and likely never would be. She had a mighty mountain to climb in overcoming Wyndham's pain—even if she were brave enough to try.

Then again, she wasn't after his heart. A week of passion to take with her into her uncertain future, a chance to experience the very thing she was reputed to be guilty of, an opportunity to possibly make all she'd been through worth the losses and the regrets.

A moment with a man like Wyndham would be more than most women had in their lifetimes.

She wished she could be as open as the marchioness was being, but she dared not expose Wyndham's plan, even to his mother. The Sirens' warnings went through her mind. No, she wouldn't risk it.

"I cannot reassure you of Wyndham's attachment, I fear," she told the marchioness. "Yet, if all goes well tonight," she said, "that might change."

The marchioness smiled. "You are a woman of increasing potential, Lady Alicia." She leaned forward and gave Alicia a wily, mischievous smile. "Have you grand plans?"

Alicia smiled back. "Why do when you can overdo?"

The marchioness's eyes went to sly slits. "Precisely. Have no mercy."

Interested eyes watched from a copse of evergreens while four fine horses thundered past, their gentleman riders upright and laughing with the speed.

Wyndham wasn't alone anymore. Perhaps he ought to have killed him earlier when the fellow wandered the woods looking for his wayward lady. Oh, well. He'd always had a weakness for the appeal of watching one's enemy in pain.

The three gentlemen in question, however . . .

Four of them.

It was them. A jolt of hot excitement shot up his spine, making his hands twitch in eagerness.

Four men. Four clever, loyal men . . . just like the legendary Quatre Royale. He felt a fierce grin stretch the ragged scars on his face, breaking the frail new skin. He ignored the hot trickles of blood and pus that ran rivulets through the furrows of his cheeks.

The Royal Four.

At last.

Greenleigh, who had escaped the clutches of the man who had suborned his father.

Reardon, who had turned on his own mentor.

Dryden, who had married that seething bitch Julia. The watcher cackled. "Sonny!"

Once upon a time, the sound of his own shattered laugh would have alarmed him, but no more.

"I'm not the man I used to be," he told the four men in the distance, his tone madly conversational. "Not as subtle, not as surgical, perhaps. Yet, there can be beauty in large gestures as well."

His vision blurred for a moment, but he scarcely noticed. The infection that had settled into the bones of his face kept his fever high and his mind euphoric. He would surprise that puny despot, Napoleon. He would return with four handsome heads in a bag along with his other prize and Bonaparte would be forced to return his lands and titles to him forthwith.

Simple, ham-handed, and crude. Oh, well. Perhaps he

could derive some enjoyment from torturing the bastards in the meantime.

Or their ladies . . .

To avoid the intimacy of disrobing in the same room with Lady Alicia, Stanton dressed early for Masque that evening. Herbert swiftly and efficiently turned him out impeccably, after which Stanton went to dawdle precious hours away on the terrace, spinning his severe black mask in his fingers.

The limitations of the house party reminded him of why he avoided such events. Here he was, only days left to prevent the kidnapping of the Prince Regent, and he was cooling his heels, waiting for a lady to curl her hair and attach her garters and—

No. Don't think about garters, because garters lead to stockings lead to knees lead to sweet, silken thighs lead to—

He barely refrained from physically smacking himself on the skull, substituting instead a quick biting of his tongue. The sharp pain helped focus his thoughts. God, she was insidious, twining into his brain when he needed to be thinking of much more important things.

Who was the conspirator? It could be Cross himself, though the man was a loud and generous supporter of George's regency and the British war effort.

A lord. That ruled out half of the present guests. They were mostly Court hangers-on, kept about for entertainment value. No one took them terribly seriously, least of all George himself. Other than helping George choose his wine, none of them could be considered to have any sort of real power.

It must be someone who had not yet arrived. Better if this unidentified suspect never arrived at all, although Stanton was itching to know who it was that dared such an impossible crime.

At any rate, the conspirator would definitely be in place

soon. The separation of the ladies and gentlemen all day was not helping Lady Alicia's efforts to identify the voice of the mystery lord among those present.

On the other hand, she seems to have no trouble getting their attention.

Stanton found himself with a strong desire to spit. That lot of fools were too easily influenced by a bright smile and a delectable pair of—

This time he did give himself a rap on the forehead. "There will be no reflecting on delectable *anything!*" His sotto voce self-scolding couldn't have reached much farther than his arm's length, yet he heard a soft laugh from the shadows.

He turned quickly. There was no one there—and yet he smelled jasmine. "Hello, Moth—my lady."

She drifted out from behind a piece of Grecian statuary that paled in comparison to herself. "Good evening, darling. Enjoying the air, I assume?"

Stanton relaxed, which was certainly not his usual response to his mother's presence. "You look miles beyond exquisite, my lady."

"I know, darling, but thank you for saying so." She walked past him to lean over the stone balustrade and peer at the dark garden. "It is cold outside. Why don't you come wait for her in the garden suite? It's very pleasant. Cross absolutely festooned it with hothouse blooms this time."

Lord Cross had been pursuing Catherine's affections for years. "I'm sure he considers it damning you with faint praise, my lady."

"Please, darling, call me 'Mother.' " She put her hand in his. He took it automatically, his surprise deep. She had always been effusively, theatrically affectionate, but this was something else—something simpler and entirely more packed with meaning.

"I realized something today . . . something about th
past."

Stanton went still. The marchioness never looked back
keeping her beautiful eyes always firmly forward as if t
look behind were to acknowledge that any of the past wa
actually true.

"And what is that . . . Mother?"

She turned toward him and for the first time he noticed th
delicate but undeniable lines about her eyes. This contradic
tion of her seeming immortality struck him hard.

"I was but sixteen when I became a mother," the mar
chioness said softly. "And a silly, careless sixteen at that."

"Mother, I—"

She shook her head sharply to halt him. "I am not a bril
liant woman, darling, but I am not quite the fool the worl
thinks me. It is possible that I could have risen to the chal
lenge. I could have been more steadfast, more selfless.
ought to have worried more about your happiness than m
own. Instead, I chose to flee Wyndham and Ilsa. To flee you.

Every word she said was the truth. Stanton watche
stunned, as the flighty, restless, inconstant creature he ha
called "Mother" transformed into a sincere, truthful woma
before his eyes.

She took both his hands in hers. He felt her cold finger
shaking through two layers of kidskin. "I'm sorry, darling.
She looked up into his eyes with more intensity than he ha
ever witnessed from her. "More sorry than I will ever be abl
to make you understand." Her face was strained, her age ap
parent in her pallor.

She had never been more striking.

For a moment, Stanton remained speechless with surprise
Then a terrible thought crossed his mind. "You're dying
aren't you?" He stepped back to peer into her face mor
closely. "That's it, isn't it? You're making amends before yo
pass on!"

For a long moment, she stared at him, lips parted.

He went cold. "We'll find the best physicians in England—in the world. We'll go to Bath. You can take the waters."

She put her hands over her face, crying . . . or was she?

No, she was laughing, gasping with hysterical giggles. Stanton straightened. "What—"

She reached to put her hand over his. "I'm sorry, darling. I—I shouldn't laugh—but you see, I'm quite well."

She did look well, of a sudden. Her eyes shone in the lantern light and her smile had never been brighter.

He shook his head. "I don't understand."

She patted his hands. "Really, darling, I'm not a bit ill. I simply thought it was time to—well, time, at any rate."

Stanton let out a slow breath. His gut was still shaking from the severity of the blow. Apparently he was more attached than he'd ever imagined.

She reached up to stroke his cheek. "I did not expect you to take on so, but I must say that I am gratified to learn that it would grieve you to lose me."

Stanton shook his head. "Of course it would grieve me. You are my mother."

She smiled a bit mistily. "I haven't been, but perhaps it is not entirely too late for you and I to be family for each other."

Family. What an odd thought. Then again, he had not sprung from an acorn, had he?

She glanced over his shoulder and smiled. "I believe there is someone waiting for you, darling."

Stanton turned to look behind him and his breath stopped.

Alicia stood in the open doorway, with the light behind her setting her hair afire and her gown to pure gold. The gown was daring and alluring, yet somehow gave her the regal air of a goddess statuette rather than simply that of a well-dressed mistress.

When she turned her head slightly, offering her profile in a
almost shy motion, the gilded half-mask she wore gleame
richly against her perfect russet hair. She was . . .

Mine, his male nature said.

All mine. Forever.

19

The marchioness leaned forward to whisper into Stanton's ear. "You should take Lady Alicia in to the ball. I find I'm not nearly so interested in this sort of affair anymore. I believe I shall go to my room to pack. Perhaps I shall see you at Christmas, if you find your way to Wyndham this year."

She swept past him on her way back inside, but paused when she came even with Alicia. To Stanton's astonishment, his lady mother deposited a kiss upon the cheek of his mistress.

"You look delightful, my dear," Catherine said. Then she went closer and whispered something that sounded very much like "Good for you, pet."

With a last little finger wave and entirely alarming smile for him, the marchioness glided away.

Alicia watched him with wide eyes. It occurred to Stanton that she was waiting for him to denigrate her gown, as he usually did.

Instead, he clicked his heels and bowed deeply. "My lady, you look—" *Ravishing. Inspirational.*

Like a beacon in the night, guiding sailors home.

And Vikings to raid.

And he was about to take this confection of fire and gol
and ripe ivory flesh into that ballroom full of lechers and de
viants.

To find a traitor, he reminded himself. There is more a
stake here than one woman's dignity and already dubiou
chastity.

Right. Think on the mission and not how she looks like
fancy foil-wrapped confection among a horde of starvin
men.

She was watching him, still waiting. "I look—"

Collecting himself, Stanton presented his arm. "You loo
ready."

She placed her hand upon it. "Of course." Behind th
mask, her lashes swept down over her eyes, but he got th
distinct feeling that she was disappointed.

That was unfortunate, but he had not come here to ply he
with compliments. They both had a job to do and time wa
running out.

Alicia was so distracted by Wyndham's contradictor
manner that she was unable to appreciate the impact Gar
rett's "princess trollop" gown made upon the party guests
When she first swept into the ballroom on Wyndham's arm
a true hush fell upon the crowd.

She was vaguely aware of white-feather-masked Lad
Davenport shooting glares of hatred at her like a quiver ful
of arrows, and the Sirens, all masked and gowned in sub
dued but elegant shades of blue, giving each other meaning
ful glances, and even the Prince Regent, masked as
feathered eagle, who watched them with a decidedly od
look upon his face of mingled anticipation and regret.

All that she could see and feel was Wyndham and th
chill depth of his glacial control.

She'd almost had him there for a moment. The light be

hind her had shone full upon his face and in his first moment of surprise he had clearly been attracted.

Then again, she had already known he was attracted. That was very nearly meaningless insofar as she seemed to have the required inches of figure to attract most men at the ball at least a little bit.

What she'd wanted was the next moment, the one after the surge of attraction. She'd wanted a smile, an intimate gaze, a tender touch—but there had been nothing. It was as if a door had slammed between them, decapitating that next moment before it even began.

Even now when they were mere inches apart, so close that she could feel the heat from his body upon the skin of her arm and shoulder and nearly bared breast—there was nothing emanating from Wyndham but that temperature that did naught to warm her.

"You look very handsome," she whispered to him, because it was true. "Rather like a dashing highwayman, in fact."

He didn't so much as glance down at her. "Thank you."

She hadn't been fishing—or at least not with much hope—but his distance was beginning to irritate her. Irritation she knew what to do with. Sadness was much harder.

So she dropped her hand from his arm and dipped a breezy curtsy. "You're being a complete stick," she said. "I'm going to see if Lord Farrington feels like dancing."

That had his attention at last. "No."

She tilted her head. "Interesting." And a bit thrilling. "Are you telling me you do not wish me to dance with Farrington?"

"Of course I am." Then he had to ruin it. "You've already discounted Farrington as a possible suspect. Dance with someone you haven't yet spoken to." He turned to look at the dancers, as if scanning for her next victim for her.

Alicia inhaled deeply. This man was going to be the death of her.

Yet who would not want such a demise? Just look at the arrogant, stubborn bastard! "If you were not so handsome, Wyndham," she muttered under her breath, "it would be much easier to box your bloody ears."

He glanced over his shoulder at her. "What?"

She folded her arms. "I look beautiful. I know I look beautiful. Everyone in this ballroom knows I look beautiful. I'll likely hear it so many times tonight that I'll become ill."

His gaze flicked down her body and back up. "I daresay that's true." He turned back to the crowd, his composure fully in place.

Behind his back, however, Alicia was smiling. *I saw that, Lord Wyndham. I saw your eyes go dark. I saw your jaw harden. I can read you now and you think I'm so beautiful that you cannot stand to look in my direction.*

She went up on tiptoe and kissed his cheek. "Thank you," she whispered. Then she spun out into the dancers, ready to take up Wyndham's search once more. There was time for her full frontal attack later.

She smiled happily, causing one man to blink in surprise and miss his dance step, seriously annoying his partner. Alicia sent him a come-hither glance from behind the coy safety of her mask, then laughed and kept going. There were more men than ever present tonight. If she wanted to find Wyndham's target tonight, she'd best get on with it.

Stanton watched Alicia flirt with the dancer. She never looked back at him, which was probably just as well. His fists were clenched at his sides and she was far too perceptive to miss that.

He could still feel her lips on his cheek and the pressure of her full breasts on his arm when she'd leaned into him. He could still smell her hair and feel the warm moist caress of her breath in his ear.

His mission seemed a thousand miles away and only one coherent thought managed to make itself across his lust-heated mind.

He was in the deepest of trouble.

When Prince George beckoned him from across the room, Stanton went. When his ruler and someday king gave him a knowing and not entirely kind smile, Stanton merely bowed. "Your highness."

"You're forgetting your duties as Lord of Misrule," George reminded him. "It's time to set the tone for tonight's celebration."

Stanton waited. George was up to no good, he could tell.

"I liked last night's misrule very much. 'Tell the truth.' Brilliant." George took a deep draught of his wine. When he'd swallowed, the empty glass disappeared into a white and gold liveried hand and reappeared full to the brim. George took it without ever letting Stanton free of his razor-sharp gaze.

"Confession is good for the soul," George went on. "I think it's time we all looked to our souls, don't you?"

Stanton kept his gaze steady, though he was aware of Alicia's bright hair and shimmering gown spiraling through the dancers, held in a stranger's arms.

"Tell the truth, Wyndham. Tell *her* the truth. Tell her what you're thinking when you watch her dancing. Tell her what you truly want when you take her to your bed."

Stanton didn't waver. "I do not lie to her."

George smiled again, that calculating gleam of teeth, tinged with bitterness. "I am not a constant man, but I know of love. I will love my dear Fitzherbert until my dying day. If I could have her as my queen, I would ne'er look astray." Then he shrugged. "Or not nearly so much, at any rate. My point is that I cannot have Maria. She and I cannot ever truly be. Such knowledge is excruciating."

George tossed back the second—or fifth, Wyndham truly wasn't sure—glass of wine. The prince wiped his mouth on the back of his hand, then gestured out to the dancers. "It does me good to see you in pain, Wyndham. I only wish the other Three could writhe before me as well." He grinned. "There, I've confessed it."

Confession. Stanton bowed crisply to George. "Thank you, your highness. I shall implement your advice at once."

He turned on his heel and strode away.

"Don't forget to beg, Wyndham!" George called out as Stanton left him behind. "Women love it when you beg!"

Stanton wasn't heading off to beg anyone for anything. George's tale of love denied had only increased Stanton's resolve to avoid that dangerous emotion at all cost.

It was the talk of confession that had sired an idea in his mind. He strode to the edge of George's dais and signaled to the musicians in the balcony to stop.

They swept the crowd up into one last swelling chord and then silenced their strings. All faces turned as one toward Stanton.

He cleared his throat. "As your Lord of Misrule, I have declared that everyone must tell the truth. Now I declare that all the gentlemen here must tell their deepest fancy—" He paused through the exclamations of shock and lascivious delight. "Every gentleman here must tell his secret longing . . . to Lady Alicia Lawrence."

20

Loud guffaws came from the contingent of Lady Alicia's most ardent admirers. Several ladies made noises of protest. Stanton glanced toward Alicia, not that he cared whether or not she protested.

She looked decidedly annoyed with him, her lips pursed beneath her mask, but she stepped forward willingly enough. She came to the base of the dais and turned toward the crowd. "You have all heard our Lord of Misrule. I will hear your secret fancies, my good sirs—" She gave them all her wickedest smile. "But I cannot promise not to tell the lady involved!"

Laughter ensued and Stanton had to give Lady Alicia credit. She certainly knew how to manage the throng.

A footman brought a comfortable chair from another room. Some wit penned a sign—THE RAKE'S CONFESSIONAL—and hung it upon the throne. Alicia was paraded to the ludicrous setting by a crowd of gentlemen who then proceeded to toss blooms stolen from Lord Cross's conservatory at her feet.

"O Lady of Lust," one man called to her. Stanton was fairly sure it was Farrington. "Are you ready to grant us our dreams?"

Alicia seated herself in the chair, but not before casting a sweetly venomous glare at Stanton across the room.

You will pay, that look said. *Someday, as God is my witness, you will pay.*

Stanton's only response was to move laterally across the ballroom so that he had a clear view of her.

Alicia relaxed slightly when she saw Stanton in clear view. He leaned one shoulder against a pillar and folded his arms over his wide chest. His chin was down so that she could not see his eyes in the shadow of his black mask, but she knew he watched.

It was a good thing, too, for the first gentleman staggered up and loomed over her, his bulk crowding her rather unpleasantly.

That wouldn't do. She clapped her hands sharply. "Kneel; wretch!"

Laughter came from around them. Of course those lechers found it hilarious. Alicia was beginning to wonder if this crowd had any sort of limits.

Perhaps there was some merit in the rules of Society, after all.

Her penitent blinked groggily—good heavens, the evening had scarcely begun!—but dropped unsteadily to one knee. "O Lady of Luss," he mumbled. "My secret fan—fan—trasy is to—to—" He swallowed and leaned forward. "Can I see your nipples?"

The dolt obviously lacked imagination. Alicia leaned forward and inhaled. He nearly drooled. "But darling," she breathed. "Don't you remember? You already have!"

He blinked slowly. "Oh. Were they pink?"

Alicia put one palm in the middle of his forehead. "The pinkest." She gave a vigorous push.

He fell backward to the loud mocking laughter of his fellows, then stumbled to his feet, his mask askew on his sweating face. Alicia caught Stanton's eye and shook her head. *Not him.*

If she had known what was to come, Alicia might have been less judgmental of the drunken man's simple fantasy. Tall and short, thin and stout—washed and unwashed—every man present came to kneel at her feet and fill her ears with lusty imaginings.

The only way Alicia was able to keep from tossing her tea was keep her gaze fixed on Wyndham—

And imagine him in every role.

Her education expanded with every muttered confession. There was so much more for two—or more!—people to do to each other than she'd ever imagined . . . or even wanted to think on.

Yet, somehow even the most distasteful acts seemed rather . . . interesting . . . when she visualized Wyndham's perfect, muscled body performing them upon her.

Some men were dogs.

Some men were wolves.

She gazed at him across the room from her and let her mind roam freely, choosing some of the more tasty fancies to pretend with him. The ballroom faded away, the men surrounding her, cheering on her subjects, became as the roar of the sea to her ears. There was no one but Wyndham.

At his post across the room, Stanton could feel the heat of her radiating across the cold marble room like that of a bonfire. Her cheeks were flushed and her eyes the green of a steaming jungle. As she gazed at him, looking over the shoulder of each man who whispered to her, he felt the pull of her desire.

When her tongue flicked out to lick her lips, he was very much afraid he groaned aloud. She was too much for him, too much for his control, too bright for his darkness.

He could not keep her gaze any longer without striding to her side and carrying her away from the voracious lechers who surrounded her. He looked away and concentrated on breathing again.

Alicia's vision was glazed with lust. Her mind was filled with him.

Wyndham caressing her *there*. Wyndham urging her mouth *there*. Wyndham's mouth *everywhere*.

Wyndham, exhausted and gleaming with perspiration, tied spread-eagle while she—

Then she heard it—that particular timbre, that habit of swallowing the softer consonants. The mystery lord was whispering into her ear!

She gazed up at him as he straightened and she met his eyes. Behind his blue velvet mask, he was a rather ordinary fellow, not too tall nor too short, with a retreating hairline and the flushed cheeks and reddened nose that came of long-term overindulgence.

He seemed cheerfully inebriated even now and not particularly inclined to guile, but one never knew. Certainly she was no great judge of character.

Apparently pleased by her extra attention, he gave her a sloppy wink while he gazed boldly into her décolletage with his other eye. "If Wyndham ever gets tiresome . . ." He trailed off.

Alicia panicked slightly at being in the presence of a criminal, but only for an instant. Then she smiled, leaned forward, and inhaled. "But without your name, my lord—"

A man with bulldog cheeks pushed between them. "Piss off, 'smy turn!"

Alicia glared at the interloper. "I don't want to hear your dirty little secret," she snarled. She stood, searching over the heads of the crowd for Stanton. He'd been standing by that post just a moment ago. He'd promised to watch diligently—where was he?

Lord Bulldog pawed at her arm. "Say, you've got to listen. The Lord of Misrule said to." He smiled a loose, smeary grin. "It's a pip of a fancy."

Alicia shook him off. "Oh, please. With your lack of imagination and whisky-stunted intelligence, I'm sure it's nothing but wearing a corset and having a hairbrush taken to your rear."

His jaw dropped and his bushy brows met in the middle. "Who told?"

"Oh, for pity's sake." Alicia shoved past him, trying to keep the mystery lord in her view. Wyndham had better have a dandy excuse for deserting her this way.

Well, she would simply keep following the man until Wyndham found her or she tripped over him, one or the other.

Lord Conspirator ambled throughout the masked dancers without any apparent purpose, at loose ends now that he'd dropped his fancy into the wishing well of Alicia's ear.

Highly unlikely.

She stayed a discreet distance behind him, trying to appear as natural as possible. The room was horribly crowded and she suspected that the guest list was growing all on its own now as others heard about the Saturnalia.

Lord Plotter began to make his way to the terrace doors. Alicia was tempted to hang back, yet what would Wyndham say when she told him she'd lost the fellow because of her own indecision?

By the time she'd followed her target through the doors to the terrace, he was already partway down the garden path.

Apparently he was a very selective vomiter, for he was wandering in a zigzag manner down the path, seemingly looking for just the right shrub.

Alicia followed him carefully, walking to one side of the path where the lesser gravel minimized the crunching of her footfalls. As she moved farther into the darkness of the garden, she became aware that they weren't the only guests to have made their way outside.

She'd lived next to the pub long enough to know what those feminine cries and male grunts signified and she was grateful for the darkness to hide her furious blush.

Lord Drunkard was still on the move, so Alicia bit her lip and kept to his trail. The only thing holding Wyndham to her side was her story and she was suddenly very desperate to prove it. After what she'd learned from his mother, she would do anything to help him believe in her.

Then a nearby cry startled her. She had to admit, the deepening darkness combined with the animal noises of carnal celebration were beginning to send shivers of alarm up her spine. She'd never been a fainting violet, but she would be very glad when Lord Sot made his way back inside.

Then she came upon him, lying across the path unconscious. She rushed toward him and knelt at his side. "My lord? My lord, can you speak?"

No, but he could snore. She would be getting no name from him now. Alicia dropped his arm to the gravel in disgust. "Oh, shut up, you miserable sot. How am I going to get you back inside now?"

She stood. There was nothing she could do but go back to the ballroom and seek out Wyndham. At least she knew the mystery lord wouldn't be going anywhere.

She turned and began to stalk back to the house, in her irritation forgetting to mask her footfalls in the gravel.

She'd gone no more than twenty steps before a shadow stepped out of the bushes into her path. She jumped slightly, suddenly becoming completely aware that she was wandering in a strange garden in the dark—not something any woman did with impunity, no matter how highborn.

"If it isn't Wyndham's new pet bitch." The figure took a step toward her. "He let you off the leash already?" The voice was flat and unfamiliar.

The faint light from the house was at his back, making his face invisible, although she was sure he could see her. In fact, her gold gown might as well be a beacon, while the stranger's dark garb made him a frightening trick of shape and shadow.

Alicia took a step back, then another, although she didn't know where she was supposed to go. Away, that was for certain, but where? Her target was passed out behind her, Wyndham was behind the stranger, doubtlessly expecting her to still be in the ballroom—which was precisely where she ought to be, now that she thought on it.

"Lovely evening," she said, forcing a light tone into the rigid fear in her voice. "But I've left my wrap inside. If you'll excuse me . . ."

The shadow man didn't step aside, not that she'd truly expected him to. A cold ball of sickening alarm began to swell in her belly.

The shadow moved a step closer. "The Lord of Misrule has declared that everyone must tell you their secret fancy. I have a very lovely fancy to relate—one where red-coated bitches are quite properly tied up and muzzled—where all their nasty habits and willfulness are beaten out of them, until they know their place . . ."

He moved closer. "Where is that place, Lady Alicia? Where do you belong in the world? You aren't a true lady, for you're even more of a whore than those unfaithful wives inside. You aren't an honest whore, if there is such a thing, for you still pretend to your birthright, the one you threw away to let a filthy manure-shoveling stable boy between your thighs. You don't even know your place, do you, Lady Alicia? You don't belong anywhere at all. A lone bitch, with no pack, taking crumbs from the lowest tables."

He laughed, a mad, strange sound. "I know where you belong, little red bitch. You belong on your knees before me, properly chastened, willing to do absolutely anything for those crumbs . . .

He reached for her, striking like a snake. She ducked violently and almost evaded him, but one merciless claw gripped her wrist.

She cried out at last, the pain setting her free of the frozen humiliation. "Wyndha—!"

The demon spun her as he twisted her arm high behind her, sending her to her knees, held upright only by his excruciating grip. He wrenched her wrist higher as if he wished to rip her shoulder right from its socket. "Keep whining, little bitch. Your master doesn't want you any more than anyone else on earth does."

God, could no one help her? "W-why?" She could scarcely form words through her gritted teeth. "Why are you angry—?"

He shook her, hard. The pain in her shoulder made her sight dim.

"Why? Why not? Do you not deserve everything I do here? Are you not a lady who turned whore? Are you not a wicked, wanton bitch in heat, mating without discretion or restraint?"

Alicia tried to deny it, but the words wouldn't come past her pain-tightened throat.

What if it was true? What if she was as unnatural as he claimed? She'd wanted Almont's body as much as she'd wanted his proposal. She wanted Wyndham until she could not sleep at night.

What if she was abnormally, innately wicked? What if her desires were the real reason she'd never been able to be the daughter her parents had wanted, the lady Society wanted . . .

The woman Wyndham could want to spend his life with.

Male voices rose through the darkness. Alicia dimly heard her name called.

The man shifted his grip, pulling her harshly to him. She

realized from some distant place of reason that he was truly no taller than she.

"Filthy, shameful whore," the stranger whispered in her ear. "I cannot stand to touch you for one more moment."

He released her, letting her slither limply down his body to fall at his feet. "Ah," he said mildly. "I see you've found your place after all."

Alicia curled away from him, sickened beyond fear by his words and the pain he'd caused her. She didn't move as she heard his footsteps recede just as the light of many lanterns began to brighten behind her closed lids.

"Wyndham." Her broken whisper couldn't have carried much beyond arm's length, yet she miraculously heard him reply.

"I'm here, Alicia." Large, gentle hands came to brush aside her hair and to gently inspect her for injuries.

"You are unhurt," he said with relief.

And by some miracle—or more likely by some sinister plan—she was completely unharmed . . . in any way someone could see. Her shoulder was immobilized with pain, but there was not a mark on her but a bit of redness about her wrist and the ache in her knees when she'd dropped to the gravel.

She could not speak of what was said to her. Never, not to anyone. The madman had read her mind, conjured up her deepest, most hidden fears, and reduced her to a helpless animal with one hand.

No, she had no proof. And she could not bear to be accused of more lies.

21

Stanton carried Alicia swiftly through the house, avoiding the ballroom entryway. He wanted no one to see her in this condition. That would invite questions and the only questions he wanted answered were his own.

Once in their bedchamber, he deposited her in the chair by the fire. Garrett rushed forward, his brow knitted in concern, and Stanton stepped back, unsure of what to do for her.

Stanton had no words to describe the emotion that had swept him when he'd seen his lovely, lively Alicia curled up on the path, so still and quiet. It had shaken him to depths he hadn't known he had—and alarmed him to the point of dread.

He could not allow himself to become so involved. He had a duty and a life that could not include an untamed creature such as Lady Alicia Lawrence. She was everything the Falcon must avoid. She was everything he'd never wanted.

As much as he wanted to take her in his arms again and hold her while she sipped the hot tea pressed upon her by Garrett, Stanton maintained his aloof pose a few feet away, one elbow braced upon the mantel. Only with that distance could he keep himself from dropping to his knees at her side and taking her hands in his.

He cleared his throat against the emotion choking him. He had work to do. He was more than some fawning swain. He was the Falcon.

"What happened to you in the garden?"

Alicia flinched slightly from his authoritarian tone, although she kept her gaze fixed on the fire. "Do not question me like that, Wyndham. I am not a criminal."

"Perhaps not, although one might call you criminally stupid to wander alone through a dark garden during an orgy!"

"I heard the voice. I tried to find you, but you had left!"

He had stepped away, of course, to take a breath and cool the rising lust within him. Only for the briefest moment, and then he'd turned back to find her gone from her throne and her flock of converts milling about like ducklings without their mother.

It had taken less than ten minutes to find her, curled on the gravel path in the garden, obviously terrified. It terrified him even now, thinking on it.

And yet, her condition raised questions, suspicions he was unable to ignore.

If someone had attacked her, why would she not accuse? Where were the bruises, the torn gown, the mussed hair?

"Was he wearing a mask?"

She looked away. "I did not see his face at all."

She was so pale. He hardened himself to her pain. "What did he do to you?"

"He grabbed my arm and . . . expressed his opinion of me."

There were plenty of people at the party with opinions about Alicia, although most of them were women. "So he did not attack you? Did he strike you? Harm you in any way?"

She leaned back in the chair and closed her eyes. "Leave me be, Wyndham. I have told you what happened."

It could have been some drunken sot who, upon finding a beautiful woman alone in the garden, had pressed his advantage. Or not.

"This is the second time, my lord," Garrett said. "Remember the box at the opera?"

Stanton had not forgotten the trip wire and the sabotaged railing—such a baroque effort was hard to forget.

If the two events were related at all . . .

This time, there was no public display of danger. There wasn't a mark on her, other than a ring of reddened flesh about her wrist that was already fading.

She did seem quite convincingly shaken, however.

"This sort of event brings out the worst in people," he told her. "Your attacker was likely some drunk who mistook you for someone who was available."

She raised her gaze to his for a moment, then flicked it away. "Perhaps."

Cradling her left arm in her right, she stood to walk behind her dressing screen. "Garrett, if you would fetch my nightdress?"

Wyndham watched her go, dissatisfied with her response though he was not sure why. She was behaving as if she'd been viciously assaulted, yet her hair wasn't even disarranged.

He reminded himself forcibly of her past reputation. Perhaps the entire matter was just a desperate grab for attention.

It made him quite furious that she was immune to his talent. He could not accustom himself to this sort of uncertainty!

"Well, if you're sure you are fine," he said gruffly. "I will go speak to our mystery lord—if I can sober him up long enough to make sense."

She thrust her head back out from behind the screen. "It is him. I am sure that is the same voice I heard behind the White Sow."

Stanton opened the chamber door to see Lady Greenleigh standing in the hallway with Lady Reardon and Lady Dryden, her fist raised to knock.

"Is Alicia all right?"

"Did you catch the man who did it?"

"Is it the Chimera?"

Stanton glowered at the three beauties. "She is perfectly well. I have someone in hand, and no, it isn't our esteemed friend 'Denny.'"

Lady Dryden folded her arms and gazed at him evenly. "Wyndham, we want to see her. She might tell us more than she's told you."

He scowled. "What makes you think she isn't talking to me?"

Lady Dryden's lips quirked. "You have that look."

Lady Reardon nodded. "Oh yes—the 'damn it' look."

Lady Greenleigh peered at him. "Actually, I think it's the 'damn it to hell!' look."

Lady Dryden tilted her head. "Indeed. You look frustrated, Wyndham. Let us in. Perhaps we can—"

Garrett popped up next to Stanton, his glorious brow creased in worried lines. "Er, my ladies . . . Lady Alicia asks me to tell you that she is indisposed at the moment, but will be happy to see you all tomorrow."

Stanton nodded shortly at the women Alicia had called 'the Sirens.' "She will see you tomorrow. In the meantime, I will continue my investigation, if you do not mind."

Lady Dryden shook her head. "You've mucked it up with her, haven't you, Wyndham?"

Lady Greenleigh nodded. "It's all over your face, my lord. And I don't think that fabulously handsome young man is speaking only to us. I think you've been banished to the morrow as well."

Stanton glanced at Garrett, who shrugged apologetically. "I'm sorry, my lord, but my lady has requested that you exit the room."

Kicked out of his own bedchamber by a mad, presumptuous vixen of a lady—who probably thought he was going to come begging on his knees to be allowed his own rotten chair to sleep in.

Stanton managed to not bang his head repeatedly against the nearest wall. He was going to need all his resources to win this contest against the conspirators. He had nothing to spare for games of the heart.

A few moments later, as Stanton stood over the limply drunken gentleman from the garden, he had to admit that the fellow didn't look like much of a danger to anyone but himself.

Then again, conspirators looked just like everyone else. He had to be careful not to fall into that trap again, the way the Liars had allowed the "harmless" valet Denny to lurk on their perimeter for so long. The way that he himself seemed willing to forget this fact that pretty Lady Alicia was a notorious liar. This fellow on the floor might be a master of disguise on a par with the Chimera himself.

And currently he was playing the role of drunken slug on Cross's parlor rug.

Stanton prodded the man with his toe. There was no response. He tried again, more firmly.

"Ow!" The sot snorted and rolled over, clapping one flapping hand to his side. "You kicked me!"

"You imagined it," Stanton said. He kneeled to bring himself more on eye level with the man. "I want you to tell me something. Do you understand?"

The man blinked and nodded. "Uhn?"

All right, so this fellow likely wasn't the brains behind the operation. Stanton leaned his crossed arms on one knee. "Where were you precisely one fortnight ago?"

The fellow blinked rapidly and pointed a finger vaguely south. "Brighton. W' Prinny."

Stanton straightened. If it were true, it would be a rather irrefutable alibi—and would certainly put the lie to Lady Alicia! He signaled to one of Cross's footmen and asked for paper and ink. When he'd received it, he scrawled a quick note to the Prince Regent—only a single line.

"Ogilvy with you a fortnight past, all night?"

The footman ran with the message. Stanton waited. Ogilvy snored.

Within moments, Stanton was in possession of one winded footman and his answer. *"Yes."* Accompanied by the distinctively scrawled *G*.

Just like that, the search was over and he had the wrong man.

If there had ever been a conspiracy at all.

What would Lady Alicia have to gain from such a lie?

Did you not see her in that gown tonight? If she wishes to take on a protector now, she will have all the offers a woman could want. And you paid for her transformation from ruined spinster to lavish courtesan from your own pocket.

The Prince Regent might have misunderstood the question. Stanton left the unconscious Ogilvy and took himself off to the prince's borrowed wing of the house.

George was huffy and resentful of losing his sleep—or rather, time with his mistress. Stanton knew that he'd best be quick.

"Ogilvy is a suspect in a kidnapping attempt against you," he said. "I need to know precisely how much you saw of him a fortnight past?"

The Prince Regent scratched at the dressing-gown-clad royal belly and yawned. "I had a small intimate party with some of the friends I would be traveling up to Sussex with. Ogilvy was there, mooching my good wine as usual. He drank too much—as usual—and spent the remainder of the night in the cloakroom sleeping on one of my best furs."

"He was identified as being at a Cheapside tavern just past midnight, fourteen days past."

"It wasn't him. See here, Wyndham, Ogilvy is brainless, spineless, and annoying, but he is no conspirator. He is a rather boring fellow who has no record of being anything but a lousy landlord and a worse gambler."

As he left the prince's chamber—whose door shut behind him with a decided slam—it occurred to Stanton that the attempts on Alicia were either bizarre or unwitnessed.

If someone had wanted to create a commotion at the opera, one might have gone to the rented box at the opera house, sabotaged the railing, and stretched a trip wire—

Except that he'd never actually seen the trip wire, had he? He'd only taken her word that something had tripped her, something thin and sharp that had cut her.

But she had almost died!

His suspicious nature would not let it rest. She'd looked very surprised just as she had gone over. Surprised that she'd been tricked, or surprised that she'd overestimated and tricked herself?

He shook his head. Alicia wasn't that sort. Alicia was—

Oh, yes. He mustn't forget. Alicia was completely unreadable to him.

22

There was only one way Stanton could think of to break down Alicia's mysterious resistance to his gift.

As he reentered their room, he moved quietly to where she stood alone by the fire, brushing out her hair. He caught her hand, making her turn with a gasp.

Her eyes were wide and shocked. Had she perhaps been expecting someone else?

He took the brush from her fingers. "Let me."

Her gaze followed the brush in his hand, then flicked to meet his. He raised the brush to the crown of her gleaming head and began to brush. She watched him for a long moment, then let her eyes fall shut to the relaxing rhythm of his brushstrokes.

As he dug his hands into the warm silk of her fiery hair, Stanton had to admit that he'd been panting to do so for days.

Yet that was not why he was stepping over this line.

He turned her gently away from him and brushed all her hair back over her shoulders toward him. The small cap sleeve of her nightdress slipped aside, falling from its perch as indeed such a nightgown was meant to do to reveal the pale female curve of her shoulder.

Experimentally, Stanton pushed aside the other side, which allowed the gown to slip down and hang dangerously low upon her luxurious breasts. She made a motion as if to clutch the gown higher.

"Don't," he ordered. Was that his voice, gone so hoarse with desire?

Yet why not? He was a man, after all, standing behind a sensuous beauty—a vantage point that allowed him a fabulous view down her cleavage. If he wasn't stirred by that, he wouldn't be much different than Garrett.

He took her hair into his fist and hefted it. Such heavy luxury. Such a gift to the man who discovered her secret beauty . . .

He wrapped her hair around his wrist, pulling it up and back to see her vulnerable neck bared to him. The scent that rose from her freshly bathed skin was an intoxicating blend of verbena and aroused woman. He bent his head to breathe her in.

Somehow his lips found the tiny tender down on the back of her neck. He brushed his mouth across her skin, breathing out so that he could breathe in again, taking her perfume into himself.

She was trembling, he realized dimly. "Are you cold?" His whisper ignited another tremor.

"N-no." Her broken sigh satisfied him. She was his for the taking, his for the discovery.

His for the revealing.

She began to turn. He stopped her with his tender, relentless grip on her hair. "Stay," he commanded.

With his other hand, he reached around her to brush his fingertips across each erect nipple. She twitched in time with his touch, her breath beginning to come in shaking gasps.

"How sensitive they are," he mused into her hair. He took a step toward the mirror. She followed as if they were already one. He shifted her until they were both reflected in the tall mirror. The angle had the added benefit of casting the firelight right through the negligible fabric of her gown. He could see every curve, every fantasy-fulfilling slope and swell.

"I see you." His voice had gone quite guttural. "I see all of you."

He took one erect nipple between his fingertips. He could see her gaze fixed upon his hand in their reflection. Rolling her hard peak gently through the spiderweb gown, he felt the quiver that went through her.

He moved closer, pressing himself to her back to take in every shiver, every erotic tremor that she made. Her soft bottom pressed into his lap, driving his own desire higher.

He directed his passion into the razor focus of his purpose. He meant to break her down and own her secrets for himself.

He moved his attention to the other nipple, which poked vigorously through her gown as if begging for his attention.

This one he plucked softly, as if pulling a ripe juicy berry from the brambles. She quivered against him, although she still did not meet his gaze in the mirror.

Suddenly he wanted her to. He needed that connection.

"Look at me," he ordered huskily.

She closed her eyes and turned her face away. Her blush was visible, even in the firelight.

"Alicia, open your eyes and look at me." Damn it, why was she being so shy? She was no fainting virgin!

He released her hair and took both her breasts into his hot grip. "Look at me," he growled.

Her eyes flew open and she looked at him. He found himself stunned by the impact of her wide, achingly hungry gaze.

Hot male satisfaction flooded him. She was his, there was no doubt about that.

With one motion, he pulled her nightdress down and let it slither down her body to pool at her feet. To tell the truth, the made-for-mistressing gown didn't put up much of a fight.

Alicia closed her eyes again. She couldn't bear to let him see into her that way, naked before him in every way, inside and out.

She felt everything. Her skin prickled to the cooler air on one side and the heat from the fire on the other. She felt the wool of his coat and the silk of his weskit on her back. She felt his erection straining tightly in his trousers. She swayed against it, rubbing her bottom lightly in order to judge its size—which seemed rather intimidating from this aspect.

He hissed when she moved and she felt his breath stir the hairs on the back of her neck. Reassured that her effect on him was as great as his on her, she opened her eyes to look at their reflection in the mirror.

She stood naked and pliant before him, a stripped harem slave before her fully clothed master. The notion excited and frightened her, for she had promised herself to never put herself into another man's power again.

Then again, this was merely a game, wasn't it? Like the ones being played out downstairs. If she was a willing playmate, then she was giving up nothing but what she chose to give up.

So she leaned back into him, pressing her bottom to his rising lust, pressing her bare shoulders into his chest, leaning her head back upon his shoulder.

"Do as you wish with me," she whispered. "Tonight I am yours to enjoy."

She felt him tense—with surprise? Had he thought the battle not won? She moved against him, pleased to have taken the initiative from his hands. He was not the only one with desires, after all.

He released her hair and it fell softly to cover her breasts. Still she did not turn, for she found that she liked to look at the two of them in the mirror. She was pale skin and bright hair, her skin cooled by the air. He was darkness and heat, which came from his body in waves to surround her.

"Do you see?" she whispered to him. "We are day and night, together."

"You are a fire goddess," he murmured, almost as if he were surprised to hear himself say such a thing.

Alicia certainly was. Her Wyndham was not one to spout flowery . . . well, to spout anything, actually.

She wanted to turn to him, but he held her shoulders, keeping her to the mirror.

"I am going to watch you come apart in my hands," he said. "I want to see you shiver and fly for me."

She wasn't entirely sure what he meant by that but she was certainly willing to find out.

He began to slide his hands from her shoulders down her arms. He pressed her hands flat to her thighs. "Stay," he commanded.

She shivered. She obeyed.

He laid one hand flat to her belly, adhering her back to his front with gentle steady pressure. "Do you feel me?"

She felt the hard rise of his trousers against her buttocks, riding the crease of her flesh. She nodded silently, her gaze trapped by his in the mirror.

He slid his other hand down to cup her furred mound. She jumped slightly as his middle finger slid along the parting of her.

"Shh." His breath was hot lava on her neck. "Do you feel me?"

His finger dipped in, dipped between the folds, making that pinpoint of her nerves pulse with pleasure. She nodded again.

He began to stroke his fingertip slowly up and down, in

and out, barely penetrating the fold. It was excruciatingly pleasurable, but it only made the throbbing worse. She tried to tilt her pelvis farther into his hand, but he pressed her back once more.

"Stay," he whispered.

Her thighs quaked, but she stayed, breathless and willing.

"I moved too quickly last night," he said softly. "I should have introduced myself more politely." His finger slipped a knuckle's depth into her. His roughened fingertip grazed her most sensitive place. "Do you know what this is called, Alicia?"

She didn't, not really. In her mind, she'd referred to it in silly ways—"lust button," for one. While she was quite sure every woman had one, she was less sure that every woman was as fond of it as she was.

"This is called your clitoris." He began to swirl his finger in a circular motion around it, his path eased by the onrush of her fluids when she shuddered with pleasure, tightening the muscles in her thighs convulsively.

"You are already so wet for me." He slid his long finger deeper, parting her with his hand as he penetrated her in a long, slow thrust.

She gasped and staggered against him. He held her steady with the pressure of his other hand. She felt his organ grow harder behind her.

"There are many names for this place," he murmured. "Some ugly, some not. I wouldn't dream of calling such a welcoming haven anything but a beautiful name." He swiveled the penetrating finger inside her. "We will call this sweet place your vulva. Perhaps not technically correct, but who will know?"

He slipped his finger out of her slowly and teasingly. She tried to follow his touch, but he held her still. He brought his hand up, and she watched in the mirror as he touched his finger to his lips. "You taste like sunlight and honey," he whispered, his breath heating the inside of her ear.

Another shudder went through her. He was a wicked, wicked man.

She ground her buttocks against him. He pressed her still. "Now I want you to take your hands and put them on your breasts."

She did so, automatically covering them with her palms. He shook his head, his dark eyes unreadable in the mirror.

"No, I want you to touch yourself as I did. I want you to touch your nipples while I touch your vulva and clitoris."

The strange words made her feel even bolder, as if they gave her power over her body. She did as he told her, cupping her heavy breasts and touching her fingertips to her nipples. It didn't feel quite the same as when he touched her there, but the way he drew his breath in a faint hiss while he watched her— that was entirely exciting!

He wanted to watch her, he'd said. Watch her come apart in his hands as she had last night. "Touch me," she whispered, emboldened by the bald hunger in his rigid expression. She traced her fingertips around her nipples, making them tighten in the chill air, and even plucked them slightly to pinken them.

Stanton could have sworn he was the one in control only moments ago. Now the unshockable monster he'd created tempted him boldly in the mirror, green eyes gone to wicked fire in the candlelight.

To reclaim the upper hand he—well, he used his hand.

Sliding his open hand down her side, he slipped it between her thighs once more. This time he plunged in, a bold invasion of a single large finger.

She gasped and shuddered against him. He withdrew slowly, then plunged in again. He repeated the motion until the teasing light of power left her eyes and her head dropped back on his shoulder and she was his willing, shivering plaything once again.

He drove her higher, fighting to ignore the grinding pressure of his own arousal and the way that her rounded bottom quivered voluptuously against his iron erection. She cried out, a senseless sound, as she rolled her head upon his shoulder. Her hands fell to clutching at the arm that crossed the front of her body, holding her still for his exploitation.

He watched every moment in the mirror. He watched the way her parted lips refused to close enough to form words. He watched as her eyelids closed against the rising pleasure. He watched the sway and quake of her full, soft breasts as she shook in ecstasy. He watched the way his fingers began to glisten with her juices and the way the flush of arousal bloomed over her belly and breasts.

But when she came, he closed his eyes to relish the way her wet heat pulsed around his finger as he plunged it deeply one last time and held his palm tight against her swollen clitoris.

She fell back against him then, her knees useless to her. Stanton allowed himself one last moment of giving her pleasure, then he changed one hand for the other and passed his dry one across her face, easing her tossed hair from his view of her expression.

"Tell me a lie," he demanded.

Alicia's eyelids fluttered open. Her confused gaze met his in the mirror. "Wh-what?"

"Tell me a lie, right now," he urged. "Any lie at all."

She raised her head and blinked at him. "Ah . . . my eyes are blue?"

Stanton froze. "Say it again, not like a question."

She was gazing at him curiously now. "My eyes are blue."

Icy reality cut through Stanton's arousal. He pulled his

hands from her and turned away, leaving her to stand naked and alone before the mirror.

The chill hit her skin immediately. Shying her gaze away from her own image in the mirror, she turned away to reach for her nightdress, drawing it swiftly over her head.

She had never experienced such pleasure as Wyndham gave her. So why did she feel so empty?

The image resurfaced of his eyes while he pleasured her. His gaze had been almost . . . distant. As if he studied her. Alicia shook off the sudden chill that riddled her spine.

He'd observed her as if she were an experiment.

"Well, if that was a test, I certainly hope I passed," she muttered uncomfortably. "I should hate to see what might constitute failure."

Failure. The word sliced to the heart of Stanton's fear. If she could not be trusted, then everything he did here was useless and possibly detrimental to the Four's tenuous control of George. If she was to be trusted, then he needed to expend everything he had in the search for the conspirator.

If he could not discern which was which, he might very possibly fail at both.

In one swift movement, he turned to her again. He took her by the shoulders and pressed her firmly to the papered wall. She jerked her head up, surprise evident in her eyes.

Her sunset-glorious hair was a mess, tangled by her earlier thrashing in his grip. He pushed back the silken disarray to look again into those eyes, desperate to divine what he could not see in her.

"What is the truth, Alicia?"

Alicia felt her heart sink—fall—dive headlong into a pit of pain. She had thought that his turning to her meant that he wanted more, that he believed her and wanted to reassure her—that her past didn't matter to him.

It wasn't true. Although it sounded like madness, somehow

he had been trying to see inside her. He had opened her up to his invasion and used her desire against her.

Just like Almont.

His face, so close to hers—his dark searching eyes that seemed to spear deep into her—

He was a stranger. She knew nothing about him but what he wished her to know. He was full of secrets and thoughts and motivations that she was never going to be privy to.

And yet he not only wanted the truth from her—which she had always given him—but he wanted her to prove the unprovable.

23

She would not run from this battle. She would not hide away. She would not disappear to make his betrayal easier.

Raising her hands, she cupped his jaw in her palms. "I am not the only one here," she whispered. "There is a man inside you who is here with me too."

Meaningless, perhaps, but it made something real flicker behind his mysterious eyes.

"I am here with you," he said.

She smiled sadly, letting the tips of her fingers trace through the hair at his temples. "No. You are somewhere else entirely. You are in another room, talking to another woman. Whoever you think you are talking to . . . she isn't me." She caressed the sharp cut of his cheekbone with her thumb. "You are talking to the notorious liar Lady Alicia Lawrence, conniving gold digger, infamous tart. You are so busy not believing her that you cannot see the truth." She stood on her tiptoes and leaned forward to whisper in his ear.

"That woman doesn't exist," she said softly. "She never did. There is only Alicia, naïve and self-important, perhaps, a mostly innocent girl tricked and trapped and thrown to the street, stripped of everything but one hundred pounds and a loyal nursemaid."

She eased back and kissed him softly on the lips. "I can introduce you to her if you like."

Stanton didn't believe her. He wanted to, for it would make everything simpler. It would make everything wonderful, in fact. But without his skill he was lost, subject to suspicion and wildly vacillating doubt. What if she was? What if she wasn't? What if she was manipulating him this very moment? What if he became so wrapped up in her that he no longer cared?

He had to know. He had to finish this, one way or the other.

As she pulled away from the kiss, he followed, diving down onto her mouth with all his desperation and urgency channeled into an intense need to *know*.

He used everything he knew, everything he'd ever heard of. His hands roved over her body like a sculptor, creating her passion, building her desire from his necessity and her isolation. It was wrong. It was trickery. It was the only avenue left open to him.

He had to know.

She was leaning back against the wall, hands spread at her side, her throat arched and her eyes closed, submitting to his manipulative ravagement like a goddess on a sacrificial altar.

He pushed up her nightdress and parted her thighs with his knee. She opened willingly, still silent, still withdrawn into feeling his touch. Stanton plunged his fingers into her two at a time, stealing her moans from her lips with hot kisses, driving her to the edge of madness again and again—then slowing, easing, robbing her of the peak. He did it again and again, until she clutched at him, protesting, begging, the broken gasping words half-formed on her lips.

He captured her hands in one of his and pulled his cravat free with the other. With the length of linen, he tied her wrists together and flipped the end of the cravat over the iron sconce on the wall to keep her hands from interfering. "Stay," he commanded.

She opened her eyes, blinking against the daze of unfulfilled arousal. Her lips moved, then she swallowed hard. "Stant—"

He drove two fingers into her wet slick opening once more, hard and fast, thrusting like a maddened lover, rotating the flat of his thumb against her clitoris. She gasped and shuddered and the protest never came into being.

He used her hard, taking her closer and closer before stopping, until she teetered on such an edge of eruption that the only thing holding her upright was the cravat tied about her wrists.

Alicia fought back the hurricane of need within her—oh, God, what was she becoming?—to look up to see that eerie detachment in Wyndham's gaze once more. She ought to stop this—it wasn't right to allow him to—

This was wrong. She couldn't remember precisely why at this moment, but deep inside she knew it was—

Wrong—it was wrong—

It was splendid.

She let her objections slip from her mind with relief, setting herself free to feel the exquisite pleasure of his skilled hands . . .

You'll be sorry.

She rolled her head against the wall, erasing the annoying whine of some disturbing insect. He was all around her, enthralling her, giving her such pleasure that she blissfully feared she might very well die from it before he finally fulfilled her.

What could possibly be wrong with that?

Finally, she exploded at his command. She cried his name out loud, amid keening gasps of pleasure. Her knees dissolved and she hung helpless from the sconce, panting.

He unhooked the cravat from its mooring and let her looped arms fall around his neck. Bending, he wrapped one arm beneath her watery knees and, with the other arm supporting her back, lifted her in his arms.

He crossed the room to lay her across the giant bed. She felt him untie the simple knot that held her wrists, distantly embarrassed to note that she likely could have untied it herself—had she wanted to.

Then she felt his weight settle next to her on the bed. "Lie to me," he growled, his voice dark and desperate. "Lie, damn you!"

She opened her eyes to look at the only man she could imagine giving herself to so wholeheartedly. If only he could see her. "I will not lie to you. I love you."

I love you. Words he never thought he'd hear a woman say.

And he couldn't tell if it was true.

24

Alicia awoke the next morning with one sore shoulder and a—well, it was a little sore, but not as much as it had been five years ago. Actually, all things considered, she felt quite good.

The frightening encounter last night had been nearly erased from her memory by Stanton's hands. There was still much to resolve between them, for he had all but fled from her when she had confessed her love for him.

She rolled over sleepily and glanced toward the fire. Stanton was sprawled in the stiff chair, his big body looking entirely uncomfortable stretched awkwardly from his slouched position.

Alicia shed her covers and padded across the room to get a better look. Stanton rarely held still long enough for truly thorough observation. She knelt on the floor before him, tucking her gown beneath her feet to fight the chill. Garrett—being Garrett—hadn't come in to light the fire yet, so sure was he that the gold gown had done its job.

Perhaps it had, at that.

Stanton sleeping was a very different sort of man. His

brow was slightly furrowed but his jaw was relaxed. He looked altogether younger and more handsome. His hair was quite mussed, hanging over his brow and curling over his ear and jaw.

His shirt was open down the front placket and Alicia was tempted by the mat of dark hair she saw there. How odd that, as intimate as they had been, she had never seen him unclothed—not even without his boots until now!

His legs stretched out on either side of her, his big feet in naught but his stockings, his big hands resting on his thighs.

His trousers tightened over his stiffened rod.

She blinked. All by itself? In his sleep?

Now, in the dim light of morning, she could see the length and breadth of his organ as it pressed tightly against the tented fabric.

Stanton had not made love to her. He had not undressed, he had not revealed himself, he had not replied when she told him she loved him. Instead, he had left her on the bed, practically running from the room.

As Alicia saw it, she was owed a bit of male . . . barter.

She didn't want to wake him too soon, but there were a few things he owed her.

Her memory buzzed with the scandalous ideas she had been exposed to last night. There had been one fancy concerning Lady Davenport and a wing chair . . .

Was it physically possible?

Well, faint heart never won fair knight! Alicia rose carefully and stood before Stanton. With a quick push at the sleeves, her gown slipped to the floor. She placed both hands on the chair arms and managed to straddle her thighs across them without so much as disturbing Wyndham's hair. Then she reached between them and slowly, carefully undid the buttons on either side of his trousers.

His erection sprang free. She imagined it looked a bit relieved, for it grew yet more as she watched. She felt her own sex throb in response. She had been satisfied last night, but her body knew there was more and was still ready for it.

She wished she dared lower her body and impale herself upon it, but that seemed a bit . . . presumptuous. Instead, she slowly dropped down to cover his hard flesh with her soft center. The position of her thighs opened her until his shaft pressed lengthwise along her cleft and pressed firmly against her lu—her clitoris. The pressure was delicious and the wicked exposure made her rotate her hips involuntarily.

Stanton shifted. His rod pressed hard to her and she gasped in response. His eyes flew open.

Instantly, his hands came up to wrap over her shoulders. She would have preferred her breasts, but he was close.

"What are you doing?"

Alicia snorted a little breathlessly. "I make it a point never to answer stupid questions," she said. "Take off your shirt."

"No. This is—" He tried to press her away, but she grabbed tight to the back of the chair.

This put her breasts swaying right before his face. He shut his eyes and moaned. Alicia inhaled deeply. Her nipple grazed his cheek, only an inch from his lips.

He twitched involuntarily and his mouth grazed her nipple. His eyes opened once more, his expression glazed with hunger.

"You owe me," Alicia said. "A gentleman always pays his debts."

Stanton swallowed hard. She was naked, in his lap, wet and hot against his aching erection, her heavy breasts before him like a feast before a starving dog—how much was a man expected to bear?

She bent forward to kiss his neck. She bit him slightly, making him jump. "Wake up, Wyndham. I want you inside me."

She was too much for him—too sweet, too hot, too irresistible. He was going to regret every moment—and he was fairly sure he was going to remember it for the rest of his life.

"Rise a little," he said finally. "Lift up to let me in."

She smiled. It was a smile he had not seen on her before—a happy soft smile with none of her usual sarcastic twist of the lips. "You'll like me," she said, as she raised her body slightly. "You'll see."

Like her? He might alternately want to ravage her or kill her, but he could not imagine ever feeling an emotion as pale and insipid as "like" regarding Lady Alicia Lawrence.

He dropped his forehead onto her shoulder and rolled his head slightly, trying for one last moment of sanity. "Sweeting, we mustn't—"

She slid her warm, slippery vulva over the pulsating head of his cock and he lost the capacity for words.

"Like this?" She pressed the blunt head of him into her, wedging it into her tightness. He was going to die, right now. It was going to be a grand and glorious death.

She was having trouble fitting him in. This caused a delay full of slippery, excruciatingly pleasurable fumblings that stretched his control until he feared bursting in her hand.

Then she caught the proper angle and he pressed inside her carefully. She gripped his shoulders with damp hands and lowered herself down, inch by inch. She paused once, hissing in discomfort, but just as he was about to withdraw, she moved on again.

Alicia closed her eyes as she drove herself down upon his last iron inch. He filled her, stretched her, made her ache with mingled pain and pleasure, and she cherished every sensation. This man was her man, whether he knew it or not, whether he loved her or not, and she was made to take him inside her.

At last her body adjusted, easing his size with more heat

and wetness. She lifted herself slightly using her hands on the chair back—

And almost lost her grip from the pleasure that coursed through her. This was so much more than last night! She saw now that this was what was meant to happen between them, arousing mirror play notwithstanding.

She let herself sink back down upon him again, relishing his groan of pleasure. His big hands dropped to wrap about her waist and he lifted her higher this time and drove her down even more slowly.

He pierced her until she gasped, then lifted her again and again. She'd thought her role would be somewhat more athletic, but he took over the rhythm, teaching her to please them both by alternating speed with devastating patience.

The lesson went on, rising—falling—sliding— throbbing—

Every motion made her pleasure swell further. Every touch of his large hot hands made her tingle with the intimacy of his skin on hers.

Every moment made the end grow in pleasure, until her climax had her tossing her head back and keening with abandon.

She was raw and open and vulnerable to him as she had never yet been and still he could see nothing when he looked in her face—nothing but a sensuous beauty who melted his knees and wormed her way past his most fortified defenses with a smile and a touch.

In that moment, he knew. It wasn't her disclosure he needed most—it was his own admission he must hide at all cost. Tangled want and need and dread encompassed him. He could not let her see—for if she was who she was thought to be, she would use it against him. She would own him and that he could not allow.

And even if she were simply sweet and giving Alicia, still

he could not bear it. He could not allow himself to ever be as exposed and naked to the world as the world was to him. If they could see what he could see—

It was not to be allowed!

He pushed her away, abruptly lifting her from his flesh and setting her clumsily aside on the carpet before the fire.

She landed awkwardly on her hands and knees and gasped. Too late he remembered her experience the night before.

Then he remembered the rest.

It isn't true. None of it is true. She is a liar.

He stood, fastening his breeches while she gazed up at him with her eyes glazed and her lips parted, still stunned from the abrupt end to her orgasm. She looked wanton and sweet and he wanted nothing more than to sweep her into the bed and stay there forever.

God, he was alarmingly close to being lost in her!

He backed away, trying to make it seem like a casual motion instead of the full-blown cowardly retreat that it was.

"You are still tired from your . . . ordeal," he said lamely. "I shall let you—I will return—"

He gave up and fled the room. Yet, no matter how much distance he put between them, he could still feel her heat on his skin.

Or perhaps it had sunk deeper than that—as deep as his soul.

25

After Stanton had fled their bedchamber, Alicia had crawled back into the covers to shiver away her half-fulfilled arousal and warm her chilled heart.

Now, she was unable to stay there one moment more, when she knew beyond doubt Stanton would not be returning to her.

She dressed herself—a surprisingly awkward task, for one who had been independent for so long. The new gowns, however, were made for a lady who never needed to reach her own buttons. The most practical garment was the fine riding habit, which prompted Alicia to consider a long ride—perhaps even one that ended far from this place.

At the stables, she asked for a horse to be readied. Any gentle mount would do. She'd been a good rider once, but she was no longer used to the saddle. As she dawdled in the cobbled yard, she saw an ungainly cart rumble around the side of the great house and aim, more or less, for the stable yard.

On the driver's bench sat a much-bundled figure, too short to be a man, too strange to be anything else. As the cart meandered nearer, Alicia was able to make out a shock of white hair, a strangely humped back and bright, twinkling eyes.

The disgruntled horse came to a halt a bit left of the graveled path and tossed his head as if to say, "Will someone get this maniac off my reins?"

Alicia took pity on the poor beast and took the pull of the reins into her own gloved hands, giving the creature's sore mouth a much-needed break from the bit. The driver applauded with glee, as if she'd done something terribly clever.

"Oh, that's a good girl!"

Alicia looked askance at him, but the driver was already clambering rather badly from the seat to the ground. He ended his precarious journey with a bit of a stagger, then turned to bestow a wide smile on her. "That's the ticket, lovey!"

Alicia had had a very long night. The last thing she wanted was to be called pet names by a strange—*very* strange—man. She frowned at the fellow. "If you call me that again, I shall not only let go, I shall swat him smartly on the rear and wave as he takes off with your goods!"

"Of course you will. Don't blame you a bit. I've atrocious manners, always have." He grinned unrepentantly. Large white teeth gleamed through the grizzle of many days unshaven and his eyes danced beneath outrageously bushy brows. "You're a tasty morsel in that fitted riding habit, so I'll endeavor not to frighten you off. I'm long past courting buxom women, but I'll never tire of gazing at them!"

She couldn't help the short laugh that bubbled up. The fellow took encouragement and bowed briskly. Good heavens, that wasn't so much a hump as it was the most horrendous slump she'd ever seen. It looked as if he spend every moment of his life bending over something that interested him so much he'd not a care for his posture. She could just see him poring over ancient manuscripts or perhaps modern marvels of clockwork.

"I am Forsythe, mad inventor and fire-starter." He nodded again, bobbing his head repeatedly. "That's why I like you, I think. You look like a candle in the gloom, yourself."

She smiled slightly. "That's a rather elegant way of saying I've red hair."

He blinked rapidly, peering more closely. "Is it really? I can't see a thing under those horrid bonnets you lot wear." He turned away to begin untying the many ropes that bound his top-heavy load upon the cart. "You don't happen to have a few stout lads hanging about, do you? Aren't all pretty ladies surrounded by stout lads?"

Alicia grimaced. "Not this one, actually."

He glanced back at her, although he had to look under his arm, not over his hunched shoulder. "Ah, then there is only one stout lad, and he's giving you fits."

Alicia leaned one arm on the withers of the stolid horse. "Absolute cat fits," she agreed wearily. "I rather think I've had enough, thank you."

"Ha." He turned back to his knots, which looked complicated and numerous enough to take up most of the day. "You're mad for the blighter, more's the pity. I'll bet he's a big lad—tall, dark and looming. He'll be as rich as Midas and titled to boot, for only a man like that could be arrogant enough to give cat fits to a fire-goddess, when he ought to be on his knees in worship."

Alicia blinked at the compliment. "Not that I disagree with your assessment, mind you, but how did you know all that? Are you acquainted with Lord Wyndham?"

The fellow rolled his head back under his armpit to blink at her. "Wyndham? That's your stout lad?" He pulled hard upon a single strand of rope—and the entire matter undid itself to slither to his feet. "There, that's done it. Now I need those strong backs." He started for the stable at a strange loping pace, looking for all the world like a stork in a hurry.

Alicia remained where she was, for now she dared not let

the horse take a single step for fear of toppling the piled cart load. It was only a moment before Mr. Forsythe returned with several eager "stout lads" from the stable staff.

One took the horse from Alicia, who stepped back out of the way to watch curiously as they began to unload the crates and boxes under the leaping, gyrating direction of Forsythe.

"No, no, you lout! You mustn't jostle the contents! Do you want the Chinese rockets to explode before they've even reached the sky?"

The stable lads were more respectful of their burdens thereafter, and Mr. Forsythe stepped back to join Alicia in watching the show.

"So you're Lady Alicia Lawrence."

Alicia turned her head to gaze at the man. Here it was again—that odd awareness people had of Wyndham and the circle of his personality. The Prince Regent had known, the Sirens had known, and now this man. Moreover, they seemed to know Wyndham himself as more than common gossip would have him.

The Four Horsemen—or whatever they called themselves—were becoming more mysterious by the moment. Prince George had enacted some sort of personal revenge upon Stanton by declaring him the Lord of Misrule. The Sirens and their husbands remained ever on the periphery of Stanton's presence, watching and waiting—for what, Alicia couldn't imagine.

And now this man, who had just arrived, knew enough about her and Wyndham to turn to her and say, "You'd be good for him. The lad's not the easiest sort."

Alicia lifted her chin. "Neither am I, I have heard." She certainly didn't seem to be easy for Wyndham to—well, to accept.

To need.

To love.

"Would you like to see my creation?" Forsythe asked, changing the subject with abrupt kindness, his rheumy gaze sympathetic without being syrupy. He stepped aside to bow her gallantly forward. "We're almost done, if you'd like to see."

The "creation" turned out to be a whimsical structure seated on a vast side lawn of the great house. As they neared it, Alicia at first thought it much larger than it was, for the scale was somehow oddly wrong. It was as if a fairy castle had been plucked from some place where people were perhaps half the size they were in this world.

It was all there, ramparts and fantastical minarets, arched windows and even a delightful drawbridge over a recently dug moat that servants were even now filling with pails of water.

"That's to keep the fire from spreading," Forsythe confided. "We wouldn't want to burn in our beds."

Alicia turned to gaze at him in confusion. "You're going to burn it down?"

"Ah," Forsythe danced away, spinning with arms wide. "We're going to burn it *up*!"

"Fireworks!" Alicia exclaimed in delight. "I haven't seen fireworks in years!"

"You've never seen fireworks like these," Forsythe boasted. "This display will be visible for miles. No one will be able to hear for a week!"

Now that she knew what to look for, Alicia could see that the castle structure was bristling with rockets and spinners and there were countless iron brackets, ready to hold more. "When?"

"On the last night of the party. It is a special commission by the Prince Regent. Georgie always did love the toys I made for him."

Alicia smiled, but it faded when Mr. Forsythe turned

away to encourage his moat-fillers. A man who called the Prince Regent "Georgie."

She turned back to the stable to tell the groom that she didn't need a horse after all. There would be no riding away not from this game.

She was playing with fire herself, coming into circles such as these, with nothing but her wits and her smile to arm her. She must keep her thoughts to herself, for she was a pawn on a board full of royalty—with her own future and her sisters' at stake.

Truth and lies. The truth we know and the lies we tell ourselves.

She was in love with Lord Wyndham.

You're a lady, more than high enough to wed a man like him.

If she wasn't notorious. Although that could be repaired.

She would be the Marchioness of Wyndham. No one in Society would dare to speak a word of her past. Her life would be wiped clean with the strength of Wyndham's wealth and power. She would be new.

She would be a fool not to want that. Her sisters would be raised back to their former level, higher even with the dowries and connections she could give them. Her parents would welcome her home with open arms, smiles wide. She could save them all.

But what of me? Am I to be sold for their sakes once more? Am I nothing to them, to myself?

Am I merely currency in this business of status and society?

She returned to the room to change. Now that she was no longer bent on escape, she felt rather silly in the riding habit.

Wyndham was there, obviously waiting for her. When she entered, he stood quickly from his seat by the fire.

He looked rather weary and worried himself. She thought perhaps he was worried about what had happened last night—or rather, this morning. She put on a warm smile to reassure him. If she could make his mind easy, then he might tell her what kept him at such a distance.

"Good day, my lord. Have you had an enjoyable morning?"

His jaw clenched visibly and he looked away. Heavens, that wasn't her meaning at all!

Stanton felt something stretch painfully inside him, as if two warring armies were pulling at his soul. She was so lovely, and all he could think about was her sweet abandon that morning. He'd been sitting in that damned chair, remembering, and getting harder by the moment.

She was also a liar, and had brought him to this bedeviled party—this shameless orgy that had trapped and haunted him with the sounds and sights of sex for days on end! He was here on the whim of an irresponsible madwoman who had tricked him out thousands of pounds and made a fool of him in a way he could never forgive.

And still he wanted her. He shook inside from the ache of wanting her—now, in the chair, on the floor, up against the mullioned window for all the world to see—

He hated her as much as he lov—

No. He cut that thought off harshly. No.

So, one last test. One last chance for her to prove her story, one last chance for him to save his heart from the razor talons of loving someone who was undeserving.

"There is something I must ask of you."

Alicia leaned away, alarmed. "You are very serious today—rather, even more serious than usual."

Please do not mean to propose! She had not resolved her emotions on that count. If he asked too soon, she could not give him the ready answer he deserved.

"Lady Alicia," he began formally, "I have a request that is of the utmost importance to us both."

She swallowed. Oh, dear.

"My lady, I must ask—nay, beg of you—to take on a most serious purpose. I must know . . ."

She held her breath. Suddenly, she was no longer unsure. Suddenly, her feelings for Stanton snapped into perfect, lovely clarity.

She loved him. She wanted to be his wife. She wanted to spend her days with him, to hell with Society and its expectations, to hell with the included reward to those who had betrayed her. Let them benefit, for she had no more reason to hate them. They had brought her to this moment, to this man.

"I must ask that you allow me to offer you as a lure to our mystery lord."

She frowned. "But we found him last night! Did he escape you?"

He worked his jaw. "That man is not the man you heard outside the White Sow. That man is a close friend of the Prince Regent's, who was with the prince—*in sight* of the prince yet—on the night you claim you heard this conspiracy."

You claim. Something was not right. Alicia stepped forward, intent on discovering what had gone so terribly wrong. "You caught the man I handed to you last night—you questioned him—you heard his voice! Is he not precisely as I described?"

Stanton nodded shortly. "He is. He is also undeniably innocent."

"But how can that be? I heard him—"

A flicker of distaste crossed Wyndham's expression—a mere shadow, but she had seen it before. The morning she'd awoken to the shocked gasps of her parents and their carefully planted 'witnesses'—the morning she had told her story

ver and over to an unreceptive audience—the moment she
ad become a liar.

Alicia felt as though a pit had opened at her feet and her
ery blood was draining from her body, leaving her hollow
nd cold. Someone wanted to harm the Prince Regent.
omeone wanted to harm *her*.

And that someone was still out there.

"A lure, you say? I'm to be bait, you mean." Her voice
vas scarcely more than a harsh whisper, when she had rather
been hoping for a scream.

He looked her in the eye, of course. Always honest, al-
vays true—to himself. She could see through him like glass
nd what she saw was nothing. He meant to throw her before
he lion, his own heart safe outside the cage.

"I shall do my best to see to your safety, but I must appre-
tend this man. You are the one thing I can offer him that will
urely bring him from hiding."

Sold again. She felt her lips stretch in a brittle smile. "At
east someone wants me."

He stiffened further, if iron could get any stiffer. "I regret
hat I can see no other way. We have only one day left. If you
begin to tell the story of what you overheard, minus a few per-
inent details, then he will hear of it and seek you out. He will
vant to know if you have more information, and whom you
lave given that information to."

She gazed at him, the man she loved, the man who had
ust proposed she tease a killer. "And while I'm flinging my-
elf bodily before the speeding pit cart, what will you be do-
ng?"

"I will be close by, watching for him. When he ap-
proaches and you have positively identified him, you will
wave to me and I will intervene."

He sighed. "I regret deeply asking you to do this."

"And yet you have done it so well," she said softly. She
net his gaze with a brittle smile. "Oh, don't let it bother you,

mate. It isn't as though I need a hero." She turned away an
took up her hat, setting it on her head with a cocky til
"What do you think? Am I tasty?"

Stanton, of course, being Stanton, could not let it go. "
must beg your forgiveness, Alicia."

She shook off his hand. "Beg, beg, beg. All you need to d
is ask. Either I will forgive or I won't. Begging won't affec
the outcome either way, unless you make me sick of it."

His pride snapped into play, just as she had counted on. H
bowed his head sharply. "Then my thanks are in order, m
lady. You are doing a greater service than you know."

He turned then and strode out of the room, his bac
straight and his brows together.

"Oh, I know what I doing," she said softly to the empt
room. "I want this man caught as well, for I am well done wit
this false love affair." She rang for Garrett and prepared her
self to reenter the social whirl of the party, this time armee
with entertaining conversation of the highest order.

"Here, kitty, kitty, kitty," she whispered to her reflection
She undid the tiny covered buttons of her riding habit
"Come and eat the helpless little bird."

At the last moment before Garrett entered, she thrust th
letter knife with the mother-of-pearl handle into her reticule
It was too long, so she repositioned it in her bodice, down be
tween her breasts. "I must remember not to slouch," she sai
archly to the girl in the mirror. " 'Tisn't proper, and it wil
hurt like hell."

She would find the bastard who had started this chain o
events. She would find him and hand him over to Stanto
and then she would disappear from their sight forever. All o
them.

After leaving their room Stanton walked slowly down th
hall. He could not—would not—allow himself to regret wha
he had just asked Alicia to do. She was the only link to thi

nad chain of seemingly unconnected events and coincidences. If—God, always "if"! Would it never be "when"?—he became able to see the truth in her, then he could dispense with such dangerous plans.

Until then, he could not allow his strange and growing attachment to her keep him from fulfilling his duty. It comforted him that he'd been able to ask her to do such a thing. Of course, if she was lying, it was all a farce anyway, so nothing was lost. If she was being truthful, then they just might be able to lay hands upon the Chimera at last—and he would find a way to explain his actions to Alicia.

He was sure he would.

26

Alicia immediately went about her assignment with brittle glee. She plunged herself into the party's afternoon entertainments and made herself alternately lust-worthy and adorable. She shot pistols on the south lawn with the ladies—she lost carelessly and laughed it aside. She invaded the male-dominated card rooms, billiard rooms and smoking rooms and made them enjoy her intrusion. She talked to men, women and servants until her throat was dry—and every one heard the story of the conspiracy at the White Sow.

Of course, she prettied up the tale, calling the filthy pub a "coaching inn" and claiming she was merely strolling through the yard. No privies, no details of the strawberry jam ignominy.

She was merry, she was stunning, she was everywhere, for she had nothing to lose now. Wyndham believed her a liar—moreover, Wyndham thought she'd lied to *him*.

She would never be free of it, never be trusted, never speak and have her words taken for simply what they were. She would be Lady All-three-cia until the day she died. All she

could hope for now was that she could avoid taking her sisters
down with her.

At last, wearied beyond smiling, beyond speech, she
made her way back to her bedchamber to dress for dinner
where, she was sure, she wouldn't be able to ask please-
pass-the-butter.

When she opened the door, she found the room dark and
the fire cold. Where was Garrett? Something papery crack-
led beneath her foot as she made her way to the candelabra
on the mantel. She absently bent to pick it up and stuck it
into her pocket as she returned to the hall and lit the tapers
from the one burning sconce several yards down the way.

The room was chill, making her weariness triple upon itself, so she rang for someone to tend the fire and to fetch
Garrett for her. While she waited, shivering, she remembered the paper on the floor.

She took it from her pocket and unfolded it in the light of
the candles. Tight, perfect letters turned frightening by the
blurred pen, as if the writer had been shaking with rage—or
madness.

> *You are the only one who knows the truth. You are not worth the
> breath you waste. I must kill you. You will die and my plan will
> succeed. I will take him away and England will be lost. I will
> kill you slowly and you shall die knowing that I have won. You
> will cry and beg and I shall listen and laugh. You will die like the
> puling bitch you are, bleeding in the mud. I shall watch and en-
> joy.*

The vicious delight in the horrible words was more frightening than the words themselves. He would enjoy it, the bastard.

Except that it wouldn't happen. She held the proof in her
hand. Wyndham would see now that the threat to the Prince
Regent was very true—and so was she.

She thrust the letter back into her pocket and flew to the door. As she sped down the dimly lighted hall, she brushed against a liveried servant toting a bucket of coal. "I shall be back momentarily," she called over her shoulder. "Find my maid, if you please!"

The man nodded and Alicia picked up speed, taking the grand stairs at a full run. She found Wyndham almost immediately, in a card room with the other of the Horsemen, ever Lord Dryden, who seemed to act as a sort of second for Lady Julia.

She skidded to a stop before the green felted card table. "Wyndham, I have it! I have your proof! He's in the house!"

The cards scattered as the gentlemen rose as one. "Where?"

"I found this in our room," she said, thrusting her hand into her pocket. "Someone had put it under the door—"

There was nothing in her pocket. She felt the other seam, although she knew there was no pocket there. She looked up at Wyndham, alarm beginning to tingle through her.

He was gazing back at her with that hateful hardness increasing in his eyes. "I ran all the way here," she explained quickly. "It must have fallen out—"

She turned to retrace her steps, casting this way and that back along her trail, bending to peer under side tables as she ran. The four lords followed her more slowly.

She found nothing, though she searched carefully all the way back to the dimly lit hallway outside their bedchamber—

Dimly lit. Never before had the hall been lit by one sconce. Lord Cross was nothing if not flagrant with his beeswax candles.

She had brushed by a servant, a small man who had averted his face—

A man who had picked her pocket like a street thief.

No. She turned back to Wyndham and the others, who stood there with varying degrees of disdain on their faces. "Lady Alicia," Wyndham stated sourly, "I am willing to wait until this man shows his face. There is no reason to prevaricate reasons to continue this investigation."

She shook her head, holding out her hands. "It is true, I vow it. He said he would kill me and laugh while I died. He said he would take the prince away and England would be lost."

"With due respect, Lady Alicia, that doesn't sound quite right." Lord Dryden rubbed the back of his neck a bit sheepishly. "While we would all miss Prince George—I hardly think England would be lost without him."

It was all happening again. She couldn't bear it. She turned to Wyndham, the only face upon which she wanted to see belief. "It is true, my lord. I can tell you everything it said, every word. It was a cruel and vicious letter, full of madness—"

"The man we seek is not mad," Wyndham said coolly. "Brilliant and cruel, yes, but not mad. Nor is he inclined to write schoolgirl notes. You have mistaken your gambit, my lady."

Julia couldn't breathe. "I—it wasn't—"

Wyndham turned away. "Gentlemen, we have a card game to finish."

The others followed him, although Lord Dryden did cast her a thoughtful look over his shoulder as he left. Lord Greenleigh paused before one of the unlit sconces briefly, sent a single unreadable look back at Alicia, then followed the others.

Sickened and unsteady, Alicia reached one hand to the wall while she fought to bring breath into her lungs. Wyndham's face—

I will kill you slowly and you shall die knowing that I have won.

She had lost the only one who had believed her. Alicia began to wonder if the madman hadn't won already.

The flame-haired girl had fallen for his ruse like a fox to the hounds.

The scarred man cackled and rubbed his hands together as much in glee as to gain warmth. He was a lord in a castle of his own once more, a sturdy castle of made of fire and death. It was a brilliant piece of work, although not truly worthy of the mind that had created this toy for that fat, infantile sot of a prince.

He reached a tremor-ridden hand out to stroke the wall of his fine, lordly abode. He must leave it soon, but he would take such fond memories away with him. He only wished he'd been there to see the look on that slut's face when she found nothing in her pocket.

He cackled again, enjoying the sound in the enclosed walls of his new kingdom. It was only a sturdy shack on the inside, but wasn't that always the way with these fine houses? All grandeur outside, all shabby former elegance within.

He would build himself a castle in Lourdes with his reward, he decided whimsically. A castle with turrets and minarets . . .

"And fireworks every night." His rasping voice filled the room, then all faded to silence once again.

But not for long.

The remainder of the "card game"—which was really a meeting of the Four masquerading as a great amount of shuffling and dealing—was called due to, as Lord Dryden put it, "an overabundance of brooding."

Stanton's fault, of course, but it had been a mighty blow to have his darkest suspicions of Alicia fulfilled so publicly—or at least, before the other Three. Damn it all to hell. Why couldn't she have been the woman he thought her? Why couldn't he have found the one woman in the world who brought him out of the prison of his own nature?

He tossed his hand down and stood. "I'll send her away," he told the others abruptly. "I'll pay her for her time and send her far away."

Lord Greenleigh leaned back in his chair and crossed massive arms. "How far do you think you can send her? Is there a city on the moon?"

Stanton frowned. "You're not suggesting—"

Lord Reardon stood as well. "Greenleigh, don't be ridiculous. The girl doesn't know anything. And no one would believe her if she did."

"I am not saying we have her terminated. I'm saying that we should consider the fact that money and distance might not entirely solve the problem."

Stanton narrowed his eyes. "And what problem might that be?"

Greenleigh gazed back evenly, undaunted by the Falcon's glare. "The problem that you're in love with her—or at least, you're infatuated with her."

Stanton gritted his teeth. *Infatuated.* "That's ridiculous. I admit that my investigation has led me to—there have been—"

"I'll wager there have been—several times, by the look of you two. Is she in love with you?"

The question bothered him far more than he could fathom why. "I don't know. I'll never know, with her."

Lord Reardon was gazing at him with sympathy that Stanton could very well have done without. "Wyndham," Reardon said, "none of us have your skill at detecting lies . . . yet we all knew, eventually."

That was all he could bear. "You lot didn't fall in love with liars!" He turned to stride from the room, but he could hear his own voice echoing in his ears, very nearly admitting to something he was not willing to own.

He burst from the card room at top speed, rushing he knew not where, but anywhere *not* here.

"Wyndham."

His mother's voice stopped him in his tracks. He turned to see her beside the card room door, obviously waiting to ambush him. He clasped his hands behind his back and tried to pull the old mask of cool aloofness over his face. "Hello Mother."

Caroline came close to him, putting one hand gently on his arm. "I was coming to see Lady Alicia before I left, to find how she'd weathered her ordeal in the garden last night . . . and I heard what you said to her in the hall."

Stanton closed his eyes briefly. How perfect. Now his mother knew things she shouldn't know. Where had his faultless control gone, and why now, when he needed it the most? "It was nothing, Mother. She—she made a mistake and I was upset with her. A trifling matter."

"You don't trust her." Caroline pressed her lips together. "I think it must be my fault that you don't trust her. She does seem to be a great deal like me, at least on the surface—"

"She is not—"

Caroline shook her head with a small smile. "No, of course not. I'm glad you see it. She is a much better woman than I have ever been, although she does give me hope for myself."

She patted his arm again, seeming much reassured. "I ought to have known you would see how perfect she is for you. I hope you'll do everything you can to staunch those horrid rumors about her being a liar. I know that awful young man who caused her difficulties. Trust me, darling, the only thing she is guilty of is trusting the wrong man."

Dark cynicism invaded Stanton's heart, easing the pain of

doubt, sparing him the thought of future loss. "Oh, I don't think she's guilty of that," he said cryptically. "I must see her now, Mother. Excuse me."

Lady Alicia had hoodwinked her last Wyndham.

27

Alone in their room, Alicia pondered what she had done to herself, all without the help of homicidal maniacs. In her obsession with vengeance, she missed the moment when she'd passed the point of no return.

So, thinking she had nothing to lose, she set out to be very, very bad—and hadn't realized how wrong she was until she'd lost the one thing she couldn't live without—the respect of the man she loved.

A man like him—an upright, ethical, demanding fellow, as demanding of himself as he ever would be of her—would not want her.

She might try to correct the mistake. She could become as demure as a nun, as circumspect as a queen. It might kill her and she feared that future, but there was no point in even trying.

At that moment, Wyndham burst into the bedchamber so hard that the door bounced back off the wall and slammed itself behind him. Alicia leaped up, startled.

Her words of surprise and admonishment died on her lips as she took in his black expression of rage and self-disgust.

"You are my worst nightmare," he growled. "You are the

woman who sails in and wreaks havoc on all around her, then sails away again laughing at the carnage."

Alicia backed a step away. "I—"

He moved closer, leaning forward, his eyes gone dark like a predator ready to strike. "You will not wreak havoc on me!"

Alicia's back hit the corner post of the bed, making her realize her own cowardly retreat. Her spine straightened and she gaze back at Wyndham with equal fury.

"You pretend that you didn't want me, but I am no virgin, Wyndham! I know when a man lusts!"

"I imagine you do," he said harshly. "I imagine it is your signal to do your worst!"

She lifted her chin. "I did nothing to you but tell you the truth every moment we've spent together. If that isn't enough for you . . . well, then nothing is. And nothing is precisely what you'll get!"

He grabbed both her shoulders in his big hands, not hurting but not gently either. "You're right. I do want you. I want to see inside of you, to get to the truth of you—but you refuse to let me in!"

He tightened his grip and then she did let out a small sound of pain, for her shoulder still stung from her encounter in the garden.

He eased his hands but he did not release her. "If you will not lower your gates," he said, his voice low and dangerous, "then I will have to storm the keep myself."

He pulled her close then, dragging her into him and bringing his mouth hard down on hers. Alicia kissed him back, just as angry, just as lost—just as alone.

Wyndham released his grip to take her fully into his arms and she wrapped her hands around the back of his neck, pulling the kiss deeper yet.

Then the floor was hard beneath her back and the carpet prickly against her bare bottom as he yanked up her skirts.

A swift adjustment at the front of his trousers and then

he threw himself upon her. She tossed her head and keened when he invaded her so harshly, but she was already slick with need and he caused more pleasure than pain.

She clung to him as he thrust violently into her, storming her gates again and again. She was swept by pleasure and longing and a wicked, shocking gratification in being conquered, in being helpless in the grasp of a virile male, her powerful lover—in being in his control.

She let him in, she let herself be his, half-naked and shamed and eager, but he could not see beyond his own walls.

She gave herself over and over again, being his goddess and his whore, his love and his creature of lust, desperate to show him that there was no other Alicia, that he had all of her there was to have—but he would not see.

He thrust into her a last, shuddering time with a deep gasping roar of self-hatred, then he rolled from her before she could breathe against the weight of him. He rose and fastened his trousers with his back to her.

Alicia pushed her skirts down and stood, raw and soul-bared and rejected, and took a deep breath. "Did that solve something for you? Did you see inside me?"

He rubbed his face with his hands, but he did not look at her. "There is nothing inside you to see."

She jerked back, the pain like ice stabbing her soul.

He went on. "The deal is cancelled. I will pay you for services rendered. I want you on your way within the hour." He turned to the door, then paused. "Have you nothing to say to that?"

Alicia moved before him, blocking his exit with her back to the door. "Oh yes, you had best believe that I have something to say to that."

28

Alicia narrowed her gaze and reinforced her spine. She might be in love with the handsome idiot, but that didn't mean she couldn't let him see one more side of her—her red-headed temper! "I have been trying to translate every move you make and every word you say and don't say—and I am through. You don't truly want me to leave. If you have something to say to me, you'll have to find your own words."

He stood in rigid silence. She relented her stance slightly, reaching to trace her fingertips down the buttons of his weskit.

"The only word you need is 'stay.'"

He wanted to—God, he wanted it more than anything—except that if he did, if he chose to believe, if he asked—

What if she didn't love him? What if, someday, once the physical ecstasy faded, she turned from him? He was not courageous enough to survive being left by a woman like her. What if he couldn't keep her flame alight, burning only for him?

Stay.

Yet the words, not even the one, wouldn't come. Her eyes,

full of wary hope and ready to promise him so much, slowly went flat. The green of spring turned to cold jade as he watched, helpless to stop her pain. No. She wasn't real.

"How can you look into my eyes and not believe?" she whispered. "How can you know so much about me and not know that I love you?"

She backed away. "You've become so dependant on this sense of yours that you do not trust your others."

So she knew that, too. "What other senses would you suggest I trust?"

She looked up at him, trying to put her heart in her gaze. "This one." Going up on tiptoe, she kissed him with all the aching tenderness and longing she had within her. His mouth remained unresponsive beneath hers. With the pain of repressed tears in her throat, she gave up, pulling her lips away, dropping down on her heels, allowing her forehead to rest upon his immobile chest in defeat. "You're a right bastard, Lord Wyndham," she whispered.

She took a deep breath and straightened, meeting his gaze without trying to hide her pain. "You can believe anything you like about me, my lord. It doesn't change a bloody thing about the truth. I only hope you figure that out someday, if not about me, then about some other woman. Otherwise, I fear you are destined to always be as alone and troubled as you are now."

She raised her hand to his face, but halted as he stiffened. Tilting her head, she smiled slightly, ignoring the tears that were beginning to fall. "You deserve better than that." She stepped back and turned away, then looked back over her shoulder. "Most of the time."

"Where will you go?"

She took up her spencer and shrugged into it. "I am going. That is all I am going to tell you. After all, this quest of yours is a fool's errand, remember? My little snipe hunt, arranged purely for your humiliation, isn't that right?"

Then she turned abruptly. "You will keep an eye on his highness, won't you? Just in case?"

Wyndham gazed at her coldly. "The Prince Regent is well guarded, as always."

Alicia almost let her shoulders fall, but the ice in her lover's eyes only seemed to strengthen the steel in her spine. "Then there is nothing more to say. You may send the money to my family. Goodbye, my lord."

Somehow she did it. Somehow she opened the door and walked through it, though she felt the pull of a thousand bindings in her heart, tying her to him. Somehow she kept her feet moving down the hall and down the stairs, until she stood blinking in the bright light of day on the steps of the grand house.

A footman approached her. "May I assist you, my lady?"

She turned to smile at him, though she could not see him well through the blurring of her vision. "I shall need a carriage back into London." Then she laughed damply. "I believe Lord Wyndham's is available."

She would go back to London and to Millie. Then she and Millie would disappear from Wyndham's long reach.

Just as he wished.

She wasn't real. She never had been.

But the pain was. It stole Stanton's breath until his vision darkened. He forced his lungs to work, forced his legs to walk, forced his voice to normal lack of emotion instead of the animal howling that tried to work its way from his throat.

She wasn't real.

But the damage she had done would be with him forever. He could feel his need for her clawing its way up through his chest, shredding the barrier around his heart in the process.

No. Letting it out would leave him open to everything he'd fled his entire life. Everything he was, everything he'd created and named "self" would change, alter, slip away.

A man like him would never fall in love with someone so inappropriate.

A man like him would never fall in love. Ever.

Love was real, he knew that. Love was a beast that took hold of a man's better nature in its teeth and shook it to death like a terrier shakes a rat.

He'd seen firsthand the lethal power of love and the way it overwhelmed and drowned a man, rather like a tempest at sea where there is nothing solid to cling to and no land in sight.

Love would not defeat him. He'd worked too hard to overcome the everlasting need to be loved. He'd made his place in the world—needed and respected, but never, ever loved.

Now it was all shot to hell.

As if something in her eyes had awakened some sense in himself, he looked about him to see that he was surrounded by love.

His mother's hopeless, wistful, regretful love. Even his mentor's love of a father for a son, expressed only in a dry, hard handclasp on his deathbed before he'd slipped away.

"Wyndham, you look a sight." The full, fruity tones of the Prince Regent's voice were tinged with real concern.

Wyndham looked up at George in horror. There it was, gleaming behind the usual twinkling wicked humor in the prince's eyes—real caring.

Love.

Stanton dropped his head into his hands. How was he to defeat something so pernicious? How was he to resist the temptation to take his mother's hand, to clap George on the shoulder, to run his fingertips over Alicia's tear-streaked cheek?

"I'm done for," he whispered aloud.

George plunked his sizable bottom onto the settee next to Stanton. "I'll say. She's a sweet little minx, though, I'll give you that. You could do worse than to lose your heart to a woman like that."

"She's a liar."

George snorted. "Do tell. So is every person I've ever met. We're deceitful creatures. I decided long ago not to hear the lies. You've got to look past them to the fear. That's why people lie, you know—it's the fear. Fear that they'll be caught out, fear that they'll be rejected, fear that someone will discover they're just as weak and petty and evil as anyone else. And just as alone."

Stanton looked at George with surprise. He knew his monarch was not a stupid man, only a supremely unhappy and rebellious one—yet he still managed to forget that it was George who had changed London with his love of beautiful art and architecture. It was George who had loved and wed the most inappropriate woman imaginable, Maria Fitzherbert, in a passionate attempt to be the man he truly was, even if the dutiful Prince Regent had been forced to dissolve the union later for a political marriage to a woman who revolted him.

"You've seen your share of liars, I suppose," Stanton said. "What would you think if a woman said she loved you but wanted to leave you?"

George looked at him pityingly. "I'd ask her which part she was lying about, you ass."

29

They rode out together again—Dane, Nathaniel, Marcus and
Stanton. The others seemed to understand Stanton's need for
silence, although he did catch Marcus giving him the "you
idiot" look now and then, much the way George had.

The four of them rode side by side. Stanton had an irreverent moment, surely influenced by too much exposure to
Alicia.

The Four Horsemen of the Apocalypse. War, famine,
plague—*and then there's you, we'll call you "heartbreak."*

The day was mild and damp and edgy, as if the weather
merely awaited an excuse to worsen into full winter. Stanton
felt the air prickle on the back of his neck, just as it did when
he was being watched—

There was a man standing in the shadows of the fireworks
structure. He ducked back when Stanton spied him, but not
quickly enough to hide the impression of a scarred, damaged
face, pale in the shadow. Stanton reined his horse about.
"There!"

The others didn't require explanation, simply turning
their mounts as one with his.

So that's what brotherhood feels like.

It was only a fleeting thought, gone as soon as they thundered up to the castle, surrounding it on four sides. There was flat lawn for many yards around them. No one had run from the building while they approached it.

"He's in there," Stanton whispered to the others. "He cannot have run without our spotting him."

They dismounted swiftly, leaving their horses a distance from the structure. They wanted no clever escapes this time. The door opened easily with a push and they moved in a great rush—to see nothing inside.

The door of the little shed slammed shut. The four of them whirled.

"Oh, hell," Marcus breathed.

Stanton threw himself at the door hard. There was not so much as a creak. The shed, after all, was newly built and made sturdy enough to support the elaborate façade throughout the upcoming series of fireworks explosions.

Stanton stepped back. "Dane, why don't you take this one?"

Dane snorted. "Stand back then."

At the impact of the big blond lord on the door, there was a definite shudder through the structure, but that was all. Dane repeated his assault several times, but all that was accomplished was a great deal of noise.

At last Dane desisted and leaned both hands on his knees. "Whose brilliant idea," he gasped heavily, "was it to make the door lock from the *outside*?"

Stanton bent to peer at the latch. It was a good one, of course. After all, the structure was designed by Forsythe, a stickler for details. "Locked properly, with a key. Who has the key?"

Nathaniel looked thoughtful. "Forsythe, I imagine. George might, as well. Or Cross. Or the carpenter who built the bloody thing. There's no way to know."

Marcus rubbed at the back of his neck. "All of whom might have left it lying about where it could be taken. After all, we know who did this, even if we don't know precisely how he got the key."

Nathaniel straightened and nodded. "The comte. He wants to blow us up."

"The Chimera," Stanton growled, "is beginning to seriously plague me off."

Dane shook his head. "What would be the point of merely locking us up? The moment someone comes in earshot, we'll be released. The promenade display isn't completed. There'll be staff all over the place in a few hours."

Nathanial frowned. "This all seems rather . . . extemporaneous. I don't think it was planned. He might have had the key because he's been hiding out in here for the past few days. Look, there are signs that someone has been using this shed."

He was quite right. A pile of what seemed to be rags in one corner turned out to be a blanket rolled about a cheap flask and battered tinderbox. Nathaniel shook the flask, then uncapped it and sniffed. "Gut-rot gin," he said, grimacing. "Sooner kill you than not. You'd think a French lord would have better taste."

"He's in pain," Stanton said slowly. "He's been ill from nearly drowning, thanks to Dane, and wounded, thanks to your lady, Marcus. By all rights he ought to be holed up somewhere, recovering. That's what I would be doing, getting well, gathering my strength to battle anew."

"God," Nathaniel breathed. "He's not, though, is he? He's running on nothing, burning himself out. Why?"

"He's lost and he knows it." Dane let out a long breath. "We thought he was dangerous before. Now, imagine that man—that twisted-minded genius—gone to desperation, with nothing left to lose."

Marcus had gone white. *"Julia."*

Stanton nodded, battling down a surge of something very like terror. *Alicia.* She'd already been targeted twice. *And you didn't believe her either time.* His worry flared higher, until he remembered that Alicia had left him.

She was gone. Gone and safe.

It was better that way.

"Quite. It is obvious that he has taken advantage of opportunity to occupy us long enough to get at someone else—" Stanton halted, gazing around the dimly lit shed. The air seemed hazy, gone sharp with—

"Fire."

Stanton drew a breath, choked on it, coughed it away. "No," he gasped. *"Smoke."*

It was coming from under the door, billowing up darker now, black and deadly in the tight, airless confines of the shed. He pulled off his jacket and tried to block the gap. "Smoking us out—like badgers from a hole." Except there was no out. Nathaniel added his coat as well. The cloud ceased. They'd stopped it all.

Dane crouched. "Get down. The air is better. The smoke might yet vent—the shed isn't that—" He choked, coughed violently. "Isn't that airtight," he finished weakly, since they could all see that the shed was, in truth, appallingly airtight.

Dane abruptly sat, shaking his head and blinking. "It's not just smoke . . ."

Stanton could feel it as well. His vision blurred, the room tilted, the hazy dimness acquiring churning colors and shapes. "What—" He realized he was on his knees. No, on all fours.

Nathaniel dropped to the floor next to him. "Opium," he hissed.

Yes, it was opium, along with something even more acrid and unpleasant that turned the air in Stanton's lungs to scorching fire. He saw Marcus sprawled unconscious, Dane

just beyond him in the same condition. He held his breath—
too late, fool—and tried to crawl across the unconscious
bodies to the other side of the shed. If he pressed his lips to
that knothole, could he—

The big form of Lord Greenleigh was an insurmountable
obstacle. "Nate—help me—"

Nathaniel was passed out, one hand still pressing his coat
into the door gap. Stanton blinked dully at the three men for
a moment. He was floating above them—no, swimming beneath them . . .

He was alone. He absorbed that fact with no concern. It
was easier that way, always had been. The earthen floor beneath his cheek was damp and cool. It became a pillow, soft
and soothing. No, a breast, full and warm. He kissed it gently. Tender fingers tunneled into his hair, soothing the
pounding in his head. *Alicia.*

"You didn't leave." Joy bubbled through his veins. He'd
been a fool, an idiot, yet she'd stayed with him anyway.

"Yes," she said softly, as she turned her body into his
and pressed her warm, naked bounty against him. "I did.
I'm quite gone, you see. Just as you wished. Never to return."

He laughed. She was teasing. "You're not gone. You're
right here. I can feel you. You stayed with me. You love me."

She kissed his neck, his chest. He could feel the heat from
between her thighs sinking into his own groin, hardening
him. "No," she whispered into his skin. "I don't. I tried to,
but I couldn't. You made sure of that."

Fear stuttered his heart. He had done her so much harm—

He reached for her. "Stay. I'm sorry. I didn't want—I
love—" His arms closed around nothing at all but the chill of
her not being there. "Alicia!" There was no one there, nothing but blank, gray, aching solitude. Forever. *"Alicia!"*

* * *

Alicia leaned back against the tufted cushions of Wyndham's carriage and refused to cry. She was only an hour or so from Cross's estate, but she felt a million miles from Wyndham.

Of course, one might feel that way while in the same room with Wyndham, when he was in one of his brooding states.

It didn't matter. All his most annoying and painful attributes meant nothing when she thought about the fine and noble man shining out from inside him. When he—if he—opened his heart someday, some lucky woman was going to be blinded by the magnificence that hid behind those careful, watchful eyes.

The Falcon Lord, Lady Greenleigh had called him. How apt.

Her eyes burned in a rather permanent way that led her to believe that she might run through numerous handkerchiefs in the next months.

Years.

No. She wouldn't allow it. Her affair with Wyndham had been ill thought out, but it had not been a mistake. Or if it had, it had been a most glorious and worthwhile mistake. She would not spend her life regretting that he could not love her as she loved him.

She leaned her head back against the cushion and let the tears leak down her temples, into her hair. He was worth crying over, damn it.

The carriage slowed suddenly and Alicia leaned from her small window to discover the reason. There was a horseman riding beside them, waving the driver to one side. A horseman in Cross livery, yet.

The driver flipped open the trap to speak to her. "What d'you want me to do, milady? 'E says Lady Dryden sent him. Ought I to stop?"

Julia? "Yes, please do."

When the carriage halted and Alicia opened her door, the young man on the horse dismounted and bobbed his head respectfully. "Milady asked me to bring you this, milady." He handed over a folded missive. "And to fetch you back straightaway, she said."

Alicia took the note and unfolded it. It contained two lines in a long, elegant hand.

"He has made his move. Our husbands are missing and so is Wyndham."

30

Stanton was lying with his head on an anvil and a large, foul-smelling smith was hammering his temples.

No, wait . . . he was sitting up, with his hands bound behind him and he was fairly sure he was snoring.

He opened his eyes and blinked. No . . . that was Dane. The giant was sitting, bound like Stanton was, with his back to the other wall of the shed. The big man's snores were the smith's hammer. Stanton wished he had something to throw—and some hands to throw with.

"Dane!" Ow. His own rasping voice hurt his brain. He tried whispering. *"Dane!"*

"It won't do any good."

Stanton turned his aching head to see Marcus gazing blearily at him from the right wall. "Why not?"

Marcus's lips twisted in a not-smile. "He must have taken in more of the smoke than we did, because I've been yelling at him for a quarter of an hour and all that happened was that you woke up." His voice was as rasping as Stanton's. He shrugged. "I'm not very loud at the moment."

Stanton looked across the shed to where Nathaniel

sagged against his own bonds. "What about Nate? Why hasn't he come around yet?"

Nate stirred and opened his eyes. "Nate came around first, thank you," he muttered. "Nate's bloody sick of listening to the rest of you snoring the roof off the place. My head hasn't hurt this much since Willa knocked my horse out from under me." He looked around them at the stark interior of the shed. "The view when I woke up was a hell of a lot better then, however."

"Ooh. Ugh." At last, Dane halted the offensive racket and opened his eyes. He shut them again instantly. "Ow."

"Oh, thank God." Marcus's voice was weak with sincerity. "He's finally stopped."

"No talking," Dane mumbled, his eyes shut tight. "He who talks, dies."

"I'm pretty sure we're going to die anyway, Dane," Nate said with a sandpaper laugh. "Also, you're not very intimidating when you drool in your sleep."

Stanton drew his knees up and tried to get his feet beneath him. He was tied cleverly—his hands bound too high to allow him to sit comfortably, too low to allow him to stand. From what he could see, the others were in the same condition.

"Dane, are you strong enough to break your bonds?"

The blond Viking glared at him through one reddened eye. "I hate you, Wyndham. I just wanted you to know that."

"Yes, right. Try anyway."

Dane took a deep breath and pulled forward. Then he pulled to one side. Then the other. The shed creaked promisingly, but the post did not give.

Stanton let out a breath. "What about you, Marcus? Have you learned any tricks from that group of gypsy lunatics you call servants?"

Marcus grimaced. "They're called 'showmen.' Or 'fair folk.' Gypsies are another thing entirely—and I think I—"

He pulled his feet in, then arched his back until he was able to pull them beneath him to sit on his heels. He went into a series of very uncomfortable gyrations that got him nowhere but red-faced and severely out of breath. At last, he gave up and stretched his legs out before him once more. "Sorry, lads."

Stanton looked at Nathaniel. Nathaniel looked back at Stanton.

"I don't suppose you have some of Forsythe's magic matches in your pocket? If we burn the ropes . . ."

Stanton shook his head. "I couldn't reach them if I did. Nor do I think fire is advisable with all these explosives above us."

Nathaniel frowned. "Yet our friend risked it. You don't think we're in danger now, do you?"

Stanton tilted his pounding head back against the post and surveyed the ceiling of the shed. "He made a small fire at the base of the door that was mostly smoke, I think. Quick to put out with a stamp of the foot, most likely. Whatever he burned knocked us unconscious fairly quickly. I don't think there was much chance he did more than scorch the door." Then he grimaced. "But that doesn't mean he isn't planning on watching us burn to death when the fireworks go off tonight."

Marcus scoffed. "That's not likely, is it? Someone will be by before then. All we have to do is call out to get their attention."

Dane opened his eyes. "Maybe, or maybe not. We're all hoarse from the smoke. The display is ready to go. The fuse is already in place several yards off. By the time someone comes near enough to hear us, it might already be lighted."

Marcus looked worried. "But our horses? Someone's going to notice four horses milling around out here."

Dane shook his head carefully. "The Chimera is everything that is thorough. I wager that our horses are even now back in their stalls, munching oats, with every appearance of being properly put away. That's what I would do."

Nathaniel considered that for a long moment. "Well, bloody hell."

Stanton didn't bother to agree. There was no point in belaboring the obvious. Unless someone noticed their absence and made the rather outrageous leap of logic that they were therefore locked in the middle of the fireworks display, they were indeed going to go to bloody hell.

"You know," Marcus said, his tone mildly gleeful. "He missed Julia entirely—and she's the most dangerous one of us all."

Greenleigh brightened slightly. "That's true. That mistake might just tilt the scales, I think. If she realizes we're missing in time. Is she expecting you back at any certain time, Marcus?"

Marcus's demeanor fell once more. "No. She might think nothing of our being gone all day."

Alicia was scarcely aware of the ride back to Cross's estate, except that the journey seemed to take twice as long, though the driver went at twice the speed. She was greeted at the door by one of Lady Greenleigh's staff and led immediately to the room where she'd spoken to Sirens before. They awaited her there, tense and pale.

The explanation came from Lady Dryden while Lady Greenleigh and Lady Reardon sat close together, their eyes on Alicia.

The men had gone riding at about the same time that Alicia had called for Wyndham's carriage. They were accustomed to conferring together out of doors, then Marcus would immediately report every detail of the meeting to Julia. "It works best that way, while we move so publicly here. It would look odd indeed for me to disappear with three other men for hours each day," Julia said wryly.

Alicia tilted her head and regarded the woman impatiently. "Are you not aware that you are at an orgy? You could have disappeared with a regiment every day after tea and no one here would have blinked an eye."

Julia looked much taken aback. "I—that is—"

Lady Reardon regarded her friend for a long moment. "I'm not sure I could pull off such a feat, but anyone would believe *you* could inspire three virile gentlemen to such . . . cooperation, Julia."

Julia opened her mouth to speak, halted, then blushed hotly. "I find it difficult enough to be the one woman working among men. You two have become my friends. I would not like minds to . . . to wander to that thought."

Lady Greenleigh flapped one hand. "Julia, don't worry about us. We don't envy you your beauty. It's too much bloody work, if you ask me."

Alicia practically shivered with impatience. "Right. You're beautiful. They aren't jealous. Wyndham is missing. Am I keeping up so far?"

Julia gazed at her evenly, though she was as pale as the others. "Yes. I knew immediately that something was wrong, especially after the incidents involving you, which seem much more sinister in retrospect."

"They were abundantly sinister in the moment, I assure you."

"Yes, well." Julia hesitated. "You must understand, Lady Alicia. Until today, we were not even sure our . . . mutual enemy was truly here."

Alicia regarded her stonily. "I was. I tried to convince Stanton—but you could have, if you had believed me."

Julia's lips twisted slightly. "I was more concerned with the effect you were having on Wyndham than in the case itself. I suppose I never truly believed that you heard what you heard."

"Because I am a liar."

Julia nodded. "Because you are believed to be a liar, yes, and because Wyndham could not read you as he can everyone else."

Alicia was weary of being left in the dark. "Speak to me. There might be something that I don't know that I know, or that I think you already know, but you don't, or—"

"We are called the Royal Four. We run England, more or less, although we try to keep ourselves to the needs of security and wartime."

"*You* run England. Not the Prime Minister? Not the Prince Regent?"

Julia lifted her chin. "Lord Liverpool answers to us, not the reverse. And George—as fond as I am of him—is not capable of truly running the country. Nor does he care to."

"So you and Wyndham and Greenleigh and Reardon . . . you are the Four." Alicia shook her head in disbelief. "I've been calling you the Four Horsemen—how close I came!"

"There is a man, a French spy who has been working against us for years, and who has been searching for what he knows as the 'Quatre Royale.'" Julia seemed serene, but she betrayed her tension by winding and unwinding her fingers. "He is doubtless the 'scarred man' you heard about in the courtyard of that public house—I did that myself, thank you—he is brilliant and ruthless and he knows far too much about us all from his days among us, pretending to be a young valet. He is not young, however. He is . . . old enough to be my father."

Lady Reardon patted Julia consolingly on the arm. Alicia half-expected Julia to pull away, as Wyndham would have done, but the pale beauty merely covered her friend's hand with her own and kept it there. "Now that we know that the attacks on you were real—" Julia waved Alicia's reputation away with one indifferent hand, as she very well could in truth, come to think of it. Lady Dryden was the talk of the town and everyone kowtowed to the exquisite beauty. If Julia supported her, Alicia could help her sisters without needing a penny—

After she found Wyndham.

"So, this enemy is here. He has been in this house, in our bedchamber. He can pass for a servant, in dim light at least—" She turned to Julia. "How badly did you slash your father? Would he be ill from those wounds?"

Julia drew back. "My, you are quick. Yes, he could very well be ill of infection."

Lady Greenleigh leaned forward. "He was ill even before that, remember? Dane almost drowned him." She went paler than pale. "The Chimera will hold that against him."

Lady Reardon shook her head slowly. "I don't think there's any shortage of hatred toward any of us."

Julia held up one hand, thinking aloud. "You heard others refuse his plan, you say? And he has done all the legwork on this himself—no lackeys in sight, correct?" She smiled grimly. "He has no money to hire help, nor is he in a position to convince even the foolhardy. He is alone and ill and possibly slipping into madness, if the tone of that letter is anything to go by."

Alicia frowned doubtfully. "Does that make him less dangerous? I would imagine it would make him more so."

Julia shook her head. "Not less dangerous, perhaps, but it may make him more predictable. With no help, he could not transport four large men any real distance. He could not overwhelm them except by subterfuge . . . poison, perhaps, although how he could trick them into taking it—" She stopped when she looked up to see some tearing eyes and quivering lips. "Oh, sorry. I'm trying to think like him, you see."

"Well, if anyone could, it would be you," Alicia said. "Let me tell you all I know." She counted on her fingers. "One, he is fevered. I could feel the heat of him behind me in the garden. I think he is perhaps very ill. Two, he is enjoying causing us all pain. He wants to *see* us hurting, I can feel it in him."

"So he would remain close, close enough to watch and relish." Willa frowned. "We have discreetly sent our servants to search all over the house and grounds. We have found nothing out of the ordinary. The men went for a ride. They did not return at their customary time. When we inquired, we learned that their horses were quite properly returned and stabled, although no one remembered seeing anyone do it."

"He does seem to slip in and out of the house very easily, for someone so disfigured," Alicia said, frowning.

Julia shrugged helplessly. "It is a very large house and there are so many unknown servants here. I'm sure he's been seen, but no one would know that he is dangerous unless we put out an alert—which would invite far too many questions."

The thought of half-dressed, drunken Society ladies and lords fleeing the manor almost made Alicia smile, until she remembered why they were here. "So he and the men are close. He is alone and ill. We have people looking everywhere. What more can we do?"

"We can wait," Julia said grimly. "Until he makes the next move."

That was logical, Alicia supposed. Sensible and well-thought out.

She didn't like it one little bit.

31

The door to the fireworks castle opened, casting a bright flare of light into four pairs of dark-accustomed eyes. Stanton blinked back the smarting ache and strained to peer through the blur.

The figure in the doorway was slight, merely a sliver of darkness against the glare.

Alicia?

No, Alicia was no longer here with him.

"Bastard," Dane growled.

Stanton warily relaxed against his bonds, careful to relate nothing of the hope which had just died within him.

The Chimera had arrived.

He strutted into the room, a small man whose face was horribly torn, whose eyes gleamed with fevered madness, who was worn so thin it did not seem possible he was still alive.

He walked to center of the floor and gazed at all of them in turn. "Look at you four, bound and helpless, overcome so easily by one man." He cackled, a mad sound that lifted the hairs on the back of Stanton's neck. "The mighty Royal Four—the legends themselves, laid low by a bit of opium and black tar. Don't they teach that particular trick in that spy school of yours?"

Stanton lifted his chin. "What spy school would that be? And who is this Royal Four you speak of?"

The Chimera smiled. Something unpleasant oozed from his scars when he did. God, the man was entirely mad to let that infection continue untended.

"You could play your little word games with Napoleon," the man said, "If I planned to let you live that long. I wish I could take you back with me, for that upstart dared to tell me I was suffering from an excess of imagination—he dismissed me because of you lot! Me!"

"Or perhaps he realized you've gone stark, staring mad," Reardon said conversationally. "I've heard that about you myself."

The Chimera smiled again, looking almost cheerful. "I've considered that. But I am not mad, you see. I am finally free. I do not work for that plebian emperor any longer. I am, shall we say, more of a bounty seeker now."

Stanton snorted. "There has been a bounty on the Prince Regent since he was twelve. He is too well protected."

The Chimera widened his eyes. "Fat Prinny? Is that who you think I'm after? I'm disappointed in you, Wyndham. I'd heard you were much more intelligent than that. Of course, it explains how I was able to catch you in this little wasp trap of mine."

He squatted before Stanton and patted his boot fondly. Stanton held very still, waiting for the moment, but the Chimera stayed just out of kicking range.

"You know," the Chimera mused aloud, "When I sent her to you, I didn't intend for you to make the poor girl your whore, Wyndham. She was only supposed to take the story to your attention, then go home to her safe, quiet slow starvation with the shreds of her reputation intact. *You* made a

ublic spectacle of her, dragging her to this den of filth,
rcing her into your bed, parading her before the world in
ose disgusting gowns that you purchased for her . . . have
ou no shame at all, my lord?"

It was all sickeningly true, and eventually, if he survived,
tanton fully intended to feel very bad about his actions. At
e moment, only one item penetrated his focus. "When you
ent her to me?"

The Chimera nodded. "I was recruiting behind a most re-
olting public house when I saw her hiding next to the privy,
stening. I followed her home to kill her—because I felt in a
illing mood, you see—"

Stanton didn't let his dismay show. How close Alicia had
ome to death that night!

"Then I thought better of it, and made use of her. Much the
ame as you did, in the end. Isn't it interesting that we both
sed her, Wyndham, but that you hurt her the most?" He lov-
ngly traced his facial scars with the tips of his fingers.
Who's the monster now, do you think?"

More scalding truth. Later, Stanton planned on feeling
ery, very bad for what he had done to Alicia.

Later.

"And you seduced her. Did she fall in love with you while
ou put her in my path again and again, like a pretty little
vorm on your hook?" He shook his head in disbelief. "You
inglish are so sentimental, and your women are ridiculously
motional." He pressed his hands over his heart. "Oh, my
earest," he said in high, quavering voice—a flawless imita-
ion of Millie, Alicia's companion—"do you really think my
ady ought to take her story to Lord Wyndham himself? He's
uch dark, brooding fellow!"

The truth struck Stanton hard, and he saw Reardon flinch
s well. The distinctive voice Alicia had heard behind the
ub—an intentional imitation of one of Prinny's closest
riends. They had forgotten something very, very important

when they had dismissed the Chimera's ability to take
disguise—the man was a perfect mimic. Their stupidity had
kept this game going on far longer than it should have—and
caused Alicia far too much pain in the process.

Later.

Now, they needed to get their hands—preferably their
fists—on this suppurating madman.

"I've sent a letter to my beloved daughter, Julia, telling
her to stay right where she is and to remain with the party at
all times, her and her three little friends. I want them sitting
in the front row, cheering on the flames that will burn you to
death. Won't that sit well with them later, when they sift
your charred bones from the ashes?"

The Chimera grinned merrily and strolled from the
shed. Just at the door, he turned. "I was going to cut your
throats while you slept and then I decided to save it for
when you woke. I didn't realize that my little smoke-bomb
would steal your voices so thoroughly that a dog wouldn't
hear you from outside this door. I rather like the idea of you
burning to death wide awake and screaming without a
sound." He tilted his head, his scars giving his face the ap-
pearance of a death mask in the shadow. "And then I shall
make off with your precious explosives and armament in-
ventor, the esteemed Mr. Forsythe. Napoleon has wanted
him for a long time and will reward me very handsomely,
but your mad genius never leaves his damned tower . . . un-
til now."

He left with a cheerful wave. They heard a clang and a
click as the Chimera locked them in.

Dane swore raspily and long. Marcus shook his head. "We
ought to have seen that coming, I suppose, although I didn't
even know there was a bounty on Forsythe."

Stanton nodded, regret and fury turning him colder than
ever. "There has been one for longer than I've been the Fal-

on . . . but Forsythe keeps to the Tower of London. There
eemed to be no need for alarm."

"Until now," Reardon said. "Do you think Forsythe could
e forced to work for Napoleon?"

Stanton shrugged. "I think Forsythe would die first—
unless Napoleon gave him some irresistible puzzle to solve.
Forsythe isn't the most political of men."

Then something else that the Chimera said came back to
Stanton.

Julia "and her three little friends."

Alicia had come back to him—just in time to watch him
die.

Alicia took the note from Julia and gazed at it in horror.
"We're simply supposed to sit there, like dolls on display,
while he does something horrible to our men?"

"At the Prince's table, in full view of everyone at all times.
All four of us—which means that he is still watching, if he
knows you are back with us."

"That's why he wants us out there during the fireworks display. He wants to watch something—but what?"

"Well, I won't do it. I love Wyndham—" Lady Reardon
made a small happy sound. Alicia glanced askance at her.
"Yes, we can go into more detail later. As I was saying, I
love Wyndham, but I don't work for your Four Horsemen. I
will take no part in some hideous mockery of a party while
Wyndham is captured—"

Julia took her hand, hard. "Alicia, look at me. If we do not
obey to the letter, he will kill them all. I *know* him."

Alicia looked back at Julia, her emotions raw upon her
face. "Julia, he's going to kill them anyway."

Julia looked away. "I know." Then she looked back. "But
as long as he thinks we're being good little dolls, we might
find something, some way—"

A footman tapped on the door, then opened it. "My ladies, there is a Lady Alberta Lawrence here to see you."

Alicia looked up in surprise to see Alberta rush into the room. Just as Alicia gained her feet, Alberta flung herself tearfully into Alicia's arms, nearly knocking the two of them back to the sofa.

"Alberta! What is wrong? Is the family all right? Oh, Alberta, what are you doing *here*?"

Across from them, Willa frowned. "Is this one of your sisters, Alicia? She ought not to be in Cross's house."

Alicia gazed back worriedly over the sobbing Alberta's shoulder. "I don't know what would make her come here. It must be something awful."

Black fears of the vicious man who had accosted her in Cross's garden swept into her mind. Someone like that was capable of anything—someone like that must know that her family lived close by. She pushed Alberta back gently but firmly. "Alberta, you must take a breath and tell me what has happened." She gave her sister a little shake for emphasis. *"Now."*

Alberta gulped a few more breaths and sniffed mightily. Four dainty handkerchiefs were instantly offered. Taking one, Alberta's eyes widened as she apparently took in her sister's companions for the first time. "Oh! I'm so sorry to have interrupted. It was terribly rude of me—"

"Stop wasting time and get on with it, girl," Julia said briskly but gently. "You're worrying your sister."

Alberta's gaze flicked from Julia to Willa to Olivia and then back to Alicia. She leaned forward. "Are they who I think they are?"

Alicia sent an apologetic glance toward the other women as Alberta's resounding whisper carried clearly through the room. "Yes, Alberta, they are. And they're very nice too, so please get on with it!"

Alberta nodded, blew her nose energetically, and settled back on the sofa. "I am ruined," she stated with finality.

Alicia's relief that apparently no one was dead was tem-
ered with guilt and regret. "Oh, Alberta. You didn't, did you?"

"I did. I walked out of our house and right over onto Lord
Cross's land and into his house. Papa said that was enough to
uin any girl, so that's what I did."

Alicia stared at her sister in disbelief. On one hand, Al-
erta was no more ruined than when she'd crawled out of
ed this morning. On the other hand, if anyone were to spot
a young, unmarried girl of good family in this house and
arry tales—yes, that would cinch matters indeed.

"But why would you do such a thing? You know perfectly
vell what I've been through. Why would you do that to your-
elf?" *And to the rest of the family*—although Alicia truly
vasn't in a position to judge on that count, was she?

"Christopher's papa let him propose finally—"

"But that's wonderful! You've been waiting for Christopher
orever!"

Alberta shot Alicia a quelling glance. "Christopher's
papa allowed him to propose on the condition that I give my
vord that I would publicly denounce you and that I would
never again acknowledge your existence and that from this
lay forward you would be worse than dead to me."

Alicia sat back. Oh, no. "Oh, Alberta. You refused, didn't
you?"

Willa came to sit on Alberta's other side and put an arm
about her. "Of course she did! Who wouldn't refuse such a
ridiculous demand? Alberta, I hope you put Christopher in
his place immediately!"

Alberta shrugged, a bit embarrassed. "I didn't precisely
do it immediately. It was after the shouting and the throwing
things and the slamming of the doors—"

"Heavens," Julia said with a frown. "Your father is a
beast, isn't he?"

"Oh, no, that wasn't Papa," Alberta said earnestly. "That
was me."

Alicia smiled ruefully at her new friends. "The red hair comes with a temper, I fear."

Olivia leaned forward, ready for a good story as always. "So what happened next? After the shouting and so on?"

Alberta dabbed at her eyes. "I told Papa and Christopher and Christopher's papa that if they wanted me not to speak to Alicia then they had better cut out my tongue, for I would never agree to it." She leaned into Alicia. "For a moment there, I thought Papa was going to do it."

Alicia wrapped her arms about Alberta. "Darling, I appreciate that you fought for me, but I think perhaps you'd better go home and agree to Christopher's demands."

Willa frowned at her. "She should do no such thing! If I had a sister, I wouldn't let anyone keep me from her."

Alicia sighed. "If you had a sister like me, you might rethink that stance."

Willa reached across to lay one hand over Alicia's. "No I wouldn't. Not for a single bloody instant."

Alberta gasped slightly at Willa's language, then giggled. Then she sat up, wiped her eyes one last time, and took a deep breath. "What's done is done, and I don't honestly know if I regret it. If Christopher thought I was capable of swearing to such a thing, then he didn't know me at all."

She looked down at herself with a sigh. "I don't know if he really loved me, or if he simply wanted me. You know, Alicia, when you look like we do . . ."

Alicia went very still. *When you look like we do.* Oh, yes, it could work . . .

Julia never missed a thing. She leaned forward. "Alicia, what are you thinking?"

Alicia shook off the thought. "No. No, we can still get Alberta out of this mess."

Julia's eyes narrowed. She looked from one sister's face to the other's. "I see. Yes, it might work."

Alicia held up her hand. "No, Julia. No. Alberta isn't part of this."

Julia tilted her head. "This is larger than simply one girl's reputation. Larger than simply four lives at stake. I would risk far more than that to have—to have a good resolution to this affair."

Alberta leaned toward Julia. "What am I not a part of?"

Julia gazed at Alberta. "Something very important. Something much more important than distancing yourself from Christopher and your father—although it would accomplish that as well."

Alicia glared at Julia. *"No."*

Olivia and Willa waited, carefully silent, but Alicia could see the hope in Olivia's eyes and the desperate worry in Willa's. Her own frantic fears threatened to drown her.

But she was the eldest. It was her duty to protect her sisters and she'd done a poor job of it so far.

Julia sat back. "Alicia, you know we must."

How could she bring in her sister, endangering her so? Yet the stakes were so very high. Alicia finally realized how it must have been for Stanton. In order to stop a madman from aiding Napoleon, he'd had to be willing to sacrifice anything.

No wonder he'd never dared allow himself to love.

Alberta, perhaps realizing for the first time that something rather more desperate than a singed reputation was at stake, looked from one woman to the other. Alberta's jaw hardened and Alicia saw the classic Lawrence stubbornness rise in her sister's eyes.

Alberta turned to Julia. "What must we do?

32

Alicia made her way through the dark wood by touch and memory. She'd climbed out her bedroom window many times to spy on Lord Cross's notorious parties.

"These are my woods," she had told Julia when she had objected. "These are my hills. What servant could find his way in the dark to the precisely perfect place to watch the house, without giving himself away?"

Julia wouldn't have agreed if she hadn't been so desperately worried. Alicia played on that shamelessly. "I know where he is. I am the only one who has a double to be at Prinny's table. I am going, Julia. The most you can do is get out of my way."

Julia had the last word, however. "What do you think you'll manage to do when you find him?"

Alicia gave her a brief hug. "I'll think of something," she said. "I always do."

Now, she was not so sure. She slowly climbed the hill, taking a path much more overgrown than it had been when she was a child. She'd dressed in her darkest green, hoping to conceal herself, but there was precious little green in the wood at the moment. She had tied her hair back tightly, but the bare branches snagged and teased strands of it down nonetheless.

At last, she had worked her way around to the bottom of the far side of the hill. She knew what was going on at the house. Prince George had declared the weather fine enough—one suspected any weather would have been fine enough—to dine outside so that the spectacle could be enjoyed over dessert. Ladies would be rolled in fur and some gentlemen as well, and all would smile and suffer and exclaim upon the fine evening.

That would all stop when dessert was brought out. Alicia only hoped that no one would notice that the girl on the giant tray, masked and covered in strategically placed spiced fruit, who was carried in by six footmen and whose distinctive red hair was spread in a great fiery fan around her head, was not the scandalous Lady Alicia—as carefully arranged gossip would have it—but truly her virtuous and pure sister Lady Alberta.

The ruination of two sisters would certainly take Antonia down as well.

Yet Alicia was having a difficult time comparing that loss to the loss of Wyndham, damn it.

She looked up to the top of the hill. A figure stood silhouetted against the sky, although from the angle of the house he would be shaded by the hill behind him. It was a smallish figure, compared to Wyndham at least, but Julia had prepared her for that.

"He is ill and not himself, but he has the strength of madness on his side. Do not underestimate him. Do not let him close to you."

As she worked her way around the small ravine that carried away the runoff from the hill, she heard the cries of startled titillation coming from Cross's party.

It seemed dessert had been served. Alicia prayed that

none of the drunken guests would stick their forks in anything that wasn't fruit.

Deep in the ravine, where it could not be seen from any angle unless one was right upon it, there burned a small, bright fire. A large bundle of some kind lay next to it. Alicia approached cautiously. It seemed that no one was about—and Julia had been quite sure that the comte had no minions at the moment . . .

In the folds of the blanket-wrapped mass, Alicia spotted a shock of white hair. The dark bundle on the ground was Mr. Forsythe. She knelt quickly and put one hand gently over his mouth before he could recognize her. She put a finger to her lips. Forsythe's brilliant eyes flashed at her impatiently. She removed her hand. "Right," she whispered. "Are you hurt?"

"I fear I am, pretty fire-goddess. He broke my legs, you see. Two swift blows with an iron rod. He says I can still work crippled, so he's going to let them heal wrong on the voyage to Paris. That way he needn't worry about me escaping." Forsythe raised his bushy brows. "Do you think that fellow might not be quite right in the head?"

Alicia kept her gaze on the capering figure on the hilltop. "I am quite sure he is not, but neither is he stupid. Have you seen Wyndham or any others of the Four?"

Forsythe blinked up at her. "I think the comte is not the only one who is not stupid. And no, I've not seen them. Are they missing?"

Alicia couldn't allow the panic to rise. "You stay here and keep warm. I will . . . I will figure something out."

The Chimera could have been well gone with Forsythe by now—so something else was keeping him here. Why would he stay simply to watch the festivities below?

He was watching—waiting—but for what?

Why don't you simply ask him?

Even as Alicia stood and began to make her way closer to

the madman, her mind was cataloguing that idea under things best thought through first. She pulled the letter opener from her bodice. It seemed a pitiful thing now—here in the dark, heading for a madman. A pistol would be worse, for she was a poor shot indeed.

What's the worst that could happen?

She could die. No, worse, she could die before she found Wyndham, and then Wyndham would die.

That would definitely be the worst thing that could happen.

She topped the hill, some distance from the madman intent on the scene below.

"One, two, three, four," he said to himself with a chilling cackle. "Four, three, two, one . . ."

Alicia stationed herself behind a tree trunk and got her bearings. As it had been when she was a girl, the panorama of Lord Cross's celebration spread out before her like a golden picnic. She could clearly see the first table where Julia, Willa and Olivia sat. She could also see the giant dessert tray, laid before the Prince Regent—with Alberta's brilliant hair and buxom displacement of fruit gaining a bit too much of his majesty's attention.

Alicia felt the damp of the night air sinking into her clothing and her bones. The estate smelled of chill and damp no longer held at bay by the greenery.

Alicia shivered. "This," she muttered to herself, "is a very bad idea." She turned on her heel.

It slipped in the muck, making her flail wildly for a moment to keep from doing a facer in the mud. When she righted herself, the man was standing only a few yards away. He was horribly scarred. Great spreading purple lines, half healed, ravaged his face. There was no telling what he'd looked like before, but now he most surely looked like a nightmare. In addition, his knife was much larger than hers.

"Good evening, pretty whore."

She would remember that voice for the rest of her life. It was him, the man in the garden. Remembering how his cruelty had twisted her own thoughts about, Alicia stepped back.

"I foolishly thought I could stop you. I have changed my mind," she said.

The man nodded politely. "As you wish. I shall simply kill you outright then."

He meant it too. She could see it in the flat depthless gray of his eyes. Truly, those eyes were more frightening than any hideous scarring could be. She had the feeling that he'd been a monster long before he'd been wounded.

And now she was alone with the monster. Her belly crawled at the way he would soon speak to her, the way he could see right into her. Why had she thought herself a match for the monster?

"You are an incredibly stupid woman, did you know that?"

At moment, it was all Alicia could not to nod her head in agreement. The smooth power of the viper's voice poisoned her from within.

He turned to gaze back over the grand spectacle being enacted before them. "They call themselves by predators' names, did you know that? Your precious Royal Four—the Cobra, the Lion, the Fox and the Falcon." He laughed, a crazed gravelly sound that made Alicia's skin tingle with fear. "I find I prefer creatures like humans." He looked at her. "Man is a clever beast—for all the cleverest beasts are the one who are both hunter and hunted."

Man. It was so very typical. Alicia felt her temper rise, with gratitude and fear combined, because right now wasn't the best time to become peppery with the man. "Then I must be twice as clever as you—" Oh, heavens, there went her mouth again. "For I am a woman and my kind has been hunted since the beginning of time." Now she was good and ery. "I left my father and my lover behind because I will not allow a man to dictate what I think of myself. I am not about to start allowing it from an ugly, rotting, scarecrow of a man!"

"That wasn't nice."

She frowned. "I never claimed to be nice. That's merely an assumption that people make because I'm pretty."

A nonsmile curled the edge of his scarred lip. "A dangerous assumption I won't make again, I assure you."

"Well, you're a fast learner, at least. Do try to retain this—we are not going to allow you to kill them."

The chilling grimace grew into a self-satisfied sneer. "Oh, but I already have."

Her belly went to ice. Then—*it isn't true.*

She didn't know how she knew it, but she did, all the way to her very bones. She narrowed her eyes at him. "Not yet, you haven't."

He didn't so much react as he did carefully not react. Too carefully. She tilted her head. "Ah. You have secured them somewhere imminently dangerous."

Again he only blinked slowly. "They are quite destroyed, believe me. The Quatre Royale are no more."

The Quatre Royale. Really, how juvenile.

She slowly backed a step away. If the four men were helpless—oh, God, Stanton!—where could this maniac have put them that would soon be "destroyed"? Something that would soon fill with water, or empty of air, or—

Or burn.

Mr. Forsythe's Spectacle of Fire.

It was perfect and deadly and awful. "You evil bastard."

He grimaced a torn smile. It was hideous. "I never claimed to be nice. That's an assumption people make because I'm pretty."

Then before she could react or even blink, he slipped the knife into her side. The blade slid past wool and silk to re-side icy cold in her belly. He stepped back, leaving the hilt jutting from her waist like a hook to hang his hat.

"Gut wounds take a while to kill. I could have stabbed you through the heart," he said conversationally, tapping himself on the chest. "There is a spot here, just between the rib bones, where the knife slides unswervingly into the heart itself and death is instantaneous. It would have been more merciful, 'tis true—but I find my capacity for mercy lately strained. I shall enjoy thinking of your endless and excruciating demise, slowly spilling your blood on the hillside, watching him burn, helpless to save your lover from his own fiery end."

Alicia moved nearly as quickly as he had. Somehow she pulled the horror from her flesh and thrust it deeply into his chest. "Thank you for the knife," she gasped. "And the explicit instruction."

Then, as the heat of her own blood began to flow down her side, she sagged against a wave of dizziness. She was barely aware of the scarred man staring stupidly down at the hilt jutting from his own chest, the handle jumping slightly in rhythm with the fading beat of his dying heart.

He looked up at Alicia. She tried to remain on her feet, preparing herself for another blow and wondering dully how many times the knife would change hands before one or both of them died.

Then the mad, ruthless gleam in his eyes flickered out like a used-up candle and his gray eyes went flat and dead.

It was awful. Even as he fell lifelessly to sprawl at her feet, Alicia wanted to take it back. Not because he deserved to live, but because she couldn't bear to be the one to make someone die. To kill.

And yet she had, without pausing for thought. A rasping sob escaped her throat. "You ought to have . . . to have listened to me, you evil bastard. I told . . . told you I wasn't nice!"

* * *

Stanton couldn't see a thing. The curtain of night had ended the hypnotic play of light through the shrinking planks. He could sense Greenleigh's growing rage, and Marcus's circling worry. He could imagine Reardon's fear for his lady—for he was feeling some of that himself.

"I hear something coming closer," Reardon said. "It sounds like some sort of parade."

Stanton rolled over, nearly pulling one arm from its socket, to peer though the chinks in the wall. "It's looks like a parade. There are several carriages and it looks like—" He peered closer. "Is that a cannon?"

Reardon sighed. "Stanton, I can hardly come over to confirm it."

Marcus nodded. "It's a cannon. Perhaps we can convince them to shoot the door in."

Dane grunted. "Oh, yes. I can see us surviving that one nicely."

Marcus began to call out. "Oy! Oy, we're in here! Halloo!"

Stanton closed his eyes, took a breath, and began to shout nonsense as well. Their voices had not returned, but perhaps they could get someone's attention with all four voices.

The approaching fanfare drowned them out.

"I hate horns," Marcus muttered. "What's a fellow to do against a phalanx of horns!"

Dane chewed his lip. "You realize that they are going to eventually light this thing on fire and we're all going to die."

"I dare say I can think of more cheerful things, but no, it doesn't look good for us now."

Stanton had to agree. Tied, too hoarse to be heard, with fireworks scheduled. The worst of it was that he was leaving Alicia when he'd just found her—

When he'd just found himself.

33

If the journey to Cross's party had been uphill instead of down, Alicia would not have made it. As it was, she was grateful every time she fell and rolled, for those were steps she need not take. Rising from her last jolting fall, she found herself nearly on the edge of the vast lawn. She felt very strange. Although she kept her hand instinctively pressed hard to her side, she felt almost nothing from the wound. Her most pressing worry was the way her vision seemed to shift from blurred to clear, and how her knees tended to simply give way.

Her brain felt as if a hundred bees were trapped inside, their droning buzz the only thing she could hear.

She skirted the seated guests and the small crowd of privileged servants who were allowed to sit on blankets to see the show. She tried to walk straight to the miniature castle, but there were ropes raised to keep back the spectators and burly footmen to police them.

One stopped her and spoke to her. She couldn't hear him for the bees. She tried to tell him that there were men inside the castle. He frowned and shook his head, speaking again

She tried to push past him, but he respectfully held her back and redirected her toward the seated guests.

She was so weary. She longed to lie down, directly on the grass, and let the bees fade.

Stanton.

He was trapped. He would burn.

Alicia caught sight of George, leaning back in his throne-like chair, gazing eagerly toward the castle. Oh, God. The Spectacle was about to begin. There was no one to stop them from lighting it. Forsythe might have, but he was lying broken in the ravine.

One thought made it through the bees—only George could stop the lighting of the rockets. No one else would dare defy the prince.

Except Julia. Alicia dully scanned the seated guests to find Julia, Willa and Olivia at the far end of the table. That made up her mind. George was closer. Closer was good.

"Well, lads, this might just be it."

Stanton shut his eyes against Dane's hoarse, regretful words. "We cannot die here," he said. "I refuse to be bested by a fevered madman and a Chinese rocket."

Reardon nodded. "That is annoying, I admit."

Marcus was still gazing out through the cracks. "I cannot believe that Forsythe would not make a final check of this—" He stopped and gazed at the others. "Right. He already has Forsythe then."

"Didn't that work out nicely for him?" Reardon leaned his head back upon his post. "I suppose we must be grateful that the women are unharmed." He turned to Stanton. "You can still see Willa, can't you?"

Stanton didn't want to look again, but Reardon so quietly, desperately wanted to know. Stanton rolled to press his face to the crack in the planks that let him see the main table of guests. Lady Reardon was indeed still seated next to Lady

Dryden and Lady Greenleigh. Stanton punished himself—perhaps 'later' was now?—by letting his gaze trail down to where Alicia lay spread before the ravening hordes as a tempting dessert. She must have had a good reason, but it pained him to see her brought so low. She looked like a courtesan, with her brilliant hair spread across the table and her bountiful figure becoming more exposed by the moment. It seemed the young men of the party had developed a sudden fondness for fruit.

He had indeed brought her low, just as the Chimera had accused him. She would not be out there now, subject to such degradation, if not for him.

He closed his eyes against the regret, then forced himself to hide no longer. When he focused again on the main table, he saw her walking toward the prince, her dark gown making her all but invisible in the flickering torch light—

Dark gown? He looked back down the table, to where the red-haired dessert lay. Then he watched as Alicia—for it truly was Alicia, it was her walk, it was the very tilt of her head—walked slowly up the table.

"Gentlemen, something interesting is going on," he said.

Alicia staggered, nearly fell. Alarm swept him. The way she pressed one hand to her side, her pallor, her disjointed gaze—she was injured!

"Alicia!" Damn his useless voice! *"Alicia!"*

As Alicia staggered to the Prince Regent's place at the grand table, she caught sight of her sister displayed upon the table as a pagan feast for the eyes. Fruit and delicacies hid the most pertinent parts of Alberta's anatomy, and the feathered mask was elaborate enough to cause confusion between them—or rather, it would have been if she herself weren't present.

Alberta caught her gaze and green eyes widened behind

the intricate feathered eyeholes. Alberta clapped one hand over her exposed mouth, dislodging some of the more essential piles of grapes covering her right breast. "Eep!"

Alicia spared her sister a single apologetic look. Alberta didn't deserve the notoriety that would soon be hers, but reputations weighed little against lives.

Stanton's life.

She wavered, staggered, her vision blurring and her head feeling light and buzzing, as if it were about to be carried off her shoulders by a military formation of brightly striped bees. She put one hand on the table and breathed slowly.

Alberta gazed up at her, frozen with alarm. "There's a ruckus on the way, Bertie," Alicia whispered. "You might want to find a spot under the table." She looked down at the expanse of creamy exposed flesh and grimaced in apology again. "And a very large napkin."

Her sister uncovered her lips to say something to her, but Alicia's attention was drawn by the sight of George standing and raising his hands for silence.

The show was about to begin.

Alicia pushed away from the table and took the last few steps on legs she could scarcely feel. Behind her, she heard a gasp of alarm as someone noticed the large smear of blood she had left behind on the snowy table linens. "Sorry 'bout that," Alicia mumbled. "Never could leave the table like a lady."

Although she was sure she still moved in the proper direction, George was beginning to shrink in her vision. Considering George's considerable girth, that took some doing . . .

She shook her head sharply. The Prince Regent was about to start the fireworks. Once the first rocket was lighted, there would be no stopping the conflagration until nothing remained by the ashes of the display—

And four charred bodies.

Stanton.

She made it to the center of the long table just as George raised his hand to signal the lighting crew.

"No!"

The buzz of excitement faded at just that instant and Alicia's voice rang loudly across the lawn. One of the Royal Guard stepped forward, but George waved him back. "Let her be." Then he leaned forward to gaze down the table to where Alberta lay like a harvest feast of the eyes. "I cannot wait to hear this," George said with smile as he looked back up at Alicia. Or rather, a point rather lower than her face.

"Your highness—they're trapped. They're inside—"

He wasn't even listening. Men and their breast fixation. Alicia was trembling with weakness, likely bleeding to death, and trying to save four lives. George was aware of none of this because he was looking at her bosom.

Alicia watched with some surprise as her right hand flashed out to slap the Prince Regent across the face. "Don't be such an infant!" she scolded with surprising force. "Listen!"

The crowd was shocked into complete silence. At that moment, she heard her name, faint and hoarse and far away.

Stanton.

George heard it as well, as did all the guests. All gazes went to the castle. The two men who stood ready to light the long fuses of the first rockets with torches yanked their flames back and away.

Alicia fell to her elbows on the table as her knees gave way. "They're inside. They're trapped inside . . ."

It was over. People were running toward the castle even now.

Alicia saw Julia, Willa, and Olivia pick up their skirts and race across the long stretch of lawn. She wanted to run but it was all she could do to straighten. The thought of walking all ιe way back around the long table seemed impossible, so she ᴦropped to her knees and crawled beneath.

Looking to her left, she saw Alberta had done the same.

And apparently, so had young Lord Farrington, who ᴇeemed to have no objection to squashed fruit all over his ⱴeskit. Alicia hesitated long enough to be sure that Alberta ⱴas a willing—nay, eager—participant, then continued out he other side. Let the future come as it may. Christopher ƚidn't deserve Bertie anyway.

At last, she was stumbling down the great lawn, her eyes ᴄasting about for any sign of Stanton. She saw Lord Green-ᴇigh sweep Olivia into his arms. She saw Lord Reardon pull ᴡilla closer than close. She saw Julia swat Marcus irritably ⱱn the chest before she dissolved into oceans of tears in his ᴇmbrace.

She saw Stanton standing alone, looking all around him. Ƚer heart gave way to something deep and painful and over-ⱴhelming, just to see him there, alive. She stopped, unable to ᴄontinue, and called his name. He made no sign of hearing ᴡer above the crowd. She waved to him. He didn't see her.

Then again, he never had.

The buzzing returned, louder than before. It stole her ᴃreath and her will to keep standing. She felt herself falling ᴃut there was no way to stop the darkness.

She didn't even feel Stanton's strong arms come about ᴡer as she slipped away.

34

Alicia awoke in her bedchamber in Lord Cross's manor. Fo
some reason that surprised her. Had she expected to b
somewhere else altogether—like dead, perhaps?

One certainly hoped heaven looked better than Cross'
manor, filled with decadent orgy participants.

She tried to roll over and discovered that she'd been cut i
half. Well, not precisely, but it certainly felt like it. Sh
pushed back to covers to see her waist where the comte ha
stabbed her was now neatly bandaged. However, that previ
ous mysterious lack of pain was definitely gone. She felt a
if she'd been torn apart and sewn back together by clumsy
blacksmiths.

It certainly seemed like she was going to live after all.

The door opened, admitting Garrett with a tray. H
brightened to see her awake. "How lovely. Now I needn'
pour soup into your open mouth. It was becoming tedious."

"I'm glad I can oblige," Alicia said tartly, before she saw
the sheen of unshed tears in Garrett's eyes. She put her hand
over his on the tray. "Thank you for taking care of me."

He shrugged off her hand with a small smile. "Oh, I've

ad a bit of help. I must say, I've never kept such high company. You don't count, being notorious and all." He leaned
close with a conspiratorial grin. "I made the Sirens do all the
unpleasant things."

The door opened again to let Willa and Olivia in. They
looked radiant as usual. Alicia wondered how horridly her
own looks were was doing.

"Oh, wonderful! You're awake!"

Alicia smiled. "So I'm told." She held out her hands and
each woman took one. They sat on either side of the mat-
tress, making Alicia feel as though she truly belonged there.

Then she remembered, sitting up straight. "Forsythe!
Oh . . . ow." The pain took her breath away and she sagged
back against the pillows.

Willa smiled. "Don't worry, we found him straightaway.
It was easy once someone spotted the trail of your blood."

Olivia grimaced. "Don't talk about blood. Please."

Willa shook her head at her friend. "Well, it's her blood.
Why don't you let her decide if we can talk about it?"

Alicia laughed, then gasped slightly. "Oh . . . ow. Please,
don't make me laugh."

Olivia sent Willa a superior look. "*I* won't make you
laugh."

Alicia laughed again. "Oh, bother. This is going to be difficult."

Willa nodded. "The Chimera really injured you. The sur-
geon said that if you had walked much farther, you wouldn't
have had enough blood in you to survive."

Alicia looked down. "I killed him."

"Of course, you did," Olivia said stoutly. "He deserved it!"

Willa seemed to understand. "But Alicia didn't deserve to
be the one who had to do it."

Alicia shrugged. "Why not me? I am not so special that I
should never be asked to do anything difficult." She bit her
lip. "Julia knows, I suppose."

Olivia nodded. "She does. She will come soon and you two can talk about it. Don't worry, Alicia. She isn't going to be angry that you killed her father."

Willa shook her head. "Unless it's that you did it before she managed to."

Alicia looked up, horrified. "Oh, no. I would rather it be me than Julia be forced to take her own father's life! Think of the pain and confusion that would cause her!"

"Well, thank you, then," came Julia's voice from the doorway. She came forward. Olivia stepped aside so that she could take Alicia's hand. Willa stepped away as well.

Alicia took a breath. "I'm sorry I killed your father."

Julia nodded. "I know, and I'm glad that you're sorry. It means that you have a heart. Killing shouldn't be easy. I am mostly sorry, however, that he *was* my father, so I forgive you readily. Of course, you saved Marcus, so I'd forgive you anything." She took a breath. "Do you forgive me for not believing you?"

Alicia shook her head. "It never crossed my mind not to. You must be very careful who you trust, in your position—and in Wyndham's." She looked away, then gazed down at her hands, then looked up to meet Julia's gaze. "Is Wyndham coming to see me?"

Julia glanced at Willa, who shook her head. "He isn't here. He took the Chimera's body back to London. There are many men who will not believe in that monster's death until they've seen it with their own eyes. He was a bad fellow and he hurt many of our people."

Alicia hid her disappointment, although not very well judging by the sympathetic expressions on her friends' faces. "He has important work. I know that." She sighed, then smiled. "So, do I win?"

Julia looked confused, but Olivia grinned. "Well, I was shot and left to die . . ."

Willa tapped her chin. "I was hunted . . ."

Julia slid a sardonic glance at her friends. "I was throt-
led . . ."

Olivia tilted her head. "But only Alicia came out better
than the Chimera, so I say she wins."

Alicia smiled, but it wasn't her side that kept her from
laughing.

Stanton hadn't come to say goodbye.

The next time Alicia awoke, the room was dark but for the
glow of the coals in the hearth. She stretched experimentally, halting with a hiss when she felt her wound pull.

"You're awake."

The deep voice came from the chair facing the fire. Wyndham stood and came to sit on the edge of the bed. He
looked wonderful, but tired and oddly ill at ease.

Her throat tightened at the look in his eyes. Something
unpleasant was in the offing, she could feel it. "Are you unwell? Did you suffer any more ill effects from your opium
poisoning?"

He clenched his jaw. "No, I am quite well now."

What was wrong with him? Alicia was becoming more
and more alarmed. "Is it one of the other gentlemen? Is
everyone well? Is it Mr. Forsythe? I thought he might recover from broken legs, but he is so old—"

He shook his head. "Everyone is quite well. You saved us
all most thoroughly."

Then what was so horrible that he couldn't bear to speak
of it? "Did something happen in London?"

"My journey to London was uneventful. The comte's
body made a gratifying display for some of our more blood-
thirsty associates." A thin smile crossed his lips. "The Prime
Minister thought that leaving the knife in his heart for eter-
nity was most appropriate."

Alicia looked down at her hands. "Your villain was an excellent teacher."

She looked up to see him gazing at her at last. "Yes," he said. "We all learned a great deal from him."

She took a breath. "Wyndham, if you don't tell me why you look so grim and unpleasant, I am going to lock you back in that castle."

He smiled thinly. "I am not grim."

She sighed. "You look like you've come to tell me you have an incurable disease and only three months to live."

"Actually, I came to ask you to marry me."

She drew back, alarmed. He couldn't mean it, not with that look of bleak determination on his face.

Was this because she had saved his life and he felt obligated? Well, she would rescue them both from his twisted concept of nobility.

"No!"

35

Stanton felt his chilled gut grow colder. He had thought about making a pretty speech, but why concoct a grand passion when cool thinking would do? "I do not understand your objection. I owe you a great deal. Wedding me would make your previous reputation very nearly disappear. Your family would benefit greatly by the connection and . . . we already know we are compatible in the bedchamber."

She was gazing at him as if he was proposing to dice up baby lizards and feed them to her. He leaned forward. He must make her see this was necessary.

"I honestly believe you would benefit from some stability and respectability, Alicia. You are too wild, too inclined to take on Society's disapproval and grind it under your heel. I could help you with that."

She let out a small bark of horrified laughter. "I'm sure you could."

She took a deep breath and gazed at him with something altogether new in her eyes—something that warmed him and hurt him at once. "Stanton, I love you. It astounds me how much I love you." She watched him for a long moment. He held her gaze, but he would not be making the response she awaited. His feelings had interfered with this entire matter from the first moment he'd met her. She'd nearly died because he'd been too absorbed with feelings to think logically about any of it. His dependence on his mysterious sense and his dismay at being without it had prevented him from thinking at all, it seemed.

She sighed. "All I have ever wanted is to laugh and live, to be allowed to be myself. So to be Lady Wyndham—to be expected to be your marchioness, to feel watched over and disapproved of, to spend the rest of my life stepping softly, fighting my own nature, tiptoeing through the rest of my days listening for endless, unanswerable, relentless disapproval— no, that I could not bear."

She leaned forward, disregarding her pain.

"One of us will always be wrong—don't you see that? And I fear that I am only too likely to believe it is me. Either you would destroy me or I would destroy myself for you."

"Every marriage must make compromises." Stanton would not—could not—relent. She must wed him. It would solve everything.

"Compromises. What a benign word for such devastation. And what will you compromise, Wyndham? Will you give up the wall around your heart for me?"

She dared too far. "My heart has nothing to do with you."

She jerked back as if struck. Then her lips thinned and her cheeks flared in her ashen face. "Then I release you from any further obligation to me. We made our deal and I caught your traitor. We need have nothing more to do with each other. Please leave."

"Alicia, I'm trying to make things right." Cool control slipped away from him. "You are the most bloody-minded, uncompromising—"

She whirled on him. "Why shouldn't I be? What has compromising ever brought me but misery? When my parents lied about my inheritance and pressed me to let Almont—"

She halted breathlessly, her expression closing as he watched.

Stanton went cold, thinking back to his first encounter with Lord and Lady Sutherland. "They made you do it—and then they threw you out."

She looked away, but her lip curled slightly. "Almont was too clever to be caught, you see. When I confessed my lack of inheritance, just afterward—he kissed me, told me it didn't matter and to go to sleep. When I awoke, he'd arranged it so that no one would ever believe a word I might say."

Almont had used her and disposed of her. As had her parents. There was a great deal of that going about. The world had refused to believe her. That seemed to be contagious as well.

Stanton was experiencing a taste of that frustration now.

She turned away and pulled the covers high.

He growled. "Alicia—"

"I believe my lady told you to leave."

Stanton looked up to see Garrett in the doorway with one of his eternal trays of tea in his hands and danger in his blue eyes. Garrett might be a bit of a Nancy, but Stanton had no doubt the lady's maid would fight to the death to keep Alicia safe.

It only bothered him that he might be considered a threat.

He stood and walked to the door. Garrett moved aside but seemed perfectly ready to defend his lady with nothing more than hot tea and biscuit missiles.

"Garrett, speak to her. Make her see reason—"

The door slammed on his words—not that he knew what to say to her. What did she expect, that he would tell her all his secrets in pretty poetry and open his heart for her perusal?

He had proposed a perfectly logical plan that would

guarantee the two of them some measure of future satisfaction.

What was so wrong with that?

A bit like a horse-trade, wouldn't you say?

He ran both hands over his face, trying to scrub away the madness that always threatened in the presence of Alicia's particular brand of logic. She was being unreasonable and unrealistic. All he asked was that she rein in her outrageous nature—and add a few inches to the bodices of her gowns—and perhaps do something a bit more elegant and restrained with her hair—

The woman he pictured in his mind was lovely and elegant, demure and very nearly of royal demeanor.

She also bore no resemblance to Lady Alicia Lawrence. He didn't like her at all.

Well, hell.

36

The Prince Regent offered Alicia a ride back to London in his carriage. She accepted because Forsythe would be joining them and because the springs on the Royal Conveyance might be good enough that the journey wouldn't be too agonizing in her wounded state.

Unfortunately, Mr. Forsythe fell into a laudenum-induced sleep shortly after leaving Cross's estate, leaving Alicia uncomfortably alone with the royal cheek she had slapped in front of a hundred spectators.

Fortunately, George had an answer for everything. "I, of course, will claim very loudly and repeatedly that nothing happened between you and I on the journey—which will ensure that everyone thinks otherwise, making your reputation and salvaging mine, thank you." He rubbed his face ruefully. "I think being slapped by a furious lover makes for better gossip than 'Don't be such an infant,' don't you?"

Alicia leaned carefully back onto the plush, soft cushions and closed her eyes. "Again, your highness, my deepest apologies—"

George shrugged. "You saved my best and most honest subjects. I cannot complain. You might have pulled your strike a bit, but such force was understandable in the heat of the moment."

"I am so sorry, your highness." Alicia could tell she was going to be saying it a great deal over the next several hours.

"You must stay with me at Carlton House," George said. "I shall throw a reception for you that will forever cement your place in Society. When people speak of Lady Alicia Lawrence in the future, it will be to wonder if they've earned an invitation into your inner circle of friends."

Alicia shook her head. "Really, your highness, that isn't necessary."

George opened his hands expansively. "But of course it is! Think of your dear sisters, my lady. If you are a reigning queen of Society, who would dare malign your lovely sisters?" He patted his chin thoughtfully. "Lady Alberta is rather nice, isn't she? Do you think—?" He caught the expression on her face. His hand went tenderly to his own left cheek. "Ah, perhaps not."

He recovered quickly, however. "Perhaps I should give you a medal, but how to honor you when the deed is a secret of national security? The Chimera's death will get back to Napoleon eventually, but we would like him to believe we had time to squeeze a few secrets from the bastard."

Alicia clapped a hand over her mouth. "Oh, no." She put her hand down but her eyes spoke volumes. "I should have—I shouldn't have killed him! I should have realized that you would have questions for him—oh, dear—"

He stared at her quizzically. "Lady Alicia, are you apologizing for not dragging back a living spy—the most dangerous and deadly spy in the history of England, mind you—to deposit at my feet the way a hardworking tabby cat might bring me a mouse?"

She frowned. "Er—yes?" She wrinkled her nose. "That doesn't sound quite right, does it?"

George's laughter threatened to wake Forsythe. Alicia smiled, but inside she only wished that the journey was over. The sooner she could pack up Millie and Garrett and leave London, the sooner she could be sure she would never see Stanton again.

Carlton House was lovely of course, being the royal residence, and George's staff was impeccably kind and attentive. Garrett was in heaven and Millie, who George had already transported back for Alicia, was in ecstasy. Alicia was served, pampered and visited by George's own personal physician.

A letter arrived from Alberta announcing her grand passion for Lord Farrington and her upcoming marriage to him. Antonia wrote as well, a stiff but pleasant letter that contained neither blame nor apology. Their parents were well, Father would soon be hitting Farrington up for a loan, etc.

All was well. Her wound was healing beautifully. Everything that had gone wrong five years ago was being made right. Alicia ought to have been happy.

Unfortunately, her heart seemed to have been left in Sussex, for she surely could feel no sign of it now. She went through the next few days in a numbed state of obedient indifference. On the night of George's party for her, Alicia allowed Garrett to dress her and let him and Millie argue for ten minutes on the best way to do her hair before she thought to intervene.

She walked into the party feeling as if she were watching from a distance. George and his current mistress, a large, bosomy woman who welcomed Alicia with a large, bosomy hug, sat her between them at dinner. Alicia was distantly conscious of the honor and behaved herself beautifully—for what did it matter if the gentleman across from her was an idiot, or that his companion was catty and unkind? Alicia simply had no claws left in her spirit nor interest left in her heart. She smiled, she nodded, she made perfectly pointless conversation.

Such irony, that when she had left Stanton behind, she had become the perfect doll-like Marchioness after all.

After the meal was served, the Prince Regent cleared his throat.

"I have in my possession a letter, written by a gentleman to the lady of his heart. He has asked me to read it to her, in public, so that all might know how he cares for her."

"To Lady Alicia—"

Alicia blinked. Oh, no. It wasn't one of those fawning swains from Cross's party, was it? How absurd. She sighed, prepared to listen with a non-committal half-smile and make polite noises after. Then she could excuse herself from this painful farce on the grounds of her "illness."

George continued.

"To Lady Alicia,

"From your first letter, I was captivated by your quick mind and your ready wit. From our first meeting, I was haunted by your lovely eyes and your subtle grace. From the first day, hour, moment—I have been bombarded with firsts. The first time I heard you laugh. The first time I made you weep. The first taste of your lips. The first caress of your skin. The first warming of a heart held too long in the cold and the dark.

"I did not understand, for I had lived too long alone. Where there was generosity, I saw recklessness. Where there was trust, I saw manipulation. Where there was love, I looked for lies.

"So I took the gold of the sun into my hand and treated it as brass.

"Rightfully so, you took it back from me . . . and took it away."

Alicia could hear the beat of her own heart thudding in her ears, almost drowning out the words of a woman seated near her.

"That's so beautiful," the woman sighed. "So passion-ate!"

George went on reading.

"I thought I was done, an accomplished man in control of his surroundings. But I was cold, so cold that I was ice in-side.

"You burn so fiercely it alarmed me, unnerved me, un-manned me. I feared that when I melted in your flame there would be nothing left—yet I could not stay away. As help-less as a moth who dies by the candle, I could not stop my circling of you.

"Too late I learn that I should not have tried. You have forged someone new with your fire, someone who might just be able to survive and flourish in close proximity to the molten core of you.

"I want more from you than I have any right to, but you will fare better without me than with me, so I will not ask. I only wish to tell you that you have left me changed. The world will not know me, so far am I from the man I was. The world will benefit, I believe, and I will ever be indebted to you for teaching the ice to thaw.

"I wish you always the joyous summer you deserve and blame you not for fleeing the stark winter you saw in me.

"Goodbye.

"Yours forever, Alicia, my love,

"Wyndham"

Alicia couldn't breathe for the emotions flooding her. All numbness had disappeared in the storm. She was furious that Stanton would let her be so miserable for so long. She was elated that he would make so free with his feelings in public. She was suddenly, irrepressibly filled with such magnificent hope that she hardly dared move for fear that she would wake from this dream.

She carefully laid her napkin on her plate. "Where is he, your highness? He's here, somewhere, I know it."

"I can't imagine why you would think so," George said smoothly.

Alicia turned her head to gaze at him, raising a brow. "Your highness, I don't care what Stanton did to you that you must avenge yourself thus. I want to know where he is. I think you'll recall that it does not go well with you if you refuse me."

George leaned away slightly. "Ah . . . he's in the music room, just through that door." He pointed obligingly, the other hand casually protecting his left cheek.

"Thank you, your highness." She stood, pushing back her chair. "I cannot stay," she called to all present. "My lover is waiting for me. Carry on with your dessert!"

She ran around the table, skidding slightly in her silk slippers. Fortunately, the door to the music room was unlocked, for she would not have allowed such a measly thing as a royal latch on a royal door to stop her headlong rush.

Stanton was there, tall and delicious and hers forever. He'd obviously been pacing worriedly, the dear. As if she could ever deny him!

He whirled at her bombastic entrance and scarcely opened his arms in time to catch her. They toppled back onto a royal settee, then rolled to the royal carpet together.

Finally, she had him just where she wanted him, trapped beneath her while she covered his face with kisses.

"I'm not—all those things—you said," she whispered between kisses.

"Of course not." He took her face between his large hands and stopped her for a moment. "You're more."

She shook her head. "You're a fool to think so."

He smiled slowly. "I think perhaps I am—for you."

She blinked back the burning in her eyes. "Don't make me cry when I'm so bloody happy."

He brought her down for a long, deep kiss that left her knees weak and various other parts humming with glee. "I love you," he told her, whispering the words into her hair. "If you'll let me up, I'll propose properly."

Alicia shook her head. "No. Absolutely not. Anything you have to say can be said perfectly well on your back."

He laughed out loud, in that easy, open way she'd heard so rarely and loved so much. She closed her eyes and simply listened, feeling the deep rumble in his chest throughout her entire body. He truly was happy.

"Very well, then," he said with a grin. "I love you. I want to marry you. I want you to be precisely who you are at every moment of every day, and if anyone in Society, the government or the Church of England doesn't like it, they should feel perfectly free to jump in the Thames."

Alicia smiled. "Your terms are acceptable. Now here are mine. I love you. I want to marry you. I want you to be precisely who you are at every moment of every day . . . except once in a while, can we wear costumes to bed? I've always fancied you as a highwayman in black."

A slow, hot smile lighted his face. With one quick motion, he rolled her over to lay heavily, deliciously upon her. "Stand and deliver," he growled.

She twined her arms around his neck, pushing her fingers deep into his thick hair. "Of course, lord highwayman—but don't you think we ought to close the door first?"

Epilogue

Alicia hopped on one foot while Stanton hurriedly did up her gown. "Blast it!" she muttered. "Where did I throw that other slipper?"

"My weskit was on the chandelier, so there's no telling." Stanton found it under the dressing table, along with his cravat. He frowned at his limp linen. "I'm going to have to call for Herbert."

Alicia snatched the slipper and donned it, then bent to fix her hair in the mirror. "But if he comes, then Garrett will too, and Garrett will never let me go out without a complete redressing and coifing and we're late as it is! Antonia will never forgive me if we aren't on time to meet her new fiancé!"

Wyndham waved his useless cravat. "But I don't actually know how to tie these things."

She looked over her shoulder at him. "Are you quite serious?"

He shrugged. "It never seemed necessary."

She turned and planted her hands on her hips. "Well, if you hadn't kissed my neck that way—"

He mocked her stance. "Well, if you hadn't filled out your bodice that way—" His eyes darkened as he looked at her now. "You're still doing it."

She crossed her arms and inhaled. "Doing what?"

His jaw worked. "Come here."

She took a step backward. "Make me."

She only had a moment to giggle wildly before he caught her. Dinner at Sutherland House would have to wait.

Outside the room, Dobbins paused at the door with a tray. Another servant came down the hall and saw him hesitating.

"At it again, are they? The honeymoon's been over for months!"

Dobbins nodded. "He ain't human."

"He never has been." The other man shook his head in admiration. "Lucky bastard."

Dobbins sighed and turned back to the kitchen. He'd best be ready with another tray. Her ladyship could be downright frightening when she didn't get her tea.

To Wed a Scandalous Spy

Willa hummed cheerfully, if somewhat out of tune, as she foraged in the meadow for a few greens to round out their noontide meal. Traveling with her husband suited her absolutely. Even with Nathaniel's strange aversion to staying at inns and his tendency to monosyllabic conversation, she was determined to enjoy his company.

Besides, she was seeing places she'd never seen before. Even though the new stone-walled sheep fields greatly resembled the previous stone-walled sheep fields of her experience, they were *new*. After a lifetime spent in the same tiny village and its monotonous environs, anything new was delightful.

Furthermore, marriage was *new*. Spending her days with such an attractive man was entirely new, and there was no point in denying the purely female pleasure she took in watching Nathaniel ride, walk—oh, heavens, that leonesque stride!—and basically breathe in and out.

Of course, she'd imagined that by now she and her husband would have managed to put that silly consummation requirement behind them . . .

Willa picked up her sack of found treasure and decided to cross the beck further down to look for watercress. Watching her feet on the damp slope, Willa didn't look up until she reached the water's edge.

When she did, her heart stopped beating, the breath left her lungs, and her mouth went dry.

He was beautiful.

Nathaniel knelt in the beck only a few yards away. With his back to her and her arrival masked by the chuckling water, he was entirely oblivious to her gaze.

He was also entirely wet.

And entirely naked.

The water was shallow, and there weren't enough bubbles in the world to cover the sheer expanse of naked man that rose from the beck.

Willa couldn't breathe. Her knees went weak at the sight of the sudsy water streaming down his broad back into the crease of his powerful buttocks. She had never seen anything so unbearably delicious in her life.

His back rippled with muscle as he soaped his hair, the cloudy afternoon light doing nothing to dim the sleek shine of soap and water on his male perfection.

Nathaniel bent to duck his head in the water, and Willa could not control the moan that escaped her at the view.

Instantly Nathaniel whirled, one fist pulled back in instinctive defense while his other hand frantically wiped soap from his eyes. Damn, he should have known he was too vulnerable here. He hadn't been thinking with the mind of a spy but had let thoughts of Willa's sumptuous thighs distract him.

His vision cleared and he saw her. The impulse to fight eased, only to be replaced by another equally ancient instinct.

It was her eyes. They were wide and hungry, with a shining ache in them that he knew from his own soul. She wanted him. He could see it in the way her chest swelled with heavy breaths and by the sheen of perspiration gilding her face and neck.

His own need rose in response to her hungry gaze, and he saw her gaze drop and her eyes widen in surprise. Then slowly, her gaze traveled back up him. Nathaniel straightened and stood motionless for her perusal.

He was the most magnificent creature she had ever seen. She knew that the thrumming within her was because of his male attraction, but the ache in her heart was from his sheer lonely perfection.

I could have her.

Surrender to a Wicked Spy

Being one of the most eligible bachelors in London Society, Dane Calwell, Viscount Greenleigh, was actually rather accustomed to saving damsels. In fact, they seemed to drop from the sky to land at his feet in various states of distress.

The Season was nearly over, and Society's mamas were becoming desperate indeed. Unbeknownst to them, Dane had every intention of marrying this year. After all, he was in his late thirties and his wild days were long done. A man with his responsibilities needed an appropriately demure, composed, well-bred hostess and mother for his heir. Therefore, he looked on all of this attempted entrapment with amused tolerance. Still, Dane had hope that he'd find a young woman with a bit more substance before the season ended.

So when a young lady fell into the Thames right before his eyes, Dane hadn't hesitated before leaping from his horse to dive into the water next to the struggling miss.

Except that this particular miss hadn't needed rescuing, at least not until she'd nearly frozen while rescuing *him.*

She lay in his arms now as he carried her up the grassy bank of the Thames. He didn't think it was precisely proper for him to be holding her so close, but the unconscious girl's mother—who only now had thought to run back down the bridge to the bank—was currently indulging in a rather overblown fit of panic and there didn't seem to be any servants or footmen with them.

Dane wrapped his sodden coat more closely about the pale chilled form of his rescuer. Her frozen state concerned him greatly. He was feeling deadly cold himself, and he was far larger than the young woman he held.

He glanced up at the gathering crowd—where had all these people been while the two of them had been floundering in the Thames?—and picked out a mild-looking young man at random.

"You there," he called. "Fetch a hackney coach here at once." The fellow nodded quickly and ran for the street. Dane glanced at the woman he was beginning to think of as "the mother from hell" and tried to smile at her reassuringly. This only sent her into a fresh bout of sobbing and carrying on as she clung to his side. She seemed to feel that she was to blame for some reason.

There was no sense coming from that quarter, so Dane tuned the woman out.

A shabby hack pulled up on the grass. It was a pretty poor specimen and small to boot, but Dane was in no mood to care. He ordered the mild young man to load the mother into the vehicle and carried the girl on himself. Seating himself in the cramped interior, he settled her into his lap, keeping a protective hold on her.

Perhaps he ought to be ashamed of noticing that she was a healthy armful and that she fit rather nicely against him. Still, it was refreshing to be this close to such a sturdy female. She felt rather . . . unbreakable. He always felt somewhat uneasy when he came too close to some of the more petite women in Society. His common sense told him that he was not going to crush them during a waltz, but his imagination supplied many an awful vision anyway.

So when his coat briefly fell away from the young woman's bodice during the jostling carriage ride, Dane fell prey to his manly instincts rather than his gentlemanly ones and didn't precisely avert his eyes from what the thin, sodden muslin wasn't covering very well.

Well, well. Very nice. Very nice indeed. He could safely change his description from "sturdy" to "buxom."

Dane saw her open eyes and smiled at her, glad to see that she was alert once more. She likely hadn't seen him peeking, and if she had, he certainly wasn't going to affirm her suspicions by appearing guilty. Besides, the brief glance at her full bosom capped with rosy points that pressed tightly to the translucent muslin had been the highlight of his rather trying day.

Her gaze left his, however, and slid to where her mother sat opposite them, now sobbing somewhat less vociferously.

"Mother," the girl said firmly through blue, chilled lips. "T–tell this nice gentleman that you're s–sorry."

The weeping woman uttered something unintelligible which seemed to satisfy the girl in Dane's lap, for she then turned to look back up at him with an air of expectation. Dane hesitated, having the feeling that he was the only one who didn't know what they were talking about. "Ah . . . apology accepted?" he said finally.

The girl seemed to relax. "You're t–taking all of this very well, I must say," she told him as her shivers continued. "That bodes well f–for your character. You must be a man of g–great parts."

Perhaps it was the fact that he'd recently been peeking at her own rather "great parts", or perhaps it was the fact that his own "parts" were becoming more and more stimulated by the motion of a curvaceous bottom being jostled against them, but the commonplace saying struck Dane in quite a different way than it was intended to. He laughed involuntarily, then covered it with a cough. Smiling with bemusement at the very unusual creature nestled on his lap, he nodded. "Thank you. I might say the same about you."

The girl eyed him speculatively for a moment, then turned to her mother again. "Mama, you should allow this gentleman to introduce himself to you."

"Mama" nodded vigorously, then visibly repressed her sobs and dabbed at her eyes with a tiny scrap of lace that truly didn't look up to the task of drying all those tears.

"That's not necessary, my dear," the woman said, with a final sniffle. "The Earl of Greenleigh and I have already been introduced."

Dane sat there for a long moment with a smile frozen on his face while he racked his memory to place the rumpled, red-eyed woman across from him. Finally, light dawned. Cheltenham. She was the wife of a destitute earl, but the family was of excellent lineage and spotless reputation. "Of course we have, Lady Cheltenham," he said smoothly, as if he'd recognized her all along.

Then he looked down at the self-possessed and voluptuous young woman in his arms. So this was Cheltenham's daughter . . .

One Night with a Spy

The scent of the rose petals beneath seep into my bare skin until I feel steeped in perfume and passion and him.

Well, damn. Marcus looked about him in alarm. The garden was a mess, all brown and dry. The rose garden he'd pictured from her diary entry was nothing but rows of skeletal sticks, truncated a foot from the ground. There was nothing but stripped vines covering the grim stone walls and nothing but yellowed grass and gravel on the ground. In the pearly morning light it looked more like a graveyard than a garden.

How was a bloke supposed to stage a seduction in such surroundings?

Lady Barrowby walked slightly ahead of him down the gravel path, her hands clasped behind her back. He noticed that her fingers were twisting together. Another display of girlish nerves from the Beauty of Barrowby?

That was reassuring, but also a reminder of their other companion, the great Beast who padded along at the lady's side, his tail twitching ominously.

Why was he having so much trouble with this mission? He knew what he needed to do and he knew how to make her respond to him. He was a charming fellow usually, prone to making ladies smile and flip their fans his way. What was it about Lady Barrowby that left him tongue-tied with mingled lust and fury?

Lust he'd felt before, so it must be the fury. He'd charmed the knickers off a few widows in his time, but he'd never faced one who held the power to destroy his dreams.

He was going to have to put his mission from his mind, that was all. He was going to have to pretend that she was just another pretty widow, albeit one with a penchant for lions and making love out of doors.

He bottled his fury, stoppered it and put it away for the day he would need it—the day he destroyed her. Finally, with a mind cleansed of anger, he stepped smartly up to her side and smiled down upon her with easy sincerity. "Lovely day, is it not?"

She blinked in surprise. Surely he'd not been all that much of a bear?

"Well," she said slowly. "It is chill and damp, I don't have a wrap, and I think I smell something dead over in the alliums."

"No," he said firmly. "It is a lovely day." He shrugged free of his coat and slipped it over her shoulders. "You do have a wrap." He steered her away from the alleged deceased down a pretty path lined by small trees whose arching branches in the summer must have met overhead in a charming shade. "And I don't smell anything but roses."

Thankfully, the Beast preferred to investigate the smellier portion of the garden and left them to their own devices.

She snorted. "Nicely done. The roses, however, exist only in your imagination, I fear."

He leaned close and inhaled deeply. Her eyes grew wide at his forward behavior.

"No," he said, his voice a caress. "I most definitely smell roses."

He saw her swallow hard and hot triumph flared within him. He fought it down. He was Marcus Blythe-Goodman now and Blythe-Goodman actually *liked* Lady Barrowby.

He straightened and grinned down at her. "Your name is not Julia," he declared, apropos of nothing.

She went very still. "W-what did you say?"

Interesting reaction, but to be stored away for later review. Now, he lightly touched a gloved finger to the tip of her nose. "I dub thee Helen, or perhaps Persephone."

Her breath gusted in a small, relieved laugh. "Oh, you are stuffed like a sausage full of blarney, Mr. Blythe-Goodman. And here I thought you a more discerning sort." She turned away, shaking her head.

He caught her hand and pulled her back to him. "Why?" He moved closer. "Because I compared you to legendary beauties?" He kept his voice low and intimate. "Or because I think you are a woman to tempt the gods?"

Her eyes locked on his. He felt her fingers tremble in his and felt his own body answer her shiver. Her lips parted and her warm breath feathered against his mouth.

"And are you tempted?" she whispered.

Hot need ignited in him and this time he let it flare. There was no chill now. Instead, there was heat, between them and around them, until Marcus feared they would set the desiccated garden aflame.

There was a ruin ahead, a garden affectation that had been fashionable a generation ago. Marcus took her hand tightly in his and dragged her several feet down the path until he came to the raised dais of the Roman-style temple.

Then he turned and wrapped his hands about her waist and lifted her to stand on the dais. She gasped, breathless from their run. Her cheeks were pink and her blue eyes alarmed. He liked her that way. "Mr. Bl—"

He couldn't wait another moment. He kissed her hard, with his hands in her hair and his body pressed to hers.

The hell of it was, she kissed him back.

She was going to hell, there was no doubt about it. Here she was, a widow of only a week, kissing another man.

And oh, sweet heaven, what a kiss!

His mouth was hot and needful and his hands were pulling her hair too hard and she felt his erection pressing into her belly through the layers of her gown—

She became aware that her own hands were fisted white-knuckled in the front of his weskit and she was making sure that her lower body didn't miss a bit of his.

And she'd never, ever heard that pleading hungry sound come from her own throat before.

No. I am not that woman.

She pushed him away, shoving hard against his shoulders until he staggered back. He stood there, his gaze blank with lust for a long moment.

"Sir, I fear you've gained the wrong impression of me."

He shook his head sharply and passed a hand over his face. "I am most assuredly impressed, my lady, but I think I am in the wrong." He laughed regretfully. "Have no fear, Lady Barrowby, I think I am definitely going to pay for overstepping so severely." He bowed. "My deepest apologies and my most heartfelt thanks. Good day."

With that confusing remark, he turned briskly on his heel and strode away, leaving his coat about her shoulders and a small helpless smile on her face.

Impressed, was he? And here that had been her very first kiss.

Marcus strode from the sleeping garden with his head down, fighting his own compulsion to return to the heat and pent-up passion that was Julia.

She'd kissed him as if she'd been waiting all her life for his lips on hers. God, she was a seductive creature. He reminded himself of all the men who had come before him. She had filled volumes with her exploits, for pity's sake!

The hell of it was, he ought to go back for the sake of his mission. He ought to press her, to work his advantage, to seduce the seducer—

"You bloody piker." There was no mistaking Elliot's supercilious drawl. Marcus lifted his head to see Elliot standing in the drive with the reins of two horses in his hands. A groom came forward to take them from him, but Elliot shook his head sharply. "No, Mr. Blythe-Goodman was just leaving."

Marcus narrowed his eyes, for it certainly seemed that he was about to embark on a journey. There stood his stallion alongside Elliot's nag, fresh and shiny from his pampering in the Middlebarrow stable, fully saddled and packed with what looked to be everything Marcus had brought with him on this mission.

"You really orta let me take them 'orses, sir."

Elliot ignored the groom, who shrugged helplessly and turned back to the stables.

"You cleaned out my room at the inn." He turned his gaze back to Elliot. "How thoughtful of you."

"Yes. I stopped by there late last night to tell you 'no hard feelings' and what did I behold? You weren't in bed as you'd claimed. I waited, thinking you'd decided to visit the privy after all the ale you drank, when it occurred to me that you spent the evening nursing a single flagon. And if you weren't drowning your sorrows, you had a reason to make me think you were."

"You came up with all that on your own?"

Elliot did not ease his glare. "I'm smarter than I look."

Marcus folded his arms. "One would hope."

"So I searched your room."

Marcus blinked. "You're bloody cool about it."

Elliot nodded slowly. "Do you know what I learned about you last night?"

Not a bloody thing. He'd made sure there was no evidence of his real identity in his belongings.

"Not a bloody thing," Elliot said. "No letters, no medals from the war, no miniatures of your mother. Tell me, what sort of fellow carries nothing personal with him?"

An idiot, apparently. Damn, he ought to have fabricated Blythe-Goodman more carefully. And he sure as hell ought to have investigated Elliot No-surname immediately!

"So I decided to give you a hand with your packing. No real point in you staying on, after all." Elliot held out the reins. "Mount up. Your visit to Middlebarrow is over."

"Leaving so soon, Mr. Blythe-Goodman?"

Marcus turned to see Lady Barrowby exit the garden. He was about to answer her when Sebastian followed her through the open gate.

The two horses went instantly mad with fear. Elliot was pulled from his feet as both his nag and Marcus's stallion reared and spun about to race away down the drive. The groom came running back at the equine screams, but he was too late to do anything but help Elliot from the gravel as they all watched the shiny haunches of the horses disappear down the long drive. All except Elliot, of course, who gaped at Sebastian, blinking forcefully as if he were trying to convince himself that he wasn't really mad.

"Told you I orta had took them 'orses," the groom muttered.

"Thank you, Quentin," Lady Barrowby said with warning in her voice. "Do put Sebastian to his breakfast, if you will."

Quentin sighed heavily. "Yes, milady. Come on, 'Bastian. Let's get you a leg o' mutton from Cook."

The groom strolled off, hands in pockets, followed by the lion with long, eager strides that boded certain ill for some mutton's leg.

Elliot remembered to inhale at last. "My lady, I must inform you that your pet cat is not what you think he is."

Julia smiled. "Do tell, Mr. Elliot."

Elliot blinked, then glared at Marcus anew. "You weren't surprised at all!"

Marcus sent a nonchalant glance after Quentin and Sebastian. "Oh, about the lion? Heavens, no. Sebastian and I are old friends."

Lady Barrowby's lips quirked. "Absolutely ancient. In fact, Mr. Blythe-Goodman was just about to help me bathe him. It seems Sebastian found something deceased to roll in."

Marcus blinked. "Er, yes . . . well . . . I would, you see— can't think of anything I'd like to do more, but now I must chase down my horse. Elliot would be more than happy to assist you, I'm sure."

Elliot blinked. "Er . . . ah . . . I fear my horse has run off as well. I hate to leave you in the lurch, my lady, but—"

"Shall I call Quentin back to aid you?" She turned to call after the groom.

"No!"

She turned to look at Marcus, surprised by the force of his refusal. The thought of Quentin strolling back with lion in tow was more than he was truly able to cope with at the moment.

Elliot was violently shaking his head as well. "Thank you but no, my lady. I'm sure Quentin has more important matters to attend to."

Lady Barrowby shook her head. "Oh, go on. Run off like a pair of spooked horses. You may return for luncheon later, if you like."

Elliot bobbed a quick bow. "I shall return, my lady, but I'm sure Blythe-Goodman wishes to get an early start—"

"I'll be but moments, my lady," Marcus said briskly. He slid a glance at Elliot. "My mount won't run far. He is well trained, unlike some."

Lady Barrowby put up a hand. "Do stop growling at each other and go fetch your horses."

They quieted, but not before Elliot got the last word in. "My horse won't run as far as yours because he can't."

"Now that I believe," Marcus shot back, as they watched Lady Barrowby stroll away.

When Julia had settled Sebastian back into his quarters—he stank after rolling in the dead thing, so she rubbed him down with dried mint leaves, leaving him smelling like something that had died from eating too much mint—she made her way slowly back to the main house.

She'd kissed Mr. Blythe-Goodman. Really, truly kissed him—open lips, battling tongues, urgent hands and all. That was a terrible thing to have done, especially since only last night she had promised herself to Mr. Elliot.

Mr. Blythe-Goodman brought out the worst in her. Every person had some devil inside them, be it drink or rich foods or the compulsion to collect great numbers of small yapping dogs. Her devil was apparently Marcus Blythe-Goodman.

The only cure for such an affliction was complete abstinence. She was going to have to avoid him most diligently in the future.

Except for luncheon, of course. But after that, she would be on a strict diet of Elliot and Elliot alone.

Blast it.

"I don't know why you had to show up." Elliot had a marvelous grasp of the acid glare.

"Now you see, that is the wrong take on matters," Marcus said conversationally as they rode back to Barrowby together on their exhausted but now-calm mounts. He was still in a very good mood after the pleasure—er, triumph—of this morning's kiss. "A man should keep his competition in plain view."

Elliot smirked. "You don't believe that her ladyship and I have come to an agreement."

"Oh, I believe you. I'm simply not sure that she does." He gave his horse a kick, pulling ahead.

"Now what is that supposed to m— Oy, hold up there, Blythe-Goodman!"

It wasn't sporting to outrun Elliot's nag. It was only that Marcus felt the pull to see her—to complete his mission.

Oh, bloody hell. He wanted to see her and he shouldn't hide it, not if he wanted to win her confidence. He should allow Marcus Blythe-Goodman to have his infatuation, for it would only make his efforts more persuasive. Look at what the fellow had accomplished with a simple stroll in the garden!

Talking about your alias as if he were real? Not sane, old man.

Nor did he care. She was less than a mile away and he wanted to see her.

Now.